Guerilla Bride

A NOVEL

Also by J. J. Zerr

War Stories
The Junior Officer Bunkroom
The Happy Life of Preston Katt
Noble Deeds
Sundown Town Duty Station
The Ensign Locker

Guerilla Bride

A NOVEL

J. J. Zerr

Primix Publishing
11620 Wilshire Blvd
Suite 900, West Wilshire Center, Los Angeles, CA, 90025
www.primixpublishing.com
Phone: 1-800-538-5788

Published by Primix Publishing   02/11/2022

ISBN: 978-1-955177-92-4(sc)
ISBN: 978-1-955177-93-1(e)

Library of Congress Control Number: 2022901110

For Karen and Susan and their forebears who
played parts in the history of that time

PART I

Spring 1860

E MERSON SHARP'S LIFE had changed abruptly and dramatically the day after his tenth birthday. That was the day Paw had taken him away from Maw. Emerson was almost eighteen now, and he hadn't thought about what had happened back then for a very long time. But his brother John was almost nine, and he'd begun to wonder if Paw'd take him too, come next year. Emerson couldn't ask. His father told a thing when he was ready. Most of the time, he never got ready to tell.

Dredged-up memories of his first day as Paw's field hand did not make Emerson smile.

He remembered that gruff voice busting into his sleep as if it came from the bottom of a well.

"What?" he'd asked.

"Git up, I said."

Emerson sat up in bed, rubbing sleep from his eyes and squinting at the huge dark figure holding back the blanket hung over the door, backlit by a kitchen lantern like a hulking bogeyman.

"Tomorra'," Paw said, "you best not make me say 'git up' twict."

Out in the field that morning, the first thing Paw had him do was shoot at a stump. Emerson raised the heavy musket and squinted his aiming eye down the barrel right into the rising sun. He lowered the weapon.

"Sun's in my eye."

He began moving to put the eye-blurring rays to the side.

"Stop," Paw barked. "Like as not when it's time to shoot a deer, bear, or Injin, the sun's gonna be in yore eyes. Git back there an' shoot that stump."

At his original spot, sun rays sliced through leaves and tree branches. He couldn't look directly at his target. Besides squinting, he had to turn his head to the side and view the stump out of the corner of his eye. He raised the heavy weapon, and the end of the barrel wobbled all around that stump. Emerson gritted his teeth, made that barrel pass through the target, and fired.

He wound up sitting on his butt, rubbing his sore shoulder. Paw stood over him, raining silent disapproval. Emerson stood up, still massaging where the gun butt smacked him.

"Listen. Hold it tight to yore shoulder. Don't close yore eyes when you fire. The gun is too heavy for you to hold steady, and you let it wobble all over the place. An' you jerked the trigger. Squeeze it. Smooth like. Now clean the dirt outta the barrel an' reload. Then shoot that *consarned* stump."

His next shot went high.

"I did like you said. But as the gun barrel lowered, I thought it was dropping too fast, and I fired too soon."

"Don't you never let me hear you complain. Ever agin. Complainin's the biggest waste a time they is. Now you shoot that stump, or I'll whip you."

His next ball hit short of the target.

"I'll hit it the next round."

"We ain't got no more time, no more powder an' ball to waste. Git over here."

Paw sat on the stump, grabbed Emerson by the arm, and said, "You bawl when I whip you, an' I'll keep whippin' till you stop."

When Paw laid him across his knees and the belt across his buttocks the first time, Emerson jerked, but he kept his jaws clamped shut. At the end, his eyes were wet and he could feel his cheeks and lips twitching around. But he did not bawl.

"Tomorra'," Paw said, "you hit that stump with the first ball, or you git anuther whuppin'."

Through the rest of his first day in the field, Paw passed on his instructions. When they stopped work to eat sandwiches, Emerson found out the rules laid down for him did not necessarily apply to his father.

"God sure screwed some things up when He made the world," Paw said before he bit off a chunk, chewed, swallowed, and drank from the water jug. Then he looked to see if Emerson was paying attention. "God separated light from dark and spread them out even over a day. Then He said, 'By the sweat of your brow shall you eat bread.' Hell, if He'd a said the sweat thing first, He'd a seen we needed more than twelve hours a daylight."

Another bite, more chewing and swallowing, and "You know what'll happen if you say what I said to yore maw?"

Emerson knew.

Late in the afternoon, as they turned furrows across a recently cleared field, Emerson walked in front of Paw with his hands up on the handles in front of his father's. The plowshare jammed into tree roots that hadn't been dug out, and the chain traces snapped. Paw said some words Emerson had never heard before.

Before Paw took him, Emerson stayed around the house, did lessons with Maw and chores for her. He gathered eggs, fed the pigs and chickens, hoed weeds in the garden, and entertained his baby brother, John. And he asked her about words he didn't understand when he did his readings in the Bible. It never occurred to him to ask Paw the meaning of a word. At supper after that first day in the field, as she was about to serve cobbler, he asked his mother about the new words he'd heard.

"Emerson!" Maw screeched and dropped the dessert pan, which set baby John to howling.

She left the mess on the floor, grabbed Emerson by the arm, dragged him over to the counter where she washed dishes, soaped up a dishrag, and scrubbed his lips and tongue. Eight years later, Emerson's taste buds still remembered that lye soap in his mouth. And, too, his buttocks had never forgotten Paw's belt whipping them just short of bleeding, which had happened first thing in the field the next morning. Never mind the words he'd asked about had come from Paw's tongue, passed through his lips, though Maw thought they came from the boys Emerson hung around with after church services.

Prior to his tenth birthday, Emerson talked to Maw about all manner of things, meanings of words from his daily reading in the Bible being one of them, but once he became Paw's field hand, he was afraid to say much to her. Besides, John—he was named after the disciple Jesus loved, not the baptizer—was beginning to say words, and Maw acted like it was a full-time job speaking with him. And it was John she carried and later walked hand in hand with every day, rain or shine, to the white- picket-fenced-off plot behind the house to pray over the four small wooden crosses.

1	1	1	1
8	8	8	8
ABEL	RUTH	ISAAC	DANIEL
4	4	4	5
4	6	8	0

Maw never spoke of those four little ones to Emerson. He wondered if she spoke to John about them.

*****

The smell of breakfast meat in the skillet woke Emerson. Bacon. And potatoes and eggs fried in the grease.

Emerson got up and trekked to the outhouse. It was the same way every morning began since those first couple of days almost eight years ago. Whenever he thought about it, which wasn't often, he expected every morning to start that way far ahead as he could see. The only thing that might change was what happened to John after his tenth birthday. Of course, he knew Paw's rules were not like the commandments, written on stone tablets and applying to everyone. Maw was awfully attached to John. She wouldn't have any more babies. Emerson heard the women talking when he'd been nine, John was an infant, and the women were there for Wednesday tea and cake.

As he walked to and from the outhouse, he wondered what would happen to his brother John. Emerson's days were filled with working, eating, shaving, sleeping, and not much wondering. John's future would unfold soon enough.

Emerson washed his hands in the basin on the porch and went inside.

"Tuesday," Maw remarked as she placed the coffeepot on the trivet on the table between Paw and Emerson.

She kept track of the days of the week and looked forward to Wednesday with her circle of women friends and especially to Sunday. Paw saw Sunday approaching and worked Emerson and himself harder to make up for losing a whole day in the field.

"Say the blessing," she said.

Emerson did and then poured a cup for Paw and one for himself.

Paw sipped, replaced the cup on the saucer, leaned back as if he had all the time in the world, and stared at Emerson with a funny little smile on his face. Paw had never acted like this before. Emerson sat forward. He noticed some gray hairs above his father's ears in the black hair Maw kept cut short. That smile of his crinkled up a passel of wrinkles at the corners of his eyes. He couldn't understand how those things had happened to his father without him noticing. Emerson gulped a mouthful of coffee.

"Boy," Paw said, "time for you to get married."

Emerson snorted coffee out his nose and set to coughing.

Paw rounded the table and pounded him on the back. Maw ran from the sink, drying her hands on her apron.

When the coughing fit quit, Maw wiped up the table with a flour-sack dish towel. Paw told him to take a bath, cut a handful of flowers from the garden, put on his go-to-church clothes, and call on Deborah Simmons.

"You court her ever' day until Saturday. Saturday's yore weddin' day."

As Paw grinned at him, Emerson thought of the gaggle of young men that huddled after church services to size up the girls. The less attractive ones were characterized finally as "Least she ain't plain as Deborah Simmons." In that moment, Emerson saw himself as the laughingstock of Terre Haute— hell, the entire state of Indiana—and for the rest of his life.

"Deborah Simmons! For Christ's sake, Paw!"

Maw slapped the back of his head for blaspheming, and Paw clouded like a July thunderstorm boiling up, a living mountain high as heaven and full of black anger flashing fire.

Paw said go, so Emerson went.

Emerson had no idea Paw coveted the Simmons farm, but it was plain as could be that's what it was. Leastwise, now it was plain.

The Simmonses were a hard-luck bunch. Well, they used to be a bunch.

The Simmonses had three boys: Amos, Bartholomew, and Casper. And they had Deborah.

A few years back, when the oldest Simmons boy, Amos, didn't come in from the field for midday dinner, the middle son, Bartholomew, went looking and found him lying next to a stump he'd been digging out. Amos had a hole from a musket ball over his heart. Around the hole a patch of shirt had burned. Bartholomew fetched his paw.

"Had his hands up when the bastard shot him," Old Man Simmons grumbled.

"Amos's hands are at his side," the youngest, Casper, pointed out.

"That's how he fell. Look at his shirt," Old Man Simmons barked. "Musket bore was touching his chest when it was fired. If a gun barrel was to your chest, wouldn't you raise your hands?"

Bartholomew picked up a tattered, rotted boot, the loose sole of which was tied to the toe with a rag. "Shot Amos for his boots."

A mile to the west of the Wabash River, the Simmons men caught up to a skinny man with wild gray whiskers and black eyes with no soul in them. He was dressed in rags held together with twine. Wore nice boots, though. He also had a pair of draft horses tethered next to his camp. It was the team Amos had been using to pull chopped loose stumps.

They hanged the man. But only after Old Man Simmons had them tie the man's arms to the workhorses and pull until one came off at the shoulder.

A year later, Casper found the remains of Bartholomew in the woods near the edge of the field he'd been planting. By the sign, it appeared Bart had gone in the woods to relieve himself, without taking the shotgun with him, and stumbled across a bear and two cubs.

Casper started having nightmares. He was unable to sleep at night. He could not close his eyes without seeing Bartholomew with his belly torn open, his guts strung across the ground, and his face ripped off, and seeing, also, a one-armed man hanging from a White Oak tree. Only after a rooster crowed could he slip into a semblance of sleep. One morning, Old Man Simmons found his last son in the barn. He'd hanged himself.

Shortly after that, Mrs. Simmons died. "Of a broken heart," people said.

"I'm a dead man, my own self," Old Man Simmons told people. "My body just don't know it yet."

Simmons had had enough of farming in Indiana. He intended to ride west. All the way. "Until the Pacific Ocean tells me I cain't go no further." He had to get his remaining child, Deborah, settled first, though.

It was clear as could be, all right. After Emerson married Deborah, Paw would add the Simmons farm to his own. Doubling his acreage.

Double the work too, Emerson thought as he rode the riding horse across fields to the Simmons place. Working as his father's field hand, or draft animal, or slave, or whatever he was had been hard enough with the smaller farm. Then he pictured what people would say when they found out he was marrying Deborah.

"Maybe, Horse," he mumbled to the beast carrying him, "Paw'll work me to death, and it'll be over soon."

As he looped the reins of the riding horse around the porch post, Deborah stepped out of the house. Emerson held the flowers out to her. "Take 'em," Old Man Simmons growled. "Take 'em inside. Put 'em in a vase. With water."

Deborah had her brown hair in a bun, like old women did. Her face wasn't hard to look at, but it was not a happy face. She glared at Emerson, snatched the flowers, and went back inside the house.

Mr. Simmons told Emerson to take one of the chairs on the porch and asked him a few questions about his maw and paw and the Sharp farm. Then he was out of words. Deborah returned and sat in the remaining chair between her father and Emerson. Her lips were pressed tight together into a straight line. Words weren't going to escape through those lips. The silence sat uncomfortable and heavy on the porch. Emerson couldn't dredge up a thing to say, though. Old Man Simmons sat there, leaning back, his legs stretched out in front of him, and chewed on a straw. After an hour, Deborah went inside to dish up midday dinner. Her father and Emerson turned his horse loose in the corral and washed up.

The meal was silent too, except for the clinking of silverware on pots and dishes. The two men cleaned their plates off while she pushed pieces of pot roast around hers with her fork as if the meat made her angry.

After dessert, the men returned to the porch while Deborah cleaned up. When she returned to the porch, Mr. Simmons said, "I got work. You two sit here."

They sat. She didn't say a word. He was tongue-tied. After a time of just sitting there, he glanced at her.

She seemed to throw off a chill, like when a person stood next to a block of ice. At the same time, he thought the anger showing on her face was as hot as a red horseshoe with a blacksmith whanging away at it. She wasn't ugly. He was sure she'd look better if she loosened up some, stop pressing her lips so tightly together. Those lips slashed across her face and made her nose look sharp and pointy. The sun had colored her smooth cheeks. Emerson liked the line of her jaw. He thought it might be nice to run his fingers over her cheek and along her jaw.

She turned her head, and it was as if her eyes burned a hole in him. He looked away and stared across the packed dirt yard to the barn and across the fields. Paw's barn was visible from the porch. Emerson noted that Old Man Simmons didn't keep his property up the way Paw did. The barn needed paint. The fence around the sty sagged with posts rotted at the base. His estimate of the amount of work to be done on Paw's new property went up. He shook his head.

Then he noticed the fenced-off cemetery plot, just like the one on Paw's farm. Like Paw's, the Simmons plot had four graves too. The three boys and their mother. A lot of bad luck had visited the Simmons family. Emerson hoped all that bad luck was buried there too. Deep.

After a long time, he snuck another peek at her profile. She was as the boys at church said of her. "Plain straight up an' down." She was flat-chested, and that was God's own truth.

She swung those eyes onto him again. He forced himself to not look away.

"I 'spect, Miss Deborah, you don't want to be here neither?" "Either," she said.

"What?"

"'You don't want to be here *either*?' That's the proper way to phrase your interrogative."

"That's what I said."

"The horse you rode over here has more education than you do."

Horse had dropped a pile of biscuits in the yard before they'd taken him to the corral. He caught a whiff of the smell. Horse manure, just then, carried a more pleasant aroma than the lilac water Deborah smelled of.

You court her ever day until Saturday. Saturday's yore weddin' day, Paw'd said.

"This how it's going to be, being married to you, Miss Deborah?"

"Until death do us part!"

The look on his intended's face reminded Emerson of Paw's bull. "A ton a pure cussed cantankerous, Bull is," Paw said.

She went into the house and returned shortly with a book. Seated again, she opened it. A tiny smile softened her face as she settled into her reading.

He thought about asking her about the book, to read it aloud, but it was likely it would only earn him a stinging, snotty put-down. He sat up straight on his chair and wondered what had happened to the silence. Before she got her book, the quiet covered the Simmons porch with a big bunch of uncomfortableness. He felt like he had to do something to bust it apart. Now the stillness worked just the opposite way. It lay over him, sort of like when he crawled into bed on a winter night, and the comforter began to keep some of his body heat inside instead of having the cold night suck it out of him.

Silently was the best way to sit with Deborah Simmons.

At supper, Old Man Simmons asked how they were getting along.

"Better than I expected," Deborah answered.

Mr. Simmons smiled. Emerson thought he was imagining the sun setting into that ocean out west.

When he entered the kitchen at home, Paw looked up from his book of figures he kept on the farm. "How'd you an' Miss Deborah get along?"

"Better than I expected," Emerson replied.

Paw smiled. It was as if Paw copied Old Man Simmons's face exactly.

That night, sleep would not come. Emerson lay on his back and blackness poured into him through his open eyes and filled him with something that made him wonder if maggots were eating him away from the inside.

Roiling in the blackness, an image formed of tomorrow's dinner with Deborah and her father as the old man smiled at visions of his future. The smile of his poured iodine over Emerson's totally raw-meat soul. That vision gave way to another, and he saw himself with Deborah day after day after day. *Until death do us part.*

He wanted to cuss out loud. He knew the words. Some from Paw, some from the boys at church. But he couldn't say them, not in Maw's house. Which told him clearly that's how it would be after the wedding. He'd live in Deborah's house. *At least,* he thought, *here Maw's fond of me. At least,* he thought, *she used to be before Christ's favorite disciple, John, showed up.*

Emerson sighed, mumbled, "Rats!" rolled onto his side, and pulled the pillow over his head as if that could shut up the voices inside. It didn't work. He saw the crowd of boys, how they would appear come Sunday when he looked at them from outside their circle. He heard what they'd be saying about him being married to Deborah Simmons. It grew hot under the covers, and he pushed them back.

Candace Barlow appeared in his thoughts as suddenly as a clap of thunder from a storm you didn't know was coming. Candace. Blonde hair in a long ponytail bound with a blue ribbon that exactly matched her eyes. Creamy complexion. Always smiling, showing her white teeth through her full pink lips. And she was not flat-chested.

Thinking about her stirred him, as it always did.

He remembered last Sunday. He'd spoken with her. She was easy to talk to, and she had placed a hand on his arm as she looked right into his eyes. It made his knees weak.

"My room is the add-on one on the ground floor," she told him.

"I'm a light sleeper," she told him.

"Paw don't keep no dogs no more," she told him.

Emerson tried to swallow, but his mouth was too dry.

The Barlow place was a twenty-minute ride northeast.

Emerson felt his face smile. The smile lasted as long as the blink of a lightning bug.

He would never know how sweet being with Candace Barlow would be. Candace might already know he was engaged to Deborah. She was probably lying in her bed at that very moment thinking about who she'd flirt with on Sunday since by then Emerson would be married.

And there's not a single solitary thing I can do about it, Emerson thought. *I'm just Paw's field hand. His slave. Another one of his draft horses.*

In the blackness above his bed, there had been nothing to see. Now he was seeing his tomorrows, and all of them were bleak and filled with drudgery and sweat, and his sweat smelled like horse sweat. And he lived in the Simmons house with Deborah. And she was cold, but at the same time hot with loathing. "Till death do us part," she'd said.

Anger flashed blinding bright behind the blackness in his eyes. It was like a nearby lightning strike. He expected to hear a clap of splitting thunder. He counted *one potato, two potato.*

But it was silent. He lay still and listened. It was so quiet, even the mice and cockroaches had to be asleep.

Emerson swung his legs off the bed, gathered his clothes, and picked up his boots. He stood still and listened.

Then he felt his face smile. He hadn't been aware he'd made a decision. Sure as shooting, though, he'd made one. He was still smiling as he tiptoed, with his arms full of clothes and boots, out of his room and out the door.

As he dressed on the porch, he thought, *I ain't no consarned draft horse!*

EMERSON RODE THROUGH the dark, more on a smooth magic carpet of giddy euphoria than bouncing on the bare back of Horse. He rode without fear or caution until he turned off the road onto the lane to the Barlow place.

There he slid off and led the animal. "Don't you go whickering to none of the Barlow stock." He whispered to him all the way to the orchard just short of the barn. Leaving Horse tied to a branch of an apple tree, he stepped cautiously, snapping his head back and forth and listening hard, across an open space to the barn. He peered around the corner at the dark two-story house.

There was no sound, no sign that anyone was awake.

An egg-shaped moon hung directly above him. It dropped not light but a soft glow on the world. Emerson had the notion he could see things in the glow, but that he, himself, would be invisible. He made out the added-on room. Candace was in there. His heart skipped a beat, and he hustled across the space between the barn to her window. He pressed his ear to the glass, held his breath, and listened. Not a sound. He smiled and *tap- tapped* on the window.

A spike of fear shot through Emerson. His taps had sounded so loud. What if Old Man Barlow heard it? Or worse, Candace's brothers. The Barlow boys were big and tough. Word was they killed three men in a barroom shoot-out down along the Ohio River.

Run! screamed inside his head.

Before he could, the window slid open.

"Emerson?" Candace stuck her head out. "I knew you'd come."

She grabbed him around the neck, pulled him to her, and kissed him hard on the mouth. Emerson was surprised and confused. His arms hung at his side. Then a great and overwhelming urge to press her to him rose. He reached for her, but she pushed him away and ducked back inside. The curtains closed over where she had been. Surprised as he'd been by the kiss, now he was horse-kicked. Was that it? Was that all there was going to be? Was he supposed to get back on Horse and ride back home?

The curtains parted, Candace stuck a bare leg out the window. Then she was through, standing barefoot on the ground, her long blonde hair cascading over her shoulders, a bundled quilt in her arms, her nightdress down to her ankles.

"Candace." His voice had gotten deep and growly.

"Shh," she whispered.

He reached for her.

"Wait."

She took his hand and led him trotting around the barn to the edge of the apple orchard. There she spread the quilt on the grass and lay down on it.

"Look at all the stars," she whispered.

He did, and when he looked back down at her, her nightdress was bunched up under her chin.

She was not plain straight up and down.

*****

A hard voice called to him from a long way off.

"What?" Emerson asked.

"Git up, I said!"

Paw stood in the doorway holding the curtain back. Emerson quickly swung his feet to the floor.

"Boy!" Paw said, shaking his head before he let the curtain drop back into place.

Emerson pulled his pants on, grabbed one of the coal oil lamps from the kitchen, and went to the outhouse. There he discovered blood on the front of his long johns. Down there.

"Rats," he mumbled.

He'd have to take a piece of soap with him and clean his underwear in a stream. He had to do that Monday mornings, occasionally, after dreaming about Candace Barlow, after seeing her on Sundays. He wasn't sure what Maw would do if she found those stains in his underwear. He didn't care to find out. He sure didn't want her finding the blood.

But, as he washed his hands before going in, he smiled, thinking about Candace. The thought stirred him.

"Boy," Paw called from inside. "Breakfast is on the table."

Paw'd drank all the coffee.

"Hustle up the eatin', boy," Paw said, "then take Bull to Oliver Teasdale's. Mind you, don't dawdle. You got supper with yore fiancée. Before that, I want to get some work out of you." He set a small box on the table and opened it. "Give this ring to Deborah tonight."

Paw said give it, so he'd give it. After, though, he'd go see Candace again.

"Eat," Paw barked. "What's the matter with you this mornin'? You best have yore mind on what you're doin' or that bull'll tromp you."

Emerson glanced at his plate. He'd barely touched his food and set to shoveling it in. Then they walked out to the pen.

Bull was a ton of red-hided, white-faced, crazy-eyed, murderous beef. He could not stand still. He was always trotting around the pen and snorting or pawing the dirt like he was about to charge into the fence. Bull did not like a man to get inside his pen.

"That vicious animal is going to hurt someone," Maw had said once.

"That bull is good *fer* what bulls is good *fer*," Paw'd responded. And Maw'd said, "Paw!" the way she did when she thought Emerson and his brother were too young to be exposed to such talk and such thinking.

Several of the farmers around them hired Bull's services, and Emerson and Paw had a way to capture him. They approached him from opposite sides of the pen, and as Bull was trying to decide which one to go after, Emerson would get a loop of rope to drop over the animal's head. When Bull turned toward him, Paw got his rope on. Paw was better with a rope than Emerson. Emerson was quicker on his feet. It made sense to do it that way. Still, Emerson wondered if Paw'd be so easy with using him as bait for the bull if he didn't have another son almost ten years old.

It was five miles to Terre Haute and another like distance to Teasdale's farm.

With Bull tied to the longitudinal frames of the wagon bed with two stout ropes around his neck, Emerson snapped the reins, and the team set off. Behind him, Bull resisted, like he always did, but finally stopped fighting when he figured out the wagon was not going to give up pulling him.

As the wagon rumbled north, Emerson could hear Bull huffing and chuffing along behind. A pile of hay in the back of the bed encouraged him to come along.

Paw'd bought Bull from Sylvester Barlow two years earlier. Besides Candace, Sylvester had two sons. Both had blond hair, like their sister, only it was a dirtier blond. Emerson didn't know what their baptism names were. Everybody called them Big and Tiny. Big was six foot two and weighed two hundred pounds. Tiny was six four and weighed two fifty. Big was strong but Tiny was stronger by a fair amount. The two boys were always together. Folks said, "Them two Barlows got the strength of five men." And someone else would say, "And the brain of half a man." Which of course they never said in earshot of Big. He was the one with the half a brain.

Tiny drooled. Once in a saloon in Terre Haute, a fellow laughed at Tiny. Big said, "Hit 'im." Tiny did. Sent the man flying and crashing into a post holding up the second story of the building. Broke the man's jaw. He wound up simple in the head and drooling more than Tiny ever had.

That day when Big and Tiny rode up the lane, each with a rope kept taut around Bull's neck, Paw'd told Emerson, "You keep your mouth shut, you hear? You say one word, one word, an' I'll beat the tar outta you."

Tiny rode a draft horse that looked like mischievous kids had dirtied the white hide with a lot of ink splatter. Next to him, the bull looked small and of little consequence, but when the Barlows pulled to a stop, the bull kept twitching its head side to side, trying to hook something with its horns.

"Mr. Sharp," Big said, "Da said tell you to watch out for them horns. Keep him in a pen. Bring the fresh cows to him. Otherwise he gores anything gits 'tween him an' the fresh ones. Where you want 'im?"

Paw rubbed his chin. "I want them horns cut off." "Da didn't say nothing about sawing horns off."

"That's the way I want him. I'll give you a dollar if you help me with it."

"A dollar each," Big said.

Big directed the operation. It was clear to Emerson that he had more than half a brain. Paw saddled the riding horse and got a rope around a rear leg of the bull. Emerson fetched a saw. Then Big had Emerson mount Tiny's horse to keep the rope stretched tight. Tiny cranked up a run and crashed into the side of the bull, and it went over on its side, bawling and slashing with the horns and making dust fly. After a bit, the bull got tired and Tiny lay across the animal's neck just behind the horns.

"Boy," Big said, "hop down an' saw them horns."

Emerson looked back at Paw. "Don't look at me, boy. Do what the man said."

Emerson sawed the horns, they tarred the bloody stubs and turned the bull loose in the pen, and Big said, "Two bucks." Paw went in the house to fetch it.

Even though he'd been dehorned, Bull continued to act as if he had them. He could still do a lot of damage to a horse or cow. Or a man. When Emerson took him to service another farmer's cows, Paw always had him use the wagon. It sure wouldn't do to try to lead it with a single riding horse.

By the time he reached Terre Haute, the sun was up. A few people were about opening stores and sweeping the boardwalk. They stopped and waved, and Emerson waved back.

As the town dropped away behind him, it occurred to him that he hadn't seen the Barlow boys at church for the last few Sundays. Having them out of town when he was … well, with their sister, that was good.

He looked back at Bull trotting along behind the wagon. He recalled how the Barlow boys had dehorned the vicious beast as easily as wringing the neck of a chicken. Emerson decided that one more night with Candace Barlow was all he was ever going to have. After that, he would just do what Paw set him to. But he would have the one more night.

Mr. Teasdale was waiting in the yard between his house and the barn with his straw hat in his hand. Emerson stopped the team. The skin on Teasdale's bald, pale head appeared stretched tight enough to split. His sunburned nose was peeling.

"You're marrying the Simmons girl."

Emerson flushed. Even his feet were sweating.

Teasdale put his hat on. "The plain ones is best for marrying."

*****

Emerson was a mile short of Terre Haute on his return trip when he spotted a stream that was suitable for scrubbing his long johns. He stopped the wagon, set the brake, and was about to hop down when he heard a heavy animal crashing through the brush ahead and to his left. He grabbed up the long rifle and cocked it.

Stupid, he scolded himself. He'd been about to go back in the trees without taking the gun. He remembered Bartholomew Simmons and the bear.

Whatever was crashing through the brush was close. He raised the rifle and aimed at the noise.

A horse and rider busted out of the trees and onto the road fifty yards ahead.

"Paw!" Emerson said. He'd never seen his father push a horse so hard.

His father jerked Horse to a stop next to the wagon, and he hopped off.

"Git down," he snarled.

He was peeved something fierce.

His father stood with his arms straight down, the hands balled into fists. Emerson could hear the air whistling in and out his nostrils as he climbed down. Paw was going to hit him.

His father ripped his hat off and smacked Emerson across the face with it. Emerson fell back against the wagon wheel. The team started. The wagon lurched forward, and Emerson fell to the ground.

"Whoa up, you goddamned fleabags!" Paw climbed up on the wagon and looped the reins tighter around the brake handle.

"Big and Tiny Barlow come calling this morning. They asked for you. I told them where you was going. Then they said you ruined their sister. 'Couldn't be Emerson,' I said. But Candace told them it was you." Emerson pushed himself to his feet.

"The boys left, and I said I was goin' to shoot you my own self. Maw said if I did, she'd shoot me."

Paw sighed with a sound like his soul was getting away from him and he was too tired to stop it. He hung his head. His shoulders slumped.

Emerson felt empty inside, from his ears to his toes. Then he was filled with a heavy, black, ugly cloud that sucked the strength from his arms and legs. He wanted to just flop down there in the road.

"Boy, the Barlow brothers are waiting for you in Terre Haute. Take the ridin' horse. Head west. Ride all night. Ride all the next day if the horse can do it."

Emerson turned and looked at the chestnut. He was a riding horse second. First he was a buggy horse. He took Maw to Wednesday teas and the family to church. He sure didn't look like an outlaw's horse. Which is what Emerson figured he was.

"Boy, go on now. I'll sit here a spell. Give you a start. WhenI go through town, the Barlows will see it's me and know what I done. But I ain't sittin' here the whole damned day. Git."

Emerson stuck a foot in the stirrup.

"Take your damned hat. Be hard enough for you to live through tomorra' if the sun fries what little brains you got."

Emerson snatched his hat up, jammed it on, and mounted.

"Boy."

Emerson faced his father.

"Don't come back. You ain't my son no more."

T HE WOODS ALONGSIDE the road were densely packed oaks, pines, elms, sycamores, walnut, hickory. Every place a tree could grow, one did. Where a tree couldn't grow, scrub brush did. A wild pig or a deer could push through it. It didn't look like a man on a horse could.

Head west, Paw'd said.

Emerson mounted and studied the brush fence in front of him. He thought about turning and looking at Paw one last time and asking him to say goodbye to Maw, but his cheek still smarted where the hat had smacked his face. *You ain't my son no more.* He felt that, too, in his chest and in his belly.

He gigged his mount with his heels. Horse turned away from the forest, apparently preferring to walk on the road.

Emerson hopped down and pushed into the scrub brush, pulling on the reins to get Horse to follow him. Some twenty yards away from the road, he found a game trail headed for the Wabash River, and he followed it. The river was down, and where the road from Terre Haute to Saint Louis crossed, there was a gravel-bottomed ford. At the ford, a wagon was crossing from the west. The water was axel deep on the wagon.

After the wagon passed, Emerson coaxed Horse to cross.

Once on the Illinois side, Emerson looked back toward ... well, *home* was the only word that came to mind. But it wasn't home anymore. Not by what Paw'd said. He looked up and down the Wabash, at the trees crowding both banks to a swath of dried reddish-brown riverbank mud. He had no idea where he was going, but it was somehow important to store up a picture of where he'd come from. Above him, an eagle floated on stretched wide wings, cutting an easy circle. The eagle was looking at him, he thought. Behind the big bird, thin, milky clouds watered down the sky's blue.

Paw'd said he wouldn't wait all day. As Emerson sat and stared, he knew he was frittering away the lead he had on the Barlows. If they caught him, he didn't know what they'd do to him. He wouldn't like it. That was clear. Still, it was hard to turn his back on Indiana. It was as if he still belonged there as long as he didn't turn away from it. It was hard to turn away.

He thought about Alfred Wiggins. Last year after church services, Alfred was telling his friend Mason about the kittens. Alfred's father had told him to put the litter in a sack, take the sack to the creek, put stones in the sack, tie the mouth shut, and toss the sack into the water. Alfred told Mason he couldn't do it, that he'd walked for a half hour and let the kittens loose in the woods. Mason said, "What?" loud enough for all the boys to hear. "That's the cruelest thing you coulda done. If a hawk caught one, it'd rip a leg off and eat while the kitty watched and listened to his bones crunch."

Emerson looked up at the eagle.

He gritted his teeth, hauled Horse around, and set him clopping toward Saint Louis.

His chest hurt, and a lump formed in his throat. That picture he'd formed of the banks of the Wabash and of the eagle overhead pulled at him like a magnet.

"We got to make tracks," he said. He gigged his heels into Horse's belly and cantered down the road.

"I sure messed up Paw's plans," he said. "He won't be adding the Simmons spread to his no more."

Then it occurred to him Paw had no field hand anymore. Maybe he'd take John away from Maw even though he wasn't ten yet.

"Aw, rats, Horse. John's a soft kid. I hope Paw doesn't take him till later. And Maw. God only knows what I did to her." He thought of Mrs. Simmons dying of a broken heart.

Horse kept slowing to a walk. He kept kicking him into a faster gait.

"Candace Barlow. I ruined her, they said. Sure as shooting, I ruined Old Man Simmons's plans."

Horse slowed again.

"Listen, Horse. If the Barlows catch us, they're liable to kill me. You they'll eat. Let's get along now."

He smacked the mount on the rump with the tail end of the reins and smacked him again. Horse broke into a run.

"Run awhile. Then maybe you'll 'preciate a trot."

A number of thoughts from Indiana kept trying to push their way into the center of his mind, but he kept pushing them out, pushing them into the background. He concentrated instead on pushing Horse down the road, on watching his surroundings.

Ahead, maybe a quarter of a mile, the road led into a town.

Emerson stopped.

"Horse, we passed wagons and riders on the road. We rode through two towns before this. Barlows will ask those people on the road. They'll ask the folks in those towns. Those people will say sure they seed us. We're going to skirt around this place. Barlows will ask. Folks here will say, 'No, ain't seed no rider on a chestnut.'"

Nothing but cleared fields lay to the south side of the road.

North was woods. He turned Horse that way.

He picked up the Saint Louis road past the west side of the town.

"Horse," he said. "Deborah Simmons. At least there'll be one person happy with what I done."

After the sun set, Emerson stopped riding around towns. The moon came up big with the sides squashed. Horse walked. Emerson was too tired to keep after him to move faster. They came to a wooden bridge over a stream. Horse didn't cross the bridge; rather, he walked down the gentle slope and drank from the trickling water.

Emerson was thirsty too. He dismounted and grabbed on to the saddle. His legs were a bit wobbly under him, and his back was stiff.

After walking a couple of paces, the legs functioned again. He stretched his back; then he lay on the bank and drank. The water was cool, and he drank a bellyful. He pushed himself to his feet, wiped his muddy hands on his pants, and wiped the back of a hand across his mouth.

Horse was munching grass.

Emerson's stomach growled like a bear's just waking up after its winter sleep.

There was the flour sack hanging from the saddle horn. Paw wanted to shoot him. Maw threw provisions in a sack for him.

Boy, Paw'd said when Emerson was first in the field with him, *you always take a gun in the field with you. Afore leaving the house, you check it.*

He went to Horse and pulled the musket from the saddle scabbard and checked the priming. He replaced it and lifted the flour sack from the saddle horn.

Boy, always look to yore animals afore you look to yourself.

Emerson pulled the saddle off and rubbed the animal's back with the blanket. Then he opened the sack. He found a skillet wrapped in his second set of long johns, a shirt, biscuits, an inch- thick slice of ham, bacon wrapped in a rag, and ten dollars. He took a big bite off the ham, and the salty meat was about as fine tasting a meal as he could recall. He took another bite and then looked around, almost in a panic.

"Rats," he mumbled through the mouthful. "Horse, we stopped here, and I didn't look around to see was it safe. And we're right here next to the road. If the Barlows was to come on us, we'd be done for. Paw never told me nothing about how to be an outlaw. You and me got to figure that out for ourselfs. Best we get moving."

The moon was higher now with its magic light again. Just like at Candace's, he thought the moonglow enabled him to see while at the same time making him invisible. Several times, both in towns and while passing farms on the road, dogs set up furious rackets until he passed by.

Dogs' noses see better'n peoples' eyes, Paw said once.

Each time a dog yapped, his heart hammered, and he spun around expecting to see Tiny Barlow reaching out his big paw to jerk him out of the saddle. He hadn't seen or heard anyone behind him, but since it had gotten dark, he felt the Barlow boys behind him coming on steady. He knew they wouldn't quit.

Emerson didn't know what time it was, but it had been dark a long time. Chances were it was past midnight. It was the day Paw mentioned.

It'll be hard for you to live through tomorra'.

"Tomorrow's here, Horse. I know you'd like to stop, but we can't."

He did dismount a couple of times and walked to rest Horse a bit and to keep his legs in working order, but he pushed them on through the night. He checked often behind him, realizing at one point the moonlight didn't make him invisible. It probably worked just the opposite way. It made him visible while it would hide the Barlows back up the dark road.

He checked behind them as often as he remembered to. It grew hard to keep his eyes open. The horse plodded along, and he rocked with it back and forth. His eyes would close. Barlows appeared in his head close behind him, and he'd snap awake and check. Then his heart rate would coast back down. Horse plodded. He rocked.

Once, he jerked awake and grabbed onto the saddle horn to keep from falling.

The second time he almost fell, the horse stopped walking.

Just stopped with its head hung low.

Emerson dismounted. His legs almost buckled. He squatted and stood up again. His legs and feet tingled as blood started flowing. The eastern sky had a splotch of dawn washing out a half circle of stars. He started walking with the reins in his hand, but Horse wouldn't budge.

Emerson stood next to the animal and patted its shoulder.

"Horse, you done right by me all night long." Behind him on the road, nothing to see, nothing to hear. "Was you a dog, maybe you could smell how close they are. I expect Barlows get tired and hungry too. Let's see can I find you some grass. Come along now."

The horse followed him into the woods as he pushed through scrub brush. A hundred yards from the road, the woods ended at a broad, stump-studded field. A long way across the field, a lantern or candle glowed in a window.

Emerson pulled off the saddle and rubbed the animal down with the blanket. Then he put a rope around the its neck, giving him enough leash to graze, but to keep him close.

After gathering stones, he shaved tinder with his belt knife and sparked up a fire. He fried bacon, turning the slices with a stick. He wanted to sleep like nothing he'd ever wanted in his life, but he knew the Barlows probably wouldn't. He'd give Horse a little rest. He'd eat. Then they'd ride on. With daylight, he intended to leave the Saint Louis road and strike off northwest.

Riding through forests and around farms, maybe he'd shake Big and Tiny. Maybe he'd ride northwest half the day and then cut back to southwest. A little smile cocked up a corner of his mouth. He'd lose those Barlows.

During the night, they'd passed a cornfield. The ears were developed, and the kernels were still filled with juice. Roasting ears. Emerson threw two ears over to Horse, and he chomped one down, cob and all. Emerson placed the other ear on the rocks by the fire. A few more minutes and the bacon would be done. He could eat that and a biscuit while the corn finished. Then he'd saddle up, douse the fire, and eat the corn as he struck out across the stump field.

A pistol cocked behind him. He froze. The hair on the back of his neck tingled. He was kneeling, sitting on his heels, and glad he was. His legs might not have held him up. Then he raised his hands slowly.

"Smelled that bacon from the road. Shit. Don't you got no coffee, Sharp?"

Big Barlow. The smart one. Tiny was bigger and mean, but only because his brother told him to be that way. Big was mean all by himself.

"Come," Big hollered. Then, "Sharp, stand up slow. Turn around."

Giant Tiny, atop his huge dirty white draft horse, entered the clearing. Emerson stared up and into empty black eyes looking back at him like he was nothing. *Death rides the pale horse.* The Bible study teacher said that once.

Big smashed a fist on Emerson's ear. He fell hard. His head filled with blackness ripped in places by lightning. Big rolled Emerson onto his belly, pulled his arms above his head, tied his hands, and looped the rope around a tree. Tiny knotted one around Emerson's feet.

"Pull it tight," Big said.

Emerson grunted as his arms stretched above his head. He spat leaves out of his mouth.

"You're lucky," Big said. "Da told us not to hurt you bad." Big kicked Emerson in the ribs.

Emerson gritted his teeth.

"Da told us to not mark up your face none. You got to look purty for your weddin'. An you probly ain't heard. It's gonna be a double. Yep. You're marrying our sister, Candace. I'm marrying Deborah Simmons. Wasn't what Da planned. But Da said, 'When opportunity knocks, you don't say we don't want none. No, sir. You holler out, *Come on in here!*'"

Emerson lost feeling in his hands. He could feel the sore spot in his side. He could wiggle his feet some. A glimpse of what people would call him blossomed in his mind. Barlow's Negro. That's what they'd call him. Actually, they'd use the other word. The one Maw couldn't abide.

Big dumped out Emerson's sack. He threw the clothes aside.

He untied the knotted handkerchief with the money in it. "Ten dollars," Big said. "And biscuits. But no damned coffee."

Big took two strides and kicked Emerson in the ribs again.

"Next time, bring coffee. Good biscuits, though, Sharp. They're real good. Right, Tiny?"

Tiny grunted, and Big sent him to fetch the whiskey.

The two brothers ate the bacon, and then they toasted the upcoming weddings. They toasted the Barlow family and the land they would own. They toasted the Sharp farm.

"Never know, Tiny," Big said. "Something could happen to Old Man Sharp."

Emerson thought Big was just trying to torture his mind to go with his physical anguish. But it was Big Barlow. It could be God's own truth he was speaking. He decided he had to watch for his own opportunity to knock. No matter how small the likelihood of success, he'd give it a try. Dying, he decided, would not be near as bad as being Barlow's Negro.

Big told Tiny to check Emerson's knots. Which he did.

"Kin I kick 'im?" Tiny asked.

"No. You'd hurt him bad. Maybe even kill him. Da said not to."

"Aw, Big."

"Just hold on, Tiny. Maybe Da will let you kill him after the weddin'. Ain't no shame in a widder woman. Come on. Bed down now. We'll grab coupla hours a shut-eye. Then we got to head back."

As the Barlows belched and farted and rustled around on their bedrolls, Emerson thought about Candace and how much trouble that hour with her was causing. He wished he'd just done what Paw had said. Deborah Simmons wasn't near as bad as this Barlow deal was working out to be.

Paw always said, "Wishing for what ain't and cain't be is the biggest waste a time they is." Lots of things were the biggest waste of time, according to Paw.

Bugs crawled on Emerson's face. Some were under his shirt collar. Ants. He shook his head and maybe got some of them off, but not all. He pulled as hard as he could against the ropes. His right foot slipped a mite inside his boot. After flexing the foot repeatedly, he tried again to pull it clear. It gave a little more. He relaxed. Breathed in. Out. Big inhale, and he pulled with everything he had.

His right foot slipped free. The left came out easily.

Getting his knees under him, he raised up and almost fell over. After a moment, the dizziness passed. With his teeth, he set to work on the knot at his wrists. Every instinct goaded him to hurry, but when he rushed things, the world spun or he pulled on the wrong part of the knot.

Ants, a handful of them, were busy in the small of his back. A fit of frantic desperation drove him to run to a tree and scratch. *Boy!* Emerson said to himself in Paw's voice. He stayed still.

The sun was up fair now, and he felt as if every passing second was a precious thing getting away from him.

He studied the knot, determined which loop to work on, bit into the fibers, and tugged. It felt as if he were pulling his front teeth out. Shifting his bite to side teeth and twisting his head and moving his hands, the knot gave a fraction of an inch. He twisted his arms against the rope. Mistake. It just tightened the knot again. With Paw's voice growling at him, he untied the knot, resisted the urge to spit the fibers and taste out of his mouth, rubbed his wrists, and squeezed and relaxed his fists. Tingling, feeling, pain, and function flowed into his hands.

Big Barlow slept with his saddle for a pillow, his hat over his eyes. Tiny was on his back, his mouth open and *snark-snarking* at the sky.

Emerson didn't have time to gather his clothes or the skillet. The money. Well, that was lost. He stuck his boots under his left arm, slung his powder horn and ball pouch around his neck, and picked up his rifle. Then, in his stocking feet, he eased to the horses and worked the bridle onto his. No time for the saddle. He slipped into his boots and untied the lead ropes around the necks of Barlows' horses.

He was ready. Big was quiet under his hat. Tiny snored at the sky.

"Now, horses," Emerson whispered slow and soft. "We're going to be real quiet." He breathed on their faces, one by one. "Just come easy." He started all three moving. "Don't step on a twig can you help it. Just come along. Reeeeeal quiet." His whispering dragged the words out. Made them long. He walked between the Barlow horses and rubbed his hands across their shoulders. "We'll cut across the grassy meadow. Make too much noise if we go through the brush toward the road. *Nooooo*, the grass'll be lots more quiet."

Behind him, a gun boomed. Emerson heard a wet smack, and Big's chestnut went down like a sledgehammered steer.

Emerson spun around.

Big stood, hatless, holding a smoking Dragoon pistol.

"Drop the rifle," Big said.

Emerson saw his opportunity snuffed as if it had been a candle flame pinched out by spit-wet fingers. A picture of himself as Barlow's Negro flashed through his mind. Paw telling him, "Boy, in the field, you best remember what happened to the Simmons boys. A robber or a bear won't give you time for a lot of ponderin'." Paw made him practice shooting rabbits with the rifle.

"Drop the rifle, I said," Big growled.

Emerson cocked the hammer as he dropped to a knee. Big cocked his pistol and fired as Emerson lurched to his right and fired.

Big went over backward.

"Big!" Tiny moved fast for such a giant. He knelt beside his brother and shook him. "Big. Get up."

Boy! Paw's voice put spurs to Emerson, and he ran toward Tiny and swung the stock of the rifle, smashing it into Tiny's jaw. Tiny fell beside his brother, both of them on their backs.

Big's eyes were dull. The eyes didn't blink even though a sunbeam found a way through the branches above them and shone on his face.

Tiny moaned. Emerson cursed. He didn't want to do what needed doing. The man was helpless, hurt. "Rats," he muttered and picked up the Dragoon. It was cocked. He aimed it at the side of Tiny's skull. Then he thought another gunshot might not be a good idea. The sun was up fair. People would be about. Maybe on the road. Definitely in that house across the open field. He let the hammer down and noticed dirt had been stuffed into the barrel. If he had fired, it might have blown his hand off.

That woulda bin bad luck.

Paw liked to say, "Bad luck. Pshaw! Most times *bad luck* is two words where one is needed. *Stupid.*"

Emerson recalled what his paw had said about living through today. Maybe it wasn't just the rough way Paw talked sometimes when Maw wasn't around. Maybe he really meant he didn't expect Emerson to live through the day.

He looked up at the sky. Not even midmorning. There were a lot of hours left in that day to live through. He needed to spend them making tracks to some other place. First, though, Tiny had to be dealt with.

The giant moaned. His eyes were closed. His jaw was off- center, busted. Tiny coughed and spewed up a cloud of mist that dewed his face pink.

The need to leave that place of death filled Emerson's brain and drove down through his limbs to where it was as if his legs were going to run away whether the rest of him ran or not. But there was Tiny.

Emerson thought about Dog. Years ago now, Paw told him Dog was so feeble he couldn't get up out of his own pee puddles anymore.

"Put it down," Paw said and handed Emerson the long rifle.

Emerson had to load the dog in a wheelbarrow to cart him to far side of the barn. When he cocked the hammer of the gun, the dog looked deep inside Emerson's soul. Dog knew what was coming. Dog didn't want that bullet to smash into his skull. But there was not one thing he could do about it. Dog wanted Emerson to know all those things. Emerson knew. Then he gritted his teeth and pulled the trigger.

Dog was a dog. Big was going to shoot him. Nothing else to do there. Tiny, lying there blowing tiny blood bubbles out the corner of his misshapen mouth, he looked like a little kid just then.

There hadn't been anything else to do with Dog.

And wasn't nothing else to do with Tiny, neither.

Or however the hell Deborah Simmons would say it.

As if saying it proper makes any goddamned difference at all.

Emerson pulled the Bowie knife from Big's belt and knelt beside Tiny. He watched the blood bubbles form and pop. "Shit," he mumbled. Then he gritted his teeth, raised the blade in a two-handed grip, and drove the Bowie down until the hilt stopped it.

4

EMERSON SNATCHED HIS rifle from the ground, ran to Horse, grabbed a handful of mane, and vaulted up onto his bare back. Getting away from the dead Barlows, especially Tiny with the knife in his chest, was close to an irresistible urgency.

"Giddup" was on the tip of his tongue. It just wanted the final release of the thought, and his hand would have snapped the reins. But Paw's voice stopped him.

You ain't got the brains to live through today.

It wasn't exactly what he'd said. But it meant the same thing.

Emerson didn't know where he was going. He'd run away from Indiana because of what he'd done there. Now he'd killed two men in Illinois and wanted to run from *this* place clean out of *this* state. If he ran, he had the clothes on his back, the rifle in his hand, powder horn and shot bag around his neck. Horse had reins. That was everything they owned.

"Horse, I hope the hell I know what I'm doing."

He hopped to the ground. Horse bobbed his head.

"I don't hear no great ideas coming from you."

Horse rolled his ears back flat against his head and then raised them again.

"What'd that mean? I don't have no great ideas neither?"

Boy! Paw's voice spoke to him in that way he had of packing *Boy, stop dawdling*, into *Boy!*

First, he loaded the long rifle and then saddled Horse. Big's chestnut was dead. After killing the Barlows, he was glad he didn't have to shoot a hurt animal too. Both Barlow mounts carried saddlebags. Inside, he found clothes, which he discarded. He kept a raincoat, powder, shot, gun-cleaning materials, a skillet, and a coffeepot. He picked up his long johns and shirt and tied Big's saddlebags onto Horse.

Tiny's dirty white had a Dragoon in a holster looped over the saddle horn. He left that where it was and picked up the pistol Big had fired at him. Another Dragoon. Emerson slipped Big's holster over his shoulder so the weapon hung under his left arm.

Big was staring up at the sky with dead fish eyes. Emerson avoided looking at them. In Big's pockets he found two dollars, plus his own ten, a watch, a Pocket Colt, and nothing else worth keeping. Tiny's eyes and mouth were open, his bottom jaw off to the side. The Bowie knife hilt was flush against his chest, the handle sticking up. Emerson took a breath and searched Tiny and took only the Pocket Colt he had stuck in his belt.

Emerson had never fired a handgun. Maybe tomorrow he could fire a couple of rounds. He figured he'd keep a Dragoon and a pocket pistol. He could sell some of the guns and Tiny's horse.

Emerson surveyed the campsite. The brothers had spread ground cloths to sleep on. He rolled them up and tied one behind each of … his horses. They were his now. Thinking about owning something was strange to him. Everything back on the farm had been Paw's. Now he owned a few items, four handguns, a rifle, and two horses. Most of what he owned, he'd killed two men to get.

Oh, Emerson! He was seeing Maw. She was sitting on her rocker with John on her lap. She wrapped her arms around the boy and said, "Don't you grow up to be like that Emerson. A killer."

"Shit," he mumbled. "I guess that means I ain't Maw's son no more, neither."

A wagon rumbled past on the Saint Louis road. He took one more look around and spied Big's hat on the ground where he'd slept. It was black and flat brimmed and looked new. He tried it on. The fit was good. It stank of Barlow a bit, but it would do him better than his own flop-brimmed rag. Then he saw Big's Bowie scabbard, took it, and walked over to Tiny. He wanted the knife. He put a boot on Tiny's chest, pulled the knife free, and wiped the blade on a Barlow shirt he'd thrown to the ground.

Both Barlows had canteens. He emptied one on the ashes of the fire he'd made.

A dead horse and a saddle this close to the road and not far from a farmhouse was one thing, but two bodies were another. He took the ropes the Barlows had tied him up with and looped one under the arms and around the chest of each. Then he tied the ropes to Tiny's horse's saddle horn. He mounted and led the dirty white by the reins as it towed the brothers. He stayed inside the trees and skirted cleared fields, heading west at first and then north around another field.

He kept his mind full of riding and watching and empty of other things.

With trees and brush screening him, he saw men working in fields, a boy driving cows toward a barn, a woman hanging wash on a line. He was pretty sure none of them had seen him.

After an hour, he was deep in forest. He came across a fallen tree and dragged and rolled the bodies next to the trunk and hid them under branches he'd hacked off with the Bowie. Animals would find them and maybe drag them into the open. There was nothing he could do about it. He wasn't going to take the time to dig a grave with a knife.

Leaving the Barlows, he decided to ride the big, dirty white. Mounting, he had to grab the saddle horn and haul himself up to get a foot in the stirrup. Once astride, his feet hung a couple of inches above the stirrups. He hopped down and adjusted the buckles to fit his legs.

Back on the white, he followed a game trail about halfway between north and west. Emerson thought he'd go that direction the remainder of the day. Come sundown, he planned to stop for the night. He couldn't go all night again.

The white was so broad across the back and belly, Emerson felt as if he was being split apart through his crotch. He raised his right leg and draped it around horn, like riding sidesaddle. A branch overhung the trail in front of him, and he ducked, but in his present posture, couldn't get low enough. The branch knocked his hat off, and it hung from the string around his neck.

"Shit," he mumbled and put his right foot back in the stirrup. "Horse," he said over his shoulder, "you best store up what rest you can, 'cause I ain't riding this damned draft animal for long."

He *gidduped* the white. Its gait had more side-to-side motion than Horse's did. Emerson found that aggravating. It was uncomfortable as hell with his legs spread so wide. His forehead stung. He reached a hand up and brought it down again smeared with blood. The tree branch that knocked his hat off had scratched him. His stomach grumbled.

"Damn, Horse, the Barlows didn't have no grub of their own, and they ate mine. Least you got to eat grass. Maybe we'll stop at a farmhouse, buy some grub from the missus."

What he wanted to do, though, was to sell the big, white horse and two of the Barlow handguns. He'd need a town for that.

He had no idea how much money he could get. Was a horse worth two hundred dollars? Or one hundred? Hell, maybe it was only twenty. Paw'd done all the buying and selling. He'd never taken Emerson along. "Buyin' a horse is a one-man job. You can still work in the field." Emerson had learned early on to not ask to go along with Paw. What about the guns? Right then, he figured, if he had the chance, he'd trade the white horse for a plateful of roast beef and fried potatoes.

It was warm under the trees. The sun peeked through the leaves and cast a soft light on the way ahead. His discomforts ebbed to annoyances.

Emerson jerked awake. He didn't think he'd slept long. A tree branch would have smacked him in the face. But nodding off worried him. He needed to be awake. He couldn't count on the horses to warn him. In the field, Paw's draft horses got skittish when bears and wolves were in the woods nearby, but the Barlows snuck up on him, and Horse hadn't even looked up from the grass he was eating.

He'd left the long rifle in the scabbard on Horse. He had the one Dragoon and a Colt in his pockets. He pulled the Dragoon and held it out as if he were aiming it. It was heavy and didn't feel natural in his hand. He recalled learning how to handle the rifle's kick. How would he handle the pistol kick? Well, it wouldn't do to pop off a couple of practice rounds.

He studied the weapon and figured out how to swing the barrel open to load the chambers of the cylinder. One of the chambers, the one that would sit under the hammer, was empty. He had Tiny's weapon. He holstered it and pulled out Big's. Big had fired at him. Twice. But three chambers were empty. He appreciated the value of having more than one shot. Why would a man leave one empty? It took a long time to reload the musket, but he'd seen Big cock and fire the Dragoon in about the space of a clock saying *tick-tock*. He understood the long rifle and considered getting it but decided he'd have to hold the weapon in his hand if he was to be ready for danger. If he carried the rifle, he'd probably drop it the next time he dozed off. No. Best to face whatever came with the handgun. He thought of Amos Simmons. He'd been killed by a ball from a musket touching his chest. Emerson thought he might hit something with a pistol if he got the barrel that close to his target.

As the dirty white plodded along the game trail, Emerson studied Big's Dragoon pistol. He cocked it and saw how the cylinder rotated. Once he understood the cocking and cylinder rotation, he dry fired the weapon a number of times, clicking the hammer down on an empty chamber. Paw didn't like dry firing a weapon, but early on, he'd had Emerson dry fire the rifle to save powder and shot. But he always insisted the rifle be live fired after a bout of that kind of practice. Emerson was deep in woods, and he worried about the noise, but, too, he needed to know how to fire a handgun.

The trail descended a gentle slope and came to a creek narrow enough for him to step across. Emerson whoaed his mount. Downstream about twenty yards, a large sycamore grew on the bank with its roots dipping into the water. About four feet above the roots, a white patch showed in the trunk where bark had peeled off. Emerson aimed the Dragoon at the white spot and fired. The white shifted weight on its feet, but it was used to guns apparently. Emerson missed the trunk to the right. He aimed and fired again. This time he missed to the left.

Despite Paw's restriction about dry firing, Emerson continued cocking, aiming, and clicking the empty pistol another half dozen times.

Then he pushed on. Before he developed any skill with a handgun, he decided, he was going to have to spend some powder and ball. And he was going to have to figure out how to reload a pistol also. When he stopped, he'd study the loaded guns and see how that was done.

Straddling Tiny Barlow's broad-backed mount, Emerson wondered if it would make him permanently bowlegged. It couldn't be helped. He couldn't stop. He hadn't yet put enough miles between him and where Big and Tiny lay. Horse was used to pulling a buggy or carrying a rider for an hour or so and then getting a bellyful of oats and a stall in a barn.

The dirty white plodded on. Horse trailed along. Above, sunlight trickled in eye-stabbing slivers through the leaves. The forest had a smell, a combination of fresh green leaves of spring not quite able to override musty, decaying leaves from last year and the year before. *Scree*: a meat-eating bird inviting a bunny to come to dinner.

You ain't my son no more.

"Huh," Emerson said.

A thought surprised him. *I was never your son, Paw. I was Maw's son for a while.*

Being somebody's son was a small thing. Having a bed to sleep in, having food and coffee provided, having days filled with not one single unfamiliar task, he saw all those not as big things. They'd been everything.

A panic-filled sense of falling into bottomless blackness jerked him awake, and he grabbed on to the saddle horn. He was breathing hard, as if he'd been running from something. The dirty white had stopped. Emerson looked around, searching for something out of place, but found nothing. "Giddup." The white walked on.

He took a deep breath and let it out and his heart rate slowed.

Boy, he told himself, *you got to pay attention.*

Paw'd told him working in the fields was dangerous. Just because he could see the barn and the house did not mean he was safe.

"Remember Amos and Batholomew Simmons," Paw'd told him.

"There's bears, wolves, wild dogs. There's men'll shoot you for yore boots."

"What about 'Thou shalt not kill'?" ten-year old Emerson had asked.

"Boy, them commandments is good to have. The way they's wrote, though, they's wrote for women and preachers. Out here where men live, there's a better way to say 'em. *You don't try to kill me, and I won't try to kill you. Don't steal from me, or I will shoot you.*"

Paw'd then grabbed Emerson's ears and went on with the longest string of words Emerson ever heard him say. "Twixt these ears, you got a mind. I don't know if it's right to say you got more than one mind in there, or if it's just one and it's like a house with rooms and you do different things in the different rooms. You cook and eat in one. You sleep in another. Anyways, when you're plowing, planting, mowing, you got to pay attention to those jobs. But you can get one of your minds to worry that business to getting done proper, while another mind watches for bears and soulless thieves after your boots. See what I'm saying?"

Emerson had not understood what Paw'd said, but once Paw'd explained a thing plain as it could be explained, further talk about it was "the biggest waste a time they is." At some point, though, he couldn't say if it was when he was eleven or last year, he began to see that how Paw explained about the mind, or minds, made a kind of sense. It was the only way to explain what happened when Big Barlow tried to shoot him. Emerson figured Big had been drunk and that's why he missed with his first shot. He wouldn't have missed with his second, though, if one of Emerson's minds hadn't compelled him to lurch to the side and fire.

Another thought tried to push into his head. It had to do with Tiny Barlow, but he did not want to deal with it. As long as he kept moving and watching for danger, he'd stay ahead of Tiny Barlow, even though he rode the man's horse.

The woods petered out a few times, and he crossed fields of hay and skirted those with grain. Trampling a farmer's crop was not something a man ought to do. He crossed roads and came close to towns, but he wasn't ready to try to sell the white horse without more distance between him and the Barlow killing and hiding places.

E MERSON LAY ON his back with a blurry, indistinct Tiny Barlow's ugly sneering face hovering over him. Tiny had a Bowie knife in a two-handed grip raised above his head.

Maw was there. She was moving her head side to side slowly and wringing her hands and saying, "Oh, Emerson. You're going to die with the sin of cussing on your soul. You're going to go to hell." Tiny's eyes were filled with yellow fire. *Hellfire*, Emerson thought.

Tiny rammed the knife down with his weight behind it. Emerson didn't feel the blade enter. He felt the hilt smack to a stop atop his breastbone. His chest hurt bad. He put his hand up, expecting to find the handle, but he didn't.

He opened his eyes. Above, sunlight flickered through leaves sashaying about in a gentle breeze. Birds twittered. A crow cawed. Large animals moved through brush. He pushed himself up with his left hand as he rubbed his chest with the right.

He looked behind him and saw the tree branch that had knocked him off the white.

The horses were fifteen yards away and still walking.

"Whoa!" Emerson hollered. The horses kept plodding on. "Horse!" Horse dug in his hooves and sat back on his haunches a bit. It jerked the big white to a stop, but then it leaned forward and started pulling Horse.

Emerson pushed himself up and ran, though it felt funny, running bowlegged. He grabbed the white's reins pulled on them and said, "Whoa."

The white whoaed, and Emerson muttered, "Dumb … animal."

Paw liked to say, "Animals is dumb 'cause they're borned that way and cain't git much smarter. Lots of humans is that way too."

"Yeah, Paw," he said.

He removed the lead rope from Horse and slipped the end of it through the ring attached to the bit of the white's harness. "Maybe if I stop your mouth, the rest of you will stop too." He turned to Horse and said, You best be rested, 'cause I'm ridin' you."

The afternoon wore on. It was time to find a town and see if he could sell the horse and guns and buy supplies.

Emerson caught a whiff of a decaying animal. "Horse, I'm almost hungry enough to find that carcass, brush the maggots off, and eat it."

Horse stopped.

They were at the edge of woods about ten feet from a road ground deep into the dirt by wheels and hooves.

To his right, east, a hundred yards or so, trees lining the road gave over to cleared fields. No houses or barns visible, though. In the other direction, the road sliced through a cluster of four buildings, two to a side. The two buildings he could see the front of had signs. He could just make them out. saloon. General store. A single horse was tied to the rail in front of the saloon. He heard a faint *ding-ding-ding*. Blacksmith.

It was just the right amount of civilization. Maybe the store would buy the guns.

As he was about to head for the town, shouts came from the woods on the other side of the road.

"Where the hell's the goddamned money, Westfall?" "Help! They're going to kill me!"

Emerson pulled the long rifle from the saddle scabbard and stepped down. Whoever the voices belonged to, they were close to the road.

"The money, goddamn it!" Another voice.

At least three of them were in the scrub brush. The rifle was a single-shot. It took close to a minute to reload. He left it.

"Horse," he whispered, "you stay still now."

He drew the Dragoon from the holster under his left arm and looked up and down the road. Nobody coming. Nobody in front of those buildings, either. He trotted across the open and slowed when he entered the scrub brush.

Two voices shouted threats. The other voice alternated cries for help and "Go to hell." Their noise covered his approach. Not that he needed much cover. He could Injun up on a grazing deer.

Peering through the brush, he saw a small clearing. A man in a suit and a white shirt was seated on the ground and tied to a tree. He was slumped forward. Unconscious. Two men in work clothes, both holding handguns, stood over him.

The two men standing were obviously trying to rob the tied-up one, but it wasn't his affair. They didn't pose a threat to him. He thought it best if he backed out of there and got on with his plan.

"Wake him up," the one with the thick black beard snarled.

"He's fakin' it. I didn't hit him that hard," a brown-haired man said.

What he'd done to Tiny popped into Emerson's head, followed immediately by the memory of a Wednesday when he was nine. He was riding with Maw on the way to Terre Haute for tea with the ladies. A voice from tall weeds along the road called out to them. Maw stopped the wagon. They didn't see a horse or anyone else around. Maw climbed down and found a man lying on his back. His face was swollen, and he was in a bad way. Even Emerson understood that. He and Maw got the man into the back of the buggy, and they continued on to town. "Snake bit me," the man said. "Ridin' in the woods. Knocked a snake off a tree limb. Copperhead." The man was dead by the time they got him to the doctor in town. Paw'd been angry with Maw for stopping. It turned out the man was wanted for murder and robbery in Indianapolis. But that following Sunday, the preacher went on about the Good Samaritan and how when God gives you the opportunity for a charitable act, an opportunity to earn grace, you best not fritter the chance away.

For an instant, he saw Maw staring at him, watching to see what he was going to do.

In the clearing, Brown Hair pulled a knife from his boot. "I'll stick 'im. He'll squeal like a pig."

Emerson had been hunkered over in the brush. He stood up and hollered, "Drop the knife!" He cocked the Dragoon.

The two men's eyes snapped to Emerson. Then they froze.

For a moment.

"Shit," Black Beard said. "He's just a kid. He won't shoot. Go ahead, stick that goddamned Westfall. Just don't kill him. We need to find the money."

Emerson aimed at Brown Hair. He didn't want to fire. He hoped they'd do what he said. He had a gun on them.

Out of the corner of his eye, he saw Black Beard pull a pistol from his belt. Emerson switched aim and fired at him. Black Beard ducked. A spike of euphoria shot through Emerson as he appreciated the power in holding a multishot weapon. He cocked the hammer and fired again. Black Beard ran across the clearing and hid behind a tree.

Brown Hair was frantically crawling for the edge of the clearing. Emerson shot at him and kicked up dirt near his boot. Black Beard stepped out from behind the tree and raised his pistol. Emerson fired at him once, twice. Then the hammer clicked.

"Empty," Black Beard said, a big grin splitting open his face hair as he aimed at Emerson.

A bullet twipped past Emerson's ear. He dropped the Dragoon and pulled the Colt from his belt. He shot at Black Beard and once at Brown Hair. Then he started walking toward Black Beard and fired. Brown Hair ran. Black Beard crashed through the brush behind his partner.

Laughter startled Emerson. The man tied to the tree was laughing his head off.

"What's so damned funny?" Emerson demanded.

"You fired nine rounds!" He laughed some more. "I, sir, am not sure you even managed to hit a tree, though we are in the middle of a forest."

Then he laughed some more.

Emerson considered shooting him. Course he'd have to get closer.

"Hey. How about cutting me loose?"

Emerson glared at him. The man was dressed fancy, and his black hair was barbered short. He didn't look quite so fancy sitting on his butt on the dirt, his arms tied behind him around a tree, his clean-shaven face cut and blood having dripped onto his white shirt.

"I think I'll leave you."

"We don't have all day. Those two scoundrels drive freight wagons. They'll round up friends and come back."

"Why were they so all-fired mad at ya?"

"I won their money at cards."

"You're a cardsharp. You cheated them."

"No, sir. I did not cheat. I didn't have to."

Emerson shrugged and turned to walk away.

"Wait, young sir. I'll pay you to cut me free."

Emerson faced him again.

"If you have a horse, I'll pay you to let me ride behind you."

"I got two horses."

"Two! Great," Black Suit said. "My bad luck just turned."

Emerson smiled at the man and started walking away.

"Hey, kid. Hey, I'm sorry I laughed. Come on. Cut me loose."

Emerson made noise walking away through the brush.

"Hey, kid. Please."

The man sounded worried. Sounding worried was better than him laughing. Emerson returned to the man and cut the rope binding him.

The man stood and pulled the ropes from his wrists. His face was a mass of cuts and bruises. The other two had beaten him pretty badly. Yet he had still laughed.

"You really have two horses?"

Emerson nodded.

"Will you permit me to ride one?"

Emerson nodded.

"You might want to let me have one of your guns. I occasionally hit what I shoot at."

"I got guns, but you ain't gittin' one. And you'll be close enough so even I can plug ya. We best be gettin' on now, mister."

At the edge of the woods, the man checked up and down the road.

"That horse at the rail by the saloon. That's mine. I'd consider getting it if you gave me a pistol. On the other hand, it was good luck you appeared to rescue me. It was extraordinary good luck you brought a horse for me. If I went back to retrieve my own steed, it would be like spitting in luck's eye."

Emerson shot a frowning glance at the man. He wasn't over having gotten laughed at for being a Good Samaritan.

They crossed the road, entered the trees, and the man walked to Horse.

"Mine," Emerson said.

"You, sir, are taller than me. The big animal will suit you better than it will me."

Emerson raised the Colt and cocked it.

"Young sir, you did not rescue me to shoot me in the back."

"I didn't rescue you so you could take my horse, neither."

The man said, "I can see that the cylinders are empty."

Emerson was stunned. He wasn't sure how many rounds he'd fired.

The man swung up onto Horse.

Then Emerson knew. The man was trying to bamboozle him. He grabbed Horse's rein with his left hand and jammed the muzzle of the pistol in the man's belly.

"How about I pull the trigger and we'll see is it empty."

The man had blue eyes. They seemed to pick up the smile from his face.

"You know, young sir, I believe I may have mistakenly mounted your fine steed."

6

T HE MAN TOOK the lead. Emerson wanted to keep his eyes on him anyway. He headed southwest.

Emerson's stomach grumbled. "Rats," he mumbled and glared at the dude's back. He'd interrupted Emerson's plan to buy supplies, to get something to eat. Those two back at the clearing said his name. West-something.

Mr. West-something looked ridiculous on the draft horse. His feet were at least two inches above the stirrups. His pants were hiked up above the tops of his boots. He looked like a kid, Emerson thought, astride a barrel, pretending it was a horse.

Emerson stopped and watched and listened behind them for signs of pursuit, but he detected none. Mr. West just kept bobbing along on the white.

They emerged from forest onto a well-used dirt road. By the low sun, it was north-south running. Mr. West stopped the white and watched to the north for a time.

"That little place where you found me, it's called Dutzow's Corner. This road intersects the one through Dutzow's. Odds are those two thieves won't come after us. They're the kind that will take a man from ambush, not facing him."

Emerson stopped in the grass bordering the road. The grass was almost knee high on Horse.

West turned and faced him. "Where are you heading, young sir?"

The question caught Emerson by surprise. He'd been thinking about food and how soon he could get some, but he didn't want the fancy-talking dude to know he had no idea where in Sam Hill he was going or ought to go. Out of the entire void in his mind, he plucked a name.

"Saint Louis," he said with the exuberance of sudden salvation appearing out of a sea of despair.

"A fortuitous happenstance."

Emerson looked at him.

"That is where I'm bound too. Would you mind if I accompanied you?"

Emerson looked away from him. The West fellow was too slick with words. He'd tried to bamboozle him about the pistol being empty.

"I'll think on it. What I want right now is something to eat. I was fixing to get something at that saloon you left your horse at."

West clucked, dug his heels into the white's belly, and turned it south.

A rabbit bolted out of the grass to their left. After two bounds in the middle of the road, it cut a square turn to the right and disappeared.

"If you had permitted me to have a pistol, I could have shot the beast for our dinner."

Emerson humphed.

When a hunter scared up a rabbit, sometimes, not always, but sometimes, another one was close by. West had the white in the road. Emerson pulled his long rifle and guided Horse through the tall grass alongside. A couple of *clip-clops* later, another rabbit burst onto the road, just as the first had.

Emerson stood in the stirrups cocking and raising the weapon. Horse stopped. As soon as the rabbit cut left, Emerson fired and the furry body spun around and lay still.

Emerson hopped to the ground and reloaded the long rifle.

Then he retrieved the carcass.

"I can see, young sir, it is a mistake to give you a weapon with more than a single shot."

"I never shot no pistol afore."

The West fellow tilted his head back and laughed. Emerson blushed, but his embarrassment burned off quickly.

He considered setting the aggravating dandy afoot. Emerson was tired and hungry and tired, too, of being laughed at.

"Young sir, if I might make a suggestion. You reloaded your rifle promptly, but you haven't reloaded the pistols. Perhaps I can reload them for you while you clean and prepare our dinner."

"Shit," Emerson said as he glared up at the mounted West fellow.

The man was hard enough to take without him being right and Emerson not.

"The rabbit ain't *our* dinner. It's mine."

"In that case, I would like to use your Colt with the two unfired rounds."

"What for?"

"When you shot the rabbit, a squirrel up in that hickory tree froze against a limb. I'd like some dinner too."

Emerson's lips pressed together, and he shook his head.

"Stand behind me. I've seen you use the long rifle. I will not try to pull something on you."

Emerson thought about it. Needing to know how to load the pistols decided it. He cocked the long rifle and stuck the pistol in the side pocket of West's suit coat. "Don't touch it till I tell you." Emerson then moved behind him, and said, "All right."

West pulled the pistol, aimed, and fired. A small tree branch and a squirrel plummeted from high in the tree, crashing through leaves and tumbling off branches to land with a thump.

After retrieving the pistol, Emerson led the two horses into the trees as West picked up the squirrel.

Emerson removed the ground cloth from behind his saddle and spread it on the ground. He laid Big's gun-loading material along with the two Dragoons and a pocket gun on the cloth.

"Load them," Emerson said. "I'll gut the meat. Then we'll ride on a piece before cookin' it."

"You know, young sir, your steed is played out. And If I might say so, you look played out."

"Your name West? I heard them fellas say a name."

"Westfall."

"Mr. Westfall. We fired guns here. If someone comes lookin', I don't want to be here. Horse is tuckered. I'm tuckered, but we're moving when we're done. A mile or so. We'll find some water. We'll cook and eat. Then we'll ride on a bit more. I don't want someone to sneak up on us by the smell of a fire and cookin'."

"Good thinking, young sir." Westfall reached up a hand as if to tip his hat, but he didn't have one. He must have lost it when the two men waylaid him.

Emerson humphed. Finally, he'd gotten something out of Westfall other than mocking laughter.

"Emerson. I'm Emerson."

"Pleased, young Emerson."

"I ain't so young."

"You, sir, I estimate, are half my age."

Westfall knelt on the cloth, swung the barrel of a Dragoon open on the hinge, and set to work pouring powder into the cylinders. Emerson took his belt knife from a saddlebag and slit the belly of the rabbit.

"How come you leave one chamber empty?"

"These weapons, young Emerson, have been known to go off with a bump or a jolt. More than one man has shot himself in the foot. So the wise man leaves the chamber under the hammer empty." He looked up at Emerson. "If you learn to shoot one of these as well as you handle your rifle, five shots will be more than enough."

Emerson knelt on the layer of last year's leaves. His rifle lay beside him. His right hand was full of entrails, but his eyes were on Westfall.

"Why you gobbing grease over the chambers?"

"Two main purposes. It keeps the powder from leaking out. Just as importantly, it keeps moisture out of the powder. If the powder gets wet, these pistols misfire."

"Sometimes they go off when you don't want them to. Other times they don't fire when you need 'em to?"

"With a modicum of proper care and attention to their peculiarities, these are fine weapons."

"Mr. Westfall, you load those 'fine weapons,' but leave the barrels broke open."

Westfall started to load a second weapon. Emerson slit the belly of the squirrel.

"What would you think, young Emerson, of sharing our kills? You eat half our squirrel; I'll eat half our rabbit."

"Tree rats, Paw called 'em. He wouldn't eat 'em." "Personally, I prefer them to rabbit. But, as you please."

Emerson wiped his hands on dried leaves, rinsed the carcasses and his hands with canteen water, and watched Westfall finish loading a Pocket Colt. The situation with Westfall felt strange. Westfall did what Emerson told him, and it was almost as if he had Paw doing what he directed. But that was a picture his mind refused to form.

"You're trying to decide whether to trust me, young Emerson. I tried to trick you back there by Dutzow's Corner, and that is bothersome to you. From my point of view, I had to see what you were made of."

Emerson wanted to believe him. But that was what was troubling, the wanting to believe the man. The man wasn't a Barlow. They were big, hard, and mean. People knew to not turn their backs on them and to be careful with what was said around them. Westfall was what Paw'd called a duded-up, silver- tongued devil. Paw once took Emerson along as he delivered Bull to a farmer who'd paid for his services. As they drove through Terre Haute, Paw'd pointed out a man on the boardwalk in front of one of the saloons. He was dressed fancier than the preacher on Sunday. "Be wary of such," he'd said. "They talk to yore face like the best friend you got whilst they reach around behind and pick yore pocket." That seemed to fit Westfall. But Emerson found himself wanting to like the man and to have to work at not liking him.

Westfall finished with the last weapon, laid it on the slicker, and stood.

"I know you are anxious for us to be on our way, but perhaps we should take a moment here with the pistols."

Westfall demonstrated how he aimed and fired a Dragoon.

Then he had Emerson dry fire the gun a few times.

"Now, young Emerson, I suggest you take it and fire a round at that tree. We have already made noise in this spot, and we can leave soon."

Emerson had Westfall check the road. It was empty of traffic. The Dragoon was heavy and hard to steady. Emerson fired and cut a sliver of bark from the edge of his target tree trunk. The Pocket Colt felt more natural and was much easier to control. He fired the Colt, and the bullet hit the center of the trunk with a satisfying splat.

"At ten yards from a tree, young Emerson, one ought to be able to score a hit. With a bit of practice, you will be as proficient with a handgun as you are with the long rifle."

They led the horses to the road. Before they mounted, Emerson handed the Colt to Westfall.

"I 'spect you 'druther have this over a Dragoon."

"Yes. Yes, I would. Thank you." Westfall slipped the pistol into a holster inside his coat. "I feel ever so much better with a weapon here." He patted his side. "How many rounds are in the Colt?"

Emerson thought about it. The Colt had five chambers in the cylinder. Only four had been loaded.

"Three."

"Correct. But, young Emerson, taking that much time to figure out the remaining rounds may have fatal consequences if you encounter someone who can shoot better than the ruffians back at Dutzow's. What I do, if it's a five-shot Colt, and one chamber is empty, I fire and in my head say, 'Three.' And I count rounds when others fire their weapons too. You recall what happened when your weapon clicked on empty? You had gained mastery of the situation, but the empty click erased your advantage and gave it to your adversary.

"It takes a bit of practice. What I do is picture a hand with fingers extended to match the rounds in the gun. I fire and a finger drops. I see the picture in my head. It's like the hand in my head is counting the rounds rather than me counting it with conscious effort. Do you see?" Westfall laughed. "Work at it. You'll see."

Emerson wasn't sure he would. He placed his foot in a stirrup.

"Young Emerson, I suggest you ride up here with me on this huge beast. He won't notice the extra weight at all. Your animal, however, most certainly will."

It was obviously the right way to proceed, but it would have sat better if it had been his idea. Which it plainly wasn't.

Oftentimes, doin' what you don't want to do is 'xactly what you got to do. Shit, Paw, Emerson thought, *you said I ain't your son no more. How come you keep talking to me, then?*

*****

They came to a creek and pushed through trees upstream to a grassy meadow. Westfall tethered the horses as Emerson dug a shallow pit and sparked up a fire. He skinned the rabbit, washed it in the stream, and skewered it on a stick.

Westfall dropped the squirrel next to Emerson. "Would you skin the squirrel, please? You obviously know what you are doing."

Emerson almost reached for it. He kept his eyes on his rabbit and turned the stick. The man was trying to bamboozle him again. If he could see a squirrel flat against a branch in the top of a tree and kill it with one shot, he'd know how to clean it. Emerson knew sure as anything. Why'd the man prod him like that? Emerson had come close to liking him. He'd trusted him enough to give him a gun. *You ain't got the sense to live through today,* popped to mind. He considered jumping up, pulling the Dragoon, disarming Westfall, tying him to a tree, saddling up, and leaving him as he found him. The smell of his rabbit over the fire started juices flowing in his mouth and punched another thought into his head.

"I gutted that tree rat. You kin eat it with the hair on if you want."

Westfall chuckled. Emerson looked up at him. He was standing there with his right hand out, the squirrel in his other. "Knife, please?"

Emerson frowned up at him for a moment and then handed him the knife. Westfall knelt by a fallen tree, chopped off the feet and head, slit the skin on the legs, and pulled the skin off. He propped the squirrel on a forked stick over the fire and knelt opposite Emerson.

Emerson studied Westfall's face, trying to see the things hidden behind it. Westfall was a puzzle. There was no mystery to Paw. None to Maw. The Barlow brothers were easy to read. Candace Barlow and Deborah Simmons, they never surprised him. Much.

"I'll show you how to load the pistol now, if you want," Westfall said.

And as he followed the older man's instruction, Emerson found his resolution to be wary of him waft away. When he loaded the last cylinder, Westfall said, "Good. As good as I would have done it." Emerson felt as if Westfall had given him a grand gift.

The rabbit was done. The squirrel wasn't. Emerson pulled a rear leg off the carcass and gave it to him.

Emerson chewed and swallowed a mouthful. "How'd them two back at Dutzow's get the drop on you, Mr. Westfall?"

"I accurately assessed their moral character but underestimated their cunning."

Emerson waited for him to continue, but he didn't.

"That's it?"

"You are merciless, young Emerson. Can you not see I'd rather not talk about it?"

"Yes, sir." Emerson took a small bite and talked around it. "I kin see that, but you bin making me uncomfortable ever since we met up. I 'spect you kin handle a minute or two of it."

Westfall raised a hand over his mouth and laughed.

"Simple, really," he said. "When I walked out of the saloon onto this step-high boardwalk, I looked up and down the street. I paid particular attention to the corner of the building, where I expected one of them to be lurking, but no one was there. When I was about to mount my horse, a pistol cocked from under the boardwalk."

"That kind of thing happen to you often?"

"That kind of thing, and worse, happened when I was … your age. Perhaps a bit younger."

"Not since?"

"Not since."

"Sharp," Emerson said.

"What?"

"My family name. I'm Emerson Sharp."

Then Warren Westfall gave his full name and more. He used different names for different days of the week. It helped him keep track of which name he was using. All he had to do was remember which day of the week he arrived in a town. He arrived in Dutzow's Corner on Wednesday, so he was Warren Westfall.

"If I'd have arrived today, Thursday, I would have been Tom Thackery."

"You don't have no real name?"

"By *real*, I assume you mean the first name I remember having. I haven't used that one for a very long time."

Emerson shook his head. Wednesday Warren Westfall was a handsome man from his slicked-back hair to his polished boots. The boots were scuffed and dirtied some now, but he was still a dandified dude. That's what Paw would call him. Maw might say he was dressed as a gentleman. He thought again of the folks in Indiana. They were easy to read. This Wednesday Westfall, however, the man had nothing but surprises inside him.

"So, young Emerson. Why don't we camp here? It's safe enough."

"Nope. It ain't. We do like I said. We ride a bit more. Then we stop."

"I see. A lesson learned from a recent experience." Westfall eyed him for a moment. "Last night?"

"You seem to see everything in me. I cain't see nothin' in you."

"Patience, young Emerson. It's said to be a virtue."

E MERSON'S EYES POPPED open. His heart thumped a sense of alarm through his veins. He lay still and listened.

Flies buzzed. A blue jay groused. A squirrel chattered. At the same time, it seemed unnaturally quiet.

Barlows!

Then he remembered what happened to them. But sure as shooting, somebody was behind him.

He was on his back with half the ground cloth draped over him. He eased his hand down to slide the Colt from his pocket. He thought about how he was going to move. Flip the cover off to his right and roll to his left as he cocked the pistol and aimed it.

He did just that and wound up pointing the gun at the white. The big draft horse snorted down at him and swished his tail at the flies bothering the other end of him. The white was at the end of its tether rope.

Emerson stood and let the hammer down on the pistol. He stretched his arms above his head.

Then it flooded back on him. Deborah Simmons. Candace and Big and Tiny. *You ain't my son no more.* All of it seemed as if it had happened a long time ago. He didn't know what day it was; Maw wasn't there to tell him.

Deborah Simmons. He got engaged to her on Tuesday. That day she was the worst thing he could imagine ever happening to him.

Early morning Wednesday, he lay with Candace Barlow under the apple trees. Candace, she was the best thing that ever happened to him. For a handful of hours.

On Thursday, Big and Tiny caught him. And he killed them. Big shot at him. He shot back. Tiny, however, lay hurt, and he'd stabbed him. Killing Tiny was like shooting Dog. Dog did not want to die. Emerson did not want to kill him, but neither of them could stop it. He would never forget shooting Dog. He would never forget killing Tiny.

Also on Thursday, he rescued Warren Westfall.

Friday. It was Friday.

But where was Westfall?

He looked around. As dusk settled the night before, they'd followed a stream away from the road forty or fifty yards into the trees and camped next to a meadow with graze. Now splatters of sunlight sprinkled through the leafy ceiling and speckled the forest floor strewn with last year's leaves. The stream trickled nearby. He could smell it—not the water but the plants growing green and thick in it and along the bank.

But Warren Westfall was gone. Horse, the saddle, the saddlebags with the powder and ball, all gone. Westfall had bamboozled him again. He stood counting up the few things he had and wishing for the many things he did not have but had need of. He had spare underwear and a spare shirt. He couldn't eat those. A coffeepot and no coffee, a skillet and no meat or grease. Owning nothing at all seemed better than owning things he couldn't use.

Emerson cut loose with a string of cuss words.

Sorry, Maw, but sometimes a man gets something in his belly so rotten and ugly it can't be dealt with, with no "Rats!"

Then Paw spoke. *Boy, I do not know how you managed to live through yestiday, but today's another matter.*

His twelve dollars. Still in his pocket.

Westfall had left both Dragoons. He had a Colt and the rifle. Five rounds plus five and four in the Colt and a single round in the rifle stood between him and starvation and salvation from whatever slicked-up dandy robbers he encountered that day.

If he managed to find Westfall, he'd spend one round on him and give it no mind at all. It'd be like shooting a wolf trying to get at a calf. Even if he was too late to save the calf, the damned wolf needed to be put down.

And the white draft horse looking at him, he still had him. It dawned on Emerson, the animal expected something to eat besides grass.

"Whitey," Emerson said, "a bag a oats may be all-fired important to you, but right now it ain't that much to me."

He scanned the campsite again, as if Westfall had to be there but he'd just overlooked the man. He cussed some more.

"Whitey, Westfall asked me to ride along with him. Shit. I believed him!"

Emerson kicked the edge of his ground cloth, glanced at the horse, and looked away, again.

"I kin say you're mine, but you ain't. You're Tiny's, and that's how I'll see you. I can't talk to Tiny's horse."

Emerson grabbed Tiny's heavy saddle and carried it to the animal. "Be nice if there was a stump nearby. Be a lot easier getting this on you." He spread the blanket on the white's back and then half flung, half hefted the saddle onto the beast. "Don't get the idea I'm talking to you, 'cause I ain't." He buckled the cinch strap. "But I got to figure out what to do, and saying it out is better than thinkin' it in." He worked the reins on and the bit in.

"First thing we're going to do, first town we come to, is see can we find you a new home. Maybe I can swap you. Maybe I'll have to sell you and then buy a ridin' horse. First thing. Second thing is I'm going to ask if Warren Westfall rode through.

"Shit.

"It's Friday. He never said what name he uses of a Friday.

Fred or Frank probably and some-last-name-or-other.

"No matter. I'll describe him. Five nine or ten. Just shy of skinny. Dresses fancy. Black hair cut short and slicked up to a fare-thee-well. That'd work better than a name.

"Well, then, standing here talking to ... talking to myself ain't gittin' none of it done."

He rolled up the ground cloth and tied the saddlebags and the roll behind the saddle. He mounted.

Then he heard someone pushing through scrub brush coming from the road. He hopped down, drew a Dragoon, and cocked it.

"Whitey," he cooed. "You keep quiet now. Don't you snort.

Don't stamp. You just stand here real quiet like."

Warren Westfall led Horse into the clearing and stopped.

"Don't shoot me, young Emerson. I've brought you breakfast."

Westfall cocked his head to the side a bit. "Ah. You thought I absconded with your animal and provisions. You were sleeping soundly. Last night when we arrived here, you spread the ground cloth, collapsed onto it with your boots still on, and, instantly, you were asleep. I thought you should stay abed as long you wanted.

"What do you say, young Emerson? Will you put the gun away and start a fire? I have pork chops and potatoes in the sack on the saddle horn. And I have coffee. I'll get the pot going. Then I have a proposition for you, if you are interested."

"I'm sure interested in the pork chop. And the coffee."

Emerson blushed. He'd sounded eager as a kid to himself.

The last cup of coffee he had, he'd snorted out his nose.

Emerson got the fire going, and Westfall brought a flat rock from the stream. It was just right to set the coffeepot on.

"You eatin' half the pork chop an' taters?"

"No. I ate at the farm where I purchased this. It's all yours." Westfall bowed his head. "Bless, oh Lord, the food You provide from the bounty You set on earth for all of us, and especially, this morning, for young Emerson."

The food was wrapped in pages torn from a catalogue. Emerson looked up from unwrapping it and dumping it into a skillet. "I hope you don't mind me saying, Mr. Westfall. You don't seem the praying kind. You seem more like my paw. He liked to say, 'Women need God. Men need guts, determination, and muscle.' Course he didn't say it where Maw could hear him."

"The odds that God exists are considerably higher than zero. Understand?" Emerson frowned.

"No matter. You should eat."

Emerson did not take time to warm up the food. He ate, wiped the back of his sleeve across his lips, and belched.

Westfall poured coffee into a shallow tin cup and handed it Emerson.

"Young Emerson, I am a sporting man. A gambler. I travel and never spend more than a couple of days in one place. When I gamble, I win. Some people get resentful. That's why I change my name. That, in a nutshell, is who I am and what I do.

"I propose to you, young sir, that we forge a partnership. What do you say?"

Emerson sipped the coffee. It was the best coffee he'd ever tasted.

"You want me to work for you, to cover your back, so nobody sneaks out from under a boardwalk and gets the drop on you?"

"Not work *for* me. Partner *with* me. We work together. What we earn, we share equally. I cover your back. You cover mine." "I'd not be working for you?"

"That wouldn't be a partnership."

"You won't try to bamboozle me no more?"

"I will not try to bamboozle you no more."

Emerson frowned at what he said and how he'd said it.

"That, young Emerson, was not a bamboozle. It was teasing banter between partners. What do you say?" "I don't know nothing about gambling."

"Quite frankly, there are a lot of things you don't know about. I will teach you."

"You're bound for Saint Louis, right, Mr. Westfall? Then what?"

"I'll get to that. Our first order of business will be to transform you. We can keep your hat, but the rest of you needs significant alteration. Right now, young Emerson, people will look at you and see a farm boy propping up a gentleman's hat."

"Mr. Westfall, you want to partner up, you best learn to speak the same language I do."

"What if, young Emerson, I teach you to speak my language? First, however, we will get you a bath to wash the smell of horse sweat and cow manure off you. With a haircut and a new suit of clothes, people will look at you and see a gentleman, and they will call you Mr. Sharp. At least until you open your mouth."

"Shit," Emerson said. "This teasin' a yours ain't no different from a bamboozle near as I kin tell."

"Ah, Mr. Sharp, you will see. This partnership will prove to be mutually beneficial."

"I don't know about that last thing you said, but I ain't said I'm in."

"Mr. Sharp, are you trying to bamboozle me down to a 49 percent share?"

"What?"

Westfall laughed, and Emerson said, "Shit."

IT WAS DARK out, but even without the smell of Maw's cooking, Emerson woke as if Paw'd just growled, "Git up, I said!"

Bedtime varied considerably during their eleven days in Saint Louis, including one occurring after sunup, but the previous night had ended early.

He turned the covers back, eased out of bed, and lit a lamp. As happened regularly now, he got out of bed with things Warren Westfall had told him playing in his head like an echo.

The day before, after they practiced with the pistols and as they cleaned and loaded the weapons, he'd said, "Going to church on Sunday, young Emerson, is not to give honor and glory to God. I do that every day when I wake, before meals, and at 'Now I lay me.' The purpose behind going to church on Sunday is to get out of scrabbling for money among people where the longest teeth, the sharpest claw, the biggest muscle, and since we are civilized, the sharpest wit is the prevailing law, and to abide for an hour in a house where the residents believe the meek are entitled to own a vegetable patch of their own. We earn our daily bread in an environment of moral toxicity. An hour a week away from that environment is salve to a rubbed- raw soul."

It was Sunday. They'd be going to services in the Catholic cathedral that morning. Last Sunday, they'd gone to a Lutheran church.

At the washstand, he poured water from the pitcher into the basin.

When Emerson looked in the mirror to shave, he saw shaving soap, but he heard Warren Westfall speaking to him. It had been a Wednesday when they arrived in Saint Louis, so he was Westfall, and he still was. During their first days together drifting south slowly, he changed his name, as he said he did, by the day of the week. But now he'd been Warren for a spell. It would be hard when they left town and he started being a different person every other day or so.

Westfall packed more talking in a day than Emerson's paw packed into a year. And the things he taught Emerson took a lot of thinking to get them to sit right in his head.

"The Sermon on the Mount, young Emerson, I don't want you to take my version of it as a new gospel. What I want you to do is to think about how I phrased it. Consider if it's right, or wrong, or somewhere between. Perhaps you will have a better way to put words to the thought."

Even when they practiced playing poker, Westfall never shut up, always going on about something.

"Consider this, young Emerson. Every variety of good and bad human behavior is in these two books: the Bible and the works of Shakespeare."

Maw'd run Emerson through the Bible often enough that he had a handle on most of the words in it. That Shakespeare fellow, though, he had some strange ways to hook up a string of letters to make a word and strange, too, in the way he strung words into sentences.

"Books and reading are among God's greatest blessings." And right here was one way Westfall and Paw were different. Paw tallied up worst things, such as "the biggest waste a time they is."

Westfall tallied up greatest blessings, and he had as many of those as Paw had the other.

"Good morning, young Emerson. Is it not a great blessing to be alive on such a fine day as this?"

On one fine morning, Emerson pointed out, "It's raining." "The rain will make the flowers grow," Westfall said.

Paw would have grumbled, "Rain. Biggest aggravation they is. It doesn't come when the crops need it to grow. It only comes at harvest time and rots a year's work in the field."

Westfall said of women, "They are God's greatest blessing. They please the eye; they please the nose; they please the ear. Mostly. And nothing else feels as good as running your hand over the skin of a woman."

Emerson moved to bring the image of the woman in the bed into view in the mirror. Her red hair splayed over the pillow, framing her face. She wasn't a beauty like Candace Barlow, more like Deborah Simmons in the face. But she was attractive sleeping with her face reflecting a soul at peace, not radiating the rancor that came off Deborah as hard to ignore as a horse stepping on your foot.

Rancor. He'd never encountered that word before he'd encountered Mr. Westfall.

Emerson glanced at the woman again and wondered if Deborah Simmons's face looked like that as she slept. Ellie. This one's name was Ellie. She slept with her arms above her head. The covers were down at her waist. She was not plain straight up and down, as Deborah was.

As much as she'd been a blessing the night before, seeing Ellie asleep and at peace, it was a great blessing.

Emerson scraped the razor over his cheek and flicked the soap into the basin.

"The second glass of whiskey is one of the greatest blessings," Warren had said at supper their first Sunday together.

"What's wrong with the first un?" he'd asked.

"One. Say *one*, not *un*."

He wouldn't answer the question until Emerson pronounced the word correctly three times in a row.

"A man is an alcohol-thirsty beast, young Emerson. A first glass tends to get guzzled down so fast the taste buds don't even know whiskey passed over them. The second glass, however, a man sips and savors on the tongue. One of God's greatest blessings."

"Jesus give His sermon from a mountain. You give yours over the feedin' trough," Emerson had observed.

Westfall was patient with his efforts to correct Emerson's speech and use of language. Paw would have told him once and then smacked him if he made the mistake again. Of course, Paw would have characterized learning proper speech and grammar as "the biggest waste a time they is."

That same night, Westfall imparted an added lesson. Shortly after a third glass, Emerson lost count of the shots. The next morning, he came to appreciate a chamber pot.

Before that morning, he considered chamber pots the strangest thing civilized people did. Cows and horses and pigs pooped and peed in a barn all the time. Unless they were very sick, uncivilized people used an outhouse. Strange, until that hangover rousted him out of bed with an urgent need to get the whiskey out his belly all in an instant when it had taken most of the night to get it all in there.

"The second glass of whiskey is a blessing. The third is a curse. You'd best remember this lesson, young Emerson."

That was as close to a threat as Westfall came in his teaching.

Emerson finished shaving, rinsed the residual soap off his face, dumped the basin into the chamber pot, and smiled. He had gotten some kind of … he had gotten quite civilized.

He put his razor in the saddlebag and walked to the side of the bed for a last look at Ellie. He was moved to leave more money on the nightstand next to her.

"You will be moved, young Emerson, to leave extra money with a young lady you spend the night with. Resist the generous impulse. It will make you memorable. Since you insist on keeping your name, it is best to seek anonymity wherever else it may be found."

Without Westfall's admonition, he would have left extra money for her.

"You have been a blessing for me, Miss Ellie," he whispered. "I hope today you find a blessing for yourself."

"Mmmm," she moaned, rolled onto her side, and pulled the covers over her head.

Emerson blew out the lamp and left. He listened at the door of Westfall's room. Quiet. He descended the stairs to the bottom floor of the Waterfront Saloon.

Emerson liked the saloon in the early morning with the sun not up yet and most of the cavernous room in shadow. Two lamps glowed, one on the bar, one on the counter behind it. Upside-down chairs sat on the tables. No one there. The piano quiet, and stilled, too, the babble of rowdy voices that made a person hoarse if he tried to talk over the noise for an extended period of time. Blessedly gone also, the tobacco smoke fog that rose from standers at the long bar, almost all of them with one leg on the brass foot rail, some facing the bar, some sideways to it, and from the table sitters ringing the round tables, and the smoke eye-stinging and sitting acrid on the tongue.

Westfall, however, liked it at night. He would say, "Look at this, young Emerson. Is it not the sight, the sound, the smell, the feel of Sodom and Gomorrah? Here in this den of iniquity, we earn our daily bread from those who earned it first by the sweat on their brows. On the eighth day, young Emerson, God created irony."

Emerson stood on the bottom step, thinking about Warren Westfall. Every time he learned something new about the man, it was as if all he did was discover how much he didn't know about him. The more he knew, the less he knew. He shook his head as he stepped onto the floor.

"Mawnin', Mistuh Shawp." "Mawnin', Mistuh Shawp."

Cato carried a tray filled with beer mugs to behind the bar. Cicero walked to the front of the bar and placed spittoons at regular intervals along its length. They were twins with glossy black skin, thick shoulders and necks, and close-cropped curly hair.

Emerson nodded to them. "You gentlemen wouldn't have a pot of coffee in the back room, would you?"

"You hear dat, Cicero? You be lookin' like some kinda genulmun wid dem spittoons!"

"Don' you mind dat uppity Cato, Mistuh Shawp. Y'all g'won an' sid at your table on dah veranda. He be bringin' dah cawfee directly."

Four small round tables, each with two upended chairs on them, had been placed near the wall of the saloon on the wide porch. Emerson righted a chair from the table nearest the door and plopped onto it. He reached his hand inside his coat to ensure he could easily pull his Colt from the holster under his left arm. "Every time you sit on a chair, the first thing you do," Westfall had instructed, "is ensure you have ready access to your pistol. You practice that until you *know* you can draw it easily, and without having to think about it, any more than you have to think about drawing a breath."

The Waterfront Saloon sat in a row of warehouses and saloons along a dirt road atop the riverbank. Up and down the road, the drinking establishments were identifiable by dim light spilling from open doors. Inside all the lighted places were men like Cato and Cicero sweeping and mopping out the signs of revelry from the night before. The warehouses came to life as the sun rose, but being Sunday, activity on the waterfront would be half what it was on a weekday.

Last Sunday, Westfall said, "The Lord asks us to keep holy the Sabbath. Mammon, in the guise of commerce on the river, tells men each and every day of the week is holy to him." Work on the river slowed down on Sunday, but it did not stop.

Westfall, Emerson thought, had eyes that saw a lot more than his did. Except even his eyes could not see in the dark. Three mornings past, Westfall and Emerson returned to the Waterfront after an all-night poker game in a hotel bar a few streets back from the river. Westfall did not like to play cards in the establishment where he roomed. They'd sat at the table Emerson occupied, and Westfall had asked Cato for coffee.

When he brought the pot and mugs, Westfall said, "Cato, why don't you and your brother sit and drink coffee with us? In the dark, we are all the same color."

"Thankee kindly, suh. Cicero. He be the smart one a us. He say we be Negroes. We gots to 'member that every minute a ever' live-long day. We be fergittin', we be fergittin' how to breathe soon after."

"You are freed men, are you not?"

"Yassuh. But there be Negro-free, an' there be white-man- free. An' dem two ain't the same, even in the dawk."

There was a glow at the edge of the world across the river in Illinois. For a moment, Emerson wondered if he was seeing all the way to the Wabash River. Cicero brought the coffee.

"Look like it be a fine mawnin', Mistuh Shawp."

"Indeed. Thank you, Cato."

Cato went back inside. When the incident had occurred at midweek, Emerson had smiled, thinking at the time that even Warren Westfall didn't know everything, that he still had lessons to learn too. Now, however, he saw that Westfall had staged that scene. Emerson had gotten too friendly with the brothers in the early-morning hours. Friendship with a Negro would be dangerous for both parties, and Westfall had orchestrated the scene so the pushback came from Cato, not as a dictum from an older man to a younger one.

Red tinged the glow in the east. Emerson sipped the coffee. It tasted as good as it smelled. The warmth from the mug felt good in his hand, and he drained it before the damp chill rising from the river could steal temperature and taste from the brew.

Watching the sunrise was what Warren Westfall would call a blessing. Colors awakened as if they had slept while the sun was down.

It occurred to Emerson that he knew what a blessing was, that he didn't need the older man to point those things out to him. He did not have Paw digging spurs into him to "Git a move on!" Coffee tasted so fine on the veranda with time to sniff the aroma, to savor the taste, while behind him it was as if the whole world slept—except for Cato and Cicero, of course—and the sunrise was just for him. He saw the dawn and the coffee as his blessings without any help. At the same time, he wondered what beauties, what wonders Westfall would see and remark on if he were there.

He thought about the night before when he'd told Warren about Candace Barlow and Deborah Simmons and Paw and Maw and Big and Tiny.

"Why did you confess all this to me, young Emerson?" Westfall asked with a bit of sharp-edged accusation.

Emerson had expected the older man to appreciate his honesty in disclosing his past. As a partner, he thought the older man should know, especially about the Barlow brothers. He stammered, searching for a reply.

"You were seeking absolution, forgiveness for killing those men, for ruining the lives of the Barlow, Simmons, and Sharp families. Do you not see, my forgiveness of those sins—I am sure you consider them such—is meaningless from me. Forgive yourself, young Emerson."

Of all the things Westfall had told him, that puzzled Emerson the most. How could it be right for men to commit sins and then just forgive themselves?

The sun edged an eye-searing spear of light above the end of the world, and it flooded Emerson's vision with white light that persisted after he squeezed the lids shut and massaged the bridge of his nose.

"Mr. Sharp, may I join you?"

Emerson made out the blurry shadow image of Westfall standing next to him.

A mistake. He hadn't heard the man approach. He'd allowed himself to be blinded.

"*Mr.* Sharp, may I join you?"

The *mister* surprised him. Always before he'd been young Emerson.

"Um, of course, Mr. Westfall."

Another mistake. Actually, he'd made two of them. He'd allowed himself to be discombob … disconcerted by the unexpected form of address, and he had clearly allowed Westfall to observe his discomfit.

Westfall sat and placed his hat on the table as Cato set a cup and a pot of coffee in front of him. He laid a five-dollar piece on the edge of the table. Cato swiped it up and went back inside.

"Mr. Westfall, you warned me about being overly generous. That appeared to be more than regular generous to me."

"Mr. Sharp, I warned you about being overly generous with female entertainers. If, within two days, you cannot see the difference between my warning and what I did, ask me and I will lay it out for you.

"Now then, Mr. Sharp. To the business at hand. I booked us on the *Bayou Belle* for a trip to New Orleans. We depart at first light tomorrow."

Emerson thought he covered the surprise at that announcement much better.

"We are partners, Mr. Westfall?" "Indeed."

"Then since you decided on New Orleans without consulting me, I have decided something for the partnership as well. Since we are departing tomorrow, I assume you listed yourself as Martin Monday?"

Westfall nodded.

"When we get to New Orleans, regardless of the day of the week, you will call yourself Weekes Daley."

"What?"

"Weekes Daley. Your name depends on the day of the week and you change it daily."

"That is the worst name I ever heard of."

"Why, Mr. Westfall, I thought you would consider it a great blessing."

PART II

Spring 1863

9

MANY TIMES OVER the last three years, Emerson Sharp had the thought that Weekes Daley had more of Maw in him than Emerson did himself.

Weekes insisted on attending Sunday church services. He frowned eloquent disapproval if Emerson swore. "A man must work at behaving like a gentleman when all those around him snuffle their supper from a trough and speak a language best confined to a sty." Maw would not have stated it that way, but she would have agreed with the idea.

He could still picture his mother after a Wednesday tea just short of his tenth birthday. Emerson had driven the buggy, and she'd turned back to the ladies on the porch and sighed. "Well," she'd said, "back to the world of man sweat and 'Time's a wastin'.'" Then she hiked her skirt up and climbed onto the seat.

When Emerson thought about Maw, it inevitably led him to think about Horse. Horse had been her buggy puller. Paw, stingy as he was, would he buy her another? He would never allow her to take one of the draft animals. Had Emerson robbed his mother of her Wednesday sip of civilized interchange with the neighbor ladies by taking away her means to travel?

After three years of gambling partnered with Weekes Daley, Emerson hid his feelings well, but Weekes always knew when his partner's conscience bothered him. "Young Emerson"— and Weekes only called him that when speaking about this particular topic—"in the bottom of a man's soul is a deep, dark pit. It's deep and dark, because over his life, a man takes his sins and his shames and shoves them down there so his mind doesn't have to deal with them. Your problem is your mind won't let those things stay there. If you forgive yourself, perhaps your mind will no longer find it necessary to keep dredging these things up and shoving them in your face."

Weekes was right, probably, but Emerson could not forgive himself for what he'd done to his mother. If he did, it would be the same as erasing her from the story of his life, as if he'd come to earth the same way Adam did. When he was in this frame of mind, Emerson could never picture himself receiving life directly from God. Furthermore, it was not as Weekes said. His mind did not go down into the pit and dredge up sin and shame. No. He, Emerson, descended body and soul into the pit, and he could not climb back out.

But Weekes had always been able to pull him up. "Assume the stance, young Emerson!"

Throughout their partnership, they practiced weekly with pistols and at open-hand boxing. Daley insisted that Emerson learn the fine art of pugilism, but when they practiced, they slapped rather than punched with fists. As gamblers, the partnership was bound to encounter those who considered their own ineptness at cards as insufficient reason for losing money. A fist to the nose could often defuse such a situation without having to kill the disgruntled card-dull. "If we, young Emerson, are cardsharps, these skill-less, luckless, belligerent simpletons are *card-dulls*. And it is best if we can avoid killing them. Killing makes us remember-able. Since you insist on us having *real* names, we must do what we can to clasp anonymity." Emerson's first boxing lessons always ended the same way: his cheeks filled with stinging fire, his head ablaze with the flames of red-yellow rage, his arms flailing like a demented windmill, and his smaller, shorter tormentor sitting on his butt with his arms raised over his head and laughing. Daley taught him to channel the heat of the anger into his hands and arms and to force cool, alert dispassion into his mind, to watch for signs that a slap was coming and to decide in a flash to strike first or to parry. When they practiced now, Emerson's reflexes were sharper, but Daley's ability to hide forecasts of his slaps was more refined. Both scored. They were evenly matched.

Except when Emerson slipped into the pit. Then Weekes would say, "Assume the stance," and Emerson would respond, "No!"

Daley would slap him until Emerson rose and tried ineffectually to parry. Daley would smack him repeatedly, backing up tall, long-armed Emerson until a sufficient number of strikes emblazoned his anger. Just before his fury reached homicidal level, Emerson would recognize his antagonist, recall where he had been, and understand how he had gotten away from there.

After such an instance, Emerson always said, "Rats!" Daley always said, "You're very welcome, Mr. Sharp." Weekes Daley always extracted Emerson from the pit.

Now, though, despair had grabbed Weekes Daley by the ankles and pulled him into darkness.

What worked on Emerson had no effect on Daley. Emerson commanded, "Assume the stance." By way of answer, Daley's face bloomed an expression indicative of indigestion, and he turned away. Emerson slapped him. He turned the other cheek. Emerson slapped him again. Daley's eyes met Emerson's but only to dump a bucketful of *I don't care how many times you hit me* into them. Emerson couldn't hit him a third time. That occurred the day before, after they arrived at the Waterfront Saloon in Saint Louis.

The night before, Daley had no interest in gambling. He took a bottle of whiskey to his room. Emerson had knocked on his door and received a muffled, "Go away," in response. Emerson descended to the ground floor. A number of card games were in progress in the saloon. He considered Daley's injunction to not gamble in the place where they roomed. Of course, they violated that rule on the riverboats, but observed it with a slight modification. On the Mississippi, they disembarked at places like Memphis and Vicksburg and gambled there for a few days before picking up another boat. In his present situation, he did not want to leave the Waterfront with Daley upstairs, suffering from some strange malady.

Emerson thought about his own bouts with what he called the "dark downs." Those always began with a sudden, unexpected recollection of Maw. He wondered if Daley had something akin to get the dark downs gnawing at him, but he could not envision such a thing gripping Weekes Daley. The man was mature, civilized, and master of any situation he found himself in. The dark downs was a juvenile malady, not something for a sophisticate. Emerson did not know what was wrong with his partner or how to help him, but he had to stay close. And that, he decided, outweighed the injunction to not gamble where they roomed.

Emerson went to the bar, ordered a beer, propped a foot on the rail, and studied the card games in progress. Of the five tables hosting poker, he focused on one with eight players. A broad-shouldered man with his back to the bar won two deals in a row. He wore pants with sewn-on suspenders. Through the spokes of the chair back, Emerson saw he also wore a belt. Under the man's left arm, a pistol barrel had been stuck under the belt.

A hand later, a man to Pistol Belt's left got up and walked away, clearly disgusted at how Lady Luck had treated him. Emerson sipped his beer and wiped foam from his mustache with the back of his hand. Two hands later, a man to Pistol Belt's right looked at his cards, threw them in, and departed.

Emerson sauntered over to stand behind the recently vacated chair. "You gentlemen mind if I sit in?"

Emerson watched Pistol Belt scan him up and down and smirk.

"Sit," he said.

Pistol Belt, Emerson judged, placed more value on skinning the fancy-dressed dude of his money than the money was worth. As Emerson sat, Pistol Belt ordered a bottle of whiskey from one of the young women floating between tables. He stuffed a bill into the top of her low-cut dress with the invitation, "You jist 'member whare that come from, little missy."

As the cards were dealt, concern for Weekes Daley evaporated. Emerson concentrated on cards and odds, on faces and mannerisms. He won a few hands and lost more as he worked to establish the demeanor of a well-heeled, naive youngster who bet recklessly.

Emerson observed Pistol Belt palm a discard every other hand or so. None of the other players cheated. After some four hours at the table, Pistol Belt had a large pile of bills and coins in front of him. Emerson dug money from a coat pocket to stay in what amounted to the largest pot of the night. To that point, ten dollars had been the largest bet any player had made.

"Fifty," Pistol Belt snarled, glaring at Emerson.

The other players all folded. "Fifty and raise a hundred," Emerson said.

"Yore hunnert and raise two hunnert more!"

Emerson was sure the man held a full house. Probably aces high. "Call." Emerson put bills into the pot.

Pistol Belt showed his cards: full house, aces over jacks. Emerson laid down four fours and a ten.

Visible highly charged emotions—astonishment, chagrin, and fury—chased, one after the other, across Pistol Belt's face.

"You cheated," Pistol Belt snarled.

Emerson smiled. "If, sir, you would care to discuss cheating, I am prepared to do so in some detail."

Wariness flickered briefly in the man's eyes, and then the fury blazed again.

Emerson could feel the man egging himself to pull his pistol.

"Was I you," Emerson growled through clenched teeth, "I'd keep them hands a yourn on the table whare I kin see 'em."

Emerson did not want to shoot the man. Odds were the man had friends. He'd have to shoot them too and then run and leave Weekes. He hoped resorting to crude speech after hours of the dandified variety would penetrate Pistol Belt's whiskey-sotted brain and find some survival instinct imbedded there.

The man's mouth fell open. Emerson kept his eyes on him but took in the two men directly opposite him. If one of the others at the table tried something, the two would show surprise. Emerson grabbed a handful of coins from the pot and stuck them in a coat pocket. He took a ten-dollar piece and slid it across the table to a man wearing a derby hat. "That's for a round of drinks courtesy of our friend here." Emerson nodded at Pistol Belt.

"Keep your hands on the table and stand up," Emerson ordered. Pistol Belt glared at him. "Stand up, I said!"

The man stood, and Emerson snatched his belt gun and laid it on the table next to the ten dollars with the barrel pointed at Pistol Belt.

"Keep this at least until I get out the door," Emerson said to Derby Hat. "I'd rather not get shot in the back. And if you're of a mind to, you might look inside this man's shirt."

Pistol Belt reached for his gun, but Derby Hat snatched it up and cocked the hammer. Pistol Belt froze.

Emerson swept the rest of the pot into his hat and jammed it on his head.

"Fred," Derby Hat said to the man to his right, "do like he said. Check the man's shirt."

Emerson made his way to the door at a pace that felt too fast and too slow at the same time. Behind him, he heard Fred discover a card in Pistol Belt's shirt. Shouts of outrage rose from the table he'd left.

Emerson passed through the swinging doors onto the boardwalk, turned left, and hurried into the alley between the Waterfront Saloon and a warehouse. He paused a moment to make sure no one followed him. No one did. As he continued through the alley, he checked behind him often. He entered the back door of the saloon and climbed the rear stairs to the second floor.

Emerson did not see anyone pay attention to him. Odds were good that no one remembered him walking down the other stairs before he joined the poker game.

Weekes did not answer when Emerson knocked on his door.

In his own room, Emerson undressed and climbed in bed. He clasped his hands behind his head and stared up at darkness as it pressed down on him. He hoped Weekes would snap out of it by morning, but then he realized Daley had been sliding into his downcast mood for some time.

He'd started complaining months ago. He liked to spend the winter in New Orleans, but war on the Mississippi River curtailed travel in that direction last year, and the situation looked worse this year. Nonmilitary traffic on the Ohio had been blocked. In 1861, Emerson and Weekes had made a trip to Joplin, Missouri.

"How about another trip to Joplin?" Emerson had suggested.

Weekes had shaken his head. "Do you not know how much fighting is going on in southern Missouri? The whole bloody western half of the state, for that matter?"

Emerson took a small amount of pleasure from not being addressed as "young Emerson."

So Weekes had decided on a winter trip through Chicago and on to Detroit. As usual on their gambling expeditions, they earned good money; however, Weekes characterized the winnings as empty victories.

"Empty victories?" Emerson asked. "We made a tidy sum on this trip. What's empty about that?"

Before the '62/'63 winter set in, Weekes always had an answer for arguments like Emerson had just posed. Weekes had always had the last word. Always. Now, though, at the first argument, he just turned away. Conceded defeat.

Emerson chided himself for not recognizing sooner what was happening to his partner when the problem had been small, when he might have dealt with it if he'd just understood what was happening to Weekes.

But he hadn't.

And at that moment, a couple of doors down from his own, odds were that Weekes Daley, who never but never had more than two drinks, was passed out drunk.

What if I can't pull Weekes out of this? What'll happen to me?

As soon as he had the thought, he knew he sounded like his nine-year-old brother, John. Then he remembered John wasn't nine anymore. John would be … he counted the years. Twelve going on thirteen.

Emerson brought his arms down and rolled onto his side. "Shit," he mumbled.

Later, sleep slipped into the room and closed his eyes. For a time.

EMERSON SAT AT the table next to the door on the veranda of the Waterfront Saloon with dawn breaking and dropping an oily sheen on the lead-hued surface of the river. The river, he thought, appeared to be filled with mercury instead of water: thick, viscous, comprised of semiliquid rotting matter, stagnant. Not moving.

"Shit," Emerson mumbled.

"You all right, Mistuh Shawp?" Cicero asked as he slid a cup and a coffeepot across the table.

"Ah, Mr. Cicero. Good morning. Thanks. For the coffee. And, yes, I'm all right. I'm worried about my partner, Mr. Daley."

"He be illin'?"

"No. Well, he does not suffer from a sickness in his body."

"Den he gots dah mugwumps. Mugwumps grab aholt a peeples time to time. Wommin, she lose her baby, mugwumps drag her down, down. Dah udder wommins, deh gadder roun' an pull her back up agin by an by. Mens git de mugwumps wen dey gits too much time to tink. Dey tink, and soon or late, deh come on de notion a what dey had befo' dey ate dat apple in de gawden a paradise. A man gits de mugwumps, you gits him back to work. Dat be dah cure."

"Huh," Emerson said. "It appears, Mr. Cicero, that you do a lot of thinking. Why don't the mugwumps grab you?"

"Oh, dey's out dere. But I'se worried 'bout dat Cato. Cain't let no mugwumps git me. I gots to take care a him."

Cicero went back inside. Emerson poured coffee. It was actual coffee. The Waterfront Saloon was able to obtain the real thing. Several places in Illinois, as they'd traveled south from Chicago to Saint Louis, had offered various substances that looked like coffee. Emerson grimaced at the recollection.

Mugwumps. Somehow, having a name to put to the dark, down moods he'd foundered in made those moods more real, more things of substance, more something his senses might recognize. *Oh, dey's out dere,* Cicero had said. Emerson felt it too. The mugwumps were out there, and they were eager to grab him. But like Cicero, he had someone else depending on him. The difference was Cicero knew what to do for Cato.

Emerson raised the coffee and sniffed the aroma and stopped the cup short of his lips.

Real coffee was a blessing. He saw, then, that it had been a long time since Weekes had toted up blessings or even mentioned a single one.

He sipped his blessing.

A man gits de mugwumps, you gits him back to work, Cicero had said.

There was enough light now that Emerson could see ripples on the surface of the Mississippi. It was moving. It was going someplace.

Cicero, he thought, *you are a smart fellow, and it was a blessing when I met you.*

*****

Behind the Waterfront Saloon, Cicero and Cato hoisted Weekes Daley up onto the bay horse, and they placed his feet in the stirrups.

"Mistuh Shawp," Cato said, shaking his head, "I bin seeing mens puke befo', but dis Mistuh Daley, I tink we come mighty close to seeing what a inside-out man look like."

"Cato, you hush. Don' you be jokin' like dat. Mistuh Shawp. Dis Mistuh Daley, he be duh finest gennulmun duh Good Lawd give me to meet up wit. He jus got tooken by de mugwumps. He need you to pull him up. I'se tinking you be duh onliest one whut kin."

Weekes Daley did not look like a fine gentleman. His gray face gave the impression it was melting to sludge and about to ooze off his skull. It was the arrangement of lines etched into his skin, Emerson decided, responsible for the impression. The corners of his mouth were pulled down forming an inverted V. Above that, a set of deep wrinkles ran from either side of the bridge of his nose down into his stubbled cheeks and formed another V.

But Cicero was right. Weekes Daley was a gentleman. He had been from the first when Emerson found him tied to a tree and about to be tortured by two ruffians. A gentleman was what he'd been through the more than a thousand days he'd known him. He'd be a gentleman again.

Cicero refused to take money for helping get Weekes cleaned up. Emerson tipped his hat to the brothers, and with the reins to Daley's horse in his hands, and Daley hanging on to the saddle horn, they set out heading west. After an hour's ride clear of the city, Emerson stopped and set up camp while Weekes curled up in his ground cloth and slept.

The next morning, Emerson built a fire and fried bacon and made coffee. With the bacon sizzling, Weekes sat up.

Emerson poured Daley a cup of coffee and gave him bacon and biscuits. When they finished eating, Emerson told him to douse the fire, saddle their horses, and pack up their gear. Emerson sat on a log with a tin cup of coffee and watched his partner do as he'd been told. Weekes labored silently. Emerson recalled the morning after he'd gotten drunk and how his physical illness symptoms were dwarfed by the shame he'd felt at Weekes Daley's moral superiority across the breakfast table from him. Now, it was the strangest thing, seeing the older man so obviously aware of his status relative to Emerson's, doing what he was told as if Emerson were an adult and sophisticated Weekes Daley were a child.

They crossed the Missouri River at Saint Charles that afternoon.

"We'll spend the night here," Weekes said.

"We're riding on," Emerson replied, and he kicked Horse into motion. Weekes followed without saying anything.

Later, Emerson killed a rabbit and field dressed it.

"You want supper," Emerson said, "you have to shoot it."

Weekes fired at squirrels three times before knocking one out of a tree.

"Build a fire while I take care of the horses," Weekes said.

"Leave the horses saddled," Emerson replied. "After supper, we'll ride on a bit. We don't bed down where we've had a cooking fire. That's my rule. It's like yours about not playing cards in an establishment where we have rooms."

Later, when they stopped for the night, Emerson helped Weekes set up camp. Then he took a bottle of whiskey from a saddlebag and covered the bottom of tin cups with the liquor. They drank, and Emerson poured each of them a second drink.

"Weekes, Cicero said the mugwumps grabbed you and pulled you down. After thinking about what happens to me, on occasion, I've concluded that mugwumps is as good a way as any to describe my symptoms. What's bothering you? Is it the mugwumps?"

Weekes held out his cup for another drink. "Nope. Two's it."

"Shit."

"Weekes! You just swore to rile me and distract me. You figured, sooner or later, I'd set the bottle down and you could grab it."

They sat atop their ground cloths. Weekes's face was hidden in shadow.

"Weekes. You guzzled your second drink as fast as you did the first one. I'm here to tell you, that second drink was one of God's great blessings."

Weekes humphed.

"So are you going to tell me what's bothering you?"

Weekes sighed and looked up. Emerson did too. Above the clearing where they camped, two stars burned holes in the dusky gray sky.

Weekes said, "Cicero is observant, intelligent, and wise."

"Perhaps, Mr. Daley, it's that the war has hemmed us in.

About the only path open to us anymore is Saint Louis to Chicago to Detroit and back again. Is that it?"

Again, a sigh. "Partly. At first, I thought the war was a small affair, concerning those along the East Coast. Now, it has washed over us in a giant polarizing wave, forcing men to choose sides, to hate not only their enemies but everyone who is not rabidly for them."

"Yes. But the war can't go on forever."

"True. It cannot go on forever. When it is over, however, the part of the world we live in will be very different from the one we had when it started."

Weekes's tone of voice had been somber and exerted a pull toward darkness. He thought about pouring both of them another drink. He jumped up, pulled the cork, and upended the bottle.

"What are you doing?"

"What you would be doing if I were in your shoes."

"Stupid!"

Emerson smiled. "In the morning, use the bottle for target practice. You need that."

"Where are we going, Emerson?"

"North."

"That's a direction, not a destination."

"That's true."

"So where are we going?" "North."

Weekes mumbled something about a most aggravating conversationalist as he rolled up in his ground cloth.

*****

"A bath, a barber shave last night, church this morning, and a roasted chicken dinner—all God's great blessings, Mr. Sharp."

The busty proprietress of Thelma's Boardinghouse passed a slice of apple pie to Weekes.

"Miz Thelma, my horse is going to groan when I sit in my saddle this afternoon. A sumptuous repast, ma'am."

The widow blushed. Emerson rolled his eyes at Weekes. The four other men at the table chipped in with their own praise, and Thelma stood up, fanning her face with her napkin.

"Coffee," she said. "I'm fetching the coffee."

After supper, Weekes and Emerson rolled up their bedrolls and walked to the livery stable.

"Where are we going, Emerson?"

"North."

"Canada's north."

They skirted a pile of horse biscuits in the road.

"I've been thinking, Emerson."

"You don't want to go north anymore?"

"Remember when we passed through Dutzow's Corner on the way to Saint Louis?"

"Of course I remember. I tried to talk you into going around the place I found you tied to a tree. It seemed out of character for you to risk seeing those two bandits again, even if the odds were small."

"I never stopped thinking about that corner. Old Man Dutzow picked that spot some fifteen years ago. He set up the saloon, the grocery store, the blacksmith shop, and a freight- hauling business. He made money hauling farmers' grain to the Mississippi. He made more money hauling whiskey and groceries back from the river to sell in his store and saloon. We, Emerson, need to find us a Dutzow's Corner of our own."

Emerson frowned.

"You thought we could live off our gambling proceeds forever?"

"Well—"

"We can't. When this war ends, prevailing conditions will be drastically different from what we know now."

"Different how?"

"I don't know, but they will be different. I have a desire to build something—if not a Dutzow's Corner, something of substance, something enduring."

"Stay in a place like that corner permanently?"

"Would that be so bad?"

"I spent the first years of my life chained to Paw's farm."

"Perhaps, Emerson, if we own it, you won't feel shackled to it."

Digging Weekes out of the mugwumps had been the most important thing. And this is what came of it. During all his years as Paw's field hand, or draft animal, he'd never imagined he could live free and fancy and leave a place when he wanted to explore wonders hundreds of miles away. Now, his partner was thinking of ending this all.

"You don't agree with what I'm proposing?"

"Well … I haven't thought about staying in one place."

"We won't be staying in just any place. It won't be some dusty, drab, uncivilized road intersection miles from the nearest neighbor. What I'm talking about is an opportunity like Mr. Dutzow found and recognized as having great potential."

"But you don't want to go north to find it?"

"No, partner. Remember when you told me about Deborah Simmons's father? I propose we take his objective as our own."

"California?" "California."

11

DURING THE TRIP heading west from Hannibal, Weekes stopped them in towns and villages. He'd had enough of sleeping on the ground.

When they stopped, they stayed overnight, occasionally for two or three days, depending on the availability of card games and whenever Weekes judged they'd taken enough money from one location. Emerson was pleased to have Weekes back to his normal self—and pleased, too, to be traveling again at a pace driven only by poker considerations.

Weekes said they'd hook up with a wagon train and follow the Santa Fe Trail. Emerson had read and heard enough about the trail to know that wagon-wheel ruts were the only markers of civilization along much of it. When he'd first partnered with Weekes, he was astounded at the things he discovered and that he could live life at such a leisurely pace with no "Git up, I said," no "Time's a wastin'." He'd grown fond of the fine things Weekes Daley had shown him in the cities they visited, and fond, too, of the life they lived. He was not fond of the idea of traveling to California.

The horses *clop-clopped* side by side on the hard-packed road. "How long do you think we'll stay in Saint Joseph?"

"Until we find a wagon train that will take us."

"You remember those fellows talking about the Indians along the trail? Apache. Comanche. They made them sound invincible. They sneak into your camp, and you don't know they're there until your throat is cut."

"I do believe the Indians of the Southwest are fierce warriors. But they are men, and therefore, they are not invincible. We will be part of a wagon train with a substantial number of well- armed men.

"I will say, Emerson, we should not underestimate these red- skinned fighters, but traveling from Hannibal to Saint Joseph was fraught with its own perils."

At a poker game a couple of nights prior, one of the players was telling about encountering bands of riders as he rode east from Kansas City. "The first band stopped me and asked me if I was for Southern rights or the federals. 'Southern rights,' said I. I could see that was the thing to say to them decked out in slouch hats and guerilla shirts. Coupla hours later, another band asked me the same question. They was guerilla hunters, looked like to me. 'I'm for the federals,' says I." The man downed his whiskey and poured another.

"This damned war has gotten to be a nuisance," Weekes had offered.

"Nuisance, my ass. If I answered wrong, they'da hung me."

Emerson checked behind them. On the trail, when he reminisced, when they talked, a survival instinct always tweaked him to be attentive, be vigilant. Weekes never seemed to worry. Emerson had asked him why he wasn't more watchful on the trail. "How'd you manage to stay alive before you partnered with me?" was the way he'd put it.

"You, Mr. Sharp, are three times the woodsman I am. You hear birds, bugs, and beast noises and can tell if the animal kingdom is at peace or disturbed by an alien presence. Before I met you, I traveled from place to place by stagecoach, train, or boat mostly. Since you refuse to part with Horse, our partnership has accommodated this attachment of yours."

Weekes had wanted Emerson to sell Horse when they first partnered, but he'd refused. They'd made a trip by horseback from Saint Louis to Joplin and back in 1861. The next year they'd traveled from Saint Louis to Saint Joseph. And like their present journey, Weekes insisted on minimal nights sleeping on the ground. Emerson was convinced Weekes had no appreciation for how difficult life was going to be on the

Santa Fe Trail. He was also convinced Weekes overestimated Emerson's skill as a woodsman. It was one thing to manage the roads, trails, and forests of the Midwest, but it would be an entirely different challenge on the Santa Fe Trail.

Emerson had voiced his concern, but Weekes had brushed him off with, "We tend to fear unfamiliar dangers much more than familiar ones even if the familiar ones are more likely and of graver consequence."

"The threat from Indians versus being in the middle of a war, is that what you mean? With your ability to read people, I think you could talk us out of any danger we encounter in Missouri. The Apache and Comanche won't ask us any questions. We won't be able to talk our way out of the danger they pose."

"Emerson, I intend to go to California. Perhaps you don't want to. It's your choice."

Emerson felt a puddle of ice water congeal in his belly. As fond as he was of the life they had, the thought of dissolving their partnership scared him more than the Indians along the trail.

"Mr. Daley, you will never make it to California unless someone watches out for you."

"Good, Mr. Sharp. It would have pained me to go alone."

Weekes stopped his mount, and Emerson pulled up beside him. The eastern edge of Saint Joseph was ahead a quarter of a mile.

It looked pretty much the same as it had the year before. A long street lined with businesses, some on both sides with the intended purpose of providing easy access to sin, and there at the end, centered on the street and marking the far end of town, sat a white church. The sight reminded Emerson of Genesis, about halfway through as he recalled, where the Lord told Abraham He was considering sweeping the wicked twin cities away. Abraham convinced the Lord to spare the place if there were ten good people. Saint Joseph was safe. The church looked as if it could hold fifty good people.

"Emerson, this is no time for daydreaming. Pay attention." All business now. "In the event a hasty retreat is required, we take the road we are on now. If that is blocked, we ride west through town and then go north. We do not want to get chased into Kansas. The Red Legs shoot anyone who is not a Red Leg."

Emerson nodded and scratched his cheek. The stubbled beard itched. Emerson was dressed in rough clothing and needed a shave. Weekes wore a suit, white shirt, and a ribbon tie. They entered card games separately and never gave indication of their partnership.

"Give me five minutes. If I find a game, I won't come out. If there isn't a suitable one, I will return to the street and try another saloon. And, Emerson, you look the part of bumpkin ruffian. Do not slip up and spout a snippet of your newfound erudition like you did two nights ago."

"I kin handle it, Paw."

"I kin handle it, Paw."

Emerson grinned, pleased anew to see evidence Weekes had put the mugwumps behind him. Weekes rode ahead. Emerson slipped the thong off the hammer of the Navy Colt in the holster on his right hip. From his saddlebags, he pulled a pocket gun. He was wearing a homespun shirt open in front over a stained long-sleeved undershirt. He stuck the pocket pistol under his belt.

After waiting the five minutes, Emerson tied Horse to a hitching rail beside three other mounts, climbed two steps to a boardwalk, entered the saloon through batwing doors, and stepped to the side with his back to the wall.

A long bar lined with patrons laughing, talking, and lounging, and two busy bartenders took up most of one wall. Girls in fancy strap dresses and bare arms and shoulders and done-up hair mingled at the bar and at tables with rough- dressed men with untrimmed face hair, and all of them, except the bartenders, wore hats. A babble of voices and cigarette and cigar smoke fog swirled over the hats and ladies' coiffures.

Nobody paid any attention to him. To his left, a wheel of chance spun, adding a clacking racket to the din. From the din, his ears sorted the sound of dice—die—rattling in a tin-sided box. Then the die clattered down a tin chute. Disappointed moans surmounted the blended murmur of fifty voices.

"Saloon, sweet saloon," Weekes liked to say. Emerson spotted him at a table playing five-card with five men.

Emerson started toward the end of the bar, intent on ordering a beer, and then joining the men at the card table.

"Emerson!"

He stopped. His hand started moving toward the Navy Colt. Then it stopped and rested on the handle.

A girl, a pretty blonde, stood up at a table two over from the card players. She said his name again, and her face lighted up. She was happy to see him evidently. He didn't know her. He didn't want to know her. He wanted to get into the card game. She started to move toward him. At the table with the girl were three men and a brunette. She was plainer than Blonde, by a considerable margin.

A red-bearded, barrel-chested lout grabbed Blonde by the arm. "Where ya think you're goin'?"

Blonde bared her teeth at the brute and jerked her arm free. Then she looked back at Emerson, and her ugly snarl metamorphosed into a warm smile, and she crossed the space between them and took his arm.

"Whiskey?" she asked. "And buy me a drink." Then she gave him a naughty grin.

The girl had some extraordinarily expressive faces she could put on.

She propelled them to the end of the bar and ordered drinks. "We'll have a drink together," she said. "Then we'll go upstairs, get you a bath, get you slicked up proper for the gamin'."

"Aw, shit," Emerson mumbled.

He remembered. The last time they'd been in that saloon, Emerson had wanted to play the well-dressed gambler.

Well-dressed gambler wasn't a role for Weekes. That was who and what he was. On the riverboats, both of them dressed as gentlemen. In the saloons, Emerson always played the common man, fitting in perfectly by appearance and speech with the rest of those habituating the saloons where they labored for their daily bread. At a card table, they never gave a hint of their relationship. Emerson played the game straight. Whether he won or lost was of no concern. Weekes, however, modified luck when necessity dictated. Emerson's part of the partnership was to cover Weekes if someone thought he won too often and to hopefully get the two of them out of the establishment and the town without getting hurt and without having to kill anyone. So far, it had worked that way. But a year ago, as they'd approached Saint Joseph, Daley agreed to let Emerson play the gentleman gambler.

They bought a suit, and after they entered the saloon, Emerson sized up the girls and picked Blonde. He bought her a drink and asked if there were facilities where he could bathe and get properly attired for the gaming. She'd scrubbed his back and shaved him with a deft hand. After he was dressed and she was dressed, she acted as if she'd swooned at the sight of him, but then she'd laughed and turned him to the mirror.

Black suit, white ruffled shirt, white cuffs showing at the sleeve. Atop his tan, his cheeks bore a blush from the shave. Black mustache trimmed and neat. Curly black hair oiled and combed. Maw would think he was a proper gentleman.

Then the girl walked arm in arm with him down the stairs and to the poker table. Weekes already had a seat. After Emerson joined the game, Weekes had a run of bad luck. Emerson saw him try to palm a discard but muff it. No one else at the table noticed. After losing steadily for an hour, Weekes got up and left. Emerson, on the other hand, won $200 on the night. At times, a player would grumble.

"Get a new deck," Emerson would say. "You deal."

It made no difference. Good cards seemed anxious to jump into his hands. A couple of times that night, Emerson said it was that girl who brought him luck. The girl had a name, but he couldn't remember it. To him, Blonde was her name now. Before he left the room the next morning, he'd left her fifty dollars on the nightstand.

No wonder she remembered him.

But he didn't need her interference with the plans he had for the night.

"You said, 'Aw, shit.' Why'd you say that?" Blonde asked, drawing him back.

"Well, ma'am, you're awful purty. I wisht I was who you said. But I ain't."

Uncertainty flashed onto her face. Then it flashed off.

"Why you acting like this?" She put her hands on her hips. "You're Emerson."

"No, ma'am." It was a Tuesday. "I'm Tom Thackery." He wasn't sure if Thackery was for Tuesday or Thursday. It didn't matter.

A bartender slid their drinks across the bar. Emerson laid money down. "That cover a round for the table this lady come from?"

The bartender grabbed the coins, and Emerson tipped his hat and walked away. All the way to the poker table, he could feel Blonde's eyes burning hot, tingly holes in his back between his shoulder blades. But he didn't hear from her again.

For a while.

At the table, Weekes had the biggest pile of winnings. The young man to Daley's left had won some too. He bore a white scar on his clean-shaven cheek that ran from his earlobe halfway to the corner of his mouth. The other three men had small stacks of silver dollars. Their bushy face hair could not hide their sullen hostility.

Emerson asked the table if he could sit in.

"Pull up a chair," Weekes said, smiling warm and friendly. "The game is draw. The ante is one dollar."

Emerson plunked a coin onto the table and sat beside the clean-shaven fellow, Scar.

Weekes hadn't been in the saloon very long. The size of his untidy pile of coins and bills indicated he'd won a couple of large pots.

The player across from Emerson had the deal. As he shuffled, periodically, a corner of his lip raised and a gold tooth peeked out. Gold Tooth slapped the deck in front of Weekes.

"Let your buddy cut," Weekes said, nodding at the man to Gold Tooth's right.

"Cut the damn cards," Gold Tooth growled.

Next to Emerson, an arm shot across the table and cut the cards. Scar. He'd cut with his left and had his right hand under the table. Emerson eased his Colt out of the holster. Gold Tooth and Scar glared at each other.

"Deal," Scar said. If the whole saloon hadn't gone quiet, Emerson wouldn't have heard Scar even though he was next to him.

Emerson and Weekes had never been in a setup like this. They'd encountered belligerent hard losers a few times. Sometimes the loser had a partner. They always focused their attention on Weekes because he took their money. They assumed he'd been cheating. Sometimes he was. But when one or two men threatened Weekes, Emerson standing up on their flank with a pistol in each hand had always gotten them out of the bind.

But Gold Tooth and the two opposite Weekes were together. Emerson was sure. Plus Scar worried him. He couldn't cover them all.

"Let the new guy deal," Weekes said. All eyes turned to him. "Just a suggestion. To get the game moving again."

Gold Tooth frowned, grabbed the cards, and started flipping them to the players.

Saloon noise resumed to its former level, as if nothing untoward had occurred. Frequenters of such a place, Emerson mused, were sensitive to the signs that bullets might soon be flying, that ducking and or running might soon be prudent. The frequenters also recognized when danger receded to tolerable levels.

Emerson won the first hand with two pair, kings and eights beating Gold Tooth's lesser pairs. After he won the second hand, he also won Gold Tooth's enmity away from Scar. Emerson dealt and Weekes won. Then the man on Gold Tooth's right picked up his hand, and his face lit up like a barn fire on a moonless night. No one bet against him.

Gold Tooth dealt. Then he bit off the end of a cigar and spat it to the floor.

"I beg your pardon!" Weekes was indignant. He pulled his breast pocket kerchief and bent over to wipe his boot.

Gold Tooth scratched a match on the table and sucked a large ember onto the end of his cigar. Then he blew a noxious cloud across the table. Emerson winced and turned his face aside toward Scar. Emerson still saw what happened. Under the table, Barn Fire passed a card to Gold Tooth.

Scar blinked but his face didn't move. Except the corner of his lips twitched once.

Weekes and Scar checked. Emerson threw a dollar. The next two each bumped the bet another one.

"Cost ya twenty to stay," Gold Tooth said, rather pleasantly.

The lower canine stared at Emerson, warm and yellow, as Gold Tooth's black eyes regarded him as a vulture would looking at dead meat just before ripping a beak-ful.

Weekes and Scar threw in twenty.

"Bump another twenty," Emerson replied.

The saloon went quiet again. Then chairs scraped and boots clumped across the wooden floor. Emerson felt the crowd press behind him.

The man to Emerson's left pulled a plug of tobacco from a shirt pocket and bit off a chunk. He was about five six. Shorty.

Shorty probably had twenty in front of him, but not much more. Finally, he was done thinking about it and threw his cards onto the discard pile. Barn Fire folded and grabbed Shorty's money and slid it and his own over to Gold Tooth.

"Call," Gold Tooth said and pushed his money into the pot.

Weekes and Scar folded.

"Cards?" Gold Tooth asked.

"Two."

Gold Tooth dealt Emerson's and said, "Playin' these." He tapped his hand. "Your bet."

"A hunnert," Emerson said. He slid bills and coins to the center of the table.

"You didn't look at your cards," Gold Tooth said.

"Hunnert to ya."

"Ya drew two cards an' you dint look."

"Put your money up, or I'm takin' this damned pot. I'm gonna count tuh three."

"What the hell are yuh tryin' tuh pull?"

"One."

"Call. Goddamn it. I call."

Gold Tooth started counting money. He had seventy-two dollars. Pulling his pocket watch, he dropped it on top of the cash.

"That ain't worth no twenty-eight dollars," Emerson said. "Two."

"Wait." Gold Tooth pulled a pistol from his belt.

Clicks of pistol hammers cocking sounded under the table. Scar had cocked his too. Scar could be aiming at Emerson's belly.

Gold Tooth held the pistol up, his finger clear of the trigger. He raised the other hand. It was empty. "This is a special modified Colt pocket gun. It's fixed so the cylinder can't move under the hammer. You kin load all five chambers and not worry none about shooting yore foot off. It's worth forty."

"I'll give you forty for it," Scar said.

"I ain't selling it. I'm bettin' it. Then I'm gittin' it back."

"Put in sixty and the Colt," Emerson said.

Gold Tooth did. He laid the pistol down with the grip in Barn Fire's direction. He turned his cards over.

"Full house. Queens an' sevens." Gold Tooth flashed his whole mouthful.

Emerson put on a lopsided grin.

Gold Tooth started reaching for the pot.

"Hold it," Emerson said.

Emerson turned over a king. Then a trey. Another king. A third king.

"You got twelve dollars left. Wanna put them up agin my last card?" Emerson asked.

"Turn the damn card."

Emerson didn't really care if he won or not. The way things were at the table just then, Emerson didn't think it would take much before lead started flying. If he won, that might tip the balance to violence. If Gold Tooth won, he'd think he'd humbled a stupid farm boy who'd gotten arrogant riding a lucky streak he had no right to enjoy. If Gold Tooth won, he'd get crazy reckless from then on. Emerson was sure he'd win everything the big guy had before the evening was over. It wasn't often Emerson thought of winning himself, rather than supporting Weekes.

Emerson turned the card. Another trey.

"Them three's in cahoots!" It was Blonde from close behind Emerson. "They cheated. I seen 'em."

Emerson had the sensation that time stopped. No one moved. It was as if he were looking at a painting of a crowded saloon. He was in the space between a tick and a tock.

Then everyone started moving.

Gold Tooth stood up, pulling his holster gun. Emerson grabbed his pistol from his lap, cocked, and fired through the table. Gold Tooth sat back on his chair with an astonished look on his face.

Barn Fire reached for the pistol on the table. Scar shot him, knocking him over backward.

Shorty fired through the table, and Weekes grabbed his throat and blood leaked between his fingers.

Emerson grabbed Shorty's pistol with his left and forced it down and smashed his Colt across Shorty's face. Then he stood and fired two shots into the ceiling. He fired and shattered the mirror behind the bar. He fired and splintered the floor near two men running for the door.

Holstering his Colt, he took Shorty's gun in his left hand and drew his own Pocket Colt. He started firing the right, and then the left, splintering more floorboards, hitting the bar near men diving over it.

He emptied both pistols and stuck them in his belt. Then he grabbed Gold Tooth's pistol from the table as Scar scraped the money into his hat.

"Let's go," Scar said.

"My partner."

"He's done for. C'mon."

Weekes lay on the floor, blood puddled under his head, unseeing eyes open.

Scar grabbed Emerson by the arm and jerked him toward the door.

A couple of men peeked up over the bar. Emerson pulled his arm free and aimed at them. They ducked.

"C'mon!" Scar hollered from the door.

Emerson fired once more, and a whiskey bottle exploded on the shelf behind the bar. Then he ran outside, crossed the elevated boardwalk, jumped down to the dirt, ripped the reins off the hitching post, grabbed the saddle horn, swung up, and said, "Horse!"

The animal took off after Scar, already a good distance ahead. Horse was running full out, but Scar was still drawing away. Emerson pulled his saddlebags from behind him and took out two Dragoon Colts and strung the holster straps over the horn.

There was gunfire from behind him. Some men were mounted and chasing him. Others were running for their horses. The two riders closest to him were firing. They were closing the distance. A bullet zipped by his ear.

"Horse," Emerson said and pulled on the reins.

Horse slowed. Emerson jerked him around to face the posse. He pulled the long rifle from the holster, stood in the stirrups, and fired.

A rider tumbled over the end of his mount. Emerson stowed the rifle, pulled a Dragoon pistol. He fired, and another rider flew out of his saddle. He fired again and a horse went down with the rider flying over the animal's head.

The rest of the posse hauled their mounts to a stop, turned them, and headed back to Saint Joseph at a gallop.

"Horse," Emerson said, and pressed his knee to the animal's side and got it walking southeast again.

Emerson pulled the rifle and poured powder down the barrel. After checking behind him, he tamped the powder and a ball and loaded a cap. Reloading the rest of the weapons, including inspecting Gold Tooth's pistol, would wait until later. It was hard to do a proper job of loading on horseback.

He kicked Horse into a trot.

Damn!

Scar had the money. The money was long gone. Emerson had ten dollars inside his gun belt. He had bills in the handles of his Colts. He wasn't broke, but all of it did not make much of a stake.

Then he remembered Weekes.

"Shit!" he said through clenched teeth.

W EEKES LYING ON the floor, blood staining his white shirt, blood trailing out the side of his mouth, blood pooling under his head. That picture was as clear in his head as if he were still in that saloon, looking at his partner.

The one he'd called Shorty had killed Weekes. And Emerson had only smacked him in the face with his pistol. A bloody lip and a lost tooth at worst. Not nearly enough for killing Weekes Daley. Emerson regretted not killing Shorty. He regretted not killing more people in that saloon. The thought of shooting Blonde flitted through his head, but he pushed it aside hurriedly. Shooting a woman was not a right thought to sit in a man's head. No matter what.

Shit!

He saw it then. It hadn't been Blonde's fault. It was his fault. He killed Weekes Daley. Last year, he had played the gentleman gambler. He had roomed where he played cards. He had tipped Blonde generously, extravagantly. Rules Weekes had taught him, he had violated. And killed his partner.

What the hell am I going to do now?

Horse was trotting down the road heading southeast away from Saint Joseph. Other than that, he had no idea about where he was going, where he ought to go. He checked behind him and found no pursuit. Still he felt like he should kick Horse into a full-out run. Get away from the town where he got his partner killed. He was also mindful of the guns in need of loading. If he had to shoot his way out of another confrontation—

Still no pursuit behind him. A hundred yards ahead, the road made a sharp turn to the right. After he rounded that bend, he'd pull Horse into the trees and reload his pistols. And he'd ride in the forest, not in the middle of a well-traveled road.

As soon as those thoughts gelled into decisions, his mind returned the image of dead Weekes to him.

He pulled on the reins to stop his mount. "Horse," he said through gritted teeth, "I'm trying to be vigilant, but right now it's hard. Do you know what's around that bend in the road?"

Swinging around in the saddle to check behind again and back to that bend, he cocked his head, listening. A crow cawed. Insects buzzed. Stillness lay over all.

"Horse. I can't see or hear anything. Wind's in our face. You smell somebody coming?"

The animal twitched its ears and swished its tail.

"A lot of help you are," Emerson remarked. "I got the sense there's someone around that bend. I don't think we should figure he's a friend. Let's go. Walk on the grass. We'll make less noise there than in the road."

Emerson guided Horse up onto the grassy swath between the packed dirt road and the edge of the woods. He drew the fully loaded Dragoon. He counted his available rounds. The long rifle, the fully loaded Dragoon, and the other one had rounds remaining.

Oaks and firs and scrub brush screened the road around the bend. Just short of the bend, Emerson dismounted, ground-hitched Horse, and stepped into the road and peered around the brush.

A horse stood on the right side of the road facing away from Emerson. A man, facing rearward, sat atop it. His legs were crossed on the animal's rump. It was Scar from the poker game.

Scar licked a cigarette paper, stuck the misshapen cylinder in his lips, struck a match on the butt of his holster gun, and grinned at Emerson. Then he put the flame to his smoke, inhaled, and blew a white cloud.

Emerson mounted and rode to within a horse length from Scar.

Scar picked up a bundle from his lap, a red bandanna tied up to be a sack. He extended it toward Emerson.

"This here's yours," Scar said.

"The money?"

Scar nodded.

Emerson studied the man. Scar puzzled him. There was something deep and undiscernible in him. As there was … had been with Weekes. "Trust no one, young Emerson," Weekes had instructed long ago. "Not even me. Be ever vigilant."

"But you ain't … viglint," Emerson had replied.

"You have vigilance enough for the two of us."

"Does that mean you trust me?"

Weekes had flashed that big grin of his, which was the only answer he ever got to the question. From their earliest days together, Emerson thought Weekes knew him as well as he would know a book he'd read carefully cover to cover. But Emerson had never been able to see into the hidden part of his partner.

He'd just met this man Scar, but Emerson perceived a deep and hidden part of him, just like Weekes. And Scar acted as if he knew all about Emerson. Just the way Weekes had. And he thought it strange to see in Scar, a man his own age, what he attributed to be Weekes's wisdom accumulated through living for a long time by his wits in a very physical, brutal world. Emerson was not ready to trust Scar. He also wondered if he could trust his perceptions with his mind so occupied with what happened to his partner.

Emerson thought Scar might be a year or two older than he was. He was smooth shaved, so the raised, angry, red welt on his cheek running from his earlobe almost to the corner of his mouth showed clear and plain. He wore his light brown hair cropped short. His dark gray shirt covered lean, muscled shoulders. Weekes wouldn't have puzzled over Scar. He'd have known exactly how to handle the situation.

"You gonna take the money?" Scar asked, holding the bandanna out to him.

Emerson guided Horse up the right side of Scar's mount so he could cover him with the Dragoon. Keeping the pistol in his right and resting it on the horn, he took the bandanna.

Scar pulled a tobacco pouch and papers from his shirt pocket and offered those to Emerson. He'd have to put the pistol away to take the offering.

"I don't use tobacco. But thanks."

"Which way you headin'?" Scar asked.

Emerson pointed ahead of them.

"Ride together a piece?"

Emerson nodded, and Scar unfolded his legs, spun around, and clucked his mount into motion. Emerson stuffed the bandanna into a saddlebag and stayed on Scar's right side.

"Sorry about yore pard," Scar said.

It was hard to envision life without Weekes Daley, but now was not the time to plow through all of that. Emerson spurred his mind back to vigilance.

The horses clopped and head-bobbed side by side.

"You a Union man?" Scar asked and faced Emerson. "You talk like one."

"I am a man. Not any particular kind of man. Just a man."

Weekes liked to say, "Calculate the odds. Always. Not just the odds in the cards but the probability that you have correctly read a player across the table from you."

Emerson put a little smile on his face. "You talk Northern too, but the odds favor your sympathies lying with the other side."

Surprise appeared on Scar's face but didn't stay long. He laughed.

"I'm Josh Ewing."

Emerson holstered his pistol, tipped his hat, and gave his name, his real one.

Josh Ewing started giving his story. His family used to own a farm in the northeastern corner of Illinois. Every Sunday at services, their preacher thumped the pulpit with his fists as he condemned the heathens who would presume to own—to *own*—other human beings.

"The preacher always tied up his sermons with, 'As if they were mules bred to be whipped to death pulling a plow. Slavery is an institution spawned in hell and practiced by devils on earth.'"

In 1857, five of the fourteen families in the congregation sold their farms, loaded furniture and tools on wagons, and headed west on a holy crusade. They would flood Kansas with righteous people. The righteous would vote to keep Kansas free, free from slavery, free from Satan.

Emerson smiled at Josh. Josh saw him.

"What?"

"An eloquent soliloquy, Mr. Ewing."

"You wanna hear this?"

"Sure."

Josh glanced behind them and then at Emerson, to see, maybe if he was paying attention. Then he went on. "After we got a new farm up and runnin', my paw joined the Red Legs. He made me join too. I went on coupla raids." Josh appeared to study the spot between his horse's ears. "I didn't cotton to how they did business. I told them all we were doing was hangin' unarmed men, burnin' helpless women outta house and home, and stealing horses.

"One of the Red Legs was Rufe Davis. He was always makin' over how he'd ridden with John Brown. He said it didn't sound like I was with the Red Legs. That meant I was against them. He crowded me, tryin' to get me to pull my pistol on him. My paw got between us. He told me that I was neither hot nor cold, I was lukewarm, and he spewed me outta his mouth. Then he slashed me across the face with a quirt he kept 'round his wrist to beat his horse when we were runnin' from a place. I walked outta that church where we were planning another raid, and I expected a bullet in the back. I don't know what it's like to get shot, but it can't feel no worse'n what I felt waitin' on a bullet. I knew Rufe was gonna shoot me. There was no point in runnin'.

"I guess my paw give me that. He wouldn't let Rufe shoot me."

You ain't my son no more. Lukewarm. He spewed me outta his mouth.

Emerson plucked a twig from a sapling beside the road. Emerson thought Josh Ewing had told all that about himself to get Emerson to talk about himself, to prime the pump, so to speak. Ewing didn't appear interested in saying more unless Emerson said something.

Emerson stuck the twig in his mouth and chewed, the way Weekes had taught him to clean his teeth. "You see, young Emerson," he'd said. "Out here in the uncivilized wasteland, I fear a rotted tooth much more than I fear a bullet, a knife, or a noose."

If Emerson was any kind of judge of character, Ewing's story was true. He and Josh were two fatherless sons.

Having decided to trust Josh Ewing opened a door in Emerson's mind. Weekes entered. He was destined for an unmarked grave. It occurred, they might dump Weekes and Gold Tooth and Barn Fire in the same damned hole.

Emerson said, "Shit."

"Thinkin' on yore pard." It wasn't a question.

Emerson humphed. "Earlier, you mentioned how your father quoted from Revelations in driving you away. Weekes—that was my partner— used to say, 'The vilest sinner on earth can find a passage in the Holy Book, which, in his mind, provides Almighty justification for his nefarious deeds.'"

Then Emerson told Josh about Weekes Daley and how they'd traveled and gambled and won money in New Orleans, Saint Louis, Chicago, and Detroit and some places that had no name but did have a saloon.

As he spoke, he watched Josh. Josh was … vigilant. Eyes always moving, checking the sides of the road and ahead. And behind. He'd cock an ear from time to time to evaluate a curious sound.

Ahead of them, a dust cloud rose above the road. Josh saw it too.

"Likely the stage. One runs between Saint Joe and Columbia." He grinned. "Gits itself held up now an agin, I hear." Josh turned right and into the trees. Back over his shoulder, he said, "Likely to have an escort of Blue Bellies."

Whether the riders under the dust cloud were Blue Bellies, Red Legs, or a pack of mongrels comprised of men like Gold Tooth, the odds were decidedly against a friendly encounter. Emerson kneed Horse, and he followed Josh.

After moving a comfortable distance away from the road, Josh turned to parallel it. He stopped at a steep descent to a trickle of a stream.

Emerson knew why. Their mounts would make noise scrabbling down one side of the gully and up the other, and even though the rumble of hooves from the road was loud, Josh was being careful. The rumble neared. Then thunder from shod horses and rimmed wheels as the dust cloud crossed a wooden bridge.

Josh leaned forward and, using a soft voice, spoke to his mount. "Don't you be a talkin' to those of yore kind up there on the road. Nooo, sir. 'Cause I'm yore family now. Why those are animals up there, they ain't human. Like you'n me."

Horse bobbed his head up and down. Emerson wondered if he thought that was funny, what Josh had said. Or maybe Horse was beginning to like the man too.

The sounds of passage receded.

"That bridge is new," Josh said. "Outlaws liked to jump the coach when it slowed to cross the stream." He grinned. "What I heard anyways."

They descended to the stream, climbed up the other side, made their way back to the road, and trotted their mounts. At a spot where wagon wheels had ground ruts from the grass leading off to the north, Josh turned and followed the ruts into the trees.

"Put yore Dragoons in yore saddlebag," Josh said.

Emerson did, and they stopped just before exiting forest to a broad, cleared expanse. In the middle of the cleared field, two men forked hay onto a wagon. To their right, a one-story square box of a house with a low-sloped tin roof snuggled under tall trees. A barn, a corral for horses, a pen with cows, a pen with pigs. All close to the house in case a bear or cougar came after the animals during the night.

"Those farmers yonder"—Josh nodded toward the two working pitchforks—"they'll have long guns. Don't do anything to spook them. If they start shootin', don't shoot back. We'll just duck into the woods and see kin we find more hospitable folks further on."

Josh clucked his mount into motion. As soon as they emerged from the trees, one of the men working the hay pointed. Both farmers dropped their pitchforks and climbed onto their wagon. The driver snapped the reins and hauled the team around to hurry to the house.

Three dogs exploded from behind the house in a fury of barking and tore down the road toward them.

"If I shoot one of them, do you think that'd spook the farmers?" Emerson asked.

Josh didn't answer. He stepped out of the saddle, knelt on the ground, and held his left hand, palm out toward the beasts charging at him. He started speaking in the singsong he and Emerson both used with their horses.

"Whoa up there, doggies. I know you don't know us. I know you got a job to do, and you're doing it."

The barking, snarling trio drew up short of Josh. He didn't move, just kept talking.

"I know you're brave doggies, an' you ain't afraid of us. No, sir, not what we think of you at all."

The dogs were dancing all excitement and pent violence constrained by some mysterious force. All three dogs were black, short-haired, but each had splotches of white on different parts of their bodies. One was slightly larger than the other two. It stopped barking and began to whimper. The other two took up the new communication. The biggest one approached Josh's hand, sniffed it, and then licked it. Another came for a sniff, lick, and the third shouldered the second aside for its turn. Then all three dogs were pressing around Josh competing for affection and all the while he kept up the singsong.

Then he said, "Pooches, let's go visit yore master."

He remounted.

"I thought those dogs would rip your throat out," Emerson said.

"Nah. Those animals are just like the rest of the citizens of Missourah. If they don't know you for a friend, they know you for an enemy until you prove otherwise."

They walked the horses toward the house, the dogs playing with each other just in front of the little parade. The farmer stood in front of his mules. A boy, seventeen or eighteen, Emerson thought, was positioned behind the rear of the wagon. Both cradled muzzle-loaders in the crook of an arm.

They have faced hard men before, Emerson thought. *Good.*

Well, it would be good if they didn't start shooting. About one hundred yards from the wagon, about where Emerson figured the farmer might raise his musket, Josh stopped and dismounted and proceeded on foot. He held his left hand up, as he had to his new friends, the canines.

"Mean you no harm, mister," Josh hollered.

"We ain't got no ridin' horses, an' we got even less money," the farmer bellowed back.

"We ain't aimin' to take none of yore money!" Josh shouted as he ambled closer. "We aim to give you some of ours!"

The farmer lowered the musket barrel so it pointed at the ground. The hammer was cocked.

The house was to the right. A porch spanned the front. A window to either side of the front door was cracked open. A gun barrel rested on each sill.

Emerson wished he had a Dragoon in his hand.

"We was wonderin'," Josh said, "can we sleep in yore barn, get some grain for our animals, and maybe get supper from yore missus? We'll pay ten dollars."

"Apiece."

"No," Josh said. "Ain't payin' that. Not unless you throw in a jug a whiskey and you let my friend fill up his powder horn; and yore wife has some kinda pie for *deesert*; and you give us some ground-up coffee to take with; and you feed us breakfast come morning."

The farmer pondered it a moment. The ponder was for show, Emerson thought. Then the farmer decided. "I'll water the horses, put 'em in a clean stall, unsaddle 'em, rub 'em down, give 'em a scoop a oats, fresh straw. And hay."

He could have just said, "I'll take care of the animals." That's what Paw would have said. Both sides would have known clearly everything that would be done.

To Josh and Emerson: "There's a basin an' soap on a bench by the back door. An' a cistern. Can a primin' water by the pump. Mind you leave it full. Supper ain't fer a hour and then some."

"Boy," the farmer said to the young man by the wagon tailgate, "go back to the field and finish loadin' th' wagon."

"I'll help him," Josh said and handed his reins to the farmer.

"An' I'll help you, mister," Emerson said, mindful of his speech. "I'm right handy around barns and manure and milking and such."

Emerson led Horse by the reins in trail behind the farmer. He looked at his palms. They'd gone soft. They'd likely get blisters. And that was fine with Emerson. Maybe blisters would help avoid thinking about Weekes. And Gold Tooth. He hadn't even thought about killing him. Gold Tooth. Maybe if Gold Tooth and his friends hadn't killed Weekes, it would be troubling killing a man over a card game. But it was like with the Barlow brothers. They crowded a man into a corner with only one way out. Gold Tooth did that too. The ones who'd chased him outside Saint Joseph, well, there was nothing else to do there, either. And all of them together did not make up for Weekes.

He wondered about Josh. He did not seem bothered by killing Barn Fire. And he never explained which side he was for. The way the question had been posed, odds were he was for a particular side. Odds were South. But because his paw was rabid North and whipped him?

Weekes would have explained it. Josh sat at Weekes's left at the poker table. Thinking back on it, Josh was watchful of Gold Tooth, Barn Fire, and Shorty. Emerson didn't think Josh considered Weekes a threat. He thought Josh must have trusted Weekes. To an extent. Weekes, he thought, probably judged Josh as a possible ally, but until he was proven to be one, Weekes would watch him.

13

EMERSON AND JOSH spread their ground cloths on the first mowed hay of the year in the loft of the barn. The alfalfa smell overrode manure, horse, and cow smells. They both lay down, and the hay rustled under Josh as he settled. Then it was quiet, and he breathed slow and deep.

Emerson, on his back, eyes open to the darkness, was thinking about when he ran away from Indiana. He was trying to remember if he'd felt then the way he did now: empty, no place to go, no vision of what to do tomorrow. And Cicero's mugwumps grasping his ankles with bony fingers and pulling him down, down.

But that wasn't how he remembered that time, three years back now. He wasn't empty. Paw had said to ride west, so he rode west. *Ride all night*, he'd said. He rode all night. Then he stopped to fry bacon. That's how the Barlows caught him. Then he had to kill them. He had to. The Barlows were no different from encountering a bear on the road. Kill the bear or it'll kill you. The Barlows were men, human. They rode horses, spoke, had a maw and paw.

And a sister.

Big and Tiny were men, but Emerson would not have been able to talk his way out of his situation with them any more than he would have been able to smooth-talk a bear. He killed them because otherwise, he'd have died.

Well, Paw, I did live through that day.

Paw would not have been pleased or proud of him. When Emerson achieved a new level of proficiency with the long rifle, Paw would say, "Took an awful lot of powder to get you to this point, boy."

Maw for sure would not have been pleased. Him living or dying would not have mattered next to *Thou shalt not kill.* He should have stayed away from Candace Barlow. If he had, Big and Tiny would not have chased him. He would not have had to kill them. And Maw would have been able to go to Wednesday tea with her head held high.

He saw then, lying on hay in the loft of a barn, that he'd taken that from Maw. Wednesday tea. He'd worried about taking Horse from her, that she wouldn't be able to get to tea. But now he saw she would not want to go to them, that the other women would not want her there.

Three years ago, he ran from the place where he'd killed the Barlow brothers. He saw then that what he'd really been running from what was he'd done to Maw. He ran, but periodically it caught up to him. It had taken Cicero to put a name to *it.*

He'd run and found Weekes Daley. Only he hadn't been Weekes Daley. Not back then. He was seven different men depending on the day of the week. But the man who became Weekes showed him a life Emerson never imagined existed. The trouble was that he never imagined it ending, either.

After a time, looking into blackness and seeing nothing but that, exhaustion pulled him down into sleep.

*****

Emerson woke when Josh kicked his foot. "You want to sleep some more or eat?"

A lantern from the ground floor threw a glow through the ladder hole in the loft floor. Emerson sat up. Out of the fog filling his head, where he was and how he'd come to be there materialized.

"Eat," Josh said, and he kicked his foot again.

Afterward, Emerson stood with the farmer and his son at the rear of the house as Josh brought the horses from the barn. Dawn threw enough light over the edge of the earth so everything looked gray and black and shadowy.

Emerson gave the farmer a twenty-dollar piece. Then he handed a silver dollar to the son.

Emerson had considered Weekes's injunction against being overly generous, but in their present situation, he didn't care if he was too dumb to see the danger in the gift; he just wanted to do something nice for the kid.

"I was you, young feller," Emerson said, "seems like an awful long time ago. Back then, I never had a penny to call my own, unless my paw gave it to me—and he was not one to give things up easy."

The youngster studied both sides of the silver coin. His father elbowed him.

"Um. Thank you," the boy stammered. Josh dropped the reins.

"You mind bringing yore missus and daughter out?" Josh asked.

"Daughter?"

"Yes, sir. When we rode up, two rifles covered us from the front of your house. If you had another son, I think we'd have seen him. Odds are that was a daughter and your wife looking at us over gun sights."

Emerson looked at Josh with a newfound respect. The farmer mulled it for a moment, and then sent his boy to summon the women.

The missus descended the steps and stood next to her husband.

The gray light, Emerson thought, did harsh things to her face. Her eyes were sunk in black shadow. Her nose and chin were cut in hard, straight lines. Her thin gray hair hung straight to her shoulders. The color had been bleached out of her flower- print sack of a dress. There was no woman shape to her. She reminded him of a thing his paw had said once. *Wimmen is mysterious creatures. Sometimes they're tougher'n any man, but unless they got another one a their kind to talk to, they wither up like flowers in a drought when you only got water enough to keep the vegetables alive.*

Another reminder of how important those Wednesday- morning buggy rides had been to Maw.

Emerson pulled off his hat. "Ma'am," he said, "it was right kind of you to feed us so well. We've been a burden to you, and I ... we want you to have something for the trouble. It isn't much, but it's what we got to give."

He clinked five dollars into her hand. She stared at the weight on her palm and then up at Emerson. He saw a tear sparkle on her cheek.

Jesus! he thought. *Hasn't anybody ever done a nice thing for you?*

Even Paw brought a hat, or ribbon, or chocolate to Maw every couple of years.

The daughter stood on the porch. She was all eyes, and when his touched hers, they grew wider, and then she looked down. In better light, he'd have seen the blush that sure as shooting colored her cheeks. Her hair was curled up above her shoulders. She was maybe fourteen but had blossomed into a shapely woman. Farming hadn't squeezed the juice out of her yet. She was attractive, and he hated seeing her standing behind her mother.

Emerson handed the woman another dollar. "For your daughter, ma'am. We were extra work for her too."

Then he took up the reins on Horse and mounted.

They tipped their hats and started down the lane at a trot.

When out of earshot of the house, Josh asked, "You always give money away like that? Keep it up an' we'll have to rob a bank."

Emerson checked behind them. The farmer and his family stood together watching their visitors ride away.

"Sometimes being generous is a mistake," Emerson replied. "It didn't seem like one back there."

Trees swallowed the lane they followed to the road. Emerson handed the bandanna with half the poker money in it to Josh.

"Givin' money away again?"

"No. Some of that is yours, and if you hadn't been at that table, I'd have wound up on the floor of that saloon, leaking blood into the sawdust. And why did you give it all to me in the first place? Why'd you even stop and let me catch up?"

Josh rubbed his chin. "I cain't figure that, neither."

The horses clopped side by side.

"You saw those three shacks out behind the barn. Were those slave shacks?" Emerson asked.

"'Spect so."

"What happened to them?"

"I don't think the man back there owned slaves. Probably a previous owner did. But in these parts, bands of armed men see horses they like, they take 'em. They do the same with slaves, and even freed Negroes. There're no markets selling Negroes nowadays, but you can always find a man who'll buy good hands."

Emerson tried to imagine what a Negro would feel if he'd been freed, then caught and sold again. He shook his head.

"What about the Emancipation Proclamation?"

"Don't apply to Missourah," Josh said. "Even if it did, wouldn't make no difference to packs of bandits roaming the roads and woods out here."

Emerson wanted to ask Josh about where he stood regarding the capture and selling of freedmen, but they exited the woods and turned onto the road that ran all the way to Columbia. Josh kicked his horse into a trot. After a time, he invited Emerson to run Horse as fast as he could go.

"Horse," Emerson said, and his animal launched into an all- out gallop. Josh kept pace but held his mount in check. After a moment, Josh loosened his reins and tore away from Emerson.

After he opened a hundred-yard lead, Josh slowed to a walk. Emerson pulled up alongside.

Horse coughed twice.

Josh pushed his hat to the back of his head. "I reckon you're some fond a this here four-legged creature."

A feeling much like he used to get when his paw asked, "Where you bin?" coagulated in Emerson's stomach. Then his belly boiled up an angry resentment.

"For a poker player," Josh said, "you sure don't hide what you're thinkin'."

"We are not playing cards."

"Not right now we ain't," Josh said. "But I expect you, or we, might be again sometime soon. You give any thought to what you're gonna do?"

"I'll think about it tomorrow."

"While you're a-thinkin'"—Josh reached over and patted Horse on the neck—"think on this. In that saloon in Saint Joe, you done a lot a shootin' but not much killin'. Scared the hell outta those people. As soon as we were gone, each one a them stopped bein' scared he was gonna die and looked around and appreciated how many a them was in that saloon. Then they got mad, alla them at the same time. And mostly they was mad 'cause you made 'em show yella. An' they posse'd up and tore after you. Woulda caught you, too, except you turned and charged 'em and killed a couple. Then they got more scareder of dyin' than they was mad."

Emerson frowned.

"You ain't got no partner no more. Maybe you're thinkin' of goin' back to that farm, in Illinois, was it?"

"Indiana," Emerson retorted.

He could not go back to Terre Haute. Whether someone stumbled across the corpses of the Barlow brothers or not, the brothers had not returned home. If Emerson did, everyone would know why the Barlows had not. And there was what Paw said. And what he'd done to Maw.

"Shit," Emerson mumbled.

Besides not being able to return home, the thought of going back to farming filled him with a sense of deep, dark, and eternal gloom. He saw how his paw was enslaved by his animals, his crops, and by the weather. Every drop of his paw's sweat was squeezed out of him by a cold, unfeeling, uncaring master personified in the cows, pigs, and chickens, in the corn, oats, and hay, and even by Maw's potatoes, tomatoes, and string beans. To Emerson, that morning, he saw farmers as slaves, every bit as much as the Negroes were slaves. He saw it that way, though if his maw knew what he was thinking, she'd smack the back of his head. At supper, Maw added a prayer for an end to the abomination that was slavery.

"So," Josh said, pulling Emerson out of his thoughts, "you wanna partner up? Or go your own way?"

"Tomorrow. I'll decide tomorrow."

Josh stopped his mount, tipped his hat to Emerson, and then turned off the road and into the woods, heading south.

"What would we do?" Emerson asked. "Gamble?"

"Some," Josh said over his shoulder.

"What else?"

"Soldierin'."

"Soldiering?" Emerson hollered at the brush swallowing Josh. "Which side do you fight for?"

"Mine!" Josh hollered back.

"Your side. What does that mean?"

Josh didn't answer. Emerson stopped Horse and listened to him plowing through the brush.

"I did not figure on being a soldier," Emerson said, and he patted his animal's neck. "I don't even know for sure which side Josh is fighting for." He looked down the empty road leading southeast. He looked at the oaks, maples, sycamores that had swallowed … his friend.

"Shit," Emerson said, and then, "Horse."

Horse started into the woods, and branches slashed at Emerson's face. He raised an arm to shield his eyes and then lowered his head behind Horse's neck. The brush ripped at his pants and scratched his legs. He thought of Blonde back in the saloon in Saint Joseph. If that vindictive … woman had kept her mouth shut, Weekes might still be alive.

Candace Barlow popped suddenly to mind. She'd dramatically altered the course of his life. She was blonde. He and Weekes had been in the middle of a war. The war hadn't been able to affect the dream of going to California. That Saint Joe saloon girl sure affected it, though. That dream was as dead as his partner. That girl was blonde.

"Shit," Emerson said. "Horse, I decided to stick with Josh for the time being. I don't know if I'm going to be a soldier, but sure as shooting, you can't be. You're too slow."

T WO DAYS LATER, Josh led them out of trees onto an east- west road and turned right, walking his mount.

"Kansas City's that way." Josh nodded, indicating ahead. "Columbia's th' other."

"You haven't told me where we're going," Emerson said.

They clopped along side by side. Josh pushed his hat back.

"I told you we were goin' to meet a man," Josh said. "First, we'll stop at Mr. Bucknell's place. He raises horses. You want a fast horse with bottom. Won't find none better'n his. Some a the guys I ride with—"

"So-called soldiers."

"Ain't nothin' so-called about it. Soldiers. Anyway, some of the guys take horses from Union sympathizers. We know who they are. Course, most of their stock is nothin' special, not like Bucknell's."

"We're going to get a Bucknell horse for me?" Emerson asked.

Josh grinned. "Ain't nothin' *we* about it. You're gonna have to fork over the money."

Josh kicked his mount to a canter.

Emerson trailed behind him a length. "Horse," he said, "you heard us talking, I guess. I'll make sure you get a good home out of the deal." Emerson shook his head. "You might be the only one of us to get a good deal."

After a time, they thundered across a wooden bridge over a deep gullied stream. Josh slowed his mount. A steep, tree- covered hill rose to their left. A bit farther, and Emerson saw that the hill was the end of a ridge stretching away to the south. Josh stopped at the base of the ridge. To his left, wagon wheels had worn ruts in the grass. The ruts led into a leafed-over tunnel.

Josh leaned forward, his elbows resting on the saddle horn. "Bucknell was on our side early on. Back at the start of the war, there was a fracas at the armory in Saint Louis. Blue Bellies shot women and kids. That soured him on the Union. Nowadays, though, Bucknell says, there's nothin' but bands of criminals roamin' the country, takin' whatever they want from whoever they want, and they'd rather shoot a man than say howdy, and one side is pretty much the same as the other."

He sat up and looked Emerson in the eye. "Keep your hand away from your gun. Stay behind me. Let me do the talking."

Josh pulled his mount around and started him down one of the ruts. A goodly distance from the road, they came to a whitewashed fence with a cowbell affixed to a gatepost. Josh rang the bell.

Ahead of them, the lane led to a wide, cleared space in front of a large, white two-story house, a mansion, with a front porch.

"Now what?" Emerson asked.

"We wait. We start ridin' toward the house before we get a 'Come on,' we're liable to get shot. There'll be a rifle on us from the barn."

To the left of the house, a red barn stood with the ground level and the hayloft doors open.

"There'll be guns on us from the right of the house—behind the high porch, maybe, off in the trees, maybe."

The house, the barn, even the fence, all wore fresh paint. It took a lot of hands to run a substantial farm and keep up appearances to boot. "This Bucknell, he owns slaves?" Emerson asked.

Josh held his hand up. It signaled *Quiet!* Josh's normally easygoing demeanor had given way to a tense watchfulness. Emerson felt it.

Another bell, like a church bell, gonged from behind the mansion as if to summon worshipers or remind them to pray in the fields. A tall, broad-shouldered, white-haired man wearing a white shirt stepped out of the house onto the porch. He cradled a long gun in the crook of his arm. He waved them in.

Josh pulled the gate open, and after they were through, a weight on a pulley shut it again.

As the horses walked toward the man on the porch, Josh said, "Don't get spooked and do somethin' stupid. Like draw a pistol."

Josh stopped ten yards from the long flight of steps leading from packed dirt up to the porch.

"Morning, Mr. Bucknell. I'm Josh Ewing. Bought this one"—he patted his mount's neck—"from you last year."

"I remember. Recently, we've had a Union man named Ewing making noise around here. You related?"

"No, sir. Not by blood. And my sympathies, well, they lie in other places than his."

Bucknell nodded. "Have you been pleased with Duke?"

"Yes, sir. Finest animal I've ever rid."

Bucknell studied Emerson. Emerson's first impression had been that the man was old because of the white hair. Up close, he didn't look old. Bucknell stood more than six feet tall. He had a tight belly, but most of the man was in his face and eyes. He exuded power, both physically and morally. Like Emerson's paw, Bucknell wouldn't take a second to figure out the right or wrong of a situation and decide what to do about it.

Emerson reached his hand up slowly and tipped his hat. "Emerson Sharp, Mr. Bucknell. I'm pleased to make your acquaintance."

"What can I do for you gentlemen?" Bucknell asked Josh.

"Mr. Sharp here asked me where he could buy a horse that was fast and had bottom. I told him there were places where he might find such, but here he'd sure find it."

"Do you want me to take the one you're on, Mr. Sharp? As part of the deal?"

"How would you use him, Mr. Bucknell?"

"With the depredations visited on farmers these days, there is always a demand for horses."

"He's not a wagon horse, Mr. Bucknell. He's a buggy horse.

Or for riding."

"I see. You're concerned that your animal be treated properly?"

"Yes, sir. I'd like that to be part of our deal."

"All right, Mr. Sharp. I expect he has a name?"

"Yes, sir. Horse."

"What?" An outraged female voice came from Emerson's left.

A girl stepped from behind the raised porch. The porch stood taller than her five feet. She wore pants and black hair chopped off just below her ears. She jammed her hands on her hips. "Horse!" she said. "You call your horse Horse?"

Bucknell hollered, "Ben!"

A man carrying a rifle with two hands and angled across his chest burst out of the shadowed doorway of the barn and ran across the open space toward them. Emerson moved his hand from his saddle horn to his thigh.

"Easy," Josh said.

Bucknell, without taking his eyes off Josh and Emerson, hollered again. "Celia."

Behind Bucknell, the front door opened. A slender woman wearing a green skirt and a white, ruffled blouse stepped through the door. Her lips were pursed as if someone had pressed a pink prune onto her pale face below her sharp nose. She had thick, blackbird-colored hair, the sides of which had been rolled into tubular curls. A dark green bow adorned the left side of her head. Green wasn't quite so green on the woman as it would have been on the girl.

The man from the barn—Ben, Bucknell had called him— skidded to a stop and grabbed the girl's upper arm. She tried to pull free, but Ben held on to her easily. He was at least a foot taller and weighed twice what she did. Ben was blond, thick through the chest and shoulders, not quite as bulky as Bucknell, but sure as shooting, he was the man's son.

"Amanda!" Bucknell's voice loaded as much sternness onto the word as it could carry.

The girl stopped struggling, but fierce defiance remained sculpted on her face as she glared up at her father.

"Amanda." This time, Bucknell's voice had the hard edges scraped off. "Go in the house. With your mother. Stay there. Let her go, Ben."

The girl jerked her arm free and crossed the packed dirt in front of the raised porch and by Emerson.

She was thirteen or fourteen, he figured.

"Horse!" Amanda huffed and stomped up the steps, stormed by her father and Celia, and into the house.

"Mr. Sharp, please accept my apology," Bucknell said. "My daughter is a reader, and she has developed some romantic notions about horses and their names." He turned to Ben. "Show him Iago."

"Iago? Are you proposing to sell me an evil, treacherous beast?" Emerson asked.

Bucknell tilted his head a bit to the side. Emerson was wearing the workingman clothing he'd worn into the saloon in Saint Joseph. Clearly, Bucknell hadn't expected him to be familiar with Shakespeare.

"Look at the animal. Judge for yourself. Ben will show you the way. I'll be out in a moment."

As his father left the porch, Ben started walking toward the rear of the house. Emerson guided Horse alongside him.

Behind the house and barn, a board-fenced, grassy field stretched for several acres alongside the ridge of high terrain. Horses, perhaps two dozen, grazed. Two of them sniffed the air and whickered. More of the horses looked up at the approaching riders. A few kept munching grass.

"My stepsister named Iago, Mr. Sharp," Ben said. "We were reading *Othello* at the time. There were illustrations in the book, and Mandy thought the ink drawing of Iago was the most romantic and exotic prince she could imagine. Our Iago is not evil or treacherous, but he is a prince among horses."

They cleared the rear of the Bucknell mansion. To Emerson's right, perhaps two hundred yards away, three small houses backed up against the board fence of the paddock. Alongside one of the houses, clothing hung on lines stirred in the gentle breeze. Ben's rifle had a cord tied to the barrel and to the stock. He shrugged the gun onto his back. Then he led them to where the reins of a chestnut mare were looped around the top of a fence post. The mare had no saddle and was a shade lighter than Horse. Ben flipped the reins over the chestnut's head, grabbed a handful of mane, and vaulted onto the animal's back. He lifted a coiled lariat hanging from the fence post and pushed through the gate. The weight and pulley mechanism closed it.

"Be right back," Ben said, and he and the chestnut cantered out toward the congregation of horses.

"Bucknell's got three boys," Josh said. "Ben's the oldest. The other two had guns on us for sure. One was in the hayloft."

"I saw the sun glint off a barrel," Emerson said.

"Probably another rifle in the woods to the west of the house. I didn't see nothin'. I just know one was there. Coulda been the other Bucknell or maybe one of his Negroes."

"Bucknell lets his slaves have firearms?"

"He doesn't hold with ownin' another man." Josh glanced at Emerson and back to Ben, who was swinging a loop over his head as he pursued three horses thundering ahead of him. "Funny. Sorta. Mr. Bucknell says he don't hold with ownin' another man, and it sits right fine with me. I admire him for sayin' it. My pa says it, and he scares me." Josh shook his head. Then he nodded toward the three houses. "Those shacks are for the families of freed Negroes. He pays 'em. He lets 'em carry guns, all right. I ain't seen 'em shoot, but I expect they can."

Ben pushed through the gate with a big black stallion trailing on his rope.

"Iago," Ben said.

Emerson stepped down and walked toward the black. He stopped a few feet away and held his hand up.

"What do you think, prince of horses?" Emerson said softly. "You think you can put up with me? I'll take care of you."

The animal tossed its head and then stepped forward. Emerson reached out to touch the animal's face, and an anticipation shiver rippled the skin of its neck. Emerson laid a hand on the side of the horse's head.

"Throw your saddle on him," Ben said. "You can run him alongside the fence. The trail cuts around the paddock, past those houses, and back to here. But Mrs. Sophie lives over there with her family. We don't want to stir dust up by her washing, so at the end of the fence, please turn around and ride back."

Emerson rode Iago down the hoof-chewed track between the fence and the wooded slope of the ridge. The horse was fast. The return trip was faster, and each additional new lap was faster still. After three down-and-backs, Emerson dismounted, grinning.

Mr. Bucknell and another of his sons were there with Ben and Josh.

"Bobby," Bucknell said, "take Horse to the barn and give him some oats. It'll make him feel better. Mr. Sharp, I take it you'd like to buy Iago."

Bobby was a handful of years younger than Ben and also blond. Lighter build, though, and perhaps an inch shorter. Seventeen or eighteen, Emerson thought. But he was every bit the horseman his older brother was.

Bobby swung onto Horse's bare back and obviously did not need reins to guide the animal. He talked to Horse all the way to the barn.

EMERSON AND JOSH spent the night in the town of Kingdom Come.

Kingdom Come had plopped itself down five miles west of the Bucknell place. The businesses sat on Main Street, which was also the road from Kansas City to Columbia. Second and Third Streets, to the north of Main, hosted houses, gardens, pens for pigs, chicken coops, and pastures for cows and horses. Travelers approached Kingdom Come from the east on a road tunneled under a ceiling of branches and leaves. The town appeared to have pushed the trees back to the north and south to make room for itself. Leaving the outskirts, the trees pushed back in to line the road to the south. To the north, it was mostly cleared fields and farmhouses and outbuildings.

They stabled their horses at the livery, ate supper, and bought baths. After the baths, Josh headed for the saloon to see about a card game. Emerson visited the general store and bought two sets of clothing. All black. Shirts and pants. A flat- brimmed hat, same color. Then he joined Josh at a poker table. Emerson lost four hands and realized he hadn't paid attention to any of the other six players. "Play the players more than you play the cards," Weekes had told him. But he couldn't force his brain to concentrate.

Emerson lost the fifth hand, threw his cards down, and pushed away from the table.

At the bar, he bought a whiskey, took a sip, winced, and said, "Shit."

He left the saloon, crossed the street, and walked to the livery. Iago was in a small corral behind the stable. A half dozen other horses occupied the corral too.

"Iago," Emerson said, and the black stallion trotted over to the fence. "I don't know, Iago—"

Emerson ripped his new hat off and slapped it against his leg. The black stallion's eyes grew big, and it backed away from the fence.

"Sorry, Iago. Didn't mean to startle you. Fact is, something is gnawing a hole in my belly. Maybe it's because I miss Weekes Daley. Of course, you didn't know him. If you did know him, I don't expect you'd have liked him. Weekes wasn't all that fond of horses. He told me I should have gotten rid of my previous mount, that I was stupid for hanging on to him. He wasn't much for saddle stock, he said. Compared to you, Iago, he wasn't."

Emerson frowned at the black. "Your name doesn't slip off the tongue comfortably." Emerson tsked. "Already I miss Horse. He was easy to talk to. His name just came out of my mouth like the most natural thing in the world. You know … Iago, right now I think I miss Horse more than I miss Weekes. That bothers me.

"Some.

"Iago, I wonder if it bothers you, carrying around all the baggage that goes with the name that saucy black-haired girl branded onto you. Amanda. I'll bet she's already renamed Horse. Probably Desdemona or Portia. No. Desdemona. She'd like the sound of that better. My partner Weekes had me read Mr. Shakespeare's works, but I'm not sure I'd ever see a horse's name in his characters. Weekes always said men hadn't changed much since the Bible was written. The Bible and Shakespeare. Everything good and bad a man can think to do is in those two books, he said. Nope. Those books are about people. Not horses."

Emerson stepped back from the fence to take in the magnificence of the animal. A black prince of a horse, all right. Iago's head was over the fence. He snorted.

"I wasn't sure you'd care to hang around here once you found out I didn't have an apple or a carrot for you." He returned and scratched in the forelock between Iago's ears. Emerson imagined he was seeing him smile. "Even a prince, at the root of it, has common and simple needs, eh?

"It's not easy to talk to someone named Iago, though I sure have blabbered on." Emerson stepped back again to look Iago in the eye. "Horse won't be needing that name anymore. Sure as shooting, that Amanda, she'll have stuck a *proper* name to him. What do you think? Horse. You are a prince of horses for sure. But I don't want to change your name unless you agree." The animal bobbed its head.

Emerson grinned. "Horse. That's settled, then."

Horse lowered his head so Emerson could scratch between his ears.

"That Amanda," Emerson said. "Feisty. Sort of like this blonde-headed girl back in Saint Joseph. She turned mean if she didn't get her way. She got Weekes killed."

A cold ball formed in Emerson's stomach.

"Fact is, Horse, I killed my partner. I violated his rule a year ago, and that's what killed Weekes Daley." Emerson kicked the toe of his boot into the packed dirt. "Candace Barlow was blonde. The Saint Joseph girl was blonde. From now on, I am steering clear of blondes.

"But here I am again, Horse. Almost like being in the exact place I was three years ago. I had a way to live. Then I … visited Candace, and the next morning, I didn't have that way to live anymore, and I was hard pressed to see a new one. Then I met Weekes. Now Weekes is gone, and with him went the way he showed me how to live.

"It just seems, Horse, like unless someone is shooting at me, I don't know what to do. Hell of a thing, eh? But don't worry. One thing I promise you, I will take care of you, prince of horses.

"Now I'm going back to the saloon, get a whiskey, and then I'm coming back here to bed down in the hayloft. I'll sleep better here. Both of us need to rest for what's ahead tomorrow. God only knows what Josh Ewing is going to lead us into."

Emerson started to turn away and stopped. "Not a time for apples," he said. "Maybe I can find a carrot for you."

*****

Emerson leaned against the front of the livery as Josh crossed the street and stuck his head in the horse trough. He held it under awhile and blew bubbles. Then he stood abruptly and flung water on Emerson.

"I was already awake and sober. Thank you," Emerson said. Josh grinned. "Now you're awaker and sob … soberer." He stuck his head in the trough again, and when he came up, he said, "More sober." Then he spun around. "Clementine's is open.

Flapjacks. C'mon."

After breakfast, with the sky behind them anxious to host dawn, Josh led them from Kingdom Come at a canter. When the horses were warmed up, he kicked his mount into a run. Horse stayed side by side with Josh's. Josh took the ends of his reins and smacked them across his animal's rump, and Josh pulled ahead for a length. Then Horse caught up and stayed abreast him.

Josh reined back and slowed to a walk.

"I shoulda bought Iago," Josh said. "Let you have Duke."

"Duke? I never heard you call him Duke."

"A horse ought to have a name so's a man can tell his horse from someone else's. But just 'cause you own a horse don't mean you gotta use his name on him. A horse don't know no different."

"Well, that's not true, is it, Horse?"

"You changed his name to Horse? Iago is just so chock-full of highfalutin trappin's. Just the name for a prince of horses." He humphed. "Horse!" He kicked Duke into a canter.

They rode west. They encountered a six-horse stagecoach. Emerson tipped his hat to the driver, but the driver didn't return the greeting. He popped the long-handled whip inspiring the team with his sense of watchfulness and comfort derived from the speed with which they ran away.

Near towns, traffic on the road picked up.

They encountered riders, mostly singles, a few pairs, and mostly farmers. A few nodded. Most didn't. The younger ones regarded them with curiosity and occasionally with envy. The older ones were invariably wary and turned in the saddle to watch Emerson and Josh after they passed. Josh didn't seem concerned with any of them. He didn't react unless someone nodded, and then he nodded back but kept his face pointed straight ahead.

They encountered wagons pulled by teams of mules or draft horses. All the wagons had a single male on the driver's seat except one. A twentysomething-year-old woman wearing a bonnet and a high-necked flowered dress sat next to a man some years her senior. Josh and Emerson both tipped their hats. The wife clutched her husband's arm and stared at the rumps of the team. Her husband was dressed in dark gray and a black hat, and he wore a black beard speckled with white. No mustache. He aimed hard black eyes at them as they passed. Emerson glanced at the lady and thought there were other ways to age a woman than to just pile years on her. Behind the couple, a girl, about six, sat on a sack of flour. She was playing with a doll on her lap. The doll, the girl, and her mother all wore dresses cut from the same cloth.

When they passed, the girl didn't look up at him, and that disappointed Emerson and brought to mind his brother, John. Thinking of his brother as Paw's field hand gnawed at him. He could never see John as tough enough for the job.

Josh slowed Duke to a walk. "Why you got the grumps? I can feel them comin' off you like heat from a blacksmith fire. You still mopin' over your partner?"

It wasn't that simple, but Emerson had no desire to talk about the things that wouldn't let him be. "Yeah," he said. "Weekes."

"Soldierin'," Josh said, "hardens a man. Every time, I mean every time, we fight the Blue Bellies, we kill some of 'em, and they kill some of us. You can't dwell on it. You can't mope about a lost friend. You say, 'Damn,' and move on."

"Damn," Emerson said, hoping that'd shut him up. It did, mostly.

With the sun hanging low over the road in front of them, Josh led them into the trees heading southwest.

They stopped to make coffee and eat the food they'd bought at Clementine's.

Emerson sat cross-legged and asked across the fire, "You going to tell me where we're going?"

"Will Nance farm. We'll get there this time tomorrow. It's a few miles east of the exclusion zone."

"Exclusion zone?"

"Yeah. It's a parcel of land some thirty miles wide right up against the Kansas border. The Blue Bellies made everybody move out of the zone. Anybody fought against leaving was shot or hung and their farm was burned. Blue Bellies said anyone they find in that area from now on is a guerilla or a Southern sympathizer, and they will be treated like the enemy."

"And that's where we're going?"

Josh nodded.

"Huh," Emerson said as he finished off his coffee and dumped the dregs. He should have seen it sooner. "Quantrill. That's who you want me to meet, isn't it?"

Josh met Emerson's stare, but he didn't answer. "Quantrill started out in Kansas, riding with what became the Red Legs. He couldn't abide with how they did things, and that drove him to switch sides and move to Missouri. That's what I've heard. Sounds like your story. Did you know him in Kansas?"

Josh doused the embers with water from his canteen. "We'll ride a half hour, put some distance between us and the fire. Then we'll bed down for the night. If we encounter anyone on the trail in this part of the country, they'll shoot first and ask if you're a friend second."

L ATE IN THE afternoon, Josh stopped in an orchard, looking through two rows of fruit trees at a two-story, wood-sided house needing paint. There were no horses in front. Behind the house stood a weathered, never-been-painted barn.

"Wait here," Josh said. "I'm goin' up to the house. If it's all right, I'll whistle. If there's shootin', I'd appreciate some cover fire." He grinned. "Do like you done back in Saint Joe. Only this time, don't be firin' at floorboards and whiskey bottles."

Josh walked Duke through the orchard and approached the open space before the house. Nothing stirred inside. He stepped down, opened the front door carefully, and then pushed his hat to the back of his head, turned, and whistled.

Emerson rode up and dismounted.

"I'll take the horses back to the pasture," Josh said. "Go on in and say howdy to the man inside. His name's Lieutenant Miller."

"Lieutenant Miller?" Emerson didn't think guerillas would bother with military ranks. "Of which army?" Josh laughed. "Go on in."

A man sitting at a table glanced up at Emerson and then back at what he was doing. Cleaning pistols. Wavy black hair, a trim black mustache. A maiden would envy his white complexion. Maybe, Emerson thought, he spent most of his outdoors time at night. On the table lay two disassembled pistols. He was working on another, and a fourth intact one was close to his right hand.

The lieutenant looked up from his work. His dark eyes scanned Emerson up and down and then seemed to bore inside and scan what was there up and down too.

"I'm Emerson Sharp, Mr. Miller."

"Lieutenant."

"Yes, sir."

Emerson didn't know where the impulse to "sir" him came from, but it felt right when the word came out.

"Josh spoke highly of you. Said you were interested in riding with us."

Emerson frowned. He hadn't committed to anything like that.

"Up to you, Mr. Sharp. Of course. If you don't want to ride with us, I'll require you to abide with us tonight. Then, come morning, you can go whichever way you want to. If you do want to ride with us, you're welcome."

Josh entered the front room from the rear. "Hell yes, he'll ride with us, Lieutenant."

"Let him answer, Josh."

"Lieutenant. Who would we be fighting, and why would we be fighting them?" Emerson asked.

"Josh," Miller said, "there's a pot of coffee on the stove.

Would you fetch it, and cups, please?"

The lieutenant pointed to a chair. Emerson scraped it across the worn wooden floor and sat.

Miller loaded powder and balls into the chambers of a Navy Colt cylinder. "I'll answer your questions, Mr. Sharp. But first, tell me where you come from and what you do."

Miller looked up from the pistol, and the penetrating eyes hit Emerson again. He had the impression that those eyes could smell truth or lie in what he said.

Emerson told him about the Barlow girl and running from her brothers.

"They caught me. I got loose and had to shoot them."

"You shot them both?"

"No, sir. I shot one. The other I killed with his brother's Bowie."

Josh placed a coffeepot and a stack of cups and saucers on the table. The cups and saucers could have come from Emerson's maw's good china.

Miller frowned.

"If the lady of the house was here, Lieutenant," Josh said. "she'd want to use the good dishes in your honor."

Josh poured a cup for Miller and related the story of the shoot-out in Saint Joseph.

"So, Mr. Sharp, you will kill a man if you have to, but you'd rather not have to. That about right?"

Emerson agreed that it was.

"Soldiers, good ones, anyway," Miller said, "endorse that sentiment too." He fingered grease over the cylinder holes and, with a rag, wiped the gun and his hands clean. "We in the army of the Confederate States certainly do. As does Captain Quantrill."

There were a lot of stories about Quantrill. Half had him as a modern Robin Hood. Others as devil spawn on horseback, raiding, robbing, burning, killing. Some said he shot captured Union soldiers. Others said he was ready with paroles, releasing captured federal troops if they promised not to bear arms against the Confederacy in the future.

"So Captain Quantrill. He's your boss?"

Miller put on a chilly smile. "The captain is my superior officer. He holds a commission in the army of the Confederacy, as do I."

The man's tone of voice put Emerson in a very inferior category and set his teeth to grinding.

"So the answer to one question, who are we fighting? We fight the Union army."

"You're fighting for slavery?" Emerson asked.

"Perhaps some are. I am fighting for the right of states to decide such matters. We fought our War of Independence so despots in England could not dictate the conduct of our affairs. Now it seems the despots have crossed the ocean and taken up residence in Washington. Somewhat ironic, don't you think?"

Josh slid a cup of coffee across the table to Emerson. "Don't mind the *loo-tenant*, Emerson. He's got a little education. What it taught 'im was how to look down his nose at others."

Emerson was on the verge of standing up and leaving. Miller's tone of voice had gotten schoolteacher-y, as if this simplest of lessons should be obvious even to such a dense pupil. Miller. Lieutenant Miller. There had been moments, listening to the man, where he'd come close to liking him, to appreciating the logic trail he unrolled, but then his superior attitude rubbed the wrong way. He'd about decided the bastard would not dictate whether he could leave. But Josh's intervention stopped him. In that moment, he saw the lieutenant had been testing him. Just as Weekes had tested him after the two of them met.

A tendril of steam wisped above the coffee. Emerson raised the cup and sniffed. "Ah, the smell of a woman, the smell of meat cooking, the smell of coffee. Those make a man glad he has a nose. More than makes up for all the stink that crawls up one's proboscis." Emerson saluted the lieutenant with his cup and sipped.

Surprise flitted across the lieutenant's face, but Emerson saw it.

Several horses, Emerson couldn't tell how many, rode into the yard behind the house.

"Some of the boys were scouting," Miller said.

A man clumped in from the kitchen. He cradled a Sharps rifle in the crook of his arm.

He reported, "We come across some sign, Lieutenant. Day or two old. A handfulla riders come in from the west. Looks like they ran into a bigger bunch heading south. Then the whole lot of them hightailed it west. The big bunch chasing the smaller one."

"A Union patrol encountered Red Legs," Miller said.

"Looks like," Sharps Rifle said.

"Will," Josh piped in and introduced Emerson. "And that's Will Nance. This is his place."

Emerson nodded. Will Nance stood about five six, stocky. Gray grizzled his bushy beard.

Two other men entered from the kitchen. They barely made a sound. Both were taller than Nance and skinny, with mustaches and clean-shaven cheeks. About Emerson's own age. They *looked* quiet. Both wore shirts with extra pockets sewed onto the front.

Miller introduced them as the Fordyke brothers, and then, "George and John, would you get supper going for us, please," he ordered politely.

Nance left to see to the horses.

"Will moved his family back to Jeff City," Josh offered.

"This area is no place for women and children," Miller said. "Frequent raids from Kansas. They indiscriminately rob and kill and burn. The Union does the same. There is no one on the side of the people who live here except Captain Quantrill." The lieutenant finished with another pistol and wiped it clean. "The Fordyke brothers. Their family was robbed by Red Legs, but Union soldiers killed their father, mother, and sister and burned the farm buildings to the ground. Will Nance stays here to try to protect his property. He keeps only a horse to ride and no hay or other provisions in the barn. He may be able to save his place, but only if Captain Quantrill keeps the Red Legs and federals from wanton destruction and pillaging."

"And why do you fight, Lieutenant?" Emerson asked. "By what you said before, I can almost see why, but I don't want to put my thinking into your brain."

The lieutenant's hard brown eyes softened up as if someone had poured melted butter into the sockets.

"Mr. Sharp, the way I see it, I do not have a country. I do not have a state. What I do have is this corner of Missouri and the people who live here. I like this place, and I like these people."

Miller stared into Emerson's eyes, looking to see if Emerson would challenge what he'd said, but Emerson wasn't inclined to argue any of the points the lieutenant made. He was thinking about something Weekes had said about five days before he died. "We have encountered many proponents for both sides of this war. I have yet to hear anyone articulate why he is Northern or Southern clearly, succinctly, logically, and in a way that satisfies." He wondered what Weekes Daley would think of what Miller had said.

Weekes. The familiar chill puddle of loss, regret, and guilt formed in the pit of Emerson's stomach as the lieutenant stowed his loading and cleaning gear in a saddlebag.

"There's times," Josh said, "when I come halfway close to sort of likin' the lieutenant."

*****

"Boys," the lieutenant ordered, "save some of the good pieces for Fred and Dick. They've been on watch and rate something better than necks and backs."

Lieutenant Miller, Will Nance, the Fordyke brothers, Josh, and Emerson were around the table. The platters of fried chicken and bowls of food were considerably diminished from when supper started.

"There's plenty of turnips left for them, Lieutenant," Josh pointed out. But he put the thigh he'd just speared with his fork back on the platter.

"Fried chicken!" Will Nance wiped his fingers on his pants and then cleaned his mustache whiskers with his shirtsleeves and patted his belly. "Sure beats coon. I eat plenty a that. Round here, ain't no farm animals left. They all been killed or stole. Deer's scared away by all the riders and the shootin'. Fried chicken! You brung me whiskey. You cook better'n my wife. I think I'll marry you Fordyke boys. You kin be my guerilla brides."

"Will," Miller growled, "take over for Dick so he can get supper."

Emerson thought Miller's tone of voice said what he, himself, was thinking. It might be his farm, his house, but Nance's comment had been unseemly. A man marrying another man. There were things a man just did not say. In the Sunday services he'd attended with Weekes, preachers had called such a thing an abomination and a sin against man, against nature, and against God.

Will didn't move and glared across the table at Miller, and an uneasy quiet settled over the lieutenant's supper table in Nance's house. Josh and Emerson faced the Fordyke brothers. Above Will's potato nose, his eyes blazed fire and defiance. Emerson slid his hands slowly below the table. If there was going to be shooting, Emerson intended to have a pistol in his hand. He only knew Josh. Josh put a restraining hand on Emerson's arm.

Emerson saw it then, and he thought so did everyone else at the table. Even Will Nance knew he wasn't going to win the stare-down. Will stood up, his chair scraped back, and he reached for the whiskey jug.

"Leave it!" Miller barked.

Will's hand froze inches from the finger hole on the jug.

"John and George," Miller said, "you take over the watches." Their chairs scraped back as they pushed back.

Miller leaned across the table. "Will, you're too drunk to stand watch. This is your place, and the Confederate army appreciates the use of it, but you are a soldier, and the rest of us need to be able to count on you." Miller pointed a finger at Will. "One more thing. You listening? Is this sinking in your whiskey-sotted brain?" Will nodded, and his eyes moved around as if looking for a place for his gaze to light and rest a spell, but those eyes could not find such a place. "What you said was an insult to Captain Quantrill. If I hear you say something like that again, I will put a bullet right between your eyes. Go upstairs and get some sleep. You'll take a later watch."

Will stood up, swayed a bit, wiped a hand across his mouth, made his way around the table, and climbed the stairs with his hand on the rail.

Miller took the jug and poured whiskey into three cups and raised his. "To the army of the Confederate States and to Captain Quantrill."

"The army and the captain," Josh said. They drained their cups.

"Will's all right," Miller said. "First time he's had whiskey in a month."

Josh stood and started stacking plates. Emerson helped him. The lieutenant divided the remaining food onto two plates and said he was going outside to check the sentry posts.

In the kitchen, Emerson and Josh scraped plates into a bucket and stacked the dishes.

"How did Will insult Captain Quantrill?" Emerson asked.

"That bit about guerilla brides," Josh said. "There's a song goin' around about Captain Quantrill and his wife, Katie. A line in the song calls her a guerilla bride. The lieutenant thought Will was pokin' fun at Katie and being disrespectful of the captain. We ain't over much on formal military manners, but in our army, nobody pokes fun at the captain. At the lieutenant, neither."

The back door opened, and a huge man filled the doorway.

"Dick," Josh said, "this is my friend Emerson Sharp. He's ridin' with us."

Dick stomped across the room. "The hell he is. He smells Union to me." Dick launched a roundhouse swing.

Emerson dropped the plate and stepped inside the blow, grabbed the big man's shirt, and was about to bash his forehead against Dick's nose and knee him in the groin.

"Stop!" Miller shouted.

Emerson felt Dick's fight go out of him, but he kept his eyes on his assailant.

"Dick, I told you he was my friend," Josh said.

"I pick my own friends," Dick growled.

"Yeah. Well, my advice is to pick Emerson for a friend. You don't want him for an enemy."

The big man snorted.

"Tell him what you were going to do to him," the lieutenant said.

"I was going to hurt you," Emerson replied.

Dick laughed.

"Dick, take my word," the lieutenant said. "He would have hurt you. In the next couple of days, we're going to be fighting Blue Bellies. Save your fight for them. There's a plate for you on the table. Go eat. Then get some sleep."

The giant lumbered past Emerson. Over his shoulder, he said, "You two oughta be wearin' aprons."

"Dick," Miller said, "I told Mr. Sharp he could ride with us. If you have an argument with that notion, argue it with me. There's food on the table. Eat it or I'll throw it out."

The big man grumbled but went to eat. Miller went up to the second floor to sleep.

"Is everybody going to brace me like that?" Emerson asked.

"Not everybody," Josh replied. "The boys are suspicious of strangers, though. The Blue Bellies have tried to stick spies among us a couple of times."

"So I'm going with you to fight Blue Bellies, and at the same time, I have to watch so somebody doesn't shoot me in the back?"

"It won't be *that* bad," Josh said.

Josh's *that* clinched it. Emerson was not riding with this bunch. In the morning, he'd tell Josh goodbye. In the morning, he'd head back east. Saint Louis first. Then Hannibal. Then Chicago maybe.

Emerson started picking up pieces of the plate he'd dropped. He thought about Will Nance's wife. He tried to picture her. An image formed of the farmer's woman at the place they stayed that first night out of Saint Joseph. If one of her plates broke, Emerson thought the woman would feel it like a pinch on her heart. He thought of his maw. She certainly placed value on things like nice dinnerware, as if those things were proof that life could be genteel and not a constant struggle for survival decided by fang and claw. Or guns. Or rains that wouldn't come because someone sinned. Or too much rain for the same reason.

"You wash. I'll dry," Josh said. He grinned and held out an apron toward him. "Shit," Emerson said.

I

T WAS SOMEWHERE around two in the morning. It was too dark to see the face of the pocket watch Emerson had taken from Big Barlow. It had to be close to two. He'd relieved John Fordyke of the watch station southwest of Will Nance's house at ten o'clock at night. The one named Fred was supposed to take over the watch at two.

Bastard's late on purpose.

Emerson's head buzzed with fatigue, and it ached as if he had an ax blade embedded in it. Through the trees, he could see the cookie-with-a-big-bite-out-of-it moon. Emerson was chilled to his core. The sun made the world warm. Maybe the damned moon made it cold. He imagined seeing ice crystals in the marrow of his bones. He cursed the medical book Weekes had given him to read. The book had showed him he was an animal comprised of meat and bone, and that his bones had marrow in them, just as a cow's did. And picturing ice crystals in his marrow, that made him feel the absence of warmth with a sharper sense. His knowledge made him colder. He mumbled a curse.

Horse had been sleeping. He raised his head and looked over his shoulder.

Adrenaline spurted and shocked Emerson to wakefulness. He oriented himself to where Nance's house was located. Horse was looking to the right of that, to the south. Fred, he expected, would come directly from the house.

"Shh," he whispered. "Shh."

He drew the Bowie with his left, the pistol with the right.

He heard it then. A horse, he thought, was walking toward him through the blackness. Which meant a man was coming also. Probably. Emerson had his thumb on the hammer of his pistol. He didn't cock it. The sound of a pistol cocking in the darkness had a way of cutting though background noise.

The silhouette of a man with a horse beside him materialized in front of the approaching noise.

Emerson cocked the pistol.

The silhouette stopped and said, "Shit!" It was Fred. "The lieutenant said I could cut your throat if I found you asleep on watch."

"Put your hands up."

"What the hell for? I'm here to take over the watch from you."

"I want to see if your hands are empty."

"You don't trust me?"

"Raise 'em." He paused. "Okay. Put 'em down and come ahead."

"I'm surprised, Sharp. If you weren't asleep here, I expected you to be gone. I told the lieutenant we couldn't trust you, that you'd run out on us. He told me if I didn't trust you, I could stand your watch and mine. Hell, I didn't distrust you that much. At least not four hours ago."

Emerson left the hilltop to Fred and rode back to the barn. He lit a lantern and turned the wick low. As he was undoing the buckle on the cinch strap, Josh rode Duke into the barn.

"I'm leavin' the saddle on," he said.

"We need to leave the horses saddled?"

"That's how I'm leavin' mine. We'll be pulling out in three or four hours."

"I'm pulling the saddle, and I'll sleep in the barn."

"Suit yourself," Josh said and ambled off to the house.

Emerson turned out the lantern and hung it on a nail. Both sets of large doors were open, and moonlight spilled in and onto a few yards of floor at both ends of the central aisle. The rest of the barn was filled with pitch blackness. He felt his way along the stalls to the ladder and climbed up to the hayloft just above Horse. At the end of the barn toward the house, a couple of boards were missing. Enough light filtered through to give him orientation. He spread his ground cloth on the loft floor, lay down, and wished like hell Will Nance had some hay. He thought about taking Horse out to the pasture and sleeping outside, but a roof over his head, well, that was something. He thought about going in the house and sleeping on a mattress on the floor, but then he'd have to leave Horse saddled the rest of the night.

"You appreciate what I'm doing for you, right, Horse?" he asked the dark barn.

Horse snorted.

Emerson smiled. "As long as you appreciate it."

He pulled one side of the ground cover over him, settled his head on the saddlebags, and exhaled, expelling exhaustion, everlasting watchfulness, and chill from the marrow in his bones. In the time it took to draw in another breath, it grew as dark and quiet inside his head as it was outside it.

Until he woke with his heart pounding and his mind identified gunfire. From the north.

Pop, pop, pop. A string of pistol shots. A pack of rifles barked reply.

Emerson pulled his boots on. Jumped up, strapped on his weapons, clattered down the ladder to the dirt floor, and rushed to the barn door. Beyond the shadow form of the house, out beyond the orchard, he saw the flashes of fire from muzzles and heard rifles, a lot of them.

He grabbed the lantern, lit it, ran to Horse, and saddled him. Then he hurried back up the ladder, slung his saddlebags over his shoulder, and threw the ground cloth down to the barn floor.

As he climbed back down, he heard the rear door of the house slam open and running feet pound toward the barn. Through the open door, he saw three figures race across the open space between the house and the barn. One of the figures stopped at the barn door and looked back toward the house. The other two continued running into the barn. When they entered the light from the dim lantern, he saw it was Lieutenant Miller and Will Nance.

Miller jerked open a stall door, pulled his horse out, and swung up onto the saddle.

"Forget the saddle, Will," Miller snapped.

"Ain't gonna," Will Nance replied as he smoothed the saddle blanket.

Miller slapped reins across the haunches of his mount, and the animal pounded out through the east door.

Emerson ran to the door where Josh stood facing the house.

"The Fordykes have not come out," Josh said.

Fordyke pistols popped from north side of the house. Rifles flashed and barked in response from the orchard.

"John! George!" Josh hollered. "C'mon. We're cuttin' out."

The Fordykes' guns continued firing.

"Goddamn," Josh said. "They're upstairs. The lieutenant hollered. Guess they didn't hear."

Another horse raced out the east barn door.

"There's probably fifteen, twenty Blue Bellies out there," Josh said, and he grabbed Emerson's arm. "I'm gonna need some cover." He turned and ran back to the house.

Emerson looked around the edge of the barn door. Two guns popped from the upstairs bedrooms. A lot of rifles responded from the orchard.

Josh made it across the open area to the rear door of the house without drawing fire. Several shadow figures emerged from the orchard, running toward the house. Rifles barked cover fire from behind the runners. The Fordykes' guns were silent. Reloading probably.

Emerson ran back to Horse and retrieved his extra Dragoon and Pocket Colt. He returned to the barn door as Josh, with the Fordykes right behind him, tore out of the back door of the house and ran for the barn. The moonlight seemed ungodly bright. They made it halfway across the open space before drawing fire.

Emerson fired three rounds at the shadows converging on the front of the house. At a barked command, the shadows knelt and aimed their rifles at the barn. Emerson dropped to his knees too. A volley of bullets smacked into the barn doorpost and through the boards above his head.

Josh and one Fordyke ran into the barn as the other went down ten yards from safety. George called out, "John!" and he grabbed Emerson's arm. "I'm out," he said. "Gimme a gun."

Emerson handed over a Dragoon and began firing again. George ran to his brother and dragged him toward the barn with one hand while he fired with the other.

Emerson holstered the empty Dragoon. Josh was firing from the other side of the barn door. George took a round in the shoulder, and it spun him around. He dropped the gun and fell. He retrieved the pistol and crawled atop his brother. He cocked the hammer and pulled the trigger. It clicked empty. But he kept cocking and clicking, cocking and clicking.

The Union soldiers' firing intensified, and George's head snapped back, and then he slumped over his brother.

Josh pulled Emerson away.

They raced out the east end of the barn with bullets zipping past them.

Emerson ducked his head behind Horse's neck as he followed Josh, tearing through brush and tree branches. After they'd put a couple of hundred yards between them and the barn, Josh stopped and listened behind them.

"Yanks fight afoot," Josh said. "We're fine now."

The sky was going gray in the east.

"Miller just left the Fordykes and ran," Emerson said.

"That's how we do it," Josh said. "Most times we're outnumbered. We knock down as many Blue Bellies as we can. Then either the captain or a lieutenant says, 'Cut out,' an' we cut."

"So it's every man for himself?"

"Yeah. We get together. Work an ambush if we can, or mount a raid. Then we split and scatter."

"Well, how come you went back for the Fordykes?"

"Damned if I know," Josh said. Then he started Duke moving again. South.

Emerson didn't start Horse. He stared at Josh's back. He thought about that saloon in Saint Joseph. If it hadn't been for Josh pulling him out of there, he'd have stayed with Weekes. Even though Weekes was dead, he'd have stayed. And been shot. Or hung. Josh got Emerson out of the saloon, but he hadn't lifted a finger to help fight off the posse.

And back there at Will Nance's farm, the lieutenant and Will ran. The two sentries, Fred and Dick, ran. Or maybe they were killed.

Emerson looked to the east. Blue Bellies were to the north. Red Legs were west. General Sterling Price, from what he read and heard, was to the south. To the east was dawn and leaving the soldiering to Josh. That's what he'd decided to do the night before.

Instead, he guided Horse to follow Duke. "Why we going this way?" he asked.

"Damned if I know."

When the sun was up fair, Josh turned west. They stopped every couple of hours to allow the animals to graze or water from a stream. They ate jerky and made coffee in the afternoon. They rode over fields lush with weeds and saplings. Emerson thought it didn't take long for the forest to begin reclaiming what years and years of sweat and effort had cleared. They rode past abandoned farms. About half the houses and barns had been reduced to piles of charred lumber and tumbled stone.

"Will Nance's place is just outside the exclusion zone. We're in it now," Josh said. "The Blue Bellies drove everybody out of here. They patrol pretty regular. But so do the Red Legs, guerilla hunters, and Captain Quantrill's guerillas. The rule in here is, you meet somebody, shoot them before they shoot you. We are as likely to be shot by guerillas as by any of the others, so pay attention. It's not a good idea to overnight in an abandoned farm. Everybody pays special attention to those. We'll bed down in the woods."

They stopped close to a trickle of a stream. A swath of pine trees and saplings skirted the creek. The trees bordered a gone- to-weed field. Graze for the horses.

Emerson watched Josh spread his ground cloth and put his coat on. His were back in Will Nance's barn.

Josh said, "I guess now you see why it's a good idea to keep the saddle on at night."

Emerson pulled the saddle off Horse and rubbed him down with the saddle blanket.

"Suit yourself," Josh said and rolled onto his side. He was breathing deeply and easily in a moment.

Emerson finished with Horse and ripped small branches from pine trees to make a bed for himself.

"You made such a pine stink," Josh mumbled, "woke me up.

A damn fire wouldn't be no worse." "Should I light one, then?" "Pilgrim!" Josh growled.

Before he settled onto his pine bed, Emerson saddled Horse.

"Soldiers got it tough sometimes, Horse," Emerson whispered. "How the hell did we get to be soldiers anyway? Bad luck, I guess."

18

EMERSON WAS GETTING tired of seeing nothing but Duke's rump. Josh had told him they'd arrive by noon. Wherever the hell he was taking them. Through the leaves of the thick forest canopy, he caught enough glimpses of the sun to tell it was well past midday.

Ever since dawn, they'd been plowing through woods without so much as a game trail to follow and most of the time in scrub brush so thick a damned rabbit wouldn't try to get through, and when the brush thinned, it usually meant there was a steep, rocky slope to descend with another to ascend shortly.

Josh stopped Duke, and Emerson pulled up beside him. Ahead of them, the terrain fell away to the floor of a narrow valley. They faced west. The valley ran north-south. In the valley floor to the south, a stream showed as if a strip had been ripped from the fabric of the sky and fluttered to earth there. Stretching away to the north, the walls of the valley rose steeply from the floor and were densely packed with trees.

Josh had his head cocked to the side, his left ear aimed at the valley floor.

Silence lay heavily on the scene. From a long distance, a crow *caw-cawed* as if it had had to go that far away to make noise. Emerson recalled a day when he traveled with Weekes Daley and they'd come across a scene and a silence just like this. Weekes had cocked his head just as Josh did. After a moment, he asked, "Do you hear that silence? This must have been like it was on the third day when God was separating land from water and there were no birds or animals around. Did you catch what a blessing this is for eyes and ears?"

Emerson felt the ache in his chest. It ambushed him occasionally. It felt as if he had a heart on both sides of his chest and both hearts ached. *Weekes.*

It was as if when he'd run for his life away from Saint Joseph, Emerson had also run away from Weekes lying in a puddle of blood on a saloon floor. The posse hadn't caught up with him, but Weekes caught him. Now and then. Always by surprise.

Rats!

He and Josh were either in Kansas or close to it. They were likely to be shot if they encountered Blue Bellies, Red Legs, and guerilla hunters, and the way Josh put it, Quantrill's guerillas would also shoot first and ask "Friend or foe?" second. Anger at his lack of vigilance spiked, and it shoved Weekes behind him.

Emerson turned in the saddle to check behind them, and leather in his saddle rubbed other leather and squeaked.

Josh put his fingers to his lips.

Emerson raised his palms, gesturing, *Now what?*

The sound of a hoof stamp whispered up from the trees below them.

Josh grinned, pulled a red bandanna from his pocket, leaned toward Emerson, and whispered, "Don't start down until I signal. Could be Blue Bellies. If it's our guys, I'll wave you down."

Emerson pulled a Dragoon and checked the loads.

As Josh made his way down into the valley, Emerson lost sight of him at times, even of the red bandanna he held aloft. But he made it to the bottom without interference. Josh stopped Duke, raised his bandanna hand high, and stayed there like a statue.

Emerson saw a flash of red halfway up the slope on the other side of the valley. He glanced at Josh, who was still holding his pose. A loosened stone clattered down the hill. Emerson heard voices but could make out none of the words. Then Josh waved for him to come down.

When Emerson pulled up alongside Josh, Lieutenant Miller walked out of the trees, hopped across the stream, and greeted Josh.

"Head up the draw a couple of hundred yards," Miller instructed. "Then climb up the slope, to your right, to where you have a good view of the trail. We expect company tomorrow before noon."

Miller nodded at Emerson and then disappeared into the scrub brush and saplings, though with the noise he made, Emerson followed his progress as he climbed back up to his hide.

Once Miller stopped, Josh walked Duke up the valley, north. Josh stared intently to his right at the rising terrain. Emerson scanned behind them and the steep slope to the west.

Josh stopped, and then he dismounted and hopped across the yard-wide stream, and Duke stepped through the stream after him. Emerson followed with Horse trailing him.

Josh picked up a stick and handed it to Emerson. "Brush out the sign of us crossing the stream."

Emerson sat on a rock and pulled off his boots and socks.

He saw Josh smirk.

"If a man takes care of his feet and his teeth," Emerson said, "and keeps the rest of himself somewhat clean, odds are he'll be healthy."

Josh humphed. "Sounds like that Weekes Daley you go on about. Your second paw."

The barb from Josh surprised Emerson. He glared at the man he trusted—*too much*—and set to work brushing out hoof marks on the far side of the stream.

When they were finished and Emerson was pulling his boots on, Josh said, "Probably close to the top of this rise, the horse holder'll have all the mounts."

Josh started climbing, leading Duke. He said over his shoulder, "Way we do it is, we put our horses together in the hands of a reliable soldier. We do our ambush. When Cap'n Quantrill says, 'Cut out,' we cut out. We grab the first horse we come to and skedaddle."

"What?"

"It makes the most sense to do it that way, Emerson. It's tactics. The Yanks patrol on horseback, but when the first shot's fired, they jump to the ground and fight afoot, so we fight long as we have the advantage.

When we lose it, the cap'n sees it and says, 'Scat,' and we scat. We all got good horses. It don't make no difference which one you ride."

"It makes a difference to me," Emerson snapped.

"You're in Cap'n Quantrill's outfit. You do things his way."

"If I'm in the captain's outfit, I got here without a say so of my own. You never told me where we were going or why. So I'm here, but I'm staying with the horses, and nobody but me rides Horse."

Horse plopped a pile of biscuits.

"Goddamn it, Horse," Emerson said, "couldn't you wait until you got in the trees?"

Josh smirked.

Emerson started pitching the droppings into the brush. Then he pulled off his boots and socks again and stepped into the stream and washed his hands.

"Mind you wash out those new tracks you made," Josh said. "Shit," Emerson said.

*****

Emerson leaned against Horse in the predawn black and chill. He drew warmth from the animal as he cursed his ground cloth back in Will Nance's barn. A night sleeping on dirt with a ground cloth and a night without one were sure two different things. The cloth kept cold out and a man's warmth in. His extra shirt and pants were back there too. The night before, he'd made a pile of pine branches to shield his backside from the earth as he tried to sleep propped against the trunk of a tree, but the branches had done nothing to keep him warm or to help him sleep. All they did was leave the seat of his pants sticky with pinesap. The long-lasting kind.

"Soldiering," Emerson mumbled.

Horse bobbed his head as if he, too, had a low opinion of that occupation.

Emerson recalled the night at Will Nance's farm. He'd resolved to cut out on his own in the morning, but the Blue Bellies attacked before he could. He and Josh had ridden away from the barn with bullets zipping past them. After they'd put some distance between them and the Union soldiers, Josh stopped for a moment and then turned south. Emerson had watched him for a moment and considered continuing on his own to the east. But he hadn't done that. He decided to follow Josh.

Why?

In the middle of his third endless night of little sleep and no rest, his head buzzing with fatigue, his legs aching from standing next to Horse for the warmth, he wasn't quite sure why or how he wound up high above a valley floor, half-frozen.

He recalled Lieutenant Miller bolting to the east out of the barn with no thought to the welfare of the men he left behind. He recalled thinking he didn't know anything about soldiering but that the lieutenant's behavior left something to be desired, that it might even be shameful. Josh had risked his skin to go back and try to save the Fordykes. He had in fact saved one of the brothers, but when a bullet knocked John Fordyke to the ground, George exposed himself to the Blue Bellies' guns to try to save him.

Josh had enlisted him in the fight to save the Fordykes, and Emerson entered the effort, if not eagerly, at least willingly. Josh clearly had seen the point where further effort to save the brothers would have been useless. Emerson, however, had needed Josh to pull him away from the barn and the two bodies sprawled one atop the other.

They'd fled east and then stopped for a moment before Josh turned Duke south. Emerson had watched him walk away, but then he decided to follow him rather than do what he'd decided.

Why?

It came out of the fuzz as a flash of clarity.

If he had continued east on his own, he'd thought Josh would have been disappointed in him.

"Stupid," he whispered so softly he wasn't sure if he said it or thought it.

As if it had been waiting for that confession, the night entered his brain like a fog bank creeping ahead on the whisper of a breeze to remind him of what winter had been like and that this particular night would never, ever end.

A violent fit of shivers woke him, and he discovered the night was ending with a faint light filtering below the forest's leafy canopy. Emerson's hands were stiff. He squeezed fists trying to loosen them up and then stuck his right in his pants pocket. If he had to draw a pistol, he thought he'd probably drop it.

From down the hillside, a man coughed. Another *shh*-ed him.

The official horse holder, Charlie, had spent the night up on crest of the ridge, some thirty yards above where a line of a dozen horses were tied to saplings and trees. Charlie had watched to ensure Blue Bellies didn't sneak up on them from that direction. Just after sunrise, he came down to check on the horses. He was about five six with long brown hair, black shirt and pants, a holster pistol, two pistols stuck in his belt, and his bedroll draped over a shoulder. Carrying a bedroll over your shoulder would be inconvenient, but so was sleeping on the ground without one.

Charlie checked that all the guerilla mounts were securely tethered, and he approached Emerson, who anchored an end of the line with Horse and Duke.

Charlie whispered, "Blue Bellies are coming. I feel 'em close by. When the shootin' starts, untie a couple of the horses and hand the reins to the guys as they come a-runnin'. I'm goin' back up to the top. Nothin' but rough country out to the east. Ain't likely, but you never know. Them Blue Bellies could try to Injun up on us."

Charlie untied one of the horses and led it up the slope. He walked slowly and made little noise.

Below Emerson's spot, there were ten men hidden in the brush and among the trees. Aside from the cough and the *shh*, there hadn't been another sound from them. Nor had any movement betrayed their presence. There was probably a like number on the other side of the valley.

Back to waiting. A mosquito sang its infernal song to Emerson's left ear. Horse swished his tail.

Stillness settled in the valley like a heavy snowfall.

Emerson shivered and rubbed his hands over his arms. He flexed his fingers.

From the valley floor, to the north, he heard a noise, from a hoof-kicked stone, perhaps. From his vantage point, he could only see patches of the valley floor through breaks in the foliage. Pine, oak, maple, walnut crowded the slopes. He moved and found a spot where he could see more of the stream to the north. A rider appeared in a window through the leaves. He stopped his horse and studied the terrain rising to both sides. He turned and held up his hand—a signal, obviously, for others behind him to stop. Then the rider disappeared, moving toward directly below Emerson. After a moment, a file of other riders paraded past his view. All of them wore blue coats. Emerson counted eight, nine of them. Then shooting started.

A single gun had fired somewhere below Emerson, and immediately, a lot of guns opened up from both sides of the valley. Pistols banged and popped. Through his window, a riderless horse ran back to the north followed by a hatless Blue Coat bent over his saddle and hanging on to the horn as his mount ran after the other.

From the valley, a horse made a noise like a human scream.

A man pleaded, "I give up. I—"

Banging and popping continued for a moment. Abruptly, it stopped.

Emerson moved lower to where he could see more of the valley floor. A few yards from the stream, bodies littered the ground. Three horses were down. Another hobbled with a front leg wounded.

The smell of gun smoke wafted up the slope to Emerson.

"Take care of those horses!" a voice hollered from below Emerson.

In the valley, two men crossed the stream to where the horses lay and the one hobbled. The men each fired a round into the head of a downed animal. One of them put the hobbler out of its misery. It collapsed as if its legs had been chopped off. A wounded Blue Coat raised himself from on his back to an elbow. One guerilla shot him.

"Shit," Emerson mumbled.

Even from the distance, he could tell the wounded Blue Coat was just a kid. About the age he'd been when he ran from the Barlow brothers. He felt old.

A moment later, from down in the valley, a man screamed as if the most unimaginable horror the devil could devise had just been visited on him. He couldn't see the two guerillas anymore. Before he could figure that out, someone hurried up the hillside, heading right for him.

Emerson drew and cocked his Navy Colt.

The noise stopped. "Emerson, it's Josh."

"Come up."

Josh broke out of the scrub brush and bent over, resting his hands on his knees and breathing hard. "Cap'n thinks these was just scouts." He stood up straight. "Cap'n wants a horse to go see if there's a bigger party comin'. Gimme yours."

"Take him another one."

"Emerson, goddamn it."

Firing broke out up the hill.

"Charlie," Emerson said.

Josh drew his pistol and charged toward the shooting.

Emerson hurried after him.

There were pistol shots and the distinctive boom of long guns.

The firing ceased, and Josh slowed to a walk. He continued pushing through the brush uphill, but he was trying to be quiet.

Josh stopped and pointed. About twenty yards away, Charlie lay draped across a log. He didn't look like he'd get up, ever.

Gunfire broke out from the opposite side of the valley.

Josh turned and listened to it for a moment, and then he turned and started up again. Emerson stayed beside him. They heard voices approaching and some rattling and clanking of equipment banging together.

Josh dropped to his belly. Emerson did too, as voices approached.

"You sure you got 'im?"

"Course I'm sure."

"He ain't shootin' no more."

"'Cause I shot him."

Three voices, Emerson thought, but it could be more.

Looking under the brush, Emerson made out four, five, six sets of legs.

Josh stood up, and Emerson started to, but Josh motioned for him to stay down.

Josh fired, and a body rolled down the hill, crashing heavily through the brush.

The Blue Coats all dropped to the ground. Closest to him was a pale man with a scraggly black beard and big eyes. The eyes didn't blink. Emerson shot him and fired again, hitting a man in the leg. The other Blue Coats jumped up, one dropped his rifle, and they started to run. Josh fired again and another one tumbled to the ground.

Josh crashed through the brush. Emerson followed. At the top of the ridge, they couldn't see any Blue Coats, but they heard them tearing through the woods and sounding like a couple of deer startled from their dens.

"If the Yanks get a serious passel of men up here, we're goners," Josh said, and he hustled down the slope.

Emerson looked at Charlie, at his bedroll. He pulled it off him, slung it over his shoulder, arranged the horse holder across the log, the way he'd been, and hurried after Josh.

As Emerson ran down the slope, gunfire raged on both sides of the valley. When Emerson got back to Horse, men were streaming up the hill. Emerson grabbed Horse's reins just before a red-faced beefy fellow did.

"Gimme the damned reins," Red Beard growled.

"Get another one." Emerson held on to the reins with his left hand.

"Horse holder goes last on the last horse left," Red Beard said. "That's how we do it."

"It's not how I do it."

Several men stopped behind Red Beard.

"Hey!" a man at the rear of the pack hollered. "There's two hundred Yanks behind us! They're afoot, but if we don't get moving right now, horses won't do any of us any good. Get mounted and skedaddle!"

Red Beard glared at Emerson for a moment, and then he followed the others selecting mounts and scattering. Some rode up the slope. Some down and across the stream and south out of the valley.

Josh and a tall, slender man with a thin black mustache mounted and headed down. Emerson swung up on Horse.

Two horses were left. For a moment, he wondered whether he should take them.

"Emerson!" Josh hollered from beside the stream on the valley floor.

Guns started blasting from behind him, from where Charlie died. Bullet-clipped twigs and leaves rained on him. Horse bolted down the slope.

19

AT THE VALLEY floor, Horse leaped the stream. Emerson was about to follow Black Mustache and Josh, who were riding hard to the south, when a gunshot boomed from up the valley. A Blue Coat and another man in a tan coat galloped hard from the north. The Blue Coat was in the lead and held a rifle in one hand. Emerson pulled his musket, stood in the stirrups, and fired. The Blue Coat tumbled back over his horse's rump. The other man hauled his mount to a stop, jumped to the ground, and pulled a long gun from a scabbard.

"Horse!" Emerson dug his heels into the animal's belly.

Horse burst into a run. Emerson could feel the animal's power, could feel that the distance between him and Josh was of small consequence to his big black. Exhilaration charged his veins. He held reins in his left hand, the rifle in his right, but he was bound physically to Horse as flesh to flesh, as if they were parts of the same magnificent beast. It was as if Horse flew, never touching the ground. The Emerson-Horse animal flew above the earth, while at the same time, the pounding of hooves on the faint trail echoed and rippled through the muscles of the man-animal, but the pounding sensation was as if it were being dreamed, not part of the awake world. The world where Emerson-Horse flew.

Emerson felt something strike Horse in the rump. He heard a rifle shot. Horse faltered for an instant and then picked up the chase again. But they weren't flying anymore.

Emerson glanced behind him. Tan Coat stood next to his horse as he loaded a breechloader rifle.

Ahead of them, the trail cut right, and Josh disappeared behind a screen of trees. As he reached the turn, Horse took another hit in the rear. He whinnied and hobbled to a three- legged halt. Emerson hopped down and ran behind the trees, leaving Horse standing in the trail. As he reloaded his musket, a riderless roan raced past, its reins streaming behind it.

Back up the trail to the north, Tan Coat mounted and, with the rifle in one hand, spurred his mount into a run down the valley. Emerson muttered curses at the son of a bitch for shooting Horse. Twice.

Emerson fired more curses as he aimed. Then he jerked the trigger. The man's hat ripped off, and Emerson cursed himself for allowing his fury into his finger.

Tan Coat reined up, turned around, and cantered back to the north.

Emerson, furious with himself for rushing the shot, spilled as much powder as he got down the barrel. He was furious that Tan Coat cantered away. Casually. As if he knew Emerson was incapable of hurting him.

"Emerson, come on," Josh said. "No time for this."

Josh held the reins of the roan out to him. "Ride on south.

I'll take care of Horse."

Emerson finished loading his weapon. The scabbard on the roan was too short for it.

Emerson said, "Shit."

He ran to Horse and pulled off his rifle scabbard, Dragoon holsters, and saddlebags and hung the straps around his neck and over a shoulder. He circled behind and then around to the front of the big black. Horse had his head hung low. Waiting.

Emerson looked at Josh.

"Better git going," Josh said.

They left Horse lying on the trail like a pile of discarded no-longer-useful black cloth.

Emerson didn't much care if they got away or not. Except for one thing. He wanted to meet the man with the tan coat again. Somewhere.

Sometime. In circumstances, he, Emerson, had some control over. He wanted that really badly.

*****

Josh was up ahead. Emerson didn't follow him, but the roan did.

"Oh, Jesus, Horse," he muttered over and over and over. "Oh, Jesus, Horse."

The image of blood oozing out of Horse's butt, trickling down his haunch, clotting his tail, stuck in Emerson's head. Flies buzzed back there. Maybe the tail was too heavy with all the blood on it. Maybe Horse knew the flies would have their way with him anyway, so why swish his tail at them?

"Oh, Jesus, Horse."

He had a vision of three buzzards circling high over that valley. *Won't be long,* he thought, *before there's a lot more of you sons of bitches. Real ones, not imagined flesh eaters.* The thought recurred every so often, the image of carrion eaters circling, floating high above and waiting and watching for the killing and dying to finish up. Buzzards. A snake neck and head with a beak instead of fangs stuck onto a filthy, black-feathered bird body.

His prince of horses bleeding to death through his butt.

That goddamned guy with the tan coat!

Emerson cursed himself for not being able to dredge up a single detail of what he looked like.

He remembered shooting the hat off, but he couldn't remember if the hat was black or white or some other damned color. When the hat blew off, was the hair light or dark? He couldn't remember. Mustache? Whiskers? Clean-shaven? Hell. He could've been naked and a Negro.

"Aw, shit, Horse," Emerson mumbled. "Maybe it was bad luck to change your name. Aw, shit, Iago. I am so damned sorry. The slings and arrows of outrageous fortune. The prince of horses bleeding to death through his butt!"

Josh appeared beside Emerson.

"What the hell're you doin', man? I check behind me, and shit if you ain't a goddamned mile back. We got to make tracks."

Josh jerked a rein from Emerson's hand and led them west at a trot.

The sun set ahead of them, and they kept riding, Josh dragging the roan to wherever he was going.

Emerson held on to the saddle horn. Every once in a while, he came back with no idea of where he'd been, but he'd been some other place. Sort of like being asleep, he thought. Each time he came back, it was a surprise to find himself in a strange saddle, on a strange animal, and then the black ugly anger at the man who shot Horse returned.

At some point during the night, Emerson realized they were heading north.

But what did north matter? What did any direction matter?

It was another long goddamned night. That mattered. All night they rode.

Then the roan stopped. Because Josh stopped.

Cold rested icy hands on Emerson's shoulders. A bit of light gray glow lit a chunk of sky. Above, the stars held on to their pieces of sky.

"Emerson." Josh said his name. From far away. "Emerson. You awake?"

Why the hell was Josh pestering him?

A slap across his face jolted Emerson.

"I need you to cover me," Josh said.

Emerson grabbed the front of Josh's shirt and cocked a fist.

Josh did not raise a hand and looked Emerson in the eye.

"Makes you feel better," he said, "go 'head. Hit me."

Emerson dropped his fist. His didn't want to hit Josh. Josh was his only—

What the hell was Josh? Was it right to call him a friend? He'd only known him a few days. Of course, he'd only known Horse a few days.

"You know why they shot Horse, don't you?" Josh asked.

Emerson shook his head, and then he realized it was still dark out. "No."

"They was hopin' to take you prisoner. They would've asked you for names of other 'Bushwhackers'—that's what they call us."

"I don't know many names."

"They didn't know that. Someone'd gone to work on you with a knife. Cut pieces off until you give up whatever you did know. Then they'd've shot you. You remember hearing that Blue Coat scream like he was slipping into hell and had nothin' to grab on to? That's what our boys was doing to him. They was asking him how many Blue Bellies was in the main bunch."

"This is soldiering?"

"It is here in Missourah and Kansas." Josh laid a hand on Emerson's arm. "You all right now, partner?"

Partner? Weekes Daley had been a partner in an enterprise they agreed to pursue. Emerson looked at Josh. There were things he admired about the man. He knew if Josh hadn't intervened in the poker game in Saint Joseph, Emerson would have wound up on that saloon floor in his own puddle of blood. Josh had gone back to get the Fordyke brothers. It hadn't worked out for them, but Josh had tried. That mattered. But that did not make him a partner.

Emerson looked around. They were on a great grassy plain dimly lit in a ghostly gray. Not a tree in sight except for a couple of hundred yards ahead of them, where a stand of trees stuck up out of the flat terrain.

"When we get to a hundred yards from those trees, cover me with your rifle. I'll ride in and make sure it's safe. You able to do that?" Josh grabbed Emerson's arm. "You going to cover me?"

It was as if Emerson had been in that stage of half wakefulness, but not yet awake fully enough, and not yet ready to endure the cold on the other side of the blankets to throw them back and get dressed. But now he was awake. He pulled the long rifle from the saddle scabbard.

"Is it loaded?"

It was loaded, but he recalled the way he'd done the job. He dismounted, cleared the barrel, and reloaded properly.

As he finished, Emerson thought about the man with the tan coat. If Tan Coat had been firing a muzzle-loader, Horse would have made it around the bend in the road before the man could have gotten a second bullet away. Then he remembered when he'd shot the man off the roan. That man had fired his rifle. He was empty. What Emerson should have done was shoot the man with the tan coat. Horse would still be alive if he'd done that.

"Goddamn it, Emerson! I'll slap you if I have to."

"Go ahead. Hit me. If it'll make you feel better."

Josh laughed and pulled his mount around and headed for the stand of trees. Emerson stopped where Josh indicated as he angled away to the left from a straight-ahead approach. Josh waved his red bandanna as he approached the trees.

Emerson kept his eyes on the trees as he sidled the roan to the right.

At ten yards from the edge of the trees, Josh stopped and stuffed his bandanna into a pocket. He appeared to be talking with someone. Then he motioned for Emerson to come.

Emerson trotted the roan across the hundred yards.

Inside the trees stood Lieutenant Miller. Next to him was the man with the black mustache he'd seen when they fled the ambush site.

Josh said, "This is Emerson Sharp, Cap'n."

"I told you, Captain," Miller said. "He looks enough like you to be your brother."

Josh dismounted. Emerson and the captain studied each other.

The captain was tall, thinner, some, in build than Emerson. He was dressed all in black. His mustache was neatly trimmed. Emerson knew what his own would look like. The ends he liked to curl, when he was in a civilized setting, would be drooped, lacking wax, and it would give him a dour mien. The captain's face, however, conveyed the impression that a bright, inquisitive mind looked out on the world. In one way, the captain reminded Emerson of Mr. Bucknell. Bucknell's demeanor showed him to be the master of the house that stood behind him. The captain equally conveyed mastery of the stand of trees and of the men assembled there.

"William Quantrill, Mr. Sharp. Step down. We'll rest here until noon. Josh, grab a cup of coffee, then see to the horses, please."

Emerson sniffed the air. The breeze was from behind him.

"It's a small fire, Mr. Sharp," Quantrill said. "If anyone is hunting us, they will check this stand of trees regardless of whether they smell smoke or not."

Emerson stepped out of the saddle but hung on to the horn until his legs steadied. He arched his back and twisted his neck. "Roan," he mumbled.

"You don't like the horse you rode here, Mr. Sharp?" Quantrill asked.

"No, sir. My horse was shot. This animal has a short, choppy gait I could not get adjusted to. My tailbone has been pounded clean up into my skull."

"That explains some of it, Emerson," Josh said as he took the reins and led the horses to the water.

Emerson sat on a log next to Captain Quantrill. The captain asked questions. Emerson answered and sipped coffee. The coffee tasted mighty fine.

After Emerson finished a second cup, with Josh sleeping and Lieutenant Miller watching from the edge of the trees, watching south, Quantrill looked Emerson in the eye.

"Sounds like you thought more highly of your horse than you did of the men we were with at the ambush. That so?" Quantrill asked.

Emerson stared back at him. "I think highly of Josh Ewing. The Fordyke brothers back at Will Nance's farm, the horse holder, Charlie, at the ambush—I think I would have admired those men if I'd had the chance to know them better."

"So, besides Josh, the ones of our company you could have admired died before you could do so. What about Lieutenant Miller?"

Miller was perhaps twenty yards away behind him. Or maybe Miller was closer and within earshot. There was an inclination to turn around and see, but Emerson did not look away.

"Lieutenant Miller was the first one to run away from the Nance farm."

"He was following my orders. The way we are forced to fight the federals, we are always outnumbered. We spring ambushes. We strike as heavy a blow as we can; then we retreat. I have told my officers their first priority, after retreat is called, is to save themselves. I have but a handful of lieutenants who are capable of sharing the leadership of our army."

"It doesn't seem like much of an army."

"It isn't much of one. Yet."

"Yet?"

"I don't know if you are one of us, Mr. Sharp."

"Neither do I, Captain. But I do know you make mighty fine coffee."

"Mr. Sharp, the men in my company, for the most part, have had a lot taken away from them. Many of them are hard and bitter. But we are united in our cause, that federals back in Washington, the Red Legs from Kansas, should not be telling us how to conduct our lives.

"I think that's enough conversation for this morning. Get some sleep. The lieutenant, Josh, and I will watch."

"Captain, if I'm caught with you, nobody is going to ask if I'm one of your band. I'll be as vigilant as any of you. I have some thinking to do. First, I'm going to check on my tailbone- pulverizing fleabag of a horse I wound up with. Josh doesn't take care of horses the way I do. Then I'll take over from Lieutenant Miller, and I'll watch for an hour. That okay with you, Captain?"

Emerson noticed the breechloader rifle lying next to Quantrill's bedroll.

"You mind if I look at your rifle?"

"Look."

Emerson picked it up.

Quantrill showed him how to open the breech and how to load it.

Emerson raised the weapon to his shoulder as if to fire, lowered it, levered open the breech, and imagined placing another cartridge and cap inside, closing the breech, and raising it to firing position. Quantrill stood hands on hips, watching him. Emerson imagined the captain reloading his muzzle-loader as Emerson went through the fire and reload motions again. The captain, the way he saw it, was still pouring powder down the barrel when Emerson was ready to fire another ball.

No wonder Tan Coat had been able to get a second bullet into Horse before they reached shelter. Even though Horse had flown over the ground. Bullets flew a hell of a lot faster.

"With minimal practice," Quantrill said, "a man with a breechloader will be able to fire four times for every ball a muzzle-loader fires."

One thing he did not like was the feel of the Sharps in the aiming position. His long rifle fit naturally to his shoulder, and his hands and arms were comfortable supporting the weapon. He grimaced.

"How long have you been shooting your long rifle?"

"Since I was ten."

"This is a Sharps carbine. There are other models of breechloaders you might find more to your liking."

Emerson thought Quantrill would want to ensure he hadn't disturbed the proper loading of the weapon, so he levered open the breech and handed it back. "Thanks."

Quantrill nodded, and Emerson walked to where Josh had tethered the roan at the edge of the trees with access to graze. He stripped the saddle and rubbed the beast down with the saddle blanket. Then as he was smoothing the blanket on the roan's back again, the beast swung its head and nipped at Emerson's arm. Emerson jumped back, but the roan's teeth tore his shirtsleeve.

Emerson said, "Let's get one thing straight. I am not the boss of much. Hell, I'm not even sure I'm the boss of my own damned self. But I am the boss of you."

The animal returned to its grazing. Emerson threw the saddle on and tightened the cinch.

Emerson patted the horse's neck, and he raised his head from the grass.

"You want to bite me again?"

The horse bit off another clump of grass.

"Roan, I wish to hell I didn't, but I like this Captain Quantrill."

Roan dumped a pile of biscuits on the ground. It was a substantial pile.

A FARMER WAITED in the yard near the house as they rode up. He cradled a long gun across his chest.

"Mr. Altmann." Quantrill tipped his hat to the man.

Altmann nodded and led Josh, Miller, and the captain into the house for supper.

Emerson entered the barn, climbed to the loft, spread Charlie's ground cover on the hay, collapsed onto it, and pulled half the cover over him. He hadn't bothered to remove his boots. He thought he'd drop into the bottomless darkness as soon as his head touched his saddlebag pillow, but his mind's eye popped open, and he was seeing Horse. Paw's horse. Weekes had prodded him to sell the animal. The beast tied Emerson to a spot when they went on a riverboat or stagecoach excursion, Weekes said. "That means," Weekes had said, "we have to go back to the place you left it. Cut yourself free of the animal. You can always get another horse."

Emerson had not been able to sell Horse. Weekes had asked him why he was so attached to the animal. Emerson had never been able to dredge up words to explain it. Horse had been Maw's buggy puller. Having a piece of Maw with him was ... comforting. Horse had taken him to Candace Barlow's window. Horse had carried him away from Candace's brothers. He hadn't been fast enough or strong enough to get away from them, though.

Big and Tiny had caught him, and he, Emerson, had had to deal with them. The fact that he'd survived was a matter of pure, dumb luck. He didn't need anyone to tell him that. Then Horse had carried him to the meeting with Weekes, and Horse had been fast and strong enough for the life he led with him.

But then Weekes had been killed and he met Josh. Josh convinced him to trade Horse for Iago. He'd changed Iago's name, and he saw now it was because he had not wanted to sever that tie to the world he had known before. Before he visited Candace, Terre Haute and a five-mile ring around it comprised the world he knew, and although Weekes Daley had shown there was a vast world outside Terre Haute and it was filled with wonders, still, at the core of himself was the Indiana farm boy. When he traded away old Horse, he traded away old Emerson too, in a way. He became a new Emerson.

But new Horse only lived a handful of days, and lying on a saddlebag pillow in filthy clothes and smelling the horse sweat and his own pungent stink inside the ground cloth, he thought, *Old Emerson is dead*. The trouble was, he thought the new Emerson had died too, along with new Horse. He couldn't stop plowing and plowing the same ground. The trouble was he never got any new ideas planted.

Then his stomach growled.

Stupid!

He wished he'd gone with the others in to supper. Altmann's missus would have her table loaded with meat, potatoes, and gravy, green beans maybe. There'd be a pie or cake. Maybe real coffee. But it was too late. If he went in now, it would be extra work for Altmann's missus. "Shit," he mumbled. He was hungry but couldn't get something to eat. He was exhausted but couldn't fall asleep. He cursed again and rolled to his other side.

He was wrong about not being able to fall asleep.

Mumbled voices from the barn floor woke him. From below, a lantern pushed a bit of glow through the loft ladder hole. "He'll be all right, Cap'n." Josh's voice.

"But it was losing his horse that affected him so?" Quantrill asked.

"Yes, sir," Josh replied.

"We're at war," Lieutenant Miller pontificated. "A man's life isn't worth all that much. How the hell can he value a horse so highly?"

"Emerson'll be all right," Josh repeated.

"We need to know we can count on him," the captain said. "Mrs. Altmann has breakfast on. Get him up, Josh, and then we need to get on the trail. Mr. Sharp will ride with me."

*****

At dawn, Emerson stood outside the barn next to the roan, waiting on Quantrill. The two of them would leave with Josh and the lieutenant following a half hour later.

When the captain led his big, black stallion out, Emerson looked away and cursed. His black looked an awful lot like Horse Two.

"Ready, Mr. Sharp?" Quantrill asked.

Emerson grabbed the saddle horn and swung up.

They set off at a canter. North. Emerson lagged a length behind. The captain motioned for him to come abreast.

"How well do you shoot with the long rifle?" Quantrill asked.

"Poorly. I had a clear bead on the man who shot my horse, but I only knocked his hat off."

"Josh told me about how true your aim was outside of Saint Joseph. After the ambush, you were trying not to hit his horse."

"Shit," Emerson said.

"What? That's not true?"

"I don't know. It could be true."

"You're here because Josh Ewing brought you, not because you want to be."

"I'm here because Josh brought me. I'd never have gotten out of Saint Joseph alive if it hadn't been for him. Back at Nance's farm, I'd decided I was going to go my own way come morning, though. I think highly of Josh, but the rest of the men in that party, not so much. The Fordyke boys, maybe, if I'd been able to know them better. Lieutenant Miller talked about what you all are fighting for. It didn't seem like my fight. Before I could leave, the shooting started and I wound up running with Josh. Then we staged the ambush. Ambushing isn't my kind of fight."

"I want to know about the horse. Why did you value it over the men you were with?"

Emerson had valued Horse Two. Highly. For the ties to home in its name, but, too, he hadn't thought about why before, but he did then. He decided it was because it was the first thing he'd ever owned that was truly his. Horse, the second one, had never been Maw's buggy puller. The long rifle was Paw's. The pistols were from the Barlows. And one was from Gold Tooth. The Bowie was Big Barlow's, and it had Tiny Barlow's blood on it. Horse, the second one, was all his. As much as a man can own a magnificent creature like him. Quantrill had no right to know any of that.

"Some things," Quantrill said, "a man can't articulate. But you will have to decide. Soon. Whether you will join us or not."

Quantrill kicked his black into a gallop. The roan followed two lengths behind.

Emerson groaned. He could not make himself adjust to the roan's choppy, butt-jarring gait. Everything he tried, from standing in the stirrups to using his thigh and calf muscles to absorb the jarring, exhausted him, so he surrendered to the pounding.

He thought about Captain Quantrill telling him how they fought, from ambush.

"It doesn't seem like much of an army."

"It isn't much of one. Yet," Quantrill had replied.

He thought about killing old dogs and cattle and pigs and chickens and game and Big Barlow and about a man killing Bartholomew Simmons for his boots.

He thought about killing Tiny Barlow. That bothered him. Some.

He thought about killing from ambush. That outright bothered him. Josh was okay with it.

Captain Quantrill had said he didn't have much of an army ... *yet*. Meaning he was on his way to having one. But from what Emerson read, he knew regular armies ambushed other regular armies.

"Shit," he muttered.

He wished he could talk to Weekes Daley. He wished he could talk to Horse. Either one of them.

"Roan," he muttered.

As night set, they slowed to a walk following roads and game trails, skirting farmers' fields, and filing through forest. Once, they hid in woods as six shadow horsemen trotted past in the starlit night. An hour after sunrise, Quantrill led them to another farmhouse, and they spent another day in another barn.

That night, Emerson rode with Lieutenant Miller, Josh with Quantrill.

The ride began the same way. Like the captain, the lieutenant had questions.

"Back at Will Nance's place," Miller said, "I told you we weren't big on military formality in our army. But there are times when Captain Quantrill or I give an order. When we give an order, it must be obeyed. You understand?"

"I understand, Lieutenant."

"Promptly. Without hesitation. And to the letter."

"I said I understood."

"The order might be to let someone else take your horse."

"Nothing ties me to this one."

"But you may get another one, and you may become as fond of it as you were of the last one. Why were you so attached to it?"

"Because it didn't pester me with questions, Lieutenant."

A couple of hours passed without questions. Miller stopped at a stream to water the animals.

"If I order you to shoot a horse, Mr. Sharp, can I count on you to do it?"

The night before, Captain Quantrill had asked his questions and gotten his answers, and that was it. Miller, however, kept picking. Like a kid with a scab. *Pick, pick, pick.* Until it bled.

"Josh already told you I shot horses outside of Saint Joseph." Emerson hoped he'd loaded enough frost on his voice. Miller had better ease up. A man could take just so much goading.

"Ah, yes," Miller said. "So he did."

They mounted and rode some more. Once they hid from men heading south. When they were clear, Miller said, "Red Legs."

The sounds of the passage receded. The croaking, cricketing, calling of night beasts and bugs came to life again. Miller led them on, still aimed north. Emerson rode beside him.

"We hid from Red Legs last night too," Emerson pointed out. "Seems to be a lot of them. Why are we here in Kansas?"

"We're here because Captain Quantrill says so. He hasn't told me why. He doesn't have to." Miller glanced at Emerson. "Fact is, the federals patrol the exclusion zone pretty heavily. There are Red Legs here in Kansas, but a lot less of them than Blue Bellies in Missourah. It makes sense to use this as the retreat route after the ambush. What doesn't make sense to me is why you are with us. Why are you?"

"I had no intention of staying with you after Nance's farm. That morning, I'd intended riding away to the east, but the shooting started, and I wound up running with Josh, and he led us west. He told me a man alone in the exclusion zone or in Kansas, unless he was pure Indian, was a goner for sure."

"We get back into Missourah and you'll leave us?"

"If you're that worried, tell me to go. You won't get an argument from me."

"You want me to make your decision for you?"

Emerson dropped back in trail on the lieutenant. He did not want the other man making his decisions for him. He did not know clearly what he wanted to do. He could stack the factors up. He liked Josh. He owed Josh. Josh had saved his life back in the Saint Joseph shoot-out. He'd saved his life again after Horse went down. He respected Josh and wanted Josh to respect him back.

The real issue for Emerson was that when he thought about leaving Quantrill and Miller, leaving Josh, there was nothing he could picture in front of him that appealed, looked interesting, or seemed worth as much as staying with Josh.

Above, thin, high clouds veiled the half-moon, and it flooded the earth with light that was like looking through watered-down milk. The milky light did not penetrate to beneath the trees bordering the trail. Emerson was comfortable with the night. His ears sorted the wilderness nocturne from the clopping of hooves and the creaking of saddle leather. The creatures who spoke and sang in the dark felt safe, secure. Miller led them at a walk. The walk did not disturb the creatures.

Then it happened again. Just as it had when the Red Legs' patrol had come thundering through the dark. The quiet occurred suddenly and completely as snuffing a lone candle made a room dark.

Emerson stopped. Miller did not. "Lieutenant, stop," he hissed.

Miller did not.

Emerson drew a Dragoon, cocked his head, and urged his ears to find a whisper of sound from the pitch blackness ahead of them.

Ahead and to the right, a muzzle flashed fire, followed by the bang of a rifle. Then a dozen other rifles flashed like a cloud of lightning bugs had just been waiting for the first one to blink on so they all could. Bullets twipped above his head. Emerson unloaded his pistol at the flashes. Then he was empty. His night vision was ruined, and his ears rang.

Miller tore past, heading back the way they came. The Jayhawks were reloading, Emerson figured. He hoped they did not have breechloaders as he wheeled his horse about and gigged his heels into the animal's belly. He tore off after Miller.

"Roan," he said.

Roan put on a burst of speed, and the wind tore Emerson's hat off, and the cord sawed at his neck. Roan caught up to Miller and blew past him. Emerson hoped Roan wouldn't step on something or in a hole. When he'd put enough distance between them, he and Roan and the ambush site, he pulled on the reins and slowed the animal gradually to a walk.

No trees roofed over that part of the trail, and the moon's milky light showed steep, rocky terrain climbing away from the trail on both sides.

Miller pulled alongside and dismounted. Emerson stopped Roan, and Miller handed his reins up. Then he walked a couple of paces back toward the ambush site and cocked his head, listening. He ran back and vaulted into saddle.

"They're coming after us."

Miller took his reins and led them at a canter as he scanned the walls of the canyon they were in. They came to a spot where the slope of walls shallowed and a V-shaped clump of pine trees had found enough dirt among the rocks to stand on. Miller hopped off his horse and led it up the slope and into the pines some twenty yards above the canyon floor.

"Put ten yards between us. Don't shoot until I do. Make your bullets count. I think there's ten or eleven of them."

The tip of the V of pines almost touched the canyon floor and widened as it climbed. Miller hid about halfway to the rim of the canyon. Emerson guided Roan to the opposite side of the V. He heard them coming. It sounded like a lot of riders. He hoped the lieutenant was right about the number of them. From the thunder of the hooves, it could have been twenty. If twenty, he and Roan were in real trouble. He hoped Miller had enough sense to just let them pass. But he'd said, *Don't shoot until I do.* Above the pounding of hooves, Emerson heard a man holler, "Stop! Stop, you goddamned idjits! Stop!" A pack of riders continued on. The moonlight exposed their entry into the steep-walled canyon. Five of them. He drew his other Dragoon and cocked it.

The riders slowed from a gallop to a trot as the leader of the file reached to just below the trees. Miller fired, and the lead rider tumbled sideways off his mount. Emerson shot the second man out of his saddle. The last in line wheeled about and started back the way they had come. Miller fired twice, and the man slumped over his mount's neck. The other two riders were hard at work trying to control their mounts. One reared. The other spun about like a dog chasing its tail. When the rearmost settled back onto four legs, Emerson knocked the rider out of the saddle. Three rounds left. Miller fired twice at the last rider, and the horse squealed and went over sideways, pinning the rider.

A bullet zipped through the trees above Emerson's head. Up the trail, a rider sat on his horse, occupied with a breechloader. Emerson pulled his long rifle from the scabbard. *Range, more than fifty yards. Say sixty-five, seventy. Downhill. Light's poor. Don't aim high.* He fired. The rider dropped his rifle and grabbed his thigh as his horse reared, throwing him off. Then the horse bolted to the north, back toward the original ambush site.

The sound of horses fleeing to the north diminished, dwindled, and faded altogether. Silence, utter and complete, filled the night. Then Emerson's ears filled with ringing. From the canyon floor, a horse huffed breath in and out as if it were a lot of work. A man moaned.

"Come on," Miller barked. "Time to get out of here."

"Go on if you want."

Emerson left Roan tied to the sapling and hustled back to the canyon floor.

A hatless man lay pinned under a horse. He had no weapon. He was maybe fourteen or fifteen. His hair looked white in the moonlight. His eyes were huge. He cried, "Please don't shoot me, mister!" Emerson cocked his pistol. The kid put his raised hands over his face, the palms toward the pistol as if he could forestay the bullet. "Please."

Emerson shot the kid's horse.

The kid dropped his hands, and those big eyes stared up at Emerson. Then the kid grimaced and squinted his eyes shut. "I'm gut-shot. Oh, Jesus, it hurts."

Emerson shot the kid before he could open his eyes again.

One shot left.

Emerson scrambled back up the hillside, untied Roan, and started up the slope, staying in the trees. At the top, Miller was waiting for him.

"The guy down there, he was just a kid."

"Yeah. Lucky for us. If they'd had enough sense to wait until we got fully into their ambush, you and I would be down there leaking blood into the dirt."

"We need to warn Josh and the captain."

"They might have heard the shooting. If not, they will find the bodies a half hour from now. Either way, they'll head east. You, Mr. Sharp, I told you we needed to leave. Instead of obeying my order, you went down and put a horse and kid out of their miseries."

"The rules, as I understand them, Lieutenant, are that once an officer says, 'Skedaddle,' it's every man for himself."

"Does that mean you are following our rules, that you want to join us?"

"Josh led me into this. I went willingly. Now there doesn't seem to be a way out other than shooting my way out. As to what I *want* to do, I don't rightly know, Lieutenant."

"None of our soldiers question their commitment to our cause."

"Then you didn't know the Fordyke brothers."

"They were committed."

"John, the oldest, he was committed. Younger brother, George, did what John led him into."

"I didn't see you talking to the brothers much. How'd you figure that out about them?"

"I spent the last three years learning how to read people. I had a good teacher."

"You can read other people, but you can't figure out what you want to do?"

Emerson sucked in a big lungful of air, held it, and then let it out. He looked up, checked the moon and the North Star.

"You know where we are, Lieutenant?"

"Kansas City is just a little north of due east."

Emerson stepped up onto Roan and guided him due east.

Miller overtook him. Miller, Emerson figured, was not about to let a man who didn't know where he was going lead him.

Emerson didn't mind. He didn't care and fell in trail.

Emerson recalled Roan's burst of speed down in the valley.

It was dark at first, but he was sure Roan was running faster than Horse, the second one, had during the race from the ambush site. He smiled and patted the animal's neck. "Roan," he whispered and patted the neck again.

Then Roan settled into his butt-jarring gait.

"Aw, shit, Roan."

PART III

Summer 1863

21

EMERSON AND JOSH Ewing set out from Kansas City bound for Saint Louis. They traveled at a leisurely pace and gambled in small towns and large ones.

Lady Luck smiled on their gaming. As they rode side by side into Saint Louis, Josh said, "I ain't never had so much money in my pockets before. Near two thousand. Whooee! Ridin' together is good l—"

"Stop!"

"What? I thought you weren't superstitious."

"I'm not. But saying a thing like that changes good luck to bad."

"That's not superstition?"

"I've seen it happen more than once. Odds are better than zero that saying such things kills good luck."

"Well, if you ain't a study, young Emerson!"

"Young Emerson!"

He led Josh to Boatman's Bank and deposited money into his account. He also informed a bank vice president, Mr. Burkemper, that Weekes Daley had died and inquired if he'd left a will. Emerson intended to help get the funds to the heir.

The bank held a copy of a will. It designated Emerson to inherit Daley's estate. Mr. Sharp would need a lawyer. Daley's death would have to be verified with authorities in Independence, and there was a legal process for transferring the funds, which, after fees, could be as much as $50,000.

"Whooee!" Josh said. "I never knowed a rich man before." "Weekes told me, 'The bank is rich. You are not.'"

Josh rubbed his chin and frowned. "What does that mean? You shouldn't live like you are rich?"

Emerson grinned. "I asked the same questions of Weekes."

"What did he say?"

"'You, young Emerson, are not nearly as ignorant as you look.'"

"Huh," Josh said. "Maybe I should rethink this business of openin' an account if all it's goin' to do is make the bank rich."

Emerson shrugged and left the bank to find the lawyer Burkemper recommended. Josh stayed and opened an account.

After departing Saint Louis, the two traveled north. One night as they ate supper in a small town a few miles west of the Mississippi, Emerson lowered his voice and asked Josh about his horse, Duke.

"I never thought about it before. I was wondering, after a"—Emerson looked around, but no one at the other tables paid them any mind— "after … like we did near the Kansas border, did a horse holder ever give Duke to somebody else?"

"Sure. Happened twice. Once I caught up to the guy with him and asked for him back. Fellow gave him over. The other time, I cut cards and won him back."

Emerson shook his head, and Josh chuckled.

"Just like I told Bucknell. Duke's the best horse I ever rid, but there's plenty almost as good. I don't get as attached to an animal as you. And why do you hang on to the roan you're ridin' now? All you do is bitch about the hard ride he gives you."

Emerson shrugged and speared a slice of fried potato and stuck it in his mouth.

"Puh!" Josh said. "Seems there's not a subject comes up you don't know somethin' about, but you don't know the answer to why you keep a horse you don't like."

"I never said I didn't like Roan."

"Like to bounce yore tailbone clean outta the top of yore skull! Seems I recall you sayin' something close to that."

"Maybe there's a card game in the saloon next door," Emerson suggested.

"And if you're so all-fired fond of an animal, why don't you give them a proper name? Iago was as fine a name as I ever heard for a horse like he was. And now you just call the roan Roan?"

"Some things, young Josh, are just a mystery. Poker?"

Their take that night covered dinner, the livery, and a room, with twenty dollars left over. They considered it a good night in a small town if they earned their keep. And some small towns only had one place for eating, drinking, and sleeping. They modified Emerson's rule to cover that case as: don't make the citizens mad even if you have to lose money.

They moved on to Hannibal and spent five days there. Every morning, Josh went off on his own for a few hours. He didn't say what he did. Emerson didn't ask. While there, they followed Emerson's rule of not gambling in the saloon where they took rooms they shared with girls. The card games were high stakes, and they piled up cash again.

Departing Hannibal, they journeyed west and camped the first night. The mosquitoes weren't quite as bad as they'd been near the river. They lay in their bedrolls, looking up at the stars.

"You ever remember any of the saloon girls?" Josh asked. "Me, I don't even remember the one I was with last night. She had black hair. I remember that."

Emerson understood it was his turn to speak, but he lay as quiet as the silent one-eyed creatures staring back at him from heaven.

"It's like I point Duke's butt at the hitchin' rail in front of the saloon where these women work, and I forget 'em."

Like you just take any horse from the horse holder and skedaddle, Emerson thought. Some things a man didn't say aloud, even to a friend and partner.

"The only girl I really remember is my maw," Josh said.

"Your maw is a girl?"

Sometimes starlight, even in the summer, seemed to be cold light. A chill settled over their camp. Josh wasn't going to respond to the jibe.

"I'd like to know, Emerson. Do you remember any of the girls?"

Emerson realized Josh was serious and that it was dark enough to ask such a question.

"Well. I remember Maw, of course. I remember Deborah Simmons. I can still picture Candace Barlow. That blonde girl in the saloon in Saint Joseph, where Weekes died. I remember Blonde. Maybe if I had one to hate, I could remember her. I don't hate her. It wasn't her fault Weekes was killed. It was mine. I broke a rule—a couple of them, actually."

"Weekes and his rules," Josh groused. "Now you spout 'em. Pain in the butt is what they are."

"Weekes gambled for twenty years. His rules kept him alive all that time, he said."

Emerson heard him mumble. Maybe he was done asking.

But no. "So you remember three girls?"

"Well, I remember Bucknell's daughter. She was feisty, sort of like Blonde, only not bitter at the core."

"Shit," Josh said. "Four girls."

Josh's bedroll rustled. Emerson waited for him to say something else, but he didn't. He fell asleep with whatever was gnawing at him.

Emerson stared up at the stars a while longer. He thought about Maw and that fenced cemetery plot near the house in Indiana. Those four crosses were there to help her remember the babies she lost. Emerson wondered if Maw remembered him. There wouldn't be a cross there with his name on it. There never would be.

"Rats," he muttered. He didn't know if any of the conversation helped Josh feel better or not, but it sure pulled Emerson down into a maudlin funk.

The next morning, with bacon in the skillet and a cup of coffee in hand, Josh radiated as much sunshine as the sliver of fire atop the horizon. It was as if the conversation and the mood of the night before had never happened. Before Emerson was awake enough to see if he was still despondent, Josh's mood elevated his own.

They'd been together on the trip for two months. They appreciated the partnership they'd forged. Both of them derived benefits from it, even if they couldn't speak about those benefits, no matter how dark it might be. For another week, they moved west, their partnership encased in the same pleasant, comfortable aura they'd enjoyed earlier. Then they came to Glasgow early one morning.

"I don't want to stop here," Josh said. "Word is this town is half-Yankee, half-Confederate. Wrong word in the wrong place gets you shot."

"Most of the western half of Missouri is like that. Is Glasgow that much worse?"

Josh looked Emerson in the eye. "I got a place to be."

Emerson sat atop Roan for a moment as Josh walked Duke down the sloped riverbank to the wooden ramp for boarding the ferry. The personal pronoun his partner had used was packed with exclusiveness. And exclusion.

Below him, the ferryman hauled on the thick guide rope and drove his raft up against the ramp. A farmer clucked the team pulling his empty wagon off the ferry and across the ramp. When he passed, a waiting freight wagon pulled on. Josh followed, and Emerson guided Roan to stand beside Duke.

The ferryman's nose and cheeks were the color of saddle leather. The rest of his face was obscured by gray and silver whiskers and by a straw hat not far removed from disintegration. The man stood no more than five six and weighed perhaps 120 pounds. He appeared to be old, emaciated, and feeble. Then he hit Emerson with his fiery brown eyes. "Keep them horses from goin' skittish. An' you watch fer driftwood. Watch good, hear? Time to time, logs git waterlogged and ride low. Watch good."

The ferryman shifted to the wagon. "You. Stay up there on the wagon." Then the ferryman growled at Josh. "Grab hold of the guide rope an' help me pull us *acrosst*. Less'n a course you're too good for such work. In which case, I'll charge you a buck 'stead a two bits."

The ferry consisted of planks lashed atop logs with three posts affixed to each side. Each of the posts had an iron eye bolted to the top with the guide rope passing through it.

"Pull smooth on the rope. You pull jerky-like, and you'll rock the raft and spook the horses. Then we're all liable to get wet. That happens, you best swim faster'n me."

They eased off the bank, and the horses stutter-stepped a couple of times and then steadied. Emerson was surprised at the power of the current he could feel at midstream, but they crossed dry and paid their two bits.

An hour beyond the crossing, they came across a body hanging by a rope around the neck and dangling from the thick limb of a tall oak next to the road.

"Hung 'im because of his shirt," Josh said.

Emerson looked at the man. One of his boots lay on the ground a yard beneath a sockless, dirty foot. The man's pants were faded and patched crudely. The shirt looked newer than the pants and was festooned with pockets. Some of the guerillas at Will Nance's farm wore shirts like that with half a dozen pockets sewn on the front.

"These people don't even need that much of an excuse to hang someone in these parts," Josh said.

"Why do you stay here if it's this bad?"

"It's not always this way. It's just that you don't know what's goin' to set guerilla hunters to bunch up and go scoutin'. Sometimes an ambush needs to be revenged, or a Red Legs Kansas raid into Missourah, or maybe the moon is full."

"So why do you stay?"

"It's like the cap'n says. Without us, half the people here got nobody on their side. Besides, I got my own rules to keep us safe."

"I didn't think you liked rules."

"Sometimes I don't like yours. Mine is that when guerilla hunters are ridin' the roads, guerillas ride in the woods."

Josh started Duke into the trees alongside the road.

"Hey," Emerson called, "we should cut him down."

Josh turned in the saddle and waved him on.

Emerson stood up in the stirrups and sliced through the rope with his Bowie. Then he dragged the dead man into the brush beside the road. There wasn't time or a shovel for burying him.

Emerson walked back out to the road, picked up the boot, and flung it into the brush. Then he turned and looked to where foliage had swallowed the image of Josh and Duke but not the noise they made crushing dried leaves and snapping twigs.

He put his hands on his hips and shook his head. He'd never wondered about Josh before.

Roan was ground-hitched a few yards from the road. Emerson walked to him, grabbed the horn, and swung up. "Roan," he said, and the horse followed the noise Duke was making.

"How the hell, Roan," he mumbled, "could Josh let his fellow guerilla just hang there beside the road? Back at the Nance's farm, before I got saddled with you—

"Well, now, isn't that funny? I got saddled with you! Shit.

Even if it was funny, I sure don't feel like laughing.

"Anyway, at Nance's, Josh ran back to get the Fordyke brothers when everybody else skedaddled. Trying to save the Fordykes and leaving that poor guy hanging in the tree, how do those two things square in the same man?"

They were riding through thick brush. Emerson had to hold his arm up to shield his face. He couldn't see Josh, only hear Duke. Then Roan came to a game trail. The brush and limbs from the trees thinned out. Josh was pushing Duke in a fast walk. Josh had a place where he needed to be. Emerson and Roan trailed along.

Late that afternoon, they stopped to cook supper. As they ate, Emerson asked, "This place you have to be, it's with Quantrill?"

Josh nodded.

"What ties you to him?"

"It's not him. It's the cause."

Emerson recollected his own favorable impression of Quantrill. He felt no attachment to their principles. He didn't like the way they fought.

"Cause! Bushwhacking and running and hiding. Where's the cause?" Emerson asked.

"It's just as the cap'n and the lieutenant say it. Washington, DC, is a thousand miles away. People back *there* got no business tellin' us how to conduct our affairs out *here*. We fight 'em with what we've got."

"Seems to me you're fighting more against your paw and the Kansas Red Legs. They're not far away."

"They've taken the federals' side."

"We have to have laws. Somebody has to make them."

"We'll make our own."

"There is no law out here. Since we crossed the river at Glasgow, we've been sneaking through the woods hiding from packs of wild men roaming the countryside, hanging anyone they don't know."

"I'm stayin' with Quantrill."

Emerson looked away from Josh and at the embers of their fire for a moment. Then he pushed up from the log they sat on side by side, tossed the dregs of his coffee, walked over to Roan, wrapped his tin cup in a rag, and stowed it in a saddlebag. He stepped up and onto the saddle and looked back at Josh.

Josh gave him that easy smile of his. "See ya, partner."

Emerson reined Roan around toward the setting sun. The trees crouching over the game trail kept the blinding rays at bay and settled an early, gloomy dusk beneath the low ceiling of leaves and pine needles.

Emerson sucked in a deep breath and huffed it out. He chided himself on how he'd conducted the argument with Josh. Weekes had told him once, "Victory in disputation, young Emerson, is 72 percent determined by the emotional control a man exercises over his statements and only 28 percent determined by the weight of logic in them." Weekes was right. If only he'd controlled his emotions. If only he'd stated his case in calm, cool terms, maybe Josh would have listened.

If only: according to Paw, the two most worthless words a man can string together.

Leaving Josh was harder than losing Weekes Daley. Weekes was killed, and then Emerson had to run for his life. Like he'd run from the Barlows.

Running for your life pushes most other thinking out of your head.

Now, though, he did have time to think. He did not want to leave Josh, but he could not abide riding with the guerillas. He didn't think many of them understood what a cause was, much less believe in *the cause*. If only Josh didn't. If only …

The game trail crossed a narrow stream. Roan stopped and dipped his head to drink. There wasn't much light left under the trees. If he continued on the game trail, odds were he'd stumble into an ambush. The way people behaved in that part of the country, they'd shoot at the sound Roan made walking on the trail.

Emerson dismounted and followed the stream until he came to a clearing with graze. The next day, he figured he'd ride on until he came to a decent-sized town. He thought he'd stay there a day or two, whatever it took to figure out what he was going to do next. He stripped the saddle off Roan and rubbed him down. "Roan," he said, "I hope to hell no guerilla hunters find Josh by smelling his fire. Like the Barlows found me." Emerson tsked. "Some people just don't listen, though."

A N HOUR AFTER sunrise, Emerson skirted a farm hacked out of the forest. A bit later, he came across another. At midmorning, the forest quit. Ahead of him, rectangular fields of wheat, oats, and corn stretched away for miles to where milky haze obscured the horizon. The layout reminded Emerson of the quilts Maw and her lady friends made on their Wednesday get-togethers. Just like those patchwork constructions showed evidence of regularity with sharply defined edges to the pattern, there was also an attractive element of the haphazard. Just so, white houses and weathered-wood barns had been dropped at random across the scene. Directly in front of him, three strands of barbed wire blocked Roan, held the woods at bay, and marked off a pasture for a dozen cows.

To the south of him, an east-west road sliced through the farms. A two-team-drawn stagecoach rattled and jangled east and passed a wagon headed the other way. To the north, nothing but farms. The road, then. Odds were the immediate area was civilized enough so a man wouldn't be shot or hung without a reason.

On the road, he cantered past a few wagons and met others and single and pairs of riders headed east. All of them regarded Emerson warily. Some of them returned his nods or hat tips.

In a single-street town, he bought oats for Roan and a meal for himself. He was told he could make Kansas City just after dark if he didn't dawdle. Another cup of coffee tempted him. He hadn't had any that morning as Josh had the pot, but he paid, retrieved Roan, and pushed on.

Late in the afternoon, a road veered off to the north. A crudely lettered sign indicated Independence was off to the north. Emerson stopped.

"What do you think, Roan? Independence should be as good as Kansas City."

Roan bobbed his head and looked due west.

"I'm driving," Emerson said and reined his mount and pointed him toward the new destination.

Roan snorted.

Emerson was inordinately pleased to have won the argument, if that was what it had been, and even if it was with a horse.

The road joined the east-west main street of Independence at a right angle and at the eastern end of town. On one side of the street was a livery stable, and Emerson paid for Roan to stay for two days. Directly across from the stable was the Little Saloon, and in small print on the sign—"Hiram Little, prop."

Emerson peered over the top of the batwing doors. Little's had a bar along most of one wall and six tables and a piano to the right of the swinging doors. It wasn't a little saloon. Neither was it large. Emerson had walked into any number of places like it any number of times. And in some of them, the same thing happened. He stepped through the swinging doors into a cloud of tobacco smoke and buzzing voices, and the noise ceased abruptly and every eye in the place locked on him as if he were a lone mouse scuttling across the dirt beneath a huge tree perched full of red-tailed hawks. In such a place, a man had about a second to measure what he sensed. Was it heavier with hostility or wariness? Then he had to spin on his heel and leave or continue inside. Hesitation was what was most dangerous. That afternoon, Emerson had not measured anything. A spike of irritation at each of the two dozen men and half dozen women in the place drove him toward a one-man opening at the bar. He didn't care what kind of men they were and if it came to shooting or not.

At the bar, Emerson heard the men on either side of him breathing. "Whiskey," he said to the bartender, who had stopped polishing a glass with a rag that was due for some cleaning itself. The bartender didn't move except to continue twirling the dirty rag in the glass.

From down the bar to Emerson's left came "Give 'im a whiskey."

Emerson leaned over the bar and saw a florid-faced, red- bearded man staring at him. Red Beard was one of the men at the ambush a couple of months prior when Emerson had served as horse holder.

Red Beard carried his glass of whiskey to where Emerson stood, and men made room for him at the bar.

Red Beard raised his glass. "Here's how," he said and drained the whiskey.

"How," Emerson said and swallowed his drink. Then he grimaced. "Barkeep, bring out a couple of bottles of the good stuff. Give everybody a drink."

Red Beard's endorsement moved the Little Saloon denizens to tolerance of Emerson. His buying *good stuff* for everyone moved him to full-blown citizenship.

Red Beard explained that many towns in that part of Missouri now had distinct areas of Southern and Northern sympathy. Since the federals had forced families to move out of the "exclusion zone," many of them had settled east of Kansas City. Some had taken to calling the area Little Dixie, but that didn't mean the area was exclusively Southern in its sympathy. What it meant was in that region where Northern sentiments had prevailed, the influx of Southern-oriented refugees from the zone now split the populace evenly.

"Round here, a man has to watch what he says and who he says it to," Red Beard said. "Lucky for you, you came in here and that I recognized you."

Emerson did not feel lucky. He was safe here with people he'd decided he wanted nothing more to do with.

Emerson studied Red Beard. At the ambush in the exclusion zone, after Captain Quantrill called skedaddle, Red Beard had come up to him and wanted to take Horse. Emerson refused, and it had angered Red Beard. That wasn't how horse holders were supposed to behave.

Apparently, Red Beard didn't remember that part, or maybe it didn't matter outside the urgency of the situation.

It occurred to Emerson that if he had allowed Red Beard to take Horse, the animal might still be alive.

In one way, he was lucky. In his years playing cards with Weekes, Emerson's face had grown quite good at hiding the thinking going on behind it. The way he'd entered Little's had been reckless. He'd pushed the odds. Now Red Beard and the others were drinking and pouring the good stuff as if it were water. Two drinks was the rule. No more. Emerson bought two more bottles of the good stuff for the crowd and, in the hubbub, slipped away and took a room upstairs.

Usually, after a couple of nights of sleeping on the ground, he slept well in a bed. Not that night. And it wasn't the noise from the rowdies down below that kept his eyes open to the empty blackness.

*****

With dawn smearing a streak of blood low across the sky, Emerson Sharp sat slumped forward, elbows on his knees, on a spindle-legged chair on the boardwalk in the darkness under the balcony roof of the Little Saloon. The mugwumps had its fangs and claws in him.

From the street behind Hiram Little's establishment, a rooster crowed as if to hurry the sun up from its too-leisurely rising.

"Shut up, you damned chicken," he mumbled and pictured the fowl rendezvousing with a skillet.

I've been here before, flitted through his head.

Except he had never been in Independence. What he thought about was sitting on the veranda of the Waterfront Saloon in Saint Louis when Weekes Daley had the downs. A few days later, Weekes got over whatever was depressing him. Then he died.

Emerson felt as if a nest of snakes filled his belly, all twining and writhing in a ball. A dew of vinegar coated his tongue.

In a corner of his mind, there lived a dim and vague notion that there was something wrong with sitting on the veranda of a saloon every couple of months as the sun came up and worrying about a partner.

What the hell am I going to do now? That thought was neither dim nor vague. He shoved that worry aside as if it wasn't honorable to harbor such selfishness in the forefront of his mind.

He worried for Josh. And if he had the decision to make all over again, he wasn't sure if he'd decide differently today. His aversion to the men in Quantrill's gang, and their outlook toward life and death, about the way a vulture would, no longer repulsed him as much as it had the day before.

Thoughts rattled through his brain like dice bouncing across the felt floor of a gaming table. Emerson shook his head as if, once he stopped shaking and the tumbling stopped, some order might settle out of the jumble. In the center of his brain, an image formed of the cubes coming to rest. Snake eyes.

It was as if every time an important thought began to form, his mind veered off onto a side trail, and the thought he wanted to latch on to got away.

Thinkin' is the biggest waste a time they is when it ain't gittin' you nowheres, Paw would say. *Git the hell up and do somethin'.*

A sliver of sun peeked over the edge of the east and big- sharp-needle-stab pain bloomed in the rear of his eyes. He squeezed the lids shut.

Emerson heard sweeping from behind him. A man wearing a white apron was vigorously swiping dirt off the boardwalk and into the street from in front of the general store three buildings farther west.

The western sky was dark. No stars showed. Black clouds curtained off the rest of the world at the end of the long street crowded with buildings along both sides. The air was still and humid and heavy, as if the air were holding its breath because it knew something was going to happen, and it would come from the west, from out of the darkness. A whisper breath of breeze brought the smell of musty straw and horse manure from the livery across from him.

Emerson mumbled a curse and stood up.

For a moment, he wished he'd paid a woman for her company the night before, but then he was glad he hadn't.

He was going to return to his room, pack his gear, and take it to the stable in case he had to leave in a hurry, and then he'd find coffee. Then he'd explore Independence.

The rooster crowed again, with great gusto.

First, he'd get a handle on the lay of the land. Then dinner.

Fried chicken.

Then he'd decide what he was going to do.

With the sun up and a course of action decided, he felt better. He pushed through the saloon doors and saw the lamp atop the piano casting a feeble glow out into the dead bar. It had been so filled with rowdy life the night before. Now the only thing alive was the smell of stale smoke, stale beer, and a whiff of vomit.

"Shit," he mumbled.

*****

The day before, he hadn't paid any attention to the layout of the town or to how he'd leave quickly if he had to.

One of Weekes Daley's rules was, when they arrived in a town, first order of business, agree on escape routes, a primary and an alternate. On the latest trip, Josh Ewing scoffed at Emerson's rules.

As Emerson descended from the second story of the Little Saloon with his saddlebags over his shoulder and his rifle in its scabbard in hand, he mumbled, "Dumb, dumb, dumb." Riding with Quantrill was dangerous. Being a guerilla with a casual disregard for his own safety was just asking for an unmarked grave. Or the eye sockets of his skull, pecked and chawed clean, lying atop the dirt and staring empty blackness up at the blue sky. Of course, he himself had been dumb the way he had charged into the saloon the night before.

"Zeekial." Hiram Little was behind the bar mopping the top with a rag, and he was speaking to a white-haired colored man with three spittoons stacked atop each other. "After you dump those, lime the outhouse. I saw flies walking out of there this morning holding their noses."

The colored man chuckled, yassuh-ed, nodded, and shuffled his burden toward the back door.

When Emerson was halfway down the stairs, Little asked, "You leaving, Mr. Sharp?"

"No. I'd like to stay another night. I'm going to check out your town. Based on the conversation last night, I thought I best be prepared in case I say the wrong thing to the wrong person."

"I got coffee on in back. Nothing to eat till noon, though.

Or maybe you'd like a hair of the dog? Course, I don't have any of the good stuff left. The boys like to strung me up last night when I run out."

"Coffee'd be good."

Emerson checked the floor. It appeared Zeekial had swept out the sawdust. He dropped his saddlebags and leaned the rifle on the bar. Little slid a mug over to him and raised his own. "Here's how," Little said.

Emerson how-ed him back and sipped. "Good stuff."

Little's grizzled, close-cropped whiskers split open and showed his missing teeth, one upper and a lower. "Nothing like an early-morning cuppa coffee before the world wakes up and starts spoiling the taste of things. That's what my pap used to say."

Over a second mug, Emerson asked for Little's take on Independence.

"Town's kinda sawed into thirds. Eastern end is Southern. Western third is businesses catering to the wagon trains. Blacksmith, a hotel. Last Chance Saloon is on that end. You want to stay clear of that place. They serve skull-splitting rotgut and they'll get your money one way or another. Wagon trains for both Oregon and Santa Fe Trails form up past the west end.

"Center part of Independence is Northern. You can tell where it starts. Two barbershops sit opposite each other across Main Street, like they was staring and daring the other side to blink. If you want a shave or a bath, use the one on the south side of the street. After you spent a night in my place, you don't want to be caught buck naked in the north-side bathtub or in a chair with a man behind you wielding a razor."

Emerson thanked Little for the coffee and information. He saddled Roan and rode down Main Street. No sign marked it as such, but that's what Little called it. Buildings snugged against each other around the sheriff's office and jail, but farther west, where the two barbershops denoted a shift of sympathies, houses and businesses were separated by empty lots, as if the Northerners not only didn't like Southerners, they didn't like each other that much. At the far end of Main, building spacing tightened up again. On the north side, narrow alleys separated a dress shop, a wide two-story building offering "Provisions for the Trail," and the even wider two-story Last Chance Saloon.

On the south side of the street, signage identified the gunsmith, Royal Arms Hotel, and blacksmith. The hotel was a four-story and appeared to be recently constructed. A hundred yards or so beyond the Last Chance, railroad tracks sliced northwest to southeast—bound for Kansas City, no doubt. Beyond the tracks, a bunch of covered wagons clustered in a field. Thin smoke from a dozen fires columned into the dark sky. Emerson hoped they'd get breakfast cooked before it rained.

He stopped in front of the gunsmith. There was a sign in the window: "For Sale. I want to go to Oregon too."

Huh. I know something about guns.

He knew about shooting them, not fixing broken firing pins or faults with the cylinder-revolving mechanism.

Maybe I should do what Weekes talked about, find myself a Dutzow's Corner. Maybe I should be thinking about finding a place to stay, permanently, instead of always thinking only about leaving and where to go to next. Maybe I could learn to repair guns. How hard could it be?

Wagons and buggies rumbled past him. He wrinkled his nose at the dust they raised. With rain coming on, the drivers all seemed intent on getting their business done before the storm cut loose.

There appeared to be more of the town to the north of Main Street than south. He turned that way and worked his way through more buggies and more wagons and riders too, and passed the Last Chance Saloon. A block later, he crossed Liberty Street, marked as such by a two-inch-wide slat tacked to a stake. The next street was Osage, also named by faded black paint lettered onto a wooden sign on a stake. He turned east. Osage was all houses set on large lots with gardens, pens for animals, and outbuildings. He came to Lexington, a north- south cross street.

Lexington continued north for a few blocks and then turned west. It looked to be well traveled and a good way out of town. He turned south and crossed Liberty. A house on a corner of the intersection identified "Myron Hofstedler, MD" as residing there.

After hitting Main, he returned Roan to the livery. A half- glass-fronted eatery sat four doors west of the Little Saloon. rosie's fine dining was painted on the window in red block letters and arranged in an arch. Smaller lettering pronounced the hours for breakfast, dinner, and supper. Dinner was eleven until one. It was 11:05 a.m. He entered.

A dozen round tables with eight chairs filled the floor, a little more packed together than the layout of the town. Three of the tables were occupied, none fully.

A young woman, trim, comely, auburn-haired, seventeen maybe, pushed through hinged half doors. She waved her hand. "Anywhere," she said.

Emerson walked to an empty table next to the doors to the kitchen and took a seat. "Do you have chicken, perchance?" He blushed. *Perchance.* He'd used the word to impress the girl. He looked again. The woman.

"Meatloaf or pork chops?" she said with what was clearly manufactured indifference. Her green eyes hit his.

She frowned. Her hands went to her hips. "Meat loaf or pork chops." Manufactured indifference had given way to annoyance, the real kind.

"Coffee. And pork chops. Please, miss."

She smiled. "We are going to have chicken for supper."

"Chicken?"

"Chicken."

The rain that had been threatening delivered a thrumming to the tin roof of Rosie's. It sounded rather pleasant, Emerson thought.

"What's your name?"

She pursed her lips, and her eyes sparked. "You said meat loaf, right?"

All he seemed capable of doing was looking at her. He became aware that his mouth was hanging open.

She huffed and turned on her heel toward the kitchen.

"Pork chops," he blurted. "Pork chops."

By the time she brought his meat loaf dinner, the rain had ceased and a crowd filed in and filled the tables. They ate as if they had businesses to get back to and then left. Emerson dawdled over his food and drank coffee until he was the only one left. Then the cream-complexioned, auburn-haired, emerald- eyed manifestation of a dream his imagination lacked the power to create stood before him, hands on hips, and inquired frostily, "Anything else, mister?"

For a moment, Emerson didn't know what to say. His mouth asked, "Have a cup of coffee with me, miss?"

She thought on it and then pulled out a chair, sat, and poured for them.

He was flabbergasted, but more than that, he was pleased.

She added about a teardrop of cream and what might have been twenty-five grains of sugar to her cup. She sipped and raised her deep-as-eternity green eyes to his. Everything from his Adam's apple to his shoulders and down to his hips melted.

He wouldn't have been surprised to see his head roll across the table.

She said something, but he missed it, as he was busy thinking about his head rolling across the table and wondering how he would see that happen if his head was—

"Beg pardon, ma'am. What did you say?"

"Nora."

"Nora," he said.

"Well!" she said.

Her face was very expressive. She was annoyed with him because he was behaving like a klutz. She was annoyed with herself for wasting time with a klutz. All that showed clearly on her face. She would not be good at poker.

"Are you going to tell me your name?"

He thought she was going to stand up and leave. "Emerson," he blurted. "Emerson Sharp. I'm pleased to make your acquaintance, Miss Nora."

She asked him questions, and he answered. Eventually, she shooed him out. He stood in front and put his hat on. He'd told her a lot about himself, but he didn't know anything about her. He hadn't even asked her last name.

"Emerson," he mumbled, "try not to be so stupid at supper."

A woman on the arm of man in a white shirt and ribbon tie approached from his right. Their hard heels thumped the boardwalk. As she walked past, her head swiveled to keep her eyes on him for a moment.

"Is Rosie serving whiskey now?" the woman asked her escort in a whisper Emerson heard clearly.

"Of course not," the man said. "Why?"

"That man. He's talking to himself."

Emerson tipped his hat and said to their backs, "They're having chicken for supper."

The woman turned her head for a last glare at him.

Just shut up, Emerson.

EMERSON'S FEET CARRIED him west down Main Street without him having thought to do so. He wasn't sure where he was going or why he was going there. The farther he walked, the scarcer boardwalks became and ankle-deep mud more plentiful. He navigated around puddles and paid attention to the riders and wagons in the street. Inside his head, a picture of Nora and her eyes appeared. He smiled at her image and stepped in a puddle. "Puh," he said and continued on to the far end of town and the gunsmith shop with the For Sale sign in the window. He used the boot scraper and went in.

The proprietor, Johannes Rottermich, was about his paw's age and an inch or two shorter than Emerson but thick through the chest and shoulders. Black chin-strap whiskers and hair framed a chiseled, stern mien. His eyes, though, betrayed pleasure to have Emerson's inquiry about buying his business. He was not pleased to hear that Emerson expected Rottermich to teach him how to repair guns.

"Ve make deal," Rottermich said. "You gif me seven tousand dollars. The business is yours. I stay and teach you to repair guns. I teach you Colts, Remingtons, Sharps, some made in Chermany. You pay me half the profits each month. But, ven first vagon train leefes next spring, I leef, vedder you still be stupid about guns or not. Ve haf deal?"

"Show me some of the broken guns you have and how to repair them."

"Bah. I show you, you not pay me to fix your gun."

"My guns are not broken, Mr. Rottermich. And I don't know whether I want to buy your business or not just yet. I need to see if I can learn this business. Let me watch you fix a broken weapon. It will help me decide."

Johannes agreed, took him to the rear of the shop where a workbench took up the wall, and showed him how to repair a Navy Colt with a broken cocking mechanism. He took parts from a gun pulled from a wooden box below his workbench. The box was filled with a jumble of handguns. All of them were nonfunctional, Johannes explained, but he kept them for parts. After installing salvaged pieces in his customer's pistol, he handed it to Emerson.

"See? Good. Like new. *Nicht?*"

Emerson took it, cocked it three times, and let the hammer back down. "Good as new," he said, handing the weapon back.

Johannes placed the repaired Colt on his workbench and disassembled it again.

"What are you doing?" Emerson asked. "*Psshht.* Vatch. Wid mouth shut, eyes open."

He reassembled both pistols in their original broken conditions and invited Emerson to effect the repair.

Johannes stepped back, removed a pair of wire-rim spectacles, hooked what looked to be identical glasses over his ears, placed his hands on his hips, and said, "You fix."

Emerson stood and stared at the two pistols lying in front of him. He understood the workbench. Three two-by-eight-inch planks had been nailed to a frame of four-by-fours. The planks were pine, the frame oak, and the bench was sturdy enough to support a horse standing on it. The planks were discolored from gun oil and cleaning solvent. The inner workings of the Navy Colts, however, were mechanical mysteries.

The gunsmith's tools were laid out in orderly fashion on a shelf above the workbench. Emerson picked up a screwdriver, sat on the stool, and bent over the Colt with the broken cocking mechanism.

"Stop," Johannes said. "I show you once more. Dis time, vatch."

Rottermich hunkered over his task, his broad shoulders making it difficult for Emerson to observe the delicate process the man's sausage fingers performed. After the gunsmith completed the repair a second time, he placed the restored Colt on the shelf next to his tools. Then he had Emerson find another Navy Colt from the box below the bench.

The bell over the front door of the shop jangled, and Johannes told Emerson to take the pistol apart, but not reassemble it until the gunsmith checked his work. Three men entered the shop. Emerson heard weapons clunk as they were placed on the wooden counter next to the glass-topped display case containing a half dozen different models of handguns.

Johannes turned from the customers and his chin-strap whiskers framed a stern glower. He waved his hand shooing Emerson to the task he'd been assigned.

Over the next two hours, as Johannes dealt with a steady stream of customers, Emerson learned how to disassemble and reassemble two Navy Colts from the box, each with different malfunctions.

"You see," Johannes said. "You can be gunsmith. You buy business now?"

"Mr. Rottermich, this is a big decision for me. I need to think about this."

"I teach you dis verk so you buy the business. If you not buy, I not teach."

Rottermich was a bull of a man, both in size and demeanor. Emerson stared into his hard, black eyes and said, "You not teach, I not buy."

Emerson wiped his hands on a rag, put his hat on his head and a smile on his face. "Good day, Mr. Rottermich." He stepped toward the door.

"Vait."

With his hand on the doorknob, Emerson turned back.

"I teach. You come back. *Morgen.*"

Emerson paused and saw the worry spike in the older man's eyes. He almost felt sorry for Johannes. Almost.

"All right, Mr. Rottermich. I will see you in the morning."

*****

Emerson walked back down Main Street to the south barbershop. After a shave, mustache trim, and haircut, he paid for a bath and having his black suit brushed and pressed and his ruffled white shirt ironed and his boots cleaned and polished. A door behind the barber's chair led to the bath. Inside, it was warm and humid. There was a flat-bottomed, galvanized tub and a large stone fireplace with a big, black kettle hanging from a hook. A low fire under the kettle heated water. A strip of a boy, maybe thirteen, dipped a wooden bucket into the bathtub and tossed the water out a door. The water in the tub was the color of coffee with milk.

Emerson held up a dime. "Take out another bucketful, will you? And put in two buckets of warm, please."

The towheaded kid hastened to earn the coin as Emerson undressed.

As the youngster scrubbed his back, Emerson thought about Johannes Rottermich's gun shop. It was strange to think he might be a gunsmith. He knew farming and didn't care to know any more about it. He knew playing cards and playing the men whose faces betrayed the hands they held. That life entailed moving constantly. People grew testy at a man taking their money day after day. Odds were that traveling to a new town every few days kept him ahead of the animosity building to violence. Most of the time. There were places where violence escalated rapidly, and it took a quick draw to convince a man that losing his life was worth more than the bills and coins in the pot he'd lost. There had been that time in Saint Joseph.

In Saint Joseph, he'd had to shoot Gold Tooth and other men after they'd formed a posse and chased him. Fact is, he reminded himself, he'd have died in that saloon, along with Weekes Daley, if it hadn't been for Josh Ewing. Gambling, he'd always had a partner. With a partner, odds were better he'd be able to avoid shooting anyone. Odds were better he'd live to move to a new town with his pockets filled with the last town's money. Gambling without a partner, thinking about it, the odds were a lot less favorable than they'd been.

The constant moving, too, was like running away. Which, when he thought over his last three years, was what he'd been doing. Maybe it was time to consider settling in one place, operating a business with good prospects. In that part of Missouri, guns were certainly in high demand. While he'd been there fiddling with Navy Colts, there'd been a steady stream of customers bringing in weapons in need of repair, to purchase or trade older ones for new ones. The wagon train forming up at the time sent many customers to Johannes. But, too, there'd been many Emerson thought he'd identified rather easily as either local North or South sympathizers. For sure, Rottermich had a good business.

Emerson Sharp: gunsmith.

He pictured the Gunsmith sign over his shop.

Nora.

He pictured her . . . if he was to have a future in Independence, she had to be in it too.

He recalled how easily he'd been able to read Johannes Rottermich. Odds were nine chances out of ten the man had been bluffing.

Why was it so hard to read Nora?

The door to the barbershop was shoved open, and Emerson grabbed his Dragoon from the stool next to the tub and cocked it.

The bald barber with the thick, gray beard, red sleeve garters, and a white apron held up his hands. "Hey, mister, um, I got another customer for the tub. Uh, he's got a gun too. Please?"

*****

Rosie's hours were 5:00–8:00 a.m., 11:00–2:00, and supper 5:00–8:00 p.m.

Emerson stepped through the door to have supper at a quarter to seven. Every table appeared to be filled with patrons. The din of conversation rivaled that in saloons when beer and whiskey had loosened constraints to where conviviality flowed easily. The smell of fresh-baked bread was strong. His nose sorted faint wisps of a pleasant pipe tobacco smoke. Rose of Sharon O'Hanrahan, followed by the other waitress, a raven- haired, brown-complexioned girl of Mexican or Spanish heritage and almost as beautiful as Nora, and Nora filed through the kitchen doors carrying plates loaded with fried chicken. The three hustled to tables, delivered supper, and picked up empty dishes and soiled silverware. A Chinaman wearing a white apron and a pigtail brought four plates to another table.

The brown-skinned girl, with one hand free, beckoned Emerson toward the rear of the place and showed him a vacant chair.

"Might I ask your name, miss?" Emerson asked.

The girl's dark eyes flashed, and anger flitted across her face as she placed a second hand on the armload of dishes and spun on her heel.

Two middle-aged couples and three men shared Emerson's table. Each of them said his or her name. He wasn't used to remembering names and couldn't remember a single one by the time it was his turn.

"Emerson Sharp. Pleased to make your acquaintance, ladies, gentlemen."

"Are you with the wagon train forming up, Mr. Sharp?" one of the women asked.

"No, ma'am. I've been moving west from Indiana, looking for a business opportunity. I may have found something here."

They wanted to know what. He explained about the gunsmith shop and that he was thinking it was time to stop roaming and settle. During dinner and dessert, Emerson learned he was dining with a banker and his wife, a lawyer, a butcher, and a whiskey salesman. The other man was a doctor, and he remembered the name from the sign he'd seen earlier, not the introductions. Mrs. Hofstedler sat between the doctor and the banker's wife.

It was funny how the mind worked. Weekes Daley had guided him in training his mind to calculate odds, to remember cards, and to read faces. If he was going to settle in Independence, he was going to have to learn to remember names. He'd watched the salesman, who obviously had a facility for remembering names.

After coffee, everyone at his table departed. The crowd had thinned out considerably. By Big Barlow's watch, it was seven thirty. As Nora passed by with hands full of dirty dishes, Emerson asked for more coffee. She nodded and continued into the kitchen. He opened his book of John Donne's poems.

"What are you reading, Mr. Sharp?"

Emerson looked up and found the proprietress glaring at him.

Rosie was about the age of his maw. Dark gray hair pulled into a bun, plump cheeks, of sturdy build, white apron immaculate. With other customers, she'd exchanged smiles and banter.

As she poured coffee into his cup, he read:

When I died last, and, dear, I die As often from thee I go ...

Rose sloshed coffee onto the saucer, and Emerson looked up from the book.

She wasn't sure about him. Emerson could see in her face she didn't often doubt her convictions.

Emerson stood. "Please, Miss Rose, join me for a cup of coffee?"

"This is a busy time."

"Running a fine establishment like this, I am sure it is always busy. Besides, *a woman's work is never done*. Please? Sit with me for a moment, and I'll wash dishes for you to make up for the time you squandered on me."

"How long?"

Emerson frowned. "How long will I wash dishes?" He pulled a chair out for her. "As long as you sit with me."

Rose smiled, placed the coffeepot on the table, sat, and called, "Isabella." The bronze-skinned waitress came over. "Bring me a cup and saucer, please. I will sit with Mr. Sharp for two hours. Then you, Nora, and I will go home, and he will wash dishes."

"Uh—"

"A deal, Mr. Sharp, is a deal."

Conversation with Rose began as it had with Nora. An interrogation. Emerson related the story he'd rehearsed with his tablemates during supper. Then he insisted Rose tell him about herself. How did she come to run Fine Dining?

She married Sean in New York twenty years prior, and the two of them worked their way west. She and he did whatever needed doing. He did the most menial of tasks, as long as it paid a bit, but he dreamed of living a better life, one where he paid a down-at-heel, holes-in-his-stockings, patched-pants Irishman to be his servant. As soon as he had a few dollars in his pocket, they moved again, searching for the wherewithal to realize his dream. They arrived in Independence. News of gold in California swept Sean up like a tidal wave and carried him away. Rosie paused, staring into her coffee.

The place in the world Rose of Sharon O'Hanrahan was meant to be was in a circle of lady friends such as the one his maw belonged to back in Indiana.

Before Rosie looked up from her moment of introspection, Emerson saw her weigh the loss of her husband as curse or blessing and settling definitely on blessing. Then she was back to business.

"After dinner, you made advances to Nora. Here at supper, you made advances to Isabella." Rosie's declaration was laced with accusation.

"I … I didn't make advances to Isabella. I wanted to know Nora's last name. I thought she might tell me. She wouldn't talk to me, though. She didn't even tell me her name."

"You traveled around the country for three years as a gambler."

Reading her face wasn't hard.

She wonders if I'm like her Sean, given to wanderlust.

"You were with many women."

"Um, well, not many."

"Many," Rose declared firmly.

Washing dishes under the supervision of the Chinaman, called Chin, Emerson understood was a test he had to pass, as was his Rosie-mandated visit to Dr. Hofstedler the next morning.

After dinner the next day, Nora told him her last name, and his courtship of Miss Ross began.

EMERSON COULD NOT come to grips with the glacial pace of his courtship of Nora Ross. His wooing of Deborah Simmons was to have been a Tuesday-to-Saturday affair. His arrangements with saloon girls had been consummated between a first drink and a second. In the week that followed, it seemed to Emerson he spoke a thousand words to Miss Rose for every one he was permitted to speak to Nora. Rose protected Nora. She wanted to be sure Emerson intended to sink roots in Independence. She wanted to be absolutely sure Emerson would not take advantage of or hurt her.

Rose was aggravating, but Nora was perfect.

Nora was beautiful. As beautiful as any woman he'd met anywhere. New Orleans, Memphis, Vicksburg, Saint Louis, Chicago. Any number of smaller towns. Candace Barlow. Nora was more beautiful than any of them. Her wavy auburn hair sparked gold in the sunlight when she turned her head. Her eyes performed feats of magic. They were at the same time jewels and pools of bottomless depth, and he sank and sank into them while feeling as if he were ascending. When he could force his eyes to leave hers, he saw her face as very much like the one Michelangelo sculpted onto the Madonna in his *Pietà*. According to Weekes Daley, Michelangelo was the only worthwhile sculptor since ancient Greece. Weekes had had an artist's drawing of the *Pietà*, and

Emerson regretted not having been able to get the drawing, or anything else of Weekes's, when he fled Saint Joseph.

But he no longer regretted losing the drawing. He admired it, but looking at Nora made his heart skip beats or spur it to thumping. Now as he went to see her, at one of three times a day Rosie permitted him, as he neared Fine Dining, his heartbeat kicked from a walk to a canter.

Rosie invited Emerson to eat with the staff at midmorning and midafternoon when the restaurant was closed. Weather permitting, they ate outside, behind the establishment, at picnic tables under a maple tree. Honeysuckle grew up a trellis near the tables. Emerson always considered the scent to be Nora's rather than the climbing vines'. For the last week, at nine at night, he walked with Nora for the scant ten minutes to Rosie's house. Always, either Rosie, or Isabella and her husband, Jose, who cooked for Fine Dining, chaperoned the walk home after work.

On Rosie's porch, Emerson was permitted to kiss Nora's hand, but he was not invited in. Each night as he walked back to his room above the Little Saloon, he recalled the Donne poem, with the line about dying some when he left his beloved. The next day, life burst anew in him when he saw Nora. Saw her beauty, her purity, her perfection. To feel so alive was almost worth the dying he experienced at their parting.

Except he felt stuck. He wasn't getting any closer to Nora. Rose of Sharon, Rose, Rosie—she had more names than Weekes Daley had before Emerson branded him—held him at bay. Nora was beautiful and pure and perfect, but at a distance he wasn't able to close. Nora was as far away from him as the beauty who'd posed for Michelangelo. Dead for four hundred years.

One thing niggled. It seemed clear she wasn't smitten with him the way he was with her. But then, how important was that? Paw sure didn't think it was important that Deborah Simmons care for him. Old Man Simmons had to know his daughter despised her intended. Deborah sure enough had a mind of her own. In the end, though, she was going to do what her father wanted. But the devils would have come up from hell to study that woman's ways to make a man miserable. Marriage wasn't supposed to be hell on earth.

Nora didn't despise him. He was sure of that. And she must be attracted to him somewhat, or she wouldn't spend all her free time with him.

Would she?

He had questions and not many answers to go with them.

But it was time to move the relationship forward.

Settling that was easier than knowing how to do it.

*****

His chin-strap whiskers not only framed Johannes Rottermich's anger but magnified it as well. Emerson explained he was not ready yet to make the decision to buy the gun shop. He also explained why he hesitated.

"Vat? Nora Ross! Ever'body knows she is damitched goots."

Johannes explained that Nora's mother was one of six wives of Mormon Daniel Ross. Daniel owned a farm amid a cluster of a dozen others of his religion to the northwest of Independence. He was a giant and a man of bestial appetites. When Nora was eleven years old, he started having relations with her—"As if six vifes vas not enough!" Nora's mother took her and ran away. She came to the sheriff in Independence.

As the sheriff was interviewing Nora's mother, Daniel Ross burst into the office and demanded his wife and daughter return with him to his farm. She called her husband a depraved and evil beast and vowed to never go back with him. Daniel lunged through the doorway, and as he grabbed his wife by the arm and reached for the daughter with the other hand, Nora's mother bit him on the arm. The sheriff pulled his pistol and ordered Daniel to let go of the woman. The giant howled at the pain in his arm and acted as if he hadn't heard the sheriff and clubbed his wife with a big fist. The sheriff shot him, but all the wound did was to further enrage Daniel. He lifted the limp form of the woman as if she were a pillow and threw her at the sheriff, who crumpled to the floor under her dead weight. A deputy responded to the ruckus and emptied his pistol into the back of Nora's father.

Rosie O'Hanrahan took the orphan in. Five or maybe six years ago, Johannes opined.

Emerson worked on a Remington pistol with a removable cylinder as he listened to Mr. Rottermich tell how Nora became damaged goods. The pistol was interesting. A man could fire it empty, remove the expended cylinder, and load one with the chambers precharged with powder and ball quicker than a man could reload a breechloader rifle. The gunsmith's story was also interesting to him, but if affected him differently from the way the narrator intended.

Rather than repel him, her "damaged" status led Emerson to admire Nora more than he already did. He was not a woman. He could not imagine what it would be like to be treated as she had been. By her father! He could imagine that it would be deeply, deeply troubling. A terrible thing to deal with. It was one thing to be used like a draft animal, as his own paw had treated him; but quite another, as a child, to be ripped from the innocence of youth for the personal gratification of her father's lust. He'd always looked on his tenth birthday as stepping from childhood to adulthood in an instant. The suddenness akin to stepping off a cliff in the dark.

Paw's "Git up, I said!" had seemed abrupt, brutal, almost cruel. What Nora endured was firmly in the realm of cruelty.

Rottermich was saying that there was a group of bankers, lawyers, merchants, and clergy who were the soul of Independence. The sheriff was also a member of the group that held the town together, enforced morality and legality, and moderated tempers even in the midst of a war between Southern and Northern sympathizers. The group made rules, decided on taxes, and managed the fire brigade. Most of the group were married. All were respectable. As the owner of Rottermich's Gunsmith Shop, Emerson would be part of the soul and conscience of Independence. None of the wives of the other members would stand for Nora's husband being included in their "above reproach" group.

Emerson finished with the repairs on the Remington and interrupted Johannes's dissertation on the political force ruling the town.

"How much for this pistol and two spare cylinders?"

"Did you listen to vat I saidt?"

"How much?" Emerson held the pistol up.

Rottermich frowned. Emerson thought the older man had just

shifted his mind from societal matters to business. It was very like actually seeing inside the man's brain.

"You vant Remington? I sell you new gun."

"I want this one. I repaired it. It's better than new."

"Puh! Apprentice! In two veeks, apprentice tinks he know better dan his master."

*****

Emerson decided his way forward.

Rose wanted proof he intended staying in Independence. He told Rottermich he wanted to buy the business.

"Seven tousand buys the building, the property. Inventory iss anudder two tousand. And you need tools. Dose are mine. I need dem."

Emerson agreed but then asked, "For nine thousand, then, I get this building, the two acres of property, the cows, pigs, and chickens, the barn, the shooting shed, the bunker where you store the powder … The powder is included with the inventory?"

"Ja, ja."

Emerson stuck out his hand. Johannes spat on his palm and then extended it. They shook.

"I will send a telegram to Saint Louis for the money. Which bank do you use?"

"Der Weiser Bank," Rottermich replied.

"The one next to the sheriff 's office?"

"Ja, ja."

Abraham Weiser owned the bank. Emerson had met him and his wife at supper at Rosie's. Weiser, Emerson learned, had built his bank next to the sheriff 's office thinking it would afford extra safety. What the sheriff couldn't provide, though, was protection against two dozen Kansas Red Legs chasing one dozen of Quantrill's guerillas into town. Unable to catch the guerillas, the Red Legs robbed the bank and went back home. Another time, twenty guerillas chased six Union soldiers into town. The soldiers forted up in the sheriff 's office, and the guerillas, unable to breech the solid structure, robbed Weiser's bank instead and left town. Maybe if the war ever ended, things would settle down, but for the present, Emerson decided he'd open an account with Weiser but keep most of his funds in Boatman's Bank.

"One more thing, Mr. Rottermich. If you stay here in my guest bedroom upstairs, I will charge rent of one dollar a day."

"Ach! You *geschaftmanns*, bizzniss mensch. You pinch pennies till dey sqveel like pigcks!" Johannes Rottermich smiled.

And his face didn't shatter like a dropped plate!

Dear Mrs. Rose of Sharon O'Hanrahan,

I dash off this quick note to explain my absence from the midmorning meal with Miss Nora Ross. I decided to stay in Independence and was occupied with purchasing Mr. Rottermich's gunsmith business. I also purchased a temporary engagement ring from Guberlow's General Store. Mrs. Guberlow informed me she could measure Nora's finger and that proper engagement and wedding rings could be ordered from Saint Louis. It is my intention to arrive at your establishment at 2:15 and take Miss Nora on a picnic for the purpose of asking her to marry me and presenting her with the temporary engagement ring.

I request, madam, that you have your staff prepare a picnic lunch for us, for which, of course, I will pay.

The judge at the courthouse can marry us tomorrow. I hope you will not be distressed over losing a valuable assistant but will be happy for us.

Sincerely yours,

Emerson Sharp

The early-summer sun shone bright, and the pleasant weight of it on his shoulders under his black coat was like a woman's hand resting there while dancing. As Roan walked the rented buggy down College Street in a flow of wagons and buggies wending through men and women pedestrians crossing and children and dogs playing in the thoroughfare, Emerson had the sensation that he was not driving a few short blocks to Rosie's Fine Dining. Rather he was driving to pick up Nora, and together they would ride to the ends of the earth. Time and distance seemed to melt together and become the same thing. The end of the earth. Forever. And Nora beside him on the seat, and he so very aware of the cloth covering her legs and the cloth covering his and the inches separating the flesh of her legs from touching the flesh of his.

Nora.

He had never felt so sure, so in command of his future, his destiny. In Indiana, Paw decided how he spent daylight minutes. Then Weekes Daley had decided their destinations. Recently, he followed where Josh Ewing led. Now, he, Emerson Sharp decided.

He'd bought Rottermich's business. He'd buy others. He recalled how Weekes had talked about Dutzow's Corner, how Mr. Dutzow made a fortune by recognizing opportunities and taking action before anyone else seized upon them. He, Emerson Sharp, would become a Mr. Dutzow, but he'd be the Mr. Dutzow of Independence.

And Nora would be Mrs. Emerson Sharp. He'd build her a grand house, and she'd hostess balls and dinners, and the snooty ladies of Independence would grovel for invitations to her soirees.

As Emerson stopped the buggy next to Rosie's backyard, birds twittered happy songs from perches in the maple shading the picnic tables. The honeysuckle perfumed the air he breathed.

But no one was at the tables. It was a beautiful day. Why weren't the staff eating outside?

Emerson stepped down and looped the reins around a picket fence post. Rosie burst out the rear door of her restaurant, stomped down the steps, clutched up her skirts, and hustled to where Emerson stood beside the buggy. He wondered what had gotten Rosie so all-fired angry.

Rosie flounced up to the fence and stopped. For a moment, Emerson thought she'd plow right through it.

"Men!" Rose hissed like a dog-cornered cat. "Hand me the buggy whip."

"What?"

"Hand me the buggy whip. Now!"

Emerson looked around at the whip standing tall in its holder.

"Why do want the whip?"

"To beat you with, you … stupid man."

Rose pulled a crumpled piece of paper from the pocket of her apron and held it across the fence to him.

"I thought you were an intelligent and cultured gentleman." Rosie looked down at the crumpled paper in her hand and seemed to deflate. She looked up at him, and he read a weariness, disappointment on her face. Then her anger flared again. She brandished the paper again. "Your letter. It is a mistake for a woman to think she has seen every way a man can mistreat a woman. I, of all women, should know that."

"What did I do to you?"

"Not to me, idiot. Nora!"

"Nora? What's wrong with wanting to marry her?"

"It's the way you put it in this … this letter."

"Rose, I know what her father did to her. I want to marry her anyway."

"'Anyway'! You want to marry her *anyway*!"

After first saying she wished she'd brought the shotgun with her, Rose lowered her voice. "If you are marrying her *anyway*, just ride away from Independence and never come back." There was more remonstrance about the contents of his letter, and then she asked if he wanted to know the proper way to court Nora.

He did.

"Go inside now, and ask Nora to accompany you on a picnic tomorrow. If you intend to offer her a ring, it cannot be something to wear temporarily. Do you see that? Men! Of course you don't see it. Take my word, then. Nora is Catholic. Nora and me, we are Catholic all day, every day. Not just on Sunday. She will be married in our church. That will take some time to arrange. You will have to take instructions in the faith and be baptized."

Softness suffused Rose's countenance. She no longer wanted to whip or shoot him, he was fairly sure, though he'd begun to doubt his ability to discern people's intentions. She walked beside him inside and hovered near as he asked Nora to accompany him for a buggy ride the next day. Then Rose took Emerson's arm and steered him back to the buggy.

"Um, Miss Rose, are you going with us on the picnic tomorrow?"

"Don't be silly. Of course not. But I will be waiting right here by the fence when you bring her back at three thirty. With the shotgun, I'll be waiting. You didn't set a time to pick her up. Be here at ten thirty."

Rose went back inside. Emerson returned to the livery stable and rented the rig for another day. He threw Roan's saddle and gear into the buggy and headed down Main Street toward his new business and his new home. He said to Roan, "I didn't know if you'd pull a buggy or not, but you did fine. I'm glad you were with me. Maybe you can tell me what the hell just happened."

25

"I THOUGHT ROSE would be pleased that I bought a business and was fixing to stay in Independence," Emerson told Roan's haunches. "I thought she'd be pleased that I'd found out about Nora's paw and wanted to marry her anyway. But no. 'Anyway' made her mad. I thought buying a temporary ring was a brilliant idea. But that made her mad too."

Halfway down Main Street, it hit Emerson how much he missed Weekes Daley. Weekes was the one man he could have talked to about Nora and Rose of Sharon O'Hanrahan. Why couldn't those women see he had dramatically changed his life? For Nora. Why couldn't they appreciate his noble commitment to Nora despite what had happened to her? Everything had seemed so certain, so clear driving up to Rosie's Fine Dining. Now, a handful of minutes later, nothing was certain and nothing was clear. He floated above the earth, suspended in a liquid confusion that wouldn't let him drown, wouldn't let him touch his toes to the bottom, and sure as hell wouldn't let him surface. Weekes would have explained it.

Traffic, of a sudden, packed Main Street. Or maybe he just now noticed the wagons, buggies, and riders going in both directions and filling the roadway from hitching rail to hitching rail and stirring up a haze of dust that hung in the air. Emerson pulled a kerchief from his pocket and held it over his nose.

As he approached the Last Chance Saloon on his right, the press of wagons and horses thinned enough for him to haul Roan into a sharp left turn. He intended to put Roan and the buggy in his barn, but his stomach grumbled. He'd had no breakfast, no dinner, and it was getting on to late afternoon. He whoaed Roan on Station Street next to the gunsmith shop—his gunsmith shop—and hopped down. Running north five blocks from Main, Station Street led to the train station. Across the street stood the new four-story Royal Arms Hotel. The hotel had a restaurant reputed to be actual fine dining, not fine dining relative to saloon fare.

Emerson took his coat off and shook the dust from it. Tapping the crown of his hat against his thigh knocked it to mostly clean. Then he crossed the street and mounted the three steps up to the wide porch fronting the Royal Arms.

"Emerson!"

Josh Ewing grinned up at him from beside his big black at the hitching rail. "Emerson Sharp," he said and bounded up the front steps and grabbed Emerson by the arms. "Didn't expect to see you here."

And clearly, Josh was glad to see him. Based on the way they'd parted company, Emerson was surprised, but the grin was real. And it was infectious.

"Good to see you too, Josh. I was about to get something to eat. Hungry?"

"What's hungry got to do with eatin'?" Josh's grin dropped off his face. "Shit. I'm meetin' someone. But maybe he's not here yet. Let's go in and see."

Emerson stepped toward the hotel door. He waited for a man and a woman to enter first.

Suddenly, Josh shoved Emerson, and he fell onto his hands and knees. A rifle banged. Pistols popped. The woman screamed and fell. Her head bounced off the porch floor. Boot heels thundered. Hooves pounded the street. Emerson tried to push himself upright, but something fell on his back. He went down again. Josh rolled off his back. He lay on the porch, his teeth gritted. He fired his pistol at four clumped-together riders in the middle of the street. They all shot back. Bullets smacked into the hotel front.

Emerson jumped up, pulled his Remington, and moved away from Josh. Now the shooters had two targets spread apart. He aimed and pulled the trigger.

A pack of riders and wagons fled north along Station Street.

Another gaggle raced east down Main.

Emerson's eyes were drawn to the biggest shooter. He was shoving a pistol into a saddle holster and drawing another. Emerson fired at him. Josh's pistol popped too. Emerson was sure he'd hit the big man with no hat. No Hat, though, fired again, aiming at Josh lying on the porch.

Emerson squeezed off three more rounds, and No Hat tumbled backward over his horse's rump. The other three riders' pistols were still barking smoke and lead. Bullets smacked into the post next to Emerson. He wished he'd loaded all six cylinders of the Remington. It was modified to be carried safely that way, but he'd felt better loading it with an empty beneath the hammer.

He cracked open the pistol, dropped the expended cylinder, pulled a full one from his pocket, slipped it onto the holding rod, closed the pistol, cocked it, aimed at the one in the center of the three riders, and fired. The man's arms flew up, and he fell out of the saddle. Emerson was aiming at another man when Josh's pistol banged and Emerson's target fell. He shifted aim to the remaining target. His pistol and Josh's *pop-pop*-ed.

The man's horse went down. He rolled clear of his mount, dropping his pistol. Three men rushed out of the Last Chance Saloon and grabbed the fallen shooter and hauled him to his feet. The three all had things to say: "Goddamned woman- shooter," "Get a rope," and "Hanging's too good for this son of a bitch."

Emerson looked for more shooters, but there were none in the street. With the danger apparently over, a crowd, all shouting at once, congregated in the street.

The woman, with her hat still on, lay facedown near the door into the hotel. Blood streaked across the back of her white blouse and puddled on the boards next to her right arm.

Josh moaned.

His pistol lay in front of him, and he had both hands clutching his leg just below the knee. There was a lot more blood from Josh's leg than from the woman. Emerson pulled his bandanna and tied it around Josh's leg just above the knee, picked up Josh's pistol, stuck the barrel through the bandanna, and turned it twice, tightening the tourniquet.

"Hold the pistol," Emerson said.

"Leg's busted bad," Josh said through clenched teeth. "Let it bleed."

"No! Hold the goddamned pistol."

Emerson grabbed Josh by the wrist and guided the hand to the butt of the gun. "Now hold it."

By the way the leg lolled, Emerson could see that the bones in the lower leg had been shattered. "Hold that gun," he snapped. "I'm going to stand you up on your good leg, sling you across my back, and carry you to my buggy." Emerson got behind Josh and put his hands under his arms. "Now don't go faintin' like a girl."

"Go to—"

Emerson hauled his friend to his foot. Josh sucked in a lungful of air. Emerson pulled Josh's right arm across his shoulder, lifted his feet off the boards, and carried him down the steps and across the street to his buggy. There, Emerson hoisted him onto the floor in front of the rear seat. Emerson took the front seat and clucked Roan into motion.

If Josh hadn't pushed him aside, Emerson could be the one with the shattered leg. Or dead. Like the woman.

"Josh—"

"Where you takin' us?"

"Doctor. Josh—"

"Don't you act like no girl, neither."

"Shit," Emerson said.

He turned left, picking up the street paralleling Main.

"Who were those guys?" Emerson asked.

"Big guy was Rufe Davis."

That was a name Emerson remembered. Josh talked about him as they were leaving Saint Joseph. "From your paw's pack of Red Legs, right?"

The buggy rattled over a bump and Josh moaned, and then he said, "Yeah."

At Lexington, Emerson turned north. As he crossed Main, he looked left. Wagons and riders moved at brisk paces in the street and the boardwalks were crowded. Ten minutes ago, a ten-minute walk away, dozens of bullets had been fired. People had been killed. A woman had been shot. But here, on the other end of town, life moved on, oblivious, apparently, to the violence a half mile and a few minutes away.

"How you doing, Josh?"

"Shit," he said.

Emerson turned right on Liberty Street, whoaed Roan in front of Dr. Hofstedler's sign, leaped down, ran to the door and banged on it twice, and ripped it open.

To the left in the room, two women sat at opposite ends of a divan. One of them was young and pregnant. To the right, an old man sat on a wooden kitchen-table chair, leaning on a cane. Mrs. Hofstedler sat behind a small narrow table. "Yes?" she asked.

She'd been busted in on before, Emerson thought.

"Got a man been shot in the leg. He's bleeding bad."

"Bring him in," Mrs. Hofstedler said, and she stood and opened the door behind her.

Emerson returned to the buggy, arranged Josh over his shoulder so Josh could help with his good leg, and brought him into the house and into the room indicated by Mrs. Hofstedler.

"On that table," the doctor said, pointing.

As Emerson was getting Josh on the table, Dr. Hofstedler lifted the wounded leg, and blood poured out of the boot onto the table and floor.

"Sorry, Doc," Emerson said, "about the blood."

Hofstedler was a skinny six footer. Thick white mustache, bald on top, a horseshoe of white fuzzy hair appeared to be held on to his head by being anchored to his big ears. His wife called, "Essie," as she placed a folded blanket under Josh's head.

"Scissors," Doc said, and his wife handed him a pair.

The doc cut along the outer seam of Josh's pants past the knee and folded the material back. The bullet had hit Josh just above the top of his boot. Slivers of white bone stuck out of the mangled flesh.

"Buffalo gun." Doc shook his head. "Nothing for it. Gotta come off."

A Negro woman entered the room from the rear, carrying a wooden bucket and a mop. "Good," she said. "It's jes blood." She set to mopping the puddle.

Josh's face was the color of ashes with the scar across his cheek pink. His teeth were gritted. He breathed in short, sharp, fast pants. He turned his face to the window. Curtains were sashed back. Out on the street, a wagon rattled by.

"Mr. Sharp, isn't it?" Doc asked.

Emerson nodded.

"I need you to hold that pistol to keep the tourniquet tight," Doc said. "I need to know I can count on you. I've seen some mighty tough men couldn't handle being next to a bone saw doing its business."

"He'll do, Doc." Josh panted. "He ain't … no girl."

"What's your friend's name?" Doc asked Emerson, and he told him.

"Josh, I'd rather have a girl for this kind of job. Comes to cuttin' and sawin', they're tougher than most men. But you best not talk anymore. Lie quiet. You're goin' to need all the strength you got left."

Hofstedler went to a sink beneath the window. His wife brought a kettle with hot water.

Emerson took Josh's wrist to pull his hand off the pistol butt, but Josh wouldn't let it go.

"Emerson," Josh whispered, "you gotta … do somethin'. Hotel. Lieutenant. Miller. Tell him. Excelsior Springs. Sunup. Tomorra'. Say it."

"Miller. You were meeting him at the hotel?"

"Excelsior Springs. Sunup," Josh gasped. "Tell him."

"Tell Lieutenant Miller, Excelsior Springs, sunup, tomorrow?"

His face was gray. He looked beat, but a weak grin tweaked at the corners of his lips. For a moment. Then his face went slack and his eyes closed. Emerson thought he died.

Josh opened his eyes. "Go! Now!" He gripped Emerson's arm. "Now."

"No more talking," Doc said. "Let your friend hold the pistol."

Josh shook his head.

"For the love of—Essie," Doc said. "Come here, please. Hold that pistol."

Essie set the bucket down and moved Emerson away from Josh's side. "Let go a dat gun now, mistuh, or you be gittin' a broke arm to go wid your broke leg."

"I'll be back as soon as I tell him," Emerson told Josh.

Emerson hurried through Hofstedler's front room and pulled open the outside door and ran into Nora as she was reaching for the knob. She stepped back. Across her face, surprise, anger, relief, and joy flashed as if she was trying on masks and in a frightful hurry. Then concern took up residence.

"Are you … have you been shot? Your shirt is bloody."

"No. Not me. My friend Josh. He was shot. I brought him here."

"Oh, Emerson." Nora threw her arms around him and pressed herself to him. Then she kissed him hard on the lips.

She stepped back, her eyes holding on to his. "A man came into Rosie's. He said there was a shooting at the hotel. Men were shot. He said one of them was you."

The look on her face, he'd gladly get shot at again to see that.

He tore his eyes away from hers and looked at the buggy. He couldn't think while those eyes pulled him into the depths … the depths of her.

He couldn't think of what to say. He looked back at her. "Nora, I got blood all over your apron."

Her eyes began pulling him in again.

"Doesn't matter. It's not your blood."

She was right. That mattered and not a single solitary other thing in the whole wide world did.

Josh's message. Josh had pushed him out of the way and got his leg shot off in saving him. Delivering the message, that mattered too. It would take fifteen minutes.

"Nora." He touched her cheek. "I'll be back in a couple of minutes."

26

AWAY FROM HER, his brain functioned. He knew what he had to do: return to the Little Saloon, change his shirt and wash the blood off, and gather his gear. Which he did.

Then he'd return to the hotel to give Miller Josh's message. Then he'd return to Nora and give her his message. He would ask her to marry him. Immediately. Well, tomorrow, actually. The judge had said tomorrow.

He drove Roan down Liberty Street. He could get to the hotel and return from it quicker if he avoided the stream of wagons on Main Street. Then it occurred there might be a commotion back at the hotel from the shooting. The sheriff would want to talk to him.

New plan.

Emerson turned left on Lexington Street. He'd return to the hotel by the same route he'd taken to Doc Hofstedler's. The hotel had a stable behind it and a rear door for stable access.

He stopped Roan behind the gunsmith shop. A pack of men clotted together in the street in front of the hotel. Emerson heard Rottermich explain, "I tell you, Sheriff. I not see nuttin'. I hear duh shootin'. I tink dey come steal guns and powder from me. I get my shotgun. I not look outside. I vait for dem to come inside."

Emerson hurried across the street and entered the rear door. He was in a corridor, a long, dark cave, leading to the front of the hotel and a large, brightly lit reception area. He clumped down the hallway. No one was behind the desk, but a man in shirtsleeves stood by the front door, watching the street.

Through the door, Emerson heard the sheriff dismiss Mr. Rottermich.

"Excuse me, sir," Emerson said to the man by the door.

The man turned and asked if he wanted a room.

"No. I'm looking for a Mr. Miller. I was told he was here."

"He just registered. He's in the bar. Would you like something to drink? I'm also the bartender."

A whiskey would be good. Two of them. And a fancy hotel like the Royal Arms would have good liquor. But then he remembered Nora's kiss. She might kiss him again, and he did not want her to kiss a whiskey mouth. Rosie didn't tolerate booze. Nora might be the same way. "No," he said. "Thanks. I just have to deliver a message."

The clerk turned back to the street, and Emerson stepped into the dimly lit bar. Not a large place. A few tables with six chairs each. The only table occupied was to his right, in a corner, with three men around it, and all of them seated so they could watch the room. The one in middle was Miller.

"Ah. Mr. Sharp," Miller said. "The sheriff was just in here asking if we were in front of the hotel when a fellow named Emerson Sharp and a woman got shot. Guess he was mistaken."

"Not about the woman, he wasn't," Emerson said. "But it was Josh Ewing took a bullet."

"Josh! Damn," Miller said. "Is he dead?"

"No. I took him to a doctor." Emerson walked up to the table. "Josh gave me a message for you."

"Sit down," Miller said.

"I'll just give you the message. Josh said—"

A pistol hammer cocked. The one to Miller's right had his hands under the table. "Sit, the lieutenant said." The man was skinny with a thin, scraggly black beard and dead black eyes. No question, he'd shoot as quickly as he'd swat a fly.

Emerson looked at the lieutenant. "Sheriff's right outside. You want Josh's message?"

"Doyel. Back down," Miller said, pronouncing it *Doy-El*. "People are skittish after the shooting. They strung up that Kansas Jayhawker. You shoot this man, and we'll have to run for it. We need to hear what Josh wanted to tell us." Then he turned to Emerson. "Please have a seat, Mr. Sharp."

Emerson placed his hands on the back of the chair. "Josh said, 'Excelsior Springs. Sunup. Tomorrow.'"

"Bullshit!" the skinny guy, Doyel, snarled. "That's the other side of the river."

"Mr. Sharp, I need you to sit down. Now." Miller's voice had that edge to it that made a man want to respond, "Yes, sir."

"Look, Lieutenant," Emerson said. "I told you what Josh said. That's all I know. I have a business to tend to. I need to get back to it."

Miller cocked his pistol below the table.

Emerson said, "Shit," and scooted the chair back and sat.

"Josh told us you weren't going to ride with us anymore," Miller said.

"That's right. I've had enough of bushwhacking."

"Why the hell we talkin' to him, Lieutenant?" Doyel asked. "He's workin' for the federals, tryin' to throw us off."

Miller didn't take his eyes off Emerson. "Shut up, Doyel," he said. Then he wanted to know about the shooting, about Josh's condition. Emerson rolled the story out, including the part about how important it had seemed to Josh to get his message delivered to Miller.

"It's all bullshit," Doyel snapped.

Miller ignored him and turned to the other man. "Elmer, you said the stagecoach was coming through Sedalia day after tomorrow."

Elmer was a puffy-cheeked, slope-shouldered, little person in a big body. Taller and heftier than Miller, his nervous eyes danced across the table.

"Info I got from them soldiers always been good before," Elmer said in a voice that squeaked like a boy breaking out in puberty.

Miller looked at Emerson. "You're probably wondering why we'd trust a man like Elmer."

Emerson was wondering just that.

"Nobody ever suspects Elmer is of any consequence. They talk in front of him like he's a piece of furniture."

"Lieutenant," Emerson said, "I gave you Josh's message. That's all there is."

"He's a damned federal," Doyel said. "You can't let him go."

Miller stared at Emerson. Emerson saw the decision gel.

"I'll git his gun." Doyel stood.

Emerson reached for his shoulder holster weapon.

"Stop!" Miller snapped. "Elmer, you check him for guns."

Elmer pulled the pistol from Emerson's shoulder holster. "It's one a them new Remingtons, Lieutenant. Comes with the extry cylinders."

Elmer, Emerson thought, was not as dumb as he looked and acted.

"Where's your horse, Mr. Sharp?" Miller asked.

"Shit," Emerson said.

*****

Miller led them—Doyel, Elmer, and Emerson—at a good pace east out of Independence. The ferry the lieutenant wanted to use to cross the Missouri stopped at sundown.

When they debarked on the northern bank, Miller, with the horses at a walk and dusk descending and dumping blackness in the trees alongside the dirt road, told Emerson to ride beside him.

"You don't want to be a bushwhacker, Mr. Sharp, and neither do we." He explained that Captain Quantrill had gone back to Richmond to ask for money to finance regular military operations. He was told to take the money from the Yankees. Which, Miller said, hurt the enemy twice. The captain's spies discovered a Union plan to sneak a payroll for the soldiers at Fort Leavenworth through western Missouri in mail sacks on a stage. "With that payroll, Captain Quantrill will be able to equip five hundred men. You're an intelligent man, Mr. Sharp. Can you not see how important this is? If we can get our hands on that money, we will be soldiers in Captain Quantrill's army rather than bushwhackers."

Miller obviously believed capturing the payroll was important.

Josh did too. But Emerson had cut his ties with Josh, who'd been more important to him than the guerillas and their cause.

"See, Lieutenant," Doyel said, "he's got nothin' to say. He's a federal. Let me shoot him. And why the hell did you listen to him? We ought to make the rendezvous with the captain. There's still time."

"Shut up, Doyel."

"Let me have my guns, Lieutenant. We might run into guerilla hunters, or more Jayhawkers, or, hell, any kind of night rider."

"You ain't gonna give him his guns are you, Lieutenant?"

Miller didn't answer. He kicked his horse into a canter. Doyel stayed close to Emerson, a half horse length behind. Elmer played caboose.

The odds of getting out of the fix he was in were low and sinking lower. He still had his Bowie. Doyel stuck close enough to dispatch him with the knife, but Elmer was behind him.

What if Josh was wrong about the stage? Would Miller let him go?

What if Josh was right and they held up the stage? Would Miller let him go?

Nora. What did she think when he didn't come back as he had promised?

*****

Miller led them around small towns. They rode in pairs through larger ones. For the last two hours, they'd ridden north through forest and along farmers' fields. They came out of trees and onto an east-west road. The half-moon was pretty near to directly overhead. It cast just enough light for Emerson to read his watch—2:00 a.m.

"Middle a goddamned nowhere," Doyel growled.

"We're an hour east of Excelsior Springs," Miller said.

"Stage isn't comin' thisaway," from Doyel.

Miller untied the roll from the rear of his saddle, walked ten yards into the woods, tied the reins of his horse to a sapling, and flapped the ground cloth out. Emerson and the other two followed.

"Damn it," Doyel said, "we don't know the stage is coming this way. If the stage does come, we don't know if it's the right one. If it is the right one, we don't know if it has a cavalry escort. Sometimes they escort the stages. Three of us ain't enough, 'specially saddled with a Union spy."

"Doyel," Miller said. "You have the first watch. Wake Elmer in an hour. Take my timepiece."

Emerson tied Roan to a tree and stripped the saddle off and rubbed his back with the saddle blanket. As he worked, he whispered, "I don't know about you, Roan, but I miss being in town in one part of me. In another, it's kind of good to be out here on the trail again." But it was not good being on another bushwhack. Roan didn't need to fret over that, though.

Under the trees, men and horses were black ghost shapes. One of the shapes crunched over dried leaves to Emerson. "What the hell you doin' talkin' to your damn horse?" *Doyel.*

"Right now, Doyel, your value as a soldier"—Miller's voice was low and even but still conveyed threat—"has been overwhelmed by the aggravation you cause. Man your post. Now. At the edge of the road. Shut your mouth and listen. And if the stage comes, we will take it. Whether there's cavalry escort or not."

Doyel stomped away.

"Wish you were with us, Mr. Sharp." Miller had spoken as if he didn't care if Doyel and Elmer heard him.

"Lieutenant, I am not against you. But your cause ... well, it's your cause."

Miller took Emerson's hand and placed a pistol in it. The Remington. He stuck it in his shoulder holster. Next came the Colt pocket gun, which he put in the holster on his hip.

"I'm going to let one of my eyes sleep now." Miller's feet whispered over the leafy forest floor.

Emerson resaddled Roan. Then he found a spot where moonlight beamed through a break in the foliage and checked his pocket gun and reloaded the empty cylinders in the Remington. He hadn't had time to do that. Didn't take much city living, Emerson reflected, for a man's sense of priorities to get skewed.

Then he got his ground cloth and rolled up in it. He pictured Nora's expressive face abloom with concern and affection for him. *I will see you tonight*. With his guns, the odds of that happening had improved considerably. Then both his eyes slept.

Emerson woke. Doyel was rousting Elmer to take the watch. Then Doyel rustled himself into position on the ground, and in a couple of heartbeats, his breathing indicated he was sinking deeper and deeper. Emerson lifted up onto an elbow and listened to the bugs and beasts going about their business. The smell of horse droppings wafted to him on a whisper of breeze. In a shaft of moonlight, he saw Lieutenant Miller leaning against a tree. He had a pistol on his lap.

Emerson woke the next time when the lieutenant asked, "You asleep, Elmer? It's got to be past four. Why didn't you wake me?"

"Just figured to give you a few extry minutes."

"Get some sleep," Miller said.

Elmer walked back into the trees. Miller rolled up his ground cloth, and Emerson did too. After tying his roll behind his saddle, the lieutenant made his way onto the roadbed. He sat cross-legged on the hard-packed dirt. Emerson leaned against a tree at the edge of the woods. Neither of them said a word.

Minutes passed, and then they dragged.

Emerson nodded forward a couple of times, and he jerked back to wakefulness.

"They're coming," Miller said, and Emerson jumped to his feet, but then he stood still. The night noises had gone silent.

Miller roused the other two men.

"Doyel, you and Emerson get in the trees on the other side of the road. Elmer, you move twenty yards east on this side."

The sound of thundering hooves came to them.

"Sounds like a lot of goddamned cavalry," Doyel groused.

"This is how we're going to do this," Miller said. "Sounds like there is an escort. Might be in front. Might be behind. Maybe some of both. Either way, the important thing is to stop the stage, so nobody shoot until I do. I will stop the stage. As soon as I fire, you guys take down the soldiers. Nobody. Shoot. Until. I shoot first. Now get in position."

"Why you puttin' me over there with him?" Doyel asked.

"Because I need you there," Miller replied.

As they worked into the saplings, Doyel hissed, "I ain't lettin' you behind me."

Emerson took Miller's approach to handling Doyel and ignored what he said, but he wasn't about to let a man he'd pegged as a back-shooter in his rear, either. But Doyel wasn't the only problem he had.

The trees were just saplings, and the slope rose slightly. No cover. And the thundering hooves were nearing.

Emerson pulled Roan up the slope and ten feet into the trees. He pulled the reins down, and the horse settled first on its knees and then rolled onto its side with the legs toward the road. He pulled his pistol and lay across Roan's neck. "Stay still now," Emerson whispered.

Sounding like a herd of horses, hooves pounded the packed dirt, trace chains rattled, a whip snapped.

Emerson could see the stage, still a way out yet. Figures of a driver and shotgun rider stuck up above the blocky shadow of the coach. He made out two riders behind the stage. There were more. Two couldn't make so much noise.

A pistol popped. From where Elmer was posted.

"What the hell, Elmer?" Doyel mumbled.

The shotgun from the stage boomed.

The driver stood up in the box and started popping the whip. "Git up, you fleabags. Run, you sons a bitches."

Then the stage was blowing past. Three teams. The driver popping his whip. The shotgun rider throwing rocks at the horses. Six cavalrymen came into view.

A rifle banged. Miller. A horse squealed. The front of the coach shot up in the air. Two bodies flew up from the driver's box. A woman screamed. From inside the coach. The soldiers whoaed their mounts.

Doyel stepped toward the road and fired, cocked and fired, and cocked and fired again. A horse went down. The other horses wheeled and milled about in the middle of the road. One rider started his horse out of the melee toward Doyel. Doyel fired again and missed and turned to run. His arms flew up, and he went down face-first. Emerson shot the soldier as he hauled his mount to a stop some fifteen feet away.

Lieutenant Miller was firing. In the melee, a rider tumbled out of the saddle. The remaining three riders bolted east. A horse without a rider chased them.

"Doyel! Elmer!" Miller hollered.

"Doyel's dead, Lieutenant. Elmer, I figure he fired a warning shot and lit out."

Emerson checked on the bodies strewn in the road. He shot a wounded horse. Two soldiers were dead. The other one was a kid, and he looked up at Emerson with big eyes. Emerson knelt beside him and whispered, "You want to live, kid, you best be real good at playing real dead."

Then Emerson hollered to Miller, "Three dead soldiers and a dead horse!"

Miller's pistol popped twice.

Up by Miller, the stage was lying on its side. Emerson wondered who Miller had shot, horses or the driver and shotgun rider.

"Check where Elmer was!" Miller hollered.

An urgent need to flee the place mounted in Emerson. *Get on Roan and ride like hell away from here.* That's what he wanted to do. That's what he would do. First, he'd check on Elmer even though he knew what he'd find.

Roan was on his feet, waiting near Doyel's horse. Emerson mounted and trotted to where the other man had been. He searched ten yards up and down the road from Elmer's last spot. He found a pile of horse droppings, but no Elmer. Emerson swung up on Roan and rode back to the coach.

Miller was pulling mail sacks out of the canvas boot and slashing their tops open. Spilled letters covered the ground around his feet.

"We killed these men, and there's no money?" Emerson asked.

Miller said, "Get my horse."

Directly in front of the coach, three dead horses lay bunched. *A woman screamed.* Emerson recalled hearing it as the coach reared up. He hopped down, ran to the coach, struck a match, and peered inside.

"Shit," he said.

He saw a woman's legs in bloomers. When the coach reared up, the door must have flown open, the woman was thrown out, and the stage crashed down on her. Then he saw the crumpled body of a girl in the forward corner of the passenger compartment. Her neck was at a funny angle. Her eyes were open. Staring.

Emerson flicked the match out and dropped it. He shivered. The sun glowed out the stars in the eastern sky. Emerson was vaguely aware of the extra cold that the night dumped on earth just before giving way to day. Inside he felt a huge emptiness.

"We killed a woman and a girl. Oh, Jesus!"

"I FOUND IT!" Miller jumped up. "I found the money."

"We killed a woman and a girl!"

"Shut up, Sharp."

"We killed—"

Miller spun on his heel. He ran across the road swinging a mailbag by the handle in each hand. Moments later, astride, he burst out of the trees and entered the woods on the other side. Heading north.

Emerson heard it then. Hooves thundering toward him. From the west. More cavalry. Had to be. They'd never believe he'd been forced to ride with the guerillas. Not a chance in hell.

He swung up onto Roan. He looked to the east. Three soldiers had fled that way.

South. Nora was in that direction. He did not want to drag what would be chasing him to her.

Emerson entered the woods the way Miller had gone, snatched up the reins to Doyel's horse, and said, "Roan." The animal charged after the lieutenant.

At first, there was no game trail. Branches and twigs tore at his legs, knocked his hat off to hang on the string, and threatened his eyes. Roan moved fast through the brush—too fast. Emerson slowed him. Catching up to Miller wasn't important. Getting away was, but he couldn't do that if Roan stepped in a hole and broke a leg.

Roan plowed through the brush. Doyel's horse trailed with slack in the reins.

"Roan," Emerson whispered, "it wasn't me that killed the woman and the girl. It was Miller."

Dawn filtered fog-like gloom through the leafy canopy.

They came to a game trail, and Roan turned west on it. Emerson reined him around to the north and into brush again.

"Shit, Roan," he mumbled. "The last thing I said didn't even convince me, so I'm sure you didn't buy it."

Emerson stopped to listen for signs of pursuit. He heard nothing. He clucked, and Roan plodded on.

"Roan, maybe you don't want a woman- and a girl-killer on your back. I could ride Doyel's horse. He won't mind. He probably saw that back-shooting son of a bitch do all manner of—

"Shit. Even Doyel never killed a woman … or a girl. Roan, if you can abide it, I'd like to ride you."

Emerson reined to a stop. The rattle of a wagon came from ahead and a bit to his left. He dismounted and led the horses forward slowly. Then he saw another horse, standing, and a man beside it. The man stared intently at the road the wagon had used. Why hadn't he turned? He had to have heard the racket the two animals made crunching leaves and twigs. Emerson dropped the reins, drew his pistol, and eased forward.

Miller. It was his chestnut.

Without turning around, Miller said, "You going to shoot me, Mr. Sharp? Or shall we ride together?"

Rage boiled up in Emerson.

Miller had shanghaied him into going with his pack. Emerson had been sure they were going to kill him. Especially Doyel wanted to. But the lieutenant gave him his guns. Odds of survival bumped up a notch. Wearing his guns again, everything felt better. He thought he might be back in Independence by late afternoon. Now, after what Miller dragged him into, he wondered if he'd ever see Nora again.

Emerson cocked the pistol.

Miller turned around. "Wouldn't want you to have to be a back-shooter."

"You already made me a woman-killer."

"There shouldn't have been anyone in that coach. We were told it would only be carrying mail and the payroll." Miller's eyes stayed on Emerson's. "Plenty of women have been killed in this war. Last year, the federals herded more than a dozen women from the exclusion zone into a rickety building in Kansas City. It collapsed and killed them all. Red Legs raid farms, steal, shoot the men, rape and kill the women. Or worse, let them live."

"So the woman and the girl in the coach, that was just an accident. Nothing to get worked up over?"

"I am not saying that. War is an ugly business. You hear about honor and glory. I haven't seen any glory and not much honor. Captain Quantrill and your friend Josh were both in Kansas. They saw John Brown and his followers spread murder and mayhem in the name of God Almighty. They both came to Missouri and both felt called to protect the people here from Red Legs and Jayhawkers. Their sense of honor required it of them. I feel the same way."

Listening to Miller had banked the fire of his anger. He hadn't wanted that to happen.

"Either shoot me or let me get on with figuring out what to do."

Once, back in Indiana, just before they harvested oats, a hailstorm ruined the crop. Paw said, "Gettin' mad at God is the biggest waste a time they is. Now get to work and we'll save what we can." Emerson took a deep breath, let it out, and holstered his Remington. Staying mad at Miller wasn't helping anything, either.

Across the road, there was nothing but cleared fields and fenced pastures and farmhouses and barns. Miller led them east and then south to skirt a small two-street town. On the far side of it, they encountered more forest to the north, and rising terrain. The lieutenant turned north again.

Around noon, ahead of him, Miller left dense forest and climbed the slope of a grassy knoll sparsely populated with man- tall saplings. A lone pine towered from the summit. A few yards short of the summit, so they wouldn't silhouette themselves, Miller dismounted and dropped his saddlebags next to the trunk of a blown-over tree. The roots rotted.

It wouldn't have taken much of a wind to topple it. Emerson pulled up beside him, alit, and dropped the reins, ground-hitching Roan and Doyel's mount.

Miller handed him a telescope. "See if anybody's following us."

Emerson hesitated a moment and then did as ordered. From the knoll, he could see above the forest canopy. He found the patch of cleared fields they'd skirted an hour prior. Most of their back trail was in dense woods. He held the magnified circle over spots for a few seconds, looking for hints of motion, but he saw no sign of pursuit.

Miller was laying wood next to a couple of stones.

"A fire?" Emerson asked.

"It's dry wood. It won't smoke. Check our back trail again."

As the lieutenant sparked up a fire, Emerson raised the glass. Tree-covered hills undulated away to the south. Haze hovered above the green. He again scanned the path they'd taken, lingering over spots until he felt as if the spyglass were not pulling circles of distance closer. Rather, it felt as if the telescope had been trying to suck his eyeball out. Nothing moved. He lowered the glass. A hawk—or an eagle, maybe—coasted on spread wings, high against the sky. Wind whistled softly through the branches of the tall pine. Emerson smelled coffee.

The fallen tree shielded Miller's small fire from the breeze. A pot sat on stones at the edge of the flames. Miller handed him a piece of jerky and a biscuit. Emerson's mouth watered. It had been a while.

They chewed.

"You going back to Independence?"

"Yes, sir."

"Word of the stage, of the woman and girl, that will get back there before you do. You best think up a good story."

The same thought had been niggling at the back of his mind.

"You might not be able to go back. You're a good man. Be good to have you with us again." "No."

Miller's mouth twisted into a whisper of a smile. "If it was me, I'd ride east for a day, then south another day before going west. Enter the town after dark. You best have someone there you can trust."

Emerson looked away and wondered how the hell he could be so stupid. He'd been smarter about surviving when he was a kid running from the Barlows. He'd forgotten everything he'd learned from Weekes. He should have thought of all that himself. Instead of thinking, his head had been filled with anger and moaning over maybe losing what he had in Independence. Hell. He hadn't even seen that Elmer was more of a threat than Doyel.

"You got a cup?" Miller asked.

Emerson retrieved one from his saddlebags.

Miller poured for Emerson and then himself.

Miller held his cup under his nose. "Ah, the smell. The taste of coffee disappoints at times. The smell of it never does."

Emerson thought the lieutenant's coffee tasted fine too. He wouldn't let himself say so. He'd decided what to do. As soon as the horses were rested, if Miller continued north, he'd turn east. If Miller turned east, he'd continue north.

Miller placed his cup on the trunk of the blown-over tree, took the saddlebags from Doyel's horse and the mail bags from his own, and carried them back to the log. He dumped Doyel's belongings on the ground near the fire.

"You can have anything of his you want." Miller started filling the saddlebags with bills from the mail sacks.

Emerson thought about it and then knelt and poked through Doyel's belongings. A flat, tin powder can, lead balls, jerky wrapped in paper—he took those. He flicked two dirty socks aside with a stick. Wadded dirty shirt and trousers. The shirt was too small. The waist of the trousers would fit. They were a couple of inches too short, but they were of sturdy fabric. Brush had ripped holes in Emerson's black suit pants.

"Here." Miller handed up a stack of bills tied with a string.

Emerson stuck them in his coat pocket. He nodded at the lieutenant and then returned to studying the dirty pants. He grimaced.

Miller sat on the log. Emerson faced the opposite direction, pulled off his boots, stood, and removed his trousers.

Emerson caught a flicker of motion at the edge of the clearing. He pushed Miller to the side and dove to the ground, pulling his Remington and firing as he fell.

Miller howled and jumped up, brushing embers from his shirt. He staggered as an arrow struck his chest. Emerson fired into the brush again, and Miller's gun barked.

Emerson jumped up, grabbed the reins to Doyel's horse. He got the animal moving toward where he'd fired, using it as a shield. No one shot at him. He found an Indian, though, lying on his back. He wore a blue soldier coat open over his bare chest. The chest leaked blood from a hole on either side. The man's black eyes stared at Emerson. There was no hostility in the eyes. Nor curiosity or interest. Then the eyelids fluttered and went still.

Emerson stepped into the brush, checking for signs of another. He didn't see anything and hurried back to Miller.

Miller was on his side behind the log. "Cut the shaft," he said through clenched teeth.

He used Miller's knife. Emerson's Bowie was back where he'd dropped his pants. After circling the shaft with the blade, he snapped it off.

Pain ruled Miller's face. For a moment. "Mr. Sharp, I need a favor." He grimaced, pulling a watch from his pocket. After flicking the cover open, he showed it to Emerson. Inside the cover was a picture of a woman and a young girl. The girl was maybe nine. About like the girl in the stage, Emerson thought.

"Picture. My wife, Amelia Loraine. And Emily Louise. Joplin. Please take this and my ring to them. Please?"

Emerson tore his eyes away from the lieutenant. The army would not have sent the Indian after them by himself. He picked up the telescope. There they were. A long file of soldiers rode along the edge of the cleared fields. An hour away. No. Less.

"Soldiers coming. Twenty of them, I think. Maybe forty minutes away."

"Mr. Sharp."

Emerson knew what he was asking.

"I'll return your things to Mrs. Miller."

"Thank you." Miller took in a big breath and grimaced. "Water."

Emerson squashed the urge to flee and brought the lieutenant's canteen to him.

Miller sipped and sighed.

"Mr. Sharp."

Emerson looked off to the south.

"Another minute," Miller said. "Take some of the money. To my wife. The rest to Captain Quantrill."

Emerson shook his head.

"Do it for your friend Josh."

"Shit."

"Next week. The town. Of Kingdom Come. Quantrill will be there. For the horse races."

"Shit."

"One more thing, Mr. Sharp."

"No."

"Put some pants on."

"I could have figured that out myself." Emerson pulled Doyel's dirty pants on.

"One more thing."

Emerson glared at the man.

"Get my Dragoons. Then, skedaddle."

Emerson gave him the pistols, and then he stripped the saddle from Doyel's horse and plopped it onto the log. He loaded the bags of money onto Roan. Emerson tipped his hat to the lieutenant and mounted.

Miller said, "I'll get … their leader."

Emerson sat up straight and saluted.

Miller coughed, and a rivulet of bloody drool trickled down his chin. He returned the salute.

Emerson led Miller's chestnut and Doyel's white-stockinged black past the pine and picked up a northbound game trail descending the knoll. He followed the trail looking for a spot where he could turn east without leaving an obvious sign of having done so. Thirty minutes later, he came to a slab of white stone weathered clean of dirt. It would do.

He stripped the bridle from Doyel's horse and smacked it on the rump. It bolted down the game trail.

Due east was thick trees and brush. "Roan, long as the army doesn't have another Indian with them, we may get away."

Emerson held the reins to Miller's horse. As Roan picked the way through the woods, Emerson was thinking about Nora and Independence and Rottermich. And Josh.

Muffled considerably by distance, the popping of pistols and booms of rifles reached him. He stopped and listened to weapons bark at each other. Miller, he thought, was probably stubborn enough to live until he emptied all three of his pistols. The firing ceased, giving the land over to silence. For a moment. Then as if they realized all that shooting wasn't aimed at them, a flock of crows cawed. Sounding indignant as usual.

Emerson rode on. He thought about Lieutenant Miller and his dead woman and his living one, his dead girl and his living one.

"Roan, those two women and those two girls, they're mine now too."

28

A COUPLE OF hours later, the country changed from mostly uncivilized to mostly cleared and cultivated. Emerson found a place with water and graze and bedded down until dark. Then he pushed the animals hard all night, switching when he felt his mount tire.

Throughout the night, Nora and Lieutenant Miller's women and girls clawed at the door at the back of his mind. But he wouldn't allow the females in. He was moving east. Men might try to stop him. He might meet sons of bitches like Doyel, who'd shoot him just because Emerson was there and the bastard had a loaded gun.

Periodically, the realization he was wearing Doyel's pants, soaked with his sweat and stink, infested with his body vermin, scratched to get in too. He ignored that also, forcing his mind to remain occupied with watching and listening.

Clouds scattered across the sky blocked swathes of star dots and the half-moon some of the time. Near towns, in the evening, he encountered few riders and fewer wagons. Passing through the one-, two-, or three-street settlements, a few people walking along boardwalks glanced at him as he clopped past. In a few of the places, bursts of laughter from a saloon overrode a piano's we're-having-a-good-time-in-here tinkle.

By midnight, the settlements he passed through were dark. When the clouds permitted, the moonlight exposed farmhouses set back from the road. Those were dark too. Dogs barked at him, but he encountered no Doyels or anyone else until close to sunup. Then it was wagons. A stagecoach thundered and jangled past. The shotgun rider turned to watch him.

With the ball of orange, yellow, and red fire above the horizon, Emerson's head buzzed with fatigue. It was hard to keep his attention focused on watching. He rode Roan, and Roan's butt-bouncing had sapped the strength from his legs.

He'd come far enough, he thought. The next town, he would stop. The horses needed rest and mash. He needed something to eat too. And a bed to sleep in. And a bath. And new pants.

Alongside the road, a telegraph wire looped from pole to pole. Telegraphs were springing up everywhere. The road topped a rise, and ahead lay a two-street town. Emerson rode past houses, a sizeable general store, and Daisy's Boardinghouse and Dining Room, and he stopped at the livery stable. A sheet of paper was tacked to the latched open door.

EMERSON SHARP
WANTED FOR MURDER
DEAD OR ALIVE
$200 REWARD

His heart rate kicked up and pumped clarity into his head. He considered courses of action. The previous afternoon and that morning, he'd glassed his back trail from every spot with a decent view. He'd seen no sign of pursuit. He hadn't spotted the Indian back on that hill with Miller. Maybe the army had another. He considered the odds.

"What do you think, Roan?"

The horse bobbed his head.

"Oats it is."

Emerson stepped down, stretched his back from side to side. "I bet I'm an inch shorter after bouncing on you hours on end."

Roan shook his head.

Emerson led the animals inside the barn and found the hostler shoeing a horse in a stall.

The man, skinny, bald on top, gray above his ears, looked up. "What day is it?" Emerson asked.

The hostler tacked a shoe-nail flat against the hoof. He spat a stream of tobacco juice at the floor, stood up, and rubbed his gray, stubbled chin between lush muttonchop whiskers.

"Tuesday, I reckon. What can I do for you, Mr. ...?"

"Tom Thackery. Brush these two down, give 'em a bagful of mash, and stable them for a day. You want me to pay in advance?"

"Nope. You don't pay, I'll keep the horses."

"How are the eats at Daisy's?"

"Daisy's my sister. She cooks as good as Maw used to."

The hostler stared for a moment at the empty saddle holsters on Miller's chestnut.

"I lost the pistols in a card game."

The man smelled a lie. Emerson recalculated the odds.

Roan shifted weight from one hind leg to the other and snorted.

"And would you check the shoes on the chestnut, please, Mr. ...?"

He spat more juice. "Bynum. Ephraim Bynum."

Across the street, he met Agnes Bynum, Ephraim's wife, behind the counter next to the cash register in the general store. He bought coarse brown pants, brown shirts, and a tan coat. In early summer, he didn't need the coat for warmth. He needed it for the pockets. He didn't buy a new hat.

Daisy was not a Bynum. She had been but married David Osgood, who died of cholera in '52. There was no barbershop in town, but Daisy cut hair, and her establishment included a bathtub room and separate outhouses for men and women. Emerson shaved his mustache. In the mirror, his newly short hair was the way Paw and he had worn it in Indiana. It didn't look strange at all. His naked upper lip, however, he couldn't look at it. Daisy served pot roast with potatoes, carrots, and onions for dinner. Then Emerson went back to the general store to buy a hat to fit his shorn head. He thought he should have waited to buy pants until after he'd eaten, but shucking Doyel's trousers had seemed awfully important that morning. With his new flop-brimmed hat, he crossed the street to Bynum's Tavern and bought two pours of the good stuff. Then he returned to his room at Daisy's, undressed, and flopped onto the bed and slept until a rooster crowed.

After breakfast, Tom Thackery owed Daisy $11.25. He was inclined to give her twenty, but he remembered Blonde back in Saint Joseph. "Generosity makes you memorable," Weekes liked to say. He found the proprietress in the kitchen.

"Missus, I had a uncommon good time here." Tom Thackery did not speak the same way Emerson Sharp did. "I've run a streak a bad luck, but I still want to leave a bit extry. Twelve ain't near enough. Thirteen'll saddle you with my bad luck. So here's fourteen. And thankee kindly, ma'am."

He'd ridden in wearing tattered fine clothes, long hair, and mustache. He was leaving in rough clothes, clean-shaven, and short-haired. People would remember those changes. Daisy would remember the fourteen dollars. But Emerson Sharp was wanted. Dead or alive. Tom Thackery shoved Emerson into the back of his mind. Tom Thackery wanted to feel like he still had some hold on normalcy, so he'd left the woman extra. Maybe it would come back on him. Maybe.

At the stable, he told Ephraim, "I'm short of cash. I bought a Dragoon for one of the saddle holsters. Will you take the saddle from the chestnut in payment for what I owe you?"

"Saddle's worth more'n you owe. I ain't giving you money for the diff'rence."

"No need." Tom spat on his palm and stuck it out.

Ephraim spat on his. "Two spit shakes is the onliest way both sides tie to a deal."

Thackery started out with his saddle on Miller's chestnut. As they cantered east past the last houses, Roan nipped the haunch of the chestnut. "Roan!" Thackery fussed.

They came to a north-south road, and Thackery reined right and kicked the chestnut into a gallop. He pushed the animals all morning. When he saw riders or wagons coming at him, he slowed to a canter or a walk. He noted how the farmers and riders studied him. They didn't appear to be as wary of him as the ones he encountered before entering the Bynum town. He thought it might be the absence of a saddle on the extra horse. They probably thought Tom Thackery was on his way to sell it, or maybe he just bought it and was taking it home. So he stayed on the roads, and his beasts ate miles.

At noon, he stopped by a stream and let the horses drink and eat grass, and he made coffee. Then he pushed on. He picked up the route Josh led him down on the way to the Bucknell place and crossed the Missouri at Glasgow late in the day.

From Glasgow, it was a day's ride to Kingdom Come. It was Wednesday, and he didn't have to be there for the races until next week. It was probably two days to Independence. A little less than that to get from there to Kingdom Come.

Nora. He had to see her, to explain what had happened. She would understand.

And Josh. He was tough. Odds were Josh pulled through. And Rottermich. He had to talk to Johannes.

He pointed Roan at the setting sun, and he chased it at a canter.

*****

Thackery waited until an hour after sunset to enter Independence. Then he skirted the south edge of town to Station Street and followed that to the gunsmith shop, where he led his animals to the barn. Inside, he lit a lantern and turned the wick low.

Rottermich intended to buy draft horses to pull his wagon west come spring but hadn't done so yet. There were hay and oats, though. Thackery changed the saddle from the chestnut to Roan, put the animals in stalls, and fed them. Then he snuffed the lantern flame and used his key to enter the rear of the gun shop. Johannes was at the workbench, repairing a pistol. He grabbed for the Pocket Colt he always kept close to hand.

"Johannes," Tom Thackery said.

"Emerson? Ah. You shave the mustache. You cut the hair."

He could not use his new name and have it tied to his old one.

"People find you here, they not bodder vit sheriff. They hang you.

People say dey alvays vonder vhere you get your money. Stagecoach robber, dey say. Killer of vimmin unt girls, dey say."

"Johannes—"

"You rob dat stagch? You kill dat voman an' dat girl?"

Thackery kept his eyes on Johannes. How the hell could he explain what happened?

"I did not want to be with those men. They were going to rob a stagecoach. They thought I knew what they were going to do. They thought I'd tell the sheriff. They made me go with them. I was there when the stage came. It was a three-team rig, and it was going fast. One of the men shot a lead horse. It fell, and the others stumbled over it and the coach crashed. They didn't think anyone would be inside the coach. But there was a woman and a girl. They were killed in the crash. I was there. So, yes. I killed them."

Johannes stared hard into Tom Thackery's eyes.

After a moment, he looked away. "Bah. You are poker player.

You hide vhat you tink."

"You're a businessman, Mr. Rottermich. You don't let your thoughts show on your face, either."

Rottermich humphed. "Vat you vant?"

"The man who was shot in front of the hotel—"

"Mr. Ewing."

"Yes. Is he alive?"

"Doctor cut off his leg. But he liffs. He is vit Rosie. Rosie and the vimmen in her house take care of him."

"I'm going to see him."

"Bah. Dat's crazy. You should get avay from here."

"Nobody comes in the shop after sundown. Nobody paid any mind to me coming here." Thackery checked his watch. "Rosie and her women will be at her restaurant. I'm going to see him. Then I'm coming back here."

Thackery returned to the barn for Roan. He rode down Station Street and turned right onto Liberty. After passing four cross streets, he said, "That's the Catholic church, Roan. That's where Rosie wanted Nora and me to get married."

The windows of most of the houses he passed spilled lamplight into the night. Rosie's did too. When he walked Nora home, they came to a dark house. Lamps were lit after the women entered.

He tied Roan to the picket fence, and his heart rate kicked up.

"Nora won't be there."

The horse snorted.

Thackery took a deep breath and walked up the planks to the porch. To the left of the door, a curtained-over window glowed. The curtains were drawn back on the window to the right. Two lighted lamps on small tables showed the sitting room to be empty.

Thackery knocked on the door. He waited, listened at the door, turned the knob, eased it open, stepped inside, and closed the door behind him.

To his right, a door stood open. Josh spoke. A woman laughed. Josh joking and charming a woman lifted a weight off him. He smiled and walked across the wood floor on the balls of feet so his heels wouldn't clomp. He looked into the bedroom.

"Nora."

She was sitting in a chair beside the bed. She frowned. "You! What are you doing here?"

His chest felt as if he'd been kicked by a horse.

"Emerson!" Josh was glad to see him. Then his face clouded. "You're takin' a chance. You don't want to let anyone else see you."

"I'm going for the sheriff." Nora stood. Determination and indignation smeared her face in equal measures.

"No!" Josh swung the coverlet back. Thackery caught a glimpse of Josh in long johns, the right leg of which had been cut off and a wad of bandage where his knee should have been. Josh swung out of bed onto his leg and lunged for Nora as she walked past the foot of the bed. Thackery stood in the doorway knowing she was going to push past him and that he wouldn't stop her.

Josh fell onto the floor with a thump. Nora stopped. Thackery recognized the look on her face. He'd seen it when he was leaving Doc Hofstedler's to deliver the message to Miller. Now, though, it was aimed at Josh.

Thackery stepped into the room and bent to help Josh.

"You let him alone," Nora snapped. "I'll do it."

Thackery rolled Josh onto his back and started lifting him up. Nora grabbed Thackery's arm. "I said I'll do it."

"Let go or you'll make me drop him."

She took her hand away. Josh stood on his good foot. Thackery helped him pivot, sit back on the bed, and swing his leg back up.

"You're bleeding, Josh."

Bright red stained the stump bandage.

"The Hofstedlers are at Rosie's. I'm going to get him."

"It's nothin'," Josh said. "I just bumped it."

"The doctor said you had to be careful."

"You were goin' after the sheriff."

"He killed a woman and a little girl."

"Emerson would shoot himself before he'd shoot a woman."

Time pressed on Thackery, and it was like being back in Indiana again when Maw and Paw talked about him like he wasn't in the room, like the last person to have anything to say about what would happen to him was he himself. It was strange being talked about with them using his old name.

"Get the sheriff if you want. Get the doctor if you want. It doesn't matter." Thackery turned to Josh. "I need to talk to you. It won't take a minute."

"Why'd you go with Miller?" Josh asked. "You said you was goin' to tell him and come right back."

"Doyel thought I was a Union spy. He wanted to shoot me. Miller wouldn't let him. They took my guns and made me go with them."

"But you didn't shoot the woman and the girl?"

"Nobody shot them. But I was with the men that made the stage crash. The crash killed them. I was with those men. I killed a woman and a little girl."

"Oh, hell, Emerson, that ain't so. How'd the stage crash?"

Thackery shook his head. "There's no time for this. I told Johannes Rottermich. If you want to know, ask him."

"Rottermich? The gunsmith you bought the business from? Why'd you tell him?"

Instead of answering, he looked at Nora. And he understood. Nora had been attracted to him from the first, as he had been to her. She'd been cautious, though. Partly because of Rosie, but Thackery was sure Nora had been hurt by a man, not her father. Then the shock of hearing he'd been shot had blown away her restraint. She showed him she loved him. Then he didn't come back to Doc Hofstedler's as he promised. But word that he killed a woman and a girl came back. He understood.

He had to force himself to look away from her green eyes. "Nora, please, will you bring me a pen and a piece of paper?"

"Why?"

He wouldn't look at her. "Just do it, please?"

Her skirts rustled. She brushed past him.

Thackery explained about learning to be a gunsmith. He spoke as he scratched out the transference of ownership to the shop, the lot, and outbuildings to Mr. Josh Ewing.

He signed it and laid the document atop the chest of drawers.

"So it's yours. If you're able to move, you can live in the shop starting tomorrow. There's rooms on the second floor, but I'm sure Johannes can fix you up a bed on the bottom floor."

"I don't know what to say. Thanks ain't near enough."

"Sure it is. Of course, I'm not sure how good you'll be at it. Sure as shootin', I won't buy a gun from you." Thackery tipped his hat to Josh. "See you."

He turned and headed for the door.

"Emerson. Aren't you going to say goodbye to me?"

"Nora. You already said goodbye to me. I won't ever be able to say it to you."

He walked out rubbing his horse-kicked chest and mounted his horse to return to the gunsmith shop.

"Roan, what do you think Johannes is going to say when I tell him he has to start all over teaching a new apprentice? Maybe I should bring you in the house with me so you can hear it. On second thought, you'll probably hear it just fine from the barn. You and Miller's chestnut will get a big laugh out of it."

At Lexington, he stopped to let a farm wagon trundle past. Nobody was driving. The wagon was loaded with sacks. A boy, maybe fifteen, lay sprawled atop the load with his arms spread, face up to the moon for it to shine on. Asleep. Passed out. He'd picked up the supplies and gone to a saloon. Maybe for the first time.

"The team knows the way home."

Roan walked on.

"Oh, Jesus, and goddamn it all to hell, Roan. I should have turned around. I should have grabbed one more look at her to take away." He huffed out a chunk of air. "I was afraid of her eyes."

29

THAT MORNING, THACKERY had ridden through two small towns.

In one, a church bell pealed, calling worshipers to assemble. The bell, clanging away the Sunday-morning stillness, implanted an image of Almighty God as Paw standing in the door to his bedroom saying, "Git up, I said!" The bell went silent as he, atop Roan, cantered past the gleaming white box of a building with wagons and buggies nuzzling up to it. Children spilled out of the conveyances and streamed up the steps and inside as men helped women climb down and enter in a statelier fashion. The men and women stopped what they were doing to watch as he passed. Thackery tipped his hat. A few of the men tipped back. But it was to God he'd tipped.

In the second town, services were in progress. The walls of that church were unable to contain "A Mighty Fortress." Thackery slowed Roan to a walk and sang a stanza with the congregation.

Josh never attended church with him. The church his family attended in Kansas was all "hell and damnation, and if you don't believe as I do, I will shoot you. Wasn't no path to heaven with that bunch." This church, however, did give off an aura of brotherly love, a place where a decent soul would go to hobnob with other souls of that kind.

With the congregation launching into the second stanza, Thackery said, "Roan," and he launched into a run that soon had the chestnut pulling against the reins, unable to keep up. Thackery slowed them and thought about something Weekes Daley had said once. "Seems like when I need to go to church the most, something conspires to keep me from it."

Roan settled into to his spine-jarring canter. "Roan," Thackery muttered. He resented the chestnut holding them back. It would have been a cleansing purgative to run Roan all out. He didn't express it, though. The horse knew he was holding them back. What Thackery said was "Good thing we had Chestnut with us. We'd never have been able to cover the miles we did without him."

An hour later, he stopped and switched the saddle, and they set off again at a canter.

"Chestnut, with your eyes where they are, they can't see it, but my butt is smiling."

Roan snorted.

On the well-traveled road, he encountered no one save churchgoers. At times, forest walled the arrow-straight thoroughfare on both sides. At other times, they passed cleared fields and farmhouses and outbuildings, the houses and buildings seeming at once to be separated by significant distances but conveying also a sense of proximity and mutual security. On a stretch with woods on both sides, Roan jerked the reins.

Far ahead, riders. Three of them, side by side. Taking up the width of the road. "Roan," he said, and the animal sidled up next to him. The reins were knotted together, and he draped them over the saddle. Roan kept pace on Thackery's right. He drew his rifle, checked the load, and slowed Chestnut to a walk. Behind him was clear. The three riders continued approaching. Thackery stopped. One rider bore down on him directly. Thackery took the rifle and reins in his left hand and pulled the Dragoon from the saddle holster.

"Chestnut, you stay still now. We are not giving way to that guy coming at us. Stay still." He cocked the rifle and then cocked the Dragoon.

The rider directly in front stopped fifty feet away. The other two continued coming on. Thackery kicked Chestnut in the ribs, and he bolted forward. He pointed the rifle in his left hand in the direction of the two and leveled the Dragoon at the other. If anyone touched a pistol, the shooting would start.

He'd surprised them. Their eyes were on him. He could see they were thinking about drawing. He grinned. Then he was past the two. Roan was right beside Chestnut. Chestnut responded to Thackery's knees and bore down on the third man. The third man scrambled his horse to Thackery's left.

Thackery dropped the rifle to the dirt, grabbed the reins, and hauled Chestnut to a stop with the third man between him and the other two. The third man's horse was dancing around, and he fought to get it quieted. Then he reached for the gun on his hip.

"I wouldn't!" Thackery growled.

The third man stayed his hand on the pistol butt. Thackery guided Chestnut alongside and jammed the Dragoon into the man's belly. Thackery swatted the man's hand off the pistol butt and pulled his pistol from the holster and dropped it to the ground.

"Tell the other two," Thackery said. "Throw their weapons down."

The man turned to look at his two companions.

"Tell them," Thackery said.

He told. They dropped them.

"Now you all skedaddle. The way you were heading."

"Our guns."

"Don't bother coming back for them. I'm going to bust them up."

"You son of a bitch!"

"A bit down the road, you'll come to a little town with a church. If I were you, I'd go in that church and thank the Almighty that it's a Sunday, and I don't like to kill people on the Sabbath. Of course, when I get to thinking on what you three intended doing to me, I have to wonder. The world would have three fewer back-shooters in it. That would be more important than not shooting people on the Lord's day."

The third man wheeled his horse and kicked it into a gallop. He raced past the other two and they chased after him.

As they thundered down the road, Thackery gathered the pistols and rifles. Junk weapons. Not even fit to go in Johannes Rottermich's busted handgun box. He used a pistol butt as a hammer, converted the weapons to real junk, and tossed the bits and pieces into the trees.

Aboard Chestnut again, Chestnut at a canter and the reins to Roan in his hand, he said, "Sure as shooting, fellows, it's a good thing those three didn't smell how much money we have on us." He patted the stuffed saddlebags. "I hope Quantrill is there when we get to Kingdom Come and we can give this to him and be shut of it."

*****

They arrived with the sun low in the sky and warm on his back.

Kingdom Come was a three-street town, but the races, which he discovered would be held on Tuesday, had swelled the population.

The handful of rooms above the saloon were not available. Mr. Bucknell always occupied those during the races, the bartender told him. During the races, everyone stayed in Tent City on the west side of town. "You come into town that way and didn't see it, you best visit a sawbones and see do you need spectacles."

The bartender, intensely pleased with his joke, flashed a smile and then moved to the other end of the bar to serve other customers, dragging his soggy mop rag across the bar, smearing spilled beer more than cleaning it.

Thackery took a sip of his race-prices beer, backed away from the bar, settled the money saddlebags across his shoulder, and walked out to look for Quantrill in Tent City.

Tent City occupied about five acres, Thackery thought. Besides the tents, there were areas for parking buggies and wagons. The tents included the Men's Sleeping Tent, the Women's Sleeping Tent, the Bar and Betting Tent, the Eating Tent, the Music and Dancing Tent, and, farthest away from the road, the Livery Stable Tent.

He paid and signed a ledger book to buy entry to the stable tent for his horses and then searched it for Quantrill. No luck. The Bar and Betting and Eating Tents were not open until tomorrow. He paid for a space in the appropriate sleeping tent and signed another ledger book. "Spread your bedroll. That stakes your claim to a spot." He staked his claim and then decided it was getting tiresome dragging the money bags with him everywhere he went, including in the men's four-hole outhouse.

He retrieved Roan and rode east out of town and looked for a spot to hide Quantrill's funds.

To his right was all forested, hilly country. The other side of the road was mostly cleared land with every now and then a swath of forest separating one farm from another.

Two miles out of town, he met a steady stream of wagons, buggies, and two-, three-, and four-man clumps of riders streaming toward Kingdom Come. The prospect of an uncommon good time seemed to be tugging at the people to get to town quickly lest they miss something. The horses all high-stepped it with their heads held up, the air of excitement infecting them too. The last wagon in the caravan passed, a man and a woman on the bench seat with a young girl between them. In the side- boarded rear, three blond, hatless boys, perhaps eight, nine, and ten, wearing identical one-strap overalls, crowded against the sideboard to watch Tom Thackery pass. He tipped his hat to them. The oldest picked up a corncob from the wagon bed and threw it at him. It landed well short of Roan.

Tom Thackery—Emerson then—was pretty sure he'd never done anything like that kid had done. For one thing, when he'd been that age, he remembered thinking Maw had eyes in the back of her head. That kid's maw stared straight ahead, apparently oblivious to the goings-on behind her.

It hit him.

"Oh, shit, Roan. You think word of Emerson Sharp, killer of women and girls, will make it back to Indiana?"

Sour fog, as if formed from vinegar vapors, filled his head.

He kicked Roan in the ribs, and the horse ran as if forty devils were chasing them with pitchforks of fire.

Up ahead to his right, a lane cut off the road and through the woods. He recognized it. The lane led to Bucknell's place. He slowed Roan. The high ridge to his right, he remembered that and the wooden bridge over the deep gulley with a stream at the bottom. He checked behind him. Clear. Clear in front too.

He stepped down and led Roan into the saplings lining the bank of the gulley. When he made some fifty paces from the road, he looked up the steep slope of the wooded ridge. Roan could climb it, he thought, but he'd leave sign.

Thackery took the saddlebags and his raincoat and climbed the rise afoot. He was huffing when he reached the top, but the spot was just what he'd been looking for. No sign that anyone had been there in a long time. Oak, maple, and hickory trees wove a thick leaf canopy above. Thick brush covered the ground. Next to a rotted fallen tree trunk, he stashed the bags wrapped in his coat and covered them with leaves and debris.

Then he descended the hill. He made sure there was no one on the road before he led Roan out of the trees and returned to Kingdom Come.

*****

In the Men's Sleeping Tent, if Thackery closed his eyes, the snoring forced them open. If he counted sheep, the wool balls *bah-ah-ah*-ed at him.

A lone lantern nailed to a tent pole leaked enough light so a man could find the path in the middle of the tent and not step on the sleepers atop their bedrolls on the straw scattered along both sides. As he dressed, Thackery wrinkled his nose. The snoring had been so loud he hadn't smelled the farts. He'd always preferred sleeping in a barn to sleeping under the stars and whatever weather God chose to dump on him. Funny, though. The smell of horse and cow droppings didn't bother his olfactory sensor as much as a man's flatulence.

Outside, he found the sky dark, overcast. No one was about. Lanterns glowed through the walls of most of the tents. The walls of the Eating Tent were rolled up. A handful of women moved about setting the tables. Thackery walked into the place. The woman who met him was Clementine, the owner of Clementine's Café. He and Josh had eaten in her establishment after he purchased Horse Two.

Thackery took his hat off.

"Food's not ready yet, mister, but the coffee is." Clementine studied him. Her face was stern, impassive. A lot was going on behind her gray eyes. Apparently, she was satisfied. "Sit over there with that man." She bustled away. Thackery remembered her chin from before. She wore it stuck out, as if trying to get it to protrude ahead of her as much as her ample bosom did.

He sat where he'd been directed. He introduced himself as Tom Thackery.

"Zeke Manley." He stuck out a hand. The hand was calloused, as Thackery's own used to be on the farm in Indiana.

Clementine returned with a pot and poured coffee for both men.

"Thanks, Maw," Zeke said.

Zeke was a talker. He was Clementine's only child. Clementine had been the first wife of Zechariah Manley. Zechariah fancied himself a prophet and left a Mormon settlement some fifty miles north to establish the Lord's Kingdom Come to earth—"Right here," Zeke said, jabbing the tabletop with a forefinger. In all, Zechariah had six wives. "The other five all had more than one child."

Clementine was laying silverware at the next table. She turned and glared at her boy. Zeke was probably thirty and some.

"Maw just reminded me there's things I do not say to strangers or anyone. She has to remind *me*, the soul of discretion?"

Thackery was repelled by Zeke's oily smile of inclusive collusion. Zeke went on to say one of Zechariah's faithful, contrary to the prophet's teaching, on a trip to Kansas City, gambled and lost his horse farm to a man named Bucknell.

Bucknell was a wastrel. He'd abandoned his family in the east and meandered west, earning his daily bread playing cards and other games of chance. He was not good at cards or particularly insightful into the things he'd bet on.

"He was uncommon lucky, though. Everybody agreed on that. Right up until the night he decided to go for a ride at midnight on one his new stallions. The stallion had never felt spurs before and reared and threw Bucknell. They found him the next morning with neck broken but gripping the bottle of applejack with iron fingers. The wastrel, to everyone's surprise, had left a will. His son, Benjamin Jr., inherited. Junior, his wife, and his three sons traveled down the Ohio River and then up the Missouri by boat to Jefferson City. From there by stagecoach. Half a day east of Jeff City, Bucknell's wife went into labor. The woman and the infant died. Bucknell buried them, went on, took possession of his property, sent for his wife's sister. Two months after she arrived, they were married. Nine months later, the new wife delivered a daughter.

"Are you entering a horse in the races, Mr. Thackery?"

"What?" The sudden shift threw him. He'd characterized Zeke as an empty-headed blabbermouth dodo. He'd listened to the man with his ears, not his mind. "Uh, no. No. I'm just here to watch them. And meet a friend."

"What's your friend's name? I'll keep an eye out for him."

"Um. Warren Westfall."

"What's he look like?"

Thackery described Weekes Daley, very accurately, he thought.

A young woman brought two plates. A pork chop, four fried eggs, and fried potatoes.

As they ate, Zeke described the races. "Short, medium, and long race. We place posts in the ground one-half mile, one mile, and two miles from the start point, which is the west edge of town. Racers have to turn around those posts and return to the edge of town where the start line is now the finish line. See?"

Thackery nodded.

"We're setting the posts at ten this morning. Would you like to come along?"

Thackery was wary of more interrogation. "Is the barbershop open today?"

"All the businesses on Main Street are closed. But Todd Manley—he's the barber—is setting up a tent right now. Near the Stable Tent. He'll probably be open in an hour. Get over there as soon as we are done here. Heck. Maybe you'll be lucky and get in the tub first. If you're finished in time, and if you want to come with us to set the posts, meet us in front of the Men's Sleeping Tent at ten."

Zeke used his handkerchief to wipe his lips. "Too many customers during the races for Maw to supply them all with napkins. It's going to be a steady mob of customers in here until after sundown on Wednesday." Zeke picked his hat up from the chair and went to the cash register table. He paid and talked to his mother. She glanced over her son's shoulder at Tom Thackery. In Kingdom Come during the races, apparently even Clementine's only son paid for breakfast.

Tom Thackery wondered how Weekes Daley had slipped so easily into and out of personae. He was not, he concluded, near good enough with this change-your-name game.

30

A T THE WEST end of Kingdom Come, the saloon sign stared across Main Street into the face of Hardware Store. The store stared back. Both buildings were two-story. Saloon had a balcony covering the porch. A banner was strung from the balcony to the top of Hardware Store. The banner proclaimed start on one side and finish on the other.

Tom Thackery and Zeke sat their horses under the banner as two men threw posts and a posthole digger onto a wagon at the rear of Zeke's store.

"Ninth-annual first-Tuesday-in-July horse race," Zeke said. "The first one was Maw's idea. She went to Mr. Bucknell. His first name is Benjamin. He's a junior. Most folks call him 'Mister.' His father, the wastrel, was Benjamin Senior. Most folks, when they talk about him, just say, 'the Wastrel.' Not around Mr. Bucknell, though. Anyway, Maw convinced Mr. Bucknell that a race would be good business for the town, and it would give him the chance to show off his horses."

The wagon rattled away from the store and headed west.

Zeke trotted his horse to keep up with the wagon.

When the driver finally hauled the wagon around, Thackery figured they were well beyond a mile away.

"See that stake there beside the road? It marks the two- mile distance for the Long Race. We had a surveyor mark the distance some years back. Racers ride from the start line to here. They have to round the post and hightail it to the finish."

One of the men began stabbing the posthole digger into the dirt.

"We plant the posts three feet deep. We plant the next one a mile from the start. That's the Middle Race. The post for the Short Race is at a half mile. I'm the race marshal. I have to witness the setting of the posts."

When the third marker had been tamped into place, the two men climbed up onto the wagon, and the driver hollered, "Heyyup!" The other man on the seat threw dirt clods at the rumps of the team.

"They want to race," Zeke said, grinning. "Giddup," he said and charged after the wagon.

"Roan," Thackery said.

Roan tore after them and flew past Zeke and the wagon. Ahead, beyond the finish line, people in the street scattered for the boardwalks to either side.

Roan passed beneath the finish line, running all out. Without Thackery having to do anything, Roan slowed, as if he knew where the race ended. They turned and headed back to the start line.

Zeke pulled off the racecourse before the finish. The wagon continued coming hard, dragging a formidable dust cloud in its wake. The driver and his passenger were both about eighteen or nineteen. Both were grinning. If they couldn't win the race, they could score another kind of victory on the spectators.

The wagon rumbled past. Thackery closed his eyes until most of the dust had settled.

"They're sore losers, Roan," Thackery said.

"Talking to your horse, are you?"

Thackery looked up. A girl, Bucknell's daughter, stood on the balcony of the saloon peering down at him, arms akimbo. But she wasn't a girl anymore. She'd ... grown up. Blossomed some. The white, lacy blouse. The skirt hugging her hips. Her short black hair, it was different and attractive. A rarity to see it so short on a woman, but he liked it. He tipped his hat. He saw recognition flash across her face.

"Tom Thackery, miss. Pleased to make your acquaintance."

"Have we met, Mr. Thackery?"

"Oh, no, miss. Sure as shootin', I'd remember if we had."

He tipped his hat again and gigged Roan in the belly with his heels. Roan started walking.

"Mr. Thackery."

"Yes, miss?"

"Are you racing tomorrow?"

"No, miss?"

"Really? You should consider entering the Short Race."

"I've never ridden in a race before, miss."

"Nothing to it. The horse does all the work. All you have to do is not fall off."

Maybe she hadn't grown up, Thackery thought. Her dress gave the impression she had. The last time he'd seen her, she'd worn pants. And sassy attitude. Still sassy, this one.

He'd given her two hat tips. That was enough.

He kicked Roan again. Roan started walking.

"Mr. Thackery."

He stopped and looked up at her. Again.

"Why don't you ask your horse if he'd like to run? Roan, you called him, right?" To the horse, she said, "What do you say, Roan? Would you like to run in the race tomorrow?"

Roan snorted.

"See, Mr. Thackery?" The girl laughed, spun on her heel, and entered the upper floor of the saloon.

*****

Tent City teemed with men and women walking and children running and screaming. It brought to mind the summer festival his church put on. The festival was held a week after Oliver Teasdale finished spring planting. Of the two dozen farmers attending Brother James's Resurrection Church, Oliver reliably finished his planting last. The church festival hadn't been jammed with near as many people as this race fandango, but the spirit of unbridled joy floating above the crowd and in the joy-filled screams of boys and girls cut loose this once a year, that was the same. Thackery recalled the dances at the festival and how unless a fellow asked early, Candace Barlow's dance card would be filled before he worked up the nerve to ask for one.

Deborah Simmons. She popped to mind. And her saucy tongue. Bucknell's daughter. She was just like Deborah. Well, both were uncommonly smart. For women. And both spoke words with an uncommonly nasty bite to them. However, Bucknell's daughter was not plain straight up and down. And if she wasn't speaking, her face was uncommonly pleasant to behold. But that was the problem. Both those women were always saying something.

Weekes Daley taught Thackery a lot about a lot of things, but not much about women. Except how to treat saloon girls. "Women," he'd said, "are one of God's great blessings." But Daley's relationships with these "blessings" generally lasted a day or two, and once in a great while as long as seven days. When it was time to move on, Weekes did, and to Thackery it appeared both parties to the arrangement left it with no emotional attachment and no regret. Which brought to mind Josh Ewing talking about saloon girls and not remembering any of them. He wondered if Weekes Daley remembered the faces of any of his blessed encounters.

Nora! Thackery would remember her forever. And her green eyes and what he could see in them and what they did to him when she looked into his soul.

Thackery sighed.

Figuring out women would have to wait for another day. What mattered was finding Quantrill and getting the money to him. Then he'd be done with everything he owed Josh Ewing, and he could be shut of Kingdom Come. And that sassy Bucknell woman.

After stabling Roan, Thackery searched Tent City, ate, and searched again, to no avail. He'd bet three dollars against two Quantrill would enter town from the west. In the afternoon, he rode Chestnut an hour west toward Sedalia. Not encountering Quantrill in the steady stream of travelers on the way to crowd into Kingdom Come, he rode back to Tent City.

After supper, Thackery stood on the edge of the Music Tent and scanned the crowd. Alone on the plank floor, two Negro men danced, high stepping, knee slapping, faces sweating, heels drumming. A fiddle, guitar, banjo, harmonica, and a hammer dulcimer hurled the reckless reel under the rolled-up sides of the tent and into the night. Among the men ringing the dance floor, toes tapped, hands clapped. Thackery's did too.

The fiddler slowly sawed his bow, and the wail he created brought the dancers, the tappers, and the clappers back to earth. When the applause began to wane, the fiddler bowed out a waltz, and the guitarist and the harmonica joined in.

"Would you like to dance, Mr. Thackery?"

The Bucknell girl!

"What? A woman shouldn't ask a man to dance."

She grabbed his arm and pulled him onto the floor. A few other couples joined them. In the center of the floor, she curtsied, grabbed his hand, put the other on her waist, and led them swirling from the center to the edge of the planks. Her waltzing, Thackery thought, was infused with lingering influence of the reel. He gave himself over to it. After a lap around the floor, Thackery saw that the other dancers had moved off. They just wanted to watch a man and woman meld music and dance the way God intended.

Then the fiddler bowed "the end," as he'd done to the reel.

The crowd applauded. The Bucknell girl curtsied and Thackery bowed.

"Thank you, Mr. Thackery."

He'd heard her name when he'd purchased Iago-renamed- Horse, but he could not remember it.

"Amanda," she said, as if reading his mind. "Come. There's a punch bowl in one corner of the Bar Tent. I'd like one. You, perhaps"—her smile vexed him—"might prefer a whiskey."

She took his arm and guided him. Lanterns hanging from poles next to tents appeared more like stars rather than serious bodies of illumination, like a moon. The stars above cast enough light to distinguish males from females. Making their way was a matter of starts and stops and "Beg pardon." The crowd wasn't necessarily thick. It was, however, comprised of numerous families. Thackery saw several men walking purposefully toward some destination, like a locomotive on rails. And like a train, it wasn't the locomotive's job to make sure the cars all followed. Behind these men, a woman held a string of children by each hand and pressed hard to remain attached to her husband.

Amanda tsked. "Everybody, for miles around, looks forward to the races every year. For a couple of days, there's no sweating in the fields, no churning butter or spinning, no confinement to a farm with nothing but chores and lessons from sunup to set. But look at the women. It's not much of a celebration for them. You'd think one of these apes could lend a hand riding herd on the children he fathered!"

A shadow figure of a man with a child in each arm said, "Beg pardon," and walked in front of them. A woman walked beside him.

After they passed, Amanda stepped out again.

Thackery smiled. "Ask and you shall receive," climbed onto the tip of his tongue, but he swallowed it.

"You're not going to gloat?"

"But, Miss Bucknell, I am gloating."

Finally, something got Little Miss Know-It-All to shut up. That he was thinking like a schoolboy flashed through his mind, but he was more concerned with how pleasant it felt to no longer be at a disadvantage to a girl some six years younger than he was.

They entered the Bar and Betting Tent, like all of them, except the Sleeping Tents, with the sides rolled up. Thackery pointed to the punch table.

"I want to show you something first."

Her hand, still tucked under his arm, guided him around a partition walling off the punch table from the bar. On the other side of the partition, three men sat behind a table, all with their hats off. Bucknell's blond-headed sons. He couldn't recall their names, but he did remember the oldest and the youngest. The one in the middle, he'd never met him, but he was obviously a Bucknell. All three Bucknell men were looking up at a tall, broad-shouldered man bent over a ledger book open on the table.

"The tall man in the black coat is the sheriff from Sedalia," Amanda Bucknell said softly. "He's been here since midafternoon. He's looking for a man named Emerson Sharp."

Thackery stared down at her. She stared up, that saucy smile pasted on her face. She knew. The smile snuffed, and she propelled them around the table.

"Still looking for that man, Sheriff?" The sheriff straightened up.

"I'm Amanda Bucknell, and this is Mr. Thackery."

The sheriff's blue eyes rested on Thackery a moment. The sheriff was a hard man and not one to trifle with. A tiny smile crinkled the corners of his eyes and curled up the corners of his mouth as he turned. "Miss Bucknell." He tipped his flat- brimmed black hat. "I've heard of you. A pleasure."

"I'm sure you've heard I'm a model of decorum lifted from the pages of *Godey's Lady's Book*."

Warmth supplanted the chill in the blue eyes. The sheriff chuckled. "That, miss, is precisely what I heard."

"You know, Sheriff, the way my father described that Sharp fellow, he might have been painting a picture of you. Tall, long black hair, full black mustache."

"Except Emerson Sharp is a good ten years younger than I am."

"I've heard he was involved in a shooting in Saint Joseph and that he rides with Quantrill."

"I've heard that too, Miss Bucknell."

"Amanda. Mind your manners!" The oldest from the far end of the table glared at his sister.

The sheriff's eyes moved back to Thackery. They were winter sky now.

"Joe Wilson, Mr. Thackery." The sheriff's handshake was a single pump. "Good luck in the Short Race tomorrow."

"What?"

"You didn't know?" the middle Bucknell boy asked. He, too, glared at his sister. "You said you were delivering the entry fee *for* Mr. Thackery."

The sheriff ahem-ed and tipped his hat, and as he turned away, he muttered, "*Godey's Lady's Book* my foot."

The oldest began, "When Mother finds out—"

"Then don't tell her." She smiled sweetly at Thackery. "These are my brothers—Ben, William, and Bobby. This is Mr. Thackery."

Ben and William were hostile.

Bobby stuck up his hand. "I'm in the Short Race, third heat. You're in the second. Maybe we'll meet in the final."

Thackery shook. "Luck."

"I'd like that punch now, Mr. Thackery."

"Bobby," Ben barked. "You take her. And don't lose her again."

"If you want to place a bet, Thackery," William said, "you place it with me. You have to use your own money, though."

As Thackery fished a twenty from his wallet, Ben smirked.

The partition separating the betting table from the punch table was three blackboards with race entrants listed by heats for the Long, Short, and Middle Races. Ben Bucknell was listed first in the first heat of the Long Race.

Thackery laid the bill on the table. "On him." He pointed to Ben.

"Most people bet against a Bucknell horse. Many of the people come here just for that purpose. To see a Bucknell horse lose."

"On him." He nodded toward Ben. "To win." He extracted another twenty. "This is on the second heat of the Short Race. On Mr. Thackery."

The rough-sawed planks of the bar still smelled of sawdust and hot saw. It wouldn't do to lean on it. A fellow would pick up a passel of splinters. He drank a whiskey and went to the stable area. Roan was in the pasture. He trotted up to Thackery. Thackery held a carrot out on the palm of his hand. As the horse crunched the treat, Thackery asked Roan if he'd really told the Bucknell girl he wanted to run in the race.

Roan put his head over the top pole of the fence and bumped Thackery's shoulder with his head.

"You want another carrot, do you? At race-time prices, I couldn't afford two. Win the race tomorrow. I put money on us. If you win, I might be able to buy two carrots."

Thackery walked through Tent City looking for Quantrill. He

didn't find him. After another whiskey, he went to the Sleeping Tent and lay on his ground cloth.

He lay looking up at the tent roof.

Amanda Bucknell was in his head. She knew who he was. He was sure of it. Her brothers Ben and William, however, did not. He was sure they'd have told the sheriff if they had.

Nora!

All the while he'd spent getting from the spot where Lieutenant Miller died to Kingdom Come, he'd been of the opinion he'd never be able to go back to Independence. At least not to live there. But he thought he might go back, at night, and talk to Nora. She might come away with him. They could go to California together. But after the way she'd looked at him, when he did go back, and the way she'd looked at Josh, no. Nora was gone.

Her green eyes weren't gone, though. They would never be corkscrewed out of his head.

He rolled onto his side. There wasn't enough straw to make that comfortable.

William goddamned Quantrill, where the hell are you?

AS RACE-DAY DAWN began melting the night, Thackery entered the Eating Tent. The tables were filled with men and a few teenaged boys. The air was still. Cigar and cigarette smoke swirled in the wake of waiters and waitresses hurrying food in one direction and armloads of dirty dishes in the other. From the cook tent, skillets rattled and banged on the iron stove, and dishwashers rattled and clattered the plates as if they knew just how much frantic abuse the dinnerware could stand without shattering. Riding just beneath the kitchen din, the diners' mingled murmurs buzzed with excitement like a far-off line of thunderstorms unable to contain all the energy boiling inside.

Clementine shooed a tableful of dawdlers over coffee away. "There's coffee in the Bar and Betting Tent," she assured them.

Someone grabbed his elbow. Zeke Manley. He propelled Thackery toward the table still being cleared. "Thanks," Thackery said.

"What, for moving us to the head of the line? Being Clementine's son gets me nowhere. I'm riding on your coattails. You're racing. You get priority on race day."

They sat. The other chairs were occupied. Plates of food appeared. Cups were filled. Thackery ate. Zeke explained how the races would be run.

The heats were ordered Long, Medium, and Short. A rider had to win his heat to compete in the final. The highlight for most people was the Short Race. Bucknell horses always won the Long and the Medium. Bucknell horses never won the Short. Zeke explained how the riders lined up on Main Street for the races.

Thackery's empty plate was whisked away. His cup was refilled. The other diners, except for he and Zeke, were invited to depart.

"You better eat," Thackery said.

"No hurry." Zeke grinned. "Long as I'm with you." Zeke chewed a forkful of scrambled eggs and fried potatoes and washed it down with coffee. "You got a regular saddle, I expect. You know how much it weighs?"

Before Thackery finished mulling an answer, Zeke said, "Soon as I'm finished, I want to show you something."

They left the Eating Tent, and Zeke led him across Main and into the rear of the hardware store. "A racing saddle." He pointed to a hornless flap of leather lying on a counter. The cinch strap was the only substantial part of the rig. The iron stirrups looked like they might bend if a man put his weight on them.

Thackery had seen them at the horse races Weekes Daley had taken him to in New Orleans. He hefted it. It wasn't a third of the weight of the saddle that had come with Roan.

"A fellow described this as a lady's hankie with a lace cinch strap," Zeke said.

"To win a final, a horse has to run two races," Thackery observed.

Zeke nodded. He didn't say anything. His customer was selling himself on the merchandise. Thackery could read it on his face.

"I can use it?"

Zeke's left eyebrow leaped to a half inch above its mate.

"Buy it?"

The corners of Zeke's straight-line lips grew a little farther apart.

*****

Next to the Stable Tent, Thaddeus Manley, owner of the livery, stood on a wagon, facing the clump of men holding the reins of their racehorses. Thackery and Roan were at the rear of the crowd.

"People call me Thadly," Manley announced. "The way this will work, I will sort you by heat and send you down Temple Street." He pointed to his right.

Thackery looked, as did everyone. Halfway down, a gleaming white building stood on the left side of the wagon-wide lane. It was a plain box of a building with no steeple or cross on top, but it was a church.

"The man wearing number one will serve as a guide for the heat. Stick with him. At the east end of town, you will enter an open gate into a pasture. Number One will lead the heat through the pasture to another gate that opens onto Main Street. One of my sons will be at that gate and open it for you at the appropriate time. When that gate opens, you file through and form a line. Stay in line and stay against the right side as you proceed toward the start line. So first heat of the Long Race, move on down to the pasture. Ben Buckley—"

"Ever' year, Buckley's Number One in the first heat."

Thadly put his hands on his hips. "And every year, Marley, you say the same thing."

Marley, a wiry five nine, about one thirty, stood next to a chestnut with three white stockings and no saddle.

"I'll move to the second heat if Marley will," Ben Bucknell said from beside his big black.

"I ain't moving to the second. Horse gets no rest before the final."

"Do it, Marley. Maybe one of us will beat him."

Thackery couldn't see who had spoken.

"I ain't moving to the second. You move to the second."

"Deal's with you, Marley," Ben said.

"Hey!" Thadly shouted. "Your choice, Marley. Forfeit, or shut up and move along to the start. Lead off, Ben."

A Negro standing by Ben cupped his hands and hoisted Bucknell up onto the black.

Bucknell was bareheaded, but he mimicked tipping his hat. "Thanks." His feet found the stirrups on the racing saddle, and he wheeled his mount around.

Marley grabbed a handful of black mane on his chestnut, swung up, and set off after the black with his legs dangling like a third set of shriveled, useless legs growing out of his horse's belly. Thackery thought the number two on his back looked sad somehow. As if Marley was in fact a long way short of second best.

Thadly called for the first heat of the Middle Race. They gaggled up and then filed away. In the first heat of the Short Race, an Indian wore a number five pinned to a tan shirt. He had a rolled red bandanna tied around his head to corral his long black hair. His bare feet hung out the bottom of tan pants. He rode bareback.

"A goddamned Injun! Wish to hell I had my pistol." The speaker was in front of Thackery and standing beside a dirty white.

"Mister," Thadly said, glaring down at him, "you better be praying nothing happens to Number Five. Middle of the next street to the north is the hanging tree."

The man next to the dirty white pushed his hat back. "Hangin' tree! You'd hang a white man for shootin' an Injun? What the hell kinda town is this?"

"You, sir, may very well find out." Thadly smiled and then shouted for the second heat of the Long Race.

When the second heat of the Middle Race was called, a Negro led a big black to congregate in front of Thadly's wagon. He too was Five. The man with the dirty white was One.

"You, gotta be … you're letting a nigger race?"

Thadly's face clouded over. "Mister, we don't hold with use of that word in Kingdom Come. Say it again, and you will be banished."

"You people! Banish me? Not likely. But I ain't racing with … him."

"Your choice, sir."

"I want my money back."

"Only way to get your money back is to win your heat."

The dirty white's rider glared at the black-skinned man.

"Do I take it, sir, you are withdrawing?"

"Hell no, I ain't."

"Then line up."

A pistol popped, and a cheer went up from the crowd along Main Street and in front of Tent City. The first heat of the Long Race was under way.

As Thackery's heat passed the temple, a groan rose from the spectators. He was Two.

Three said, "Damned Ben Bucknell won his heat."

Thackery followed One through the pasture and down Main Street to wait on the right side of the street behind the start sign.

Down the track, about at the half-mile marker, the second heat of the Middle Race appeared to be a pyramid-shaped cloud of dust framing a black horse in the center, a whitish horse to the right, and a brown to the left. The thundering of hooves spurred a buzz of voices from spectators on the boardwalk next to Thackery and from those lining the course in front of Tent City. Heads craned out to see past the press of those down course.

The black led. A brown and a white appeared to trail by a length. A couple of lengths farther back, two other racers were visible now. Suddenly, how fast the black was running became apparent. The black flashed under the finish line and past Thackery. An image of the black-skinned man's face stuck in his mind. On his face had been not exactly joy, not exactly ecstasy, but not exactly *not* those things, either.

Thackery could taste the feeling he'd sensed when he'd been Emerson Sharp after the bushwhack and he and Horse were running down the valley and the sense of that flying so far removed from a man's walking that distance and time had been superseded by speed in such a pure form only an angel would understand.

As he sped past, Thackery saw red spots, like crimson tears below the black-skinned man's left eye.

From the porch in front of the hardware store, Zeke Manley hollered, "Five won!"

From the porch in front of the saloon, Mr. Bucknell hollered, "Five won!" Then he cupped his hands around his mouth. "Short racers, hold your positions!" He faced the hardware store. "Mr. Race Marshal, would you have Numbers One and Five of this heat brought back to the finish line, please?"

Zeke hollered down the street, and spectators passed the call along.

A rider from down course cantered up to the finish line. "Mr. Marshal, Rider One cut the turn pole short. He didn't go around it."

Zeke acknowledged the message.

Roan's front legs danced in place. His rear legs pranced out into the street. Thackery patted him on the neck. Thackery sensed it too. Leashed violence, aching to bust loose.

The dirty white walked past. The rider swiveled his head one way and then the other, glaring malevolence at both sides of the street. A quirt dangled from a strap around his right wrist. A young man with a pistol in his hand walked behind the white. At the start line, the young man said, "Stop." One sawed back on his reins. Five on the opposite of the street halted his black. "Number One here, Uncle Zeke," the young man with the pistol said, "didn't want to come see you."

Mr. Bucknell stepped down from the porch of the saloon and into the street. "Absalom, turn Romeo around."

Romeo. Thackery glanced up at the balcony of the saloon. Clementine Manley, Mrs. Bucknell, and Amanda were seated on chairs. Amanda had named the black. It had to be her.

Clementine stood, placed her hands on the balcony railing, and stared down at the scene. Thackery returned his gaze to the street.

Three lines of red cut Absalom's cheek below his left eye. The rump of the black also bled from three lines as if the hide had been sliced by claws.

Mr. Bucknell approached the dirty white. It shied back from him. He spoke to it. Roan's ears stood up straight at the voice. The white quieted. Bucknell lunged and grabbed the front of One's shirt and pulled him off the horse and threw him onto his back on the dirt. He stepped on the man's wrist and jerked the quirt, snapping the strap. One coughed, and then he started to push himself up. A pistol hammer clicked into cocked.

The young man who'd escorted One back to the finish pointed his pistol at One's head. "I'd lie still."

Bucknell looked up at the balcony. "I request a magisterial hearing."

Clementine Manley's sun-bonneted silhouette grew a couple of inches. Thackery blinked his eyes. "The magistrate will hear Mr. Bucknell." Her voice rang clear and strong.

A hush settled over Kingdom Come, like in the forest, when a man makes a noise that bugs and birds find worrisome.

"This man's quirt has barbs of iron tied to the strips of leather." Bucknell pointed to a bloody patch of the white's rear haunch. "Much more of this and the horse would have to be put down." Thackery saw Bucknell study the white's mouth. Bloody drool dripped from it to the ground. He didn't say anything about that, though. He pointed to the black in front of the Hardware Store. "Plus he struck Absalom and my horse and drew blood from both."

"He strike you?" Clementine inquired of Absalom.

"He whipped Romeo, ma'am. And me."

"Are you all right, Mr. Absalom?" "Mister! You call a goddamned—"

The young man with the pistol jammed the barrel against One's forehead.

"Are you all right, Mr. Absalom?"

"Yes, ma'am. A dab a horse liniment, we bote be good."

"You there, Number One. Do you have anything to say for yourself?"

"I ain't explaining nothing to no damned woman!"

"Very well." Clementine looked down on the prostrate man. "Your horse is forfeited to the township of Kingdom Come."

One howled, swatted the pistol aside, and lunged to his feet. Bucknell hit him with a looping uppercut. One's head snapped back, and he flopped onto the dirt again.

"Zeke Manley."

"Yes, ma'am."

"Administer ten lashes to the man with his own whip."

Zeke called for a Solomon and a Lawrence to help him. The two were thick-chested six footers. They tied a rope to One's right wrist and lashed the other end of it to a post supporting the saloon's balcony. They tied another rope around his other hand, and the two of them pulled it taut.

One was held facing the saloon. He kept swinging his head, frantically searching for Zeke behind him. Suddenly he went still, staring at someone on the saloon porch.

"Sheriff. Sheriff Wilson. You ain't gonna let them whip me."

"Mister, I think more lowly of you than I do of a chicken- killing skunk. And Kingdom Come. Why, it's the only town in my jurisdiction where I never get no trouble to deal with. Zeke, I think you should do what the magistrate ordered."

The sheriff's big black mustache couldn't hide all his smile.

Zeke raised the quirt. One went still, grimaced, and closed his eyes.

Zeke brought it down and tapped One's shoulder with the handle.

There were some giggles from the spectators on the saloon porch.

Thackery heard, "Peed his pants," "Wet himself."

Zeke administered seven more taps. Thackery couldn't see One's face. He imagined it, though. One was going to escape with nothing worse than pissed pants. If he could see the man's face, that would be written all over it.

Then Zeke laid the whip across One's back. The "1" tag tore free. A strip was torn from his shirt to expose bloody flesh. One screamed like a demon who just poked his head out of hell. Zeke struck again writing a red *X* where the "1" had been.

One coughed, choking on his scream, and moaned.

The silence that had been there before returned.

For a moment, Clementine leaned on the railing and stared at the dirt street. Then she stood up straight. "Solomon, David. Get your horses. Take his boots away from him. Then walk him or drag him a half hour south into the woods. Let him go there."

"Yes, ma'am." Duet. A high-end baritone and a low-end tenor.

"Zeke."

"Yes, ma'am?" "The race."

Zeke looked down at the bloody straps of the quirt. He walked to the side of the street, flung the whip back along the side of his store, and mounted the two steps to the boardwalk.

Zeke looked up at Clementine. Then he hollered, "Short Race! Second heat! Riders, take your positions!"

Thackery didn't want to race. He'd never wanted to. The Bucknell girl had maneuvered him into it. He had to wait for Quantrill. What the hell. He'd race. But now ... the hell with his obligation to Josh Ewing. The hell with Quantrill. The hell with the goddamned money.

"Roan," he muttered, "let's just turn around, head east, ride the hell away from here."

Short-race One cut across the street.

Bucknell backed away from under the center of the start banner unstringing a ribbon.

Thackery tugged the left rein, but Roan shook his head and followed the black with one white stocking on its rear leg.

"Good luck."

He looked up. Amanda Bucknell had her hands on the balcony rail and a beatific smile on her face. A sip of cold blood pumped through his heart. Her smile was for his horse.

Roan seemed to know what to do better than Thackery did. He stopped next to the black, and just like it, his nose was above the ribbon stretched across the course.

Thackery noticed something stuck in the middle of one of the gray splotches dotting Roan's neck. He plucked it off with a thumb and forefinger.

"Riders, get ready," Zeke warned from his boardwalk post.

Thackery studied his fingers. Bloody horsemeat. Or human flesh. He wiped the sticky stuff on edge of the blanket under the saddle.

A pistol fired.

Roan shot forward. Thackery barely grabbed the front of the racing saddle to keep from going over backward. He righted himself. Roan was in front. Thackery looked over his left shoulder and then the right. The closest was a length behind.

The turn post was coming up fast. Thackery tugged on the reins. "Roan." The horse planted his forelegs, and Thackery flew against Roan's neck. The horse tossed his head back, setting him in the saddle again. Thackery hauled on the left rein and the horse turned. The post brushed Thackery's leg.

Roan faced the finish. Another rider, crowded off the course by the other three, was right in front of them, as if it wanted to make the turn in the wrong direction. Roan faltered. Thackery dug his heels into Roan's belly and, with the reins, guided him just to the left of the oncoming animal. Roan shot ahead. The off-track horse dug in his forelegs. The rider flew over the horse's head and past Thackery. Thackery was sure he would smash his leg against the shoulder of the horse.

Busted leg. Like Josh's.

But the animal leaped to the side. Roan flew past and flew over the course. The finish flew over them.

It took the length of Main Street to coast to a walk. "Oh, Jesus, Roan. Oh, sweet Jesus!"

He turned in through the gate into the pasture at the east end of town, hopped down, and checked Roan's forelegs.

"You all right, Roan? Didn't bust anything?"

Roan started walking to the far end of the pasture. "Where you going? Back to the Stable Tent? Oh. I know.

You want a carrot. All right. I'll walk with you. Maybe by the time we get there, I can figure out what I want to do: laugh or cry. I gotta figure it because, sure as shooting, I have to do one or the other."

AS ROAN WALKED down Temple Street, headed for the stable tent, his head bobbed up and down. Thackery walked beside him. Periodically, he wagged his head side to side.

They passed the gleaming, pure-white temple.

"I haven't been to church two weeks in a row, Roan. My friend Weekes Daley believed it was important for a man to get out of the world and into a church for an hour once a week. For an hour, sit there and soak in the notion his pew-mates loved him as much as they loved themselves."

Thackery smiled. "The challenge, Weekes said, was to love them back just like that."

One head bobbed. The other wagged.

"When Weekes was alive, we stayed clear of the war. Oh, we came close to it a time or two, but Weekes always knew how steer us around it. Now, the damned war is all around. Every time I turn around, another part of it grabs hold of me."

He looked up, squinted at the midday sun, and wished he had his hat between it and his head.

"That Lieutenant Miller, Roan. I don't know what you thought of him, but I couldn't keep my mind made up. I disliked him. Then I'd see a side of him he brought out from hiding and I'd admire him. I always thought I could read a man. And, of course, Josh Ewing. I never did anything but admire him. We differed on the war and bushwhacking, but there was never any question about the kind of man he was—hell, still is. Quantrill too. Miller and Josh both admired … admire the hell out of him. And I did too, after talking with him. But I don't understand how that thing inside him that I admire, or admired, countenances bushwhacking.

"And those damned Jayhawkers. They just rode into Independence. One of them hated Josh and started shooting. Then they all started shooting. Never mind Josh was in the middle of a crowd. They killed a woman. Could have been a lot worse. Thank you, God, they couldn't shoot worth a damn.

"Sometimes I wonder, Roan, if in the core of a man's soul is a demon itching to get back to hell, but that demon is covered over by the good a maw and paw cover it over with. As he grows up, all kinds of things in the world try to help that demon come out. And it sure as shooting doesn't take a war. But a war, a big one, cuts loose herds of devils."

Thackery kicked the dirt in the street, and said, "Shit," then, "Whoa." Roan did. Thackery looked back at the temple.

In a pew in that house of worship, the worshipers would never love Emerson Sharp as they loved themselves. Emerson Sharp killed a woman and a girl.

So he was no longer Emerson Sharp.

He pictured Tom Thackery in a crowded pew inside. His mind knew how to paint a picture of men and boys in Sunday clothes and women and girls in their best dresses loving him as they loved themselves. His mind knew, but it would not paint the scene.

"I used to say things to Weekes like I just did to you, Roan. He'd listen. Then he'd ask if I was done. I'd nod. Then he'd start off with, 'Young Emerson.' Always it was 'Young Emerson.' And then he'd reel off a handful of words. It would be like the clouds parted in an overcast so thick it was darned near dark as night, and it suddenly became so bright it made my eyes squint. It was so simple after he explained it."

Thackery patted the horse on the shoulder just forward of the hankie saddle. Roan started walking again.

"Weekes told me once that I was a good man. I told him I didn't feel like one. 'Precisely,' he said. I had to think on that one a while."

He shook his head. "I wonder if Weekes would tell me I'm a good man if he knew I killed a woman and a girl."

From Main Street, the crowd roared. The last heat of the Long Race just started.

"Roan, this is what we're going to do. We're going to gather our gear and get the hell out of Kingdom Come. I'll just leave that damned money where I hid it. We're going to Independence. We'll have to sneak into town like a bushwhacker, but I want to see Nora. I have to see her. Maybe it'll be to tell her that goodbye I said I could never say to her. I don't know. I won't know until I can see her."

Thackery felt as if the weight of the world had just lifted off him.

They skirted the edge of Tent City and entered under the rolled-up sides of the Stable Tent. He stripped off the racing saddle, took a rag from the hostler's toolbox, and began to wipe the lather from the horse.

"You rode a hell of a race, Mr. Thackery." He spun around. Quantrill.

"Fred Green," Quantrill said.

The last time Thackery had seen him, he'd worn a black mustache. Quantrill was clean-shaven now. His hair was short too. He looked behind him. No one was near.

"Clever, Mr. Thackery. Hiding in plain sight."

Thackery frowned. He dug, looking for a new plan in the rubble of his old one. "Uh, Cap—"

"Fred. Fred Green."

"Okay, Mr. Green. Let me get my gear. I'll give you what you're looking for, and then we go our separate ways."

"We cannot do that. Sheriff Wilson is here. He's looking for me, and he knows me, and he's looking for a fellow named Emerson Sharp. If you don't run in the final, he will come looking for you. If you want to remain Tom Thackery, you have to run in the race."

"Shit!"

"Mr. Thackery, Josh Ewing explained your conviction to not ride with us anymore. Have you had a change of heart? I would be pleased to have you with us again."

"I have not had a change of heart. I owe Josh Ewing, and I promised Lieutenant Miller. That's why I'm here. All I want is to give you … your property and then get on about my own business."

Quantrill raised a finger to smooth his mustache, which no longer resided on his lip. He looked at his finger as if he were disappointed in it and then raised his cool blue eyes. "I think the postrace festivities will tie you up the rest of today. Can you pick a place to rendezvous tomorrow morning?"

"Yes, sir. Five miles east of town. A treed-over ridge just before you come to a stream with a wooden bridge. You can wait in the woods this side of the creek. I'll be there at five."

Quantrill stuck his hand out. They clasped hands and then both turned at the sound of running feet. Quantrill pulled his hand free and put it on the butt of his sidearm.

Amanda Bucknell ran through the tent, her petticoats rustling. Her face shone as she stopped next to Roan, put her arm up over his neck, and embraced him.

"He's lathered up some, Miss Bucknell."

She stepped back, still beaming at the horse. "Oh, Roan. You were magnificent! I saw you with Father's spyglass as you rounded the pole and that other horse was bearing down on you. You didn't even flinch. You just charged straight ahead. You were magnificent!"

She looked down and pulled her moist blouse loose from her skin, not a hint of embarrassment in her action or on her face.

Thackery looked away and glanced at Quantrill. He didn't want Quantrill to be watching Amanda arranging her clothing. But Quantrill was smiling at him. Thackery blushed.

"I'm Amanda Bucknell."

Her bright, intelligent, dark eyes scanned Quantrill down and back up again.

"Fred Green, Miss Bucknell."

He doffed his hat and dipped his head, and she bobbed a hint of a curtsy. Then she stared at Quantrill for a moment. Thackery frowned.

"I'm going back to the race, Mr. Green. My brother Bobby is racing in the next heat of the Short Race."

She hiked up her skirts and ran toward Main Street. An irritation itched at Thackery. She hadn't looked at him once.

"You have an admirer."

"Me? She admired you. And your ruffled shirt. She admired my horse."

Quantrill chuckled. "Good luck on your race, Mr. Thackery."

A man waited with two horses next to the fence around the pasture behind the Stable Tent. Quantrill started walking toward him.

*****

In the final of the Short Race, Thackery drew number three, which would have been bad luck. Number One started on the left, with the inside track to the turn pole. Thackery, however, viewed it as good luck. It gave him an excuse to lose. After losing, he could slip out of town without creating interest or suspicion.

Spectators jammed the boardwalks along Main Street as the three riders walked their mounts toward the start. Thackery heard his name shouted.

Bobby Bucknell, number two and aboard a white-faced, white-stockinged sorrel and next to Thackery, said, "Lot of money on you, Mr. Thackery."

"On me?"

"Sure. My brother Ben won the Long Race. Bucknell's Negro, that's what they"—Bobby nodded his bare head at the boardwalk to his left—"call our employee Absalom. Anyway, he won the Middle Race. This is the first time my father let me ride. People think they are finally going to see a Bucknell get beat in a race. After Absalom won a race, they sure don't want to see Ottawa Joe win."

The number-one rider was the Indian Thackery had seen earlier. He was bareback on his pinto.

"Look at the faces, Mr. Thackery. Even the women are excited. I imagine a Christian seeing those faces in the Coliseum crowd. Imagine what the crowd would have done to a Christian who killed a lion."

Thackery glanced at the crowd to his right and then to his left, past

Bobby grinning at him, and past the Indian, riding stiff-backed and staring straight ahead, to the men's, women's, and children's faces alight with anticipation. It wasn't a stretch to embrace Bobby's metaphor.

"There's my sister." Bobby pointed at the balcony of the saloon.

Amanda stood at the railing and waved.

"Aren't you going to wave back?"

"She isn't waving at me, Mr. Thackery."

"Shit."

As they approached the tape strung across the street under the start banner, Bobby's sorrel shied and tried to turn away, bumping his butt into Roan. Roan sidestepped. As Bobby turned his horse around and again approached the line, he spoke to the sorrel. This time, the sorrel, though still nervous, stood in place. Thackery moved Roan into position.

The crowd hushed.

"Ready!" Zeke Manley hollered.

Roan stood still. As Thackery leaned forward, he felt the horse shiver.

The pistol banged, and Roan shot away from the line.

With each stride, Roan gained lead on the sorrel and the pinto. Halfway to the pole, Roan was a length ahead of the other two running side by side.

As the turn pole bore down on them, Thackery glanced behind. A length-and-a-half lead. Thackery tugged on the reins. Roan planted his forelegs, hopped once, and Thackery hauled left on the reins, cutting in front of the two. The pinto rounded the pole with his nose almost touching Roan's tail.

Rounding the pole, Roan bounded for the finish. A few strides later, the pinto's nose evened with Roan's haunch on the left. The sorrel was a nose behind the pinto to Thackery's right. "Run, you son of a bitch!" Race bloodlust infected even a kid like Bobby.

The Indian cut loose with an ululating cry that prickled the hair on Thackery's neck. The pinto's nose inched ahead of Thackery's knee. The sorrel stayed with the pinto, gaining with each stride. The finish was bearing down.

The race, Thackery thought, was between the other two. He hadn't cared before. But he cared now. He growled, "Roan." Thackery could feel it. Roan had saved a little. He dug it out.

The other two were unable to gain. Then Roan inched ahead more. Thackery felt the other two horses concede before Roan flew under the banner, with the pinto half a length behind. Bobby was perhaps a nose behind the pinto.

*****

As Thackery started slowing Roan, the crowd on the boardwalks started spilling into the street. He pulled on the reins, and the three racers wound up surrounded by a sea of upturned happy faces. Thackery was pulled from the saddle, hoisted onto the shoulders of two men, and carried to the Bar and Betting Tent. His feet were placed upon the trampled grass next to the bar and hands grabbed his arm and thrust drinks at him and slapped his back.

Elation-gilded voices surmounted the general excited clamor. "Best damn race I ever see'd." "Best damn horse race Kingdom Come ever run."

A drink was shoved into his right hand. A beaming man holding a six-year-old boy in his arm took the drink from him and asked, "Mr. Thackery, will you shake hands with my son?"

Thackery wiped spilled whiskey onto his trousers and extended the hand.

As the father threaded his way out of the press of bodies, he kept repeating, "My Petey shook Tom Thackery's hand." The boy, though, Thackery could see was bewildered and frightened, and his eyes searched frantically, for his mother probably.

The crowd of men around him stirred up dust. The dust woke Thackery's smeller to horse sweat, man sweat, and whiskey aromas. To that point, Thackery hadn't tasted a drop of whiskey. He picked up a half-spilled glass from the bar and drained it.

"Mr. Thackery!"

He found Bobby Bucknell at the rear of the half circle of well-wishers trying to get his attention.

"Boys," Bobby said, "Mr. Thackery is needed at the Stable Tent. It's time to present the winners' pots."

The crowd parted for him.

Bobby greeted him with a big grin and an outstretched hand. Thackery took it, and Bobby gave it a pump. "Congratulations. A heck of a race!"

"Thanks. A shame we couldn't all win. Three fine horses ran in that final."

"I don't feel like I lost anything, Mr. Thackery. It was … I don't even know how to say what it was like."

They started walking.

"I'll tell you how I feel. When I was little, brother Ben had me by the hands and was swinging me in a circle. My hands slipped out of his and I went flying. Right before I hit the dirt, I was thinking, *This is so much fun!* The difference between then and now is the dirt isn't rising to smack me.

"Ah, Mr. Thackery. You're a hero to the people hereabouts. They came to see something exciting. I didn't see you run your heat, but people are talking about when you rounded the turn pole and there was Ollie Winchel, completely off the course and about to plow right into you. You didn't even hesitate. Half the people here are talking about that heat. The other half are talking about the final of the Short Race. Over there." Bobby pointed.

Ben Bucknell stood beside the black he'd ridden. Absalom was beside his mount, a white-faced black. Amanda Bucknell held the reins to Roan.

"Father wanted another of our employees to take care of your horse. My sister, though, well, she's headstrong. Too headstrong, my stepmother says."

Then Thackery saw the camera positioned to photograph the three race winners.

Mr. Bucknell grabbed Thackery's arm, dismissed his son, and led the way toward the horses.

"Think about it, Mr. Thackery," Bucknell whispered. "You're

worried about a picture being taken of you. But think about it. It will be a picture of you as Tom Thackery."

Thackery frowned. Maybe a photograph would be a good thing. But that thought had no power to diminish the sense hard-packed dirt was rushing up at him.

"Will you visit tomorrow?"

"At your place?"

"Yes."

Thackery nodded.

Amanda handed the reins to him. "I told you Roan wanted to race."

Then she sauntered off to where her mother stood wearing her own dark frown.

Ben didn't look at him.

Absalom smiled. "Fine race you run, Mistuh Thackry." "You too, Mr. Absalom."

Thackery took a breath, let it out, and faced the cameraman, who ducked under the drape.

33

T HE DAY BEFORE, after he won the race, everybody loved Tom
Thackery. This morning, everybody he met wanted to shoot him.
Well, Quantrill didn't, but the fellow with him did.

A few yards off the road and in the trees, the dusky light of dawn
carved two statues of black. One was of a man standing beside a horse
with the hatted head of the man showing above the saddle. The other
was mounted. "Captain?"

"Mr. Thackery." Quantrill. "I told you he'd come."

Thackery couldn't see the astride man's face. The man didn't say
anything. Still, Thackery sensed hostility radiating off him. Odds were
Quantrill's companion wouldn't shoot him until he had the money.
Thackery didn't worry about the captain. Quantrill had a reputation
for respecting bravery, for offering paroles to those he captured if they'd
behaved honorably.

Thackery had Roan and Chestnut with him, and he tied the reins
to saplings. "I'll get it."

"I'll go with him."

"Stay here." Quantrill's voice said it didn't want to hear an argument.

"You trust him?"

"I trust him."

"You trusted Elmer too."

A pistol hammer clicked.

"Give me a reason to not shoot you."

"Cap'n, I, uh—"

"A reason, quick."

"I've rid with you. I've covered your back."

"A reason." Quantrill's voice conveyed, *You best get it right this time!*

"It won't happen again, Cap'n."

The drama had played out in darkness, but Thackery had seen it clearly. It was not a good idea to question Captain Quantrill's authority.

It was time for Tom Thackery to get the captain his money.

He checked the road and then crossed it, climbed the ridge, retrieved the saddlebags, and retraced his steps. He handed the bags to the captain.

"Would you like compensation for your troubles, Mr. Thackery?"

"Lieutenant Miller gave me some money. I'm going to give it to Josh Ewing. He also gave me money for his wife. I'll get it to her. You have a purpose for that money. I don't."

"Luck, Mr. Thackery."

"Luck to you, Captain."

They walked their horses out of the trees and headed east. Thackery followed them and watched them canter away and rumble across the wooden bridge. He trusted Quantrill, but he also knew how important the money was to him. And Elmer had betrayed the captain.

Trust was something he never thought about before he met Weekes Daley. From him he learned to trust Weekes but no one else. He met Josh Ewing and trusted him. Still did, even though they disagreed about the war and guerilla fighting. Trust, he concluded, was pretty thin soup in the midst of the hatreds of Jayhawkers for guerillas, of Southern sympathizers for Kansans and federals. The strongest glue cementing the opposing forces together was revenge for injustices each side had perpetrated on the other. Trust didn't weigh much compared to revenge.

He waited in the woods until the sun was above the trees and above the sash of haze girdling the world atop the forest. Then he mounted Chestnut and went to meet Mr. Bucknell.

*****

Bucknell sat at one end of the breakfast table. After a colored woman, Amanda, and Mrs. Bucknell served plates of food to the men, Mrs. Bucknell sat at the other end. Ben—Benjamin III, Thackery figured—and William sat across from each other and next to their stepmother. Bobby wasn't there. Thackery sat at Mr. Bucknell's right. His host rose and seated the colored woman to his left. Thackery was surprised, and as Bucknell took his seat again, a smile curled up the corners of Bucknell's lips. Thackery had allowed his surprise to show. Bucknell noticed and enjoyed his guest's discomfit. Then he introduced the woman as Clarice, Absalom's wife.

Clarice looked him in the eye, jolting Thackery anew. He'd never seen a colored woman look a white man in the eye. He glanced left. Bucknell's smile had broadened.

"Um, ma'am, I'm pleased to make your acquaintance. I saw your husband win his heat yesterday. An admirable performance."

A softness suffused her countenance. "Thank you, and I'm pleased to meet you too, Mr. Thackery."

"Amanda," Bucknell said. "Say grace, please."

Thackery bowed his head. She said familiar words of thanks for blessings and nourishment, and a warmth and contentment seeped into his core. It was a feeling he hadn't experienced in a very long time.

"Amen."

Thackery looked up. He nodded at Bucknell and smiled at Clarice. Amanda's eyes were still cast down. Then he saw black- haired Mrs. Bucknell and her blond stepsons. Not one of them wanted him at their table, in their house, or on their property, or anywhere near Kingdom Come. Ben wanted to shoot him.

Thackery stood up. "I apologize, Mrs. Bucknell. I brought animosity and discontent to your table."

"Sit down, Mr. Thackery, please?" Bucknell said. "Let the woman-killer go," Ben III said.

"Ben," his father directed. "Take your plate and eat in the kitchen. Now."

"Mr. Bucknell, I very much appreciate your kind invitation, but if your wife does not want me here, I cannot stay."

For a moment, glances as charged as lightning bolts flickered back and forth, from one end of the table to the other.

Mrs. Bucknell raised her eyes. The part of her face below her nose smiled. "Please. Eat with us, Mr. Thackery."

"Thank you, ma'am." He faced the colored woman. "Is it all right with you too, ma'am?"

Her smile was small, but genuine. "Of course, Mr. Thackery."

He sat, and Bucknell sliced through an egg, and the yolk flooded into the fried potatoes. Knives and forks clinked. Thackery hadn't eaten the night before. He picked up his utensils, and they joined the symphonic tribute to the cook. Everyone ate. No one spoke. Amanda still hadn't looked at him. She moved slices of potato around on her plate. Clarice didn't seem bothered by the anger boiling off William and Mrs. Bucknell at the far end of the table. Neither did Mr. Bucknell. He ate at a leisurely pace, showing appreciation for a fine meal.

"Why didn't you turn me in to the sheriff, Mr. Bucknell?"

Mrs. Bucknell answered, "I would have."

William echoed the sentiment with conviction.

Mr. Bucknell placed his silverware on his plate and asked William to get the coffee.

"Do you ride with Quantrill?" Mrs. Bucknell asked.

Her black eyes shot fierce condemnation at him. He didn't look away from them. "I rode with him." He was going to say *once*, but that wasn't right. "I rode with him, but I don't anymore." Amanda looked up and at Thackery. Her face was a mask.

A disappointment mask.

"Quantrill was there last night." There was accusation in Mrs. Bucknell's statement.

"Yes. I saw him too, ma'am."

"And you say you don't ride with him!"

"Celia!"

Her father's bark startled Amanda, and William jerked as he poured coffee for Clarice, spilling some on the table.

Celia rose and mopped up the spill with her napkin. William finished serving the coffee and sat.

"Why didn't you turn me in, Mr. Bucknell?"

Bucknell's blue eyes twinkled. "I have no part in this war. As to men, and women, I make my own mind up about them."

Thackery nodded.

"Then I have a question for you. Will you sell your horse to me? Roan, you call him?"

"I hadn't thought about it."

"Ask Roan." Amanda's fiery independence had returned. "Ask a dumb animal?" William scoffed.

Celia glared at her daughter.

Thackery noticed Clarice. She cared for both the mother and the daughter. The two of them were fighting over something. Clarice wished they'd get the fight settled. He looked at Mr. Bucknell and wondered if the father played a part in that fight.

Amanda came around the table. "What do you say, Mr. Thackery? Shall we go ask him? Will you come too, Father?" She took Thackery's arm and guided him to the front porch. Bobby stood at the foot of the steps. He held the reins to two horses. One was Horse, the animal he'd traded to Bucknell in the deal for Iago. The other was a big black.

"I'm betting you changed his name. What do you call him?" Thackery asked.

"Why, Horse, of course." Amanda smiled sweetly. "It's bad luck to change a horse's name."

That was like a slap in the face. An image of the beautiful animal that had taken him flying over the earth and then got left for vultures to fly down out of the sky—

Mr. Bucknell brought the session back to business. "The black there comes from the same stallion and mare as produced Iago."

"You raise magnificent animals, Mr. Bucknell."

"Well, are you going to ask Roan?"

"Miss Amanda, you ask him."

An hour later, Thackery was cinching his saddle to the black. His name was David. Bucknell was beside him. The three brothers stood side by side on the porch. Amanda sat on the top porch step.

"Mr. Thackery," Bucknell said in a soft voice with his back to his house, "I'm going to ask something of you. Please do not come back here again."

There was no pleading on Bucknell's face, not much real *please*, either.

"It was an honor to meet you, sir. I will do my best to cause you no more trouble. Okay if I say goodbye to Bobby?"

Bobby and Amanda walked down the steps to meet him. He and Bobby shook. He kissed Amanda's hand. She curtsied. He returned to the black, mounted, and tipped his hat to Mr. Bucknell. On the other side of the spring-loaded gate, he said, "David. David. It's a fine name. Doesn't roll off the tongue like Horse or Roan, but don't worry. I'm not going to change it on you. It's bad luck to do that."

*****

Two nights later, after traveling only in darkness, Thackery entered Independence from the south, paralleled Main Street to Station Street. He dismounted in the shadow of the gunsmith shop.

Across Station Street, a few scattered windows in the four- story structure glowed with lamplight. Otherwise, the Royal Arms Hotel looked across Main Street with regal indifference to the Last Chance Saloon.

The saloon spilled a hundred male voices, all insisting that they be heard first, and piano tinkles occasionally surmounting the clamor into the night. A glass shattered. A man came flying out through the batwing doors and lay sprawled facedown in the street. Light from inside the saloon backlit two men who stepped through the batwings.

"He ain't movin'. You think he's okay?"

"Hell if I know. Check on 'im in a bit, if you want."

"We can't leave him there. He'll git runned over by a wagon."

"Shit," the second fellow said, but he stepped down into the street and grabbed the unconscious fellow by an arm. Then the two men dragged the other around the side of the saloon, dropped him there, and went back inside.

Thackery peeked around the front of the gunsmith shop and saw no one on the boardwalk on his side of the street. He stepped out and peered in through the half-glassed front. Nora stood behind the counter. Josh was behind the counter too. Part of his crutch stuck out from under his arm. She was looking at Josh. Josh was looking at her.

Thackery turned away. He returned to his horse. "Shit, David. It was sure stupid changing my mind about saying goodbye to her."

He considered riding away down the middle of Main Street, not giving a good goddamn if anyone recognized him or not, but he remembered what had happened to Iago-renamed-Horse. Pushing his own luck was one thing. Pushing David's luck was another. Thackery stood in the shadow next to … Josh Ewing's shop. "Shit," he said again.

Stars filled the sky overhead. The Last Chance continued to blare whiskey-fed exuberance. The evening was warm. A pleasant, honest-labor aroma arose from David. Thackery took a deep breath and let it out, and he waited for rational thinking to find a way into his head. David nudged his shoulder with his nose.

"All right, partner," Thackery said. "We have a plan. I told Quantrill I'd give the money Miller gave me to Josh."

He led David to the rear of the shop and left him at the corner. Thackery used his key and inched open the back door.

Nora said, "Are you sure you can handle walking down the aisle tomorrow? You can use the wheelchair. Or we can even wait a few days for you get more used to the crutch."

Josh said, "Nobody's pushing me in that chair. I'll walk. Tomorrow. Heck. I'll walk to the moon and back if I have to."

Something soft and tender and nice smoothed their voices, and each one of those things was a strand of barbwire whipping his heart.

He tossed the money and his key onto floor, slammed the door, and swung up onto David, and the black galloped away and swung left at the first cross street. Thackery slowed them to a trot. They'd leave town the way they came.

"They're getting married tomorrow, David. Tomorrow. Mrs. Rosie was going to make Nora and me wait months. What the hell?"

As they left town, they encountered a few riders in pairs. Thackery kept his head straight ahead. The riders, though, all turned to watch him.

When the last one was clear, Thackery said, "For a moment, I was hoping one of those guys would do something to give me an excuse to shoot him. Wanting to shoot a man for no damned reason. Hell of a way for a man to feel, David."

They passed a field, and he caught the scent of alfalfa. "Farmer scythed that field today, David."

They picked up the road running to Sedalia and on to Kingdom Come and from there to Jefferson City.

"David. It's getting so I like to say your name. A king's name. Makes me feel like plain old Tom Thackery has moved up in the world.

"David," he said, and the big black tore off down the road like he was racing Bucknell's freeman Absalom in the Middle Race. When Thackery figured they'd run about as far as the turn pole, he slowed them.

"We're leaving the big road here, David. It leads to Kingdom Come. I don't want to go through there. We need to go to Saint Louis. I have money in a bank there, but I have to put my new name on it. Then we'll spend a couple of days there while we figure out what we're going to do next."

A lesser road cut off to the left. They took it.

"You know, David. I think I like the night better than I do the daytime. That just made me think of something my paw said once. He thought God should have made days longer and nights shorter. One of these days, or nights, I'll tell you about Maw and Paw and the Barlows. And the Simmonses. Huh. Old Man Simmons, he wanted to go to California."

Weekes, too, had wanted to go to California. Thackery hadn't wanted to before, and his search for his own Dutzow's Corner in Independence hadn't worked out. He thought of Zeke Manley and his mother. They'd sure made their place in Kingdom Come. Just then, nowhere in Missouri seemed to hold a promise of a place for him. There was nothing for him east of the Mississippi.

"David, maybe we need to rethink California?"

34

T HEY CAME TO the Missouri River with the sun just up. A farm wagon, the load covered with a tarpaulin, waited atop the bank sloping down to where a ferry would touch the shore. Thackery stopped David behind the box-bed rig. The driver, a kid, maybe sixteen and wearing a ratty straw hat close in color to his dirty blond hair, glanced around, studied him briefly, and looked away.

A ferry was midstream, carrying another wagon, with the ferryman hauling on the shore-to-shore rope, inching the raft across, slowly but steadily. Across the river, the terrain was higher. From this side, Thackery had a good view of the layout of a three-street town.

Thackery sniffed at the musty, musky, swampy river perfume. The smell was half decay and half the aftermath of the act of procreation, he thought. He'd been thinking of a saloon girl. It seemed like it had been a long time since he'd been with one. A short time ago, he thought he'd never visit one again.

A hawk *screeee* sliced a hole in the peaceful morning. The kid on the wagon glanced at Thackery again. The morning wasn't peaceful for him.

How did I get to be a fellow that scares people?

He would have asked David, but the farm boy was spooked enough without him talking to his horse.

When he got to Saint Louis, he'd have to do business in daylight. That little town across the way. It was far enough away from Independence and the people looking for the fellow he used to be. He'd stay a couple of days and get himself adjusted to the other twelve hours.

*****

Two days later, Thackery stopped David and looked back at the town. The general store, saloon, barber, restaurant, livery stable, and blacksmith all sat on the uphill side of River Street facing the Missouri as if those establishments had to watch carefully so that business unloading from the ferry or debarking from a riverboat could be captured before it got away up the slope and on the road heading east. The other two streets housed dwellings, gardens, outbuildings, and small pastures for a horse or two, a cow or two. A goat.

The ferry was at midriver, carrying four horses with riders beside them, heading for Center City.

Center City. "Smack-dab in the middle a the state a Missourah," the locals liked to say. "Take a small map of the state, put a fat thumb over the middle of it, and under that thumb is Center City. Smack-dab in the middle. Jist like I said." Then the locals laughed like hell while the visiting drummers and gamblers who'd gotten off a riverboat to skin these locals frowned. Occasionally, an avaricious gleam would light the eyes of a gambler at the prospect of easy pickings. Thackery had replenished his stake at their expense. He'd gotten to the point where he would have to use the money he had for Lieutenant Miller's widow, which he would have replenished in Saint Louis, but he preferred to put the actual bills Miller had placed in his hands into the hands of Miller's wife. He was pleased that, now, leaving Center City, he would be able to do so.

Thackery nudged David with a knee, and the horse faced the risen sun and kicked into a canter.

David was a pleasant ride. He had that thought every time he climbed onto the saddle. Of course, he'd only had the horse a handful of days, but his butt and spine were pleased to be shut of Roan.

It brought to mind Horse and Iago/Horse. Both of them had gaits naturally suited to him. He thought about Weekes Daley and Josh Ewing. He respected and admired both men.

Weekes, he thought, had not been a friend. He was more like a father. Or half of one. Paw, in retrospect, had been half a father. Weekes had been the other half. A half he'd been looking for but unaware he was doing so.

Josh Ewing had been a friend. "Still is, I guess," he mumbled. Their friendship ran up against the war, and it divided them. Then, Josh had taken a bullet, saving Thackery from it. In return, he'd given Josh a new life and a wife to go with it. As if Nora had ever been his to give. As if friendships rested on something like the balance sheet Rottermich kept in the gunsmith shop.

Horse and Iago/Horse never argued or disagreed with him, and they'd seemed, to him, to be content and even happy to carry him around. Maybe they were better friends than Josh. Did always agreeing and never arguing define friendship? He'd never thought about it before. He'd never had occasion to. Never really had a friend before.

Then there was Roan. He seemed to want to punish Thackery for having to carry a man around, and he was feisty. Especially after he first had him. The damned animal nipped at him on more than one occasion. But Roan had heart and he had bottom. Like that little firebrand Bucknell girl. Although, at the breakfast table, something had tamed the wildness in her. Mostly. Thackery smiled, remembering the return of her spunk at the end of the meal.

But Bucknell told him to not come back. He had every intention of doing what the man said.

"This is what we're going to do, David. We're going to Saint Louis and take care of our business there. Then we'll go to Joplin and deliver the lieutenant's things to his missus. Then we'll skirt the Indian Territory and head down to Texas and figure out how to get to California from there."

Hell of a thing, Tom Thackery, a man of your age, and your best friends have all been horses.

He thought about telling David. Some things, though, a man didn't say, even to a best friend.

He leaned forward and patted the horse's neck, and David burst into a run. David ran hard. Thackery knew, though, he had something left. Thackery knew David was digging it out. Thackery knew David was going to take him flying.

Then just before it happened, David backed off. Inside Thackery, where elation had been all set to bloom, disappointment did.

Then Thackery saw it. He was hunched low. "David," he said, and the animal coasted down to a trot. Up ahead, on the side of the road, a catawampus wagon sat with a rear wheel missing and a pants-wearing woman standing next to it.

David stopped behind the wagon. The woman wore a holster gun, cross-draw fashion. Pocket Colt, he thought. She had watched him intently as he approached. Now he noticed her eyes. His heart skipped a beat, or maybe kicked in an extra one. She had Nora's green eyes.

The way she stared at him, she wasn't afraid. Neither did she expect specifically good or specifically bad from him. Whichever he delivered, she would handle. *Without raising a sweat.*

"Tom Thackery, miss."

"Missus."

"Yes, ma'am. Okay if I step down and help?" Asking for permission to help seemed like the best thing.

"You looked like you were in an all-fired hurry to get someplace."

"No real hurry, ma'am. David and me, we just felt like running."

It was as if sunshine found a hole in the clouds and lit her face.

She approached David and held her hand out to him. He nuzzled it with his nose. Then she looked at Thackery. He expected her to wipe the horse snot off on her pants. She didn't, though.

"Step down, Mr. Thackery."

He did. "Do you have the axle nut, ma'am?"

She opened her left hand, exposing the nut resting on her black-greased palm. She placed the nut on the bed of the wagon.

"How about if you get the wheel, ma'am. I'll see if I can lift the wagon bed. If I can lift it, I won't be able to hold it long. Or you can lift and I'll get the wheel back on."

"The first way you said it." She picked up the wheel from where it lay next to her team, half on the grassy shoulder and half over the roadbed, which was scoured clean of grass. She rolled it to the rear.

He took off his coat and draped it over the saddle. Then he backed up to the sagging corner of the wagon bed, bent his knees, gripped the bed, and strained. It didn't budge. He walked in a tight circle, shaking his arms and breathing deeply. Then he gripped the bed again. "Wagon," he said through clenched teeth. He heaved and it budged, but he couldn't get his legs straight. They started quivering. He took a deep breath, held it, and gave it everything, and the wagon lifted. His legs were straight under him. It was as high as he could lift it.

"Get the wheel on," he grunted.

"Higher," she said.

Something like a howl or a scream escaped as he strained harder. The wheel clunked into place on the axle. At least that's what that sound had to be. He collapsed onto his knees.

"My arms are a foot longer and my legs that much short—"

He looked between David's legs. Four riders. Coming from Center City. At a canter.

"Get up," the woman said. "Quick."

As he pushed himself up, she smeared grease across his cheek. Some got in his mouth.

"Move. Put the axle nut on."

"I don't want to get grease on my right hand."

"Then use your left."

The riders split just behind David. Three of them took the middle of the dirt road and stopped, looking across the wagon at Thackery. The other rode on the grassy strip. The woman, Thackery saw, faced the one on the grass. She knew something, that one did.

"What's your name?" The question came from the middle of the three riders. He wore a pinto vest. All of them, Thackery saw, wore two belt guns. They all had two pistol holsters slung from their saddle horns.

"He's my hired hand," the woman said.

"I asked him." Pinto Vest.

"I answered you."

"Well, ma'am, since you're the talker. You know him long?"

"A while."

Pinto Vest looked at the coat on David's saddle. "Purty fancy clothes for a farm hand."

"I sold a load of apples in Center City this morning. I brought him along. He needed a new Sunday go-to-church suit. His old one was worn out and a couple of inches short in the sleeves."

Pinto Vest pointed to the saddle holster on David. "Purty well-heeled for a farm hand."

"There are bands of cutthroat, back-shooting thieves roaming around the countryside. They are almost as well-heeled as you are. They call themselves guerilla hunters."

Thackery stopped screwing the axle nut. Each one of the four riders bristled. They hadn't liked the woman's insult one bit. What she'd done was like coming across a bear waking up in the springtime and poking it with a stick and then running away. The bear was going to eat the next person he came to, whether it was the stick-poker or not. Those guerilla hunters wouldn't get even with the woman. They'd take it out on him.

"Where you live, woman? I want to talk to your husband."

"Talk to my husband all you want. Only to do that, you have to ride to Pea Ridge and holler through six feet of dirt."

That set Pinto Vest back on his heels for a moment. Then, "Which side he fight for?"

"Your side. And your side killed him, not the rebs. Eleven men got sick and died before the fighting even started."

"Come on, Lieutenant," the man who had his horse on the grass said. "Let the woman alone."

"Lieutenant!" The woman's voice dripped disdain as black and sticky as the axle grease.

Jesus, woman. Didn't you see we had a chance of getting out of this without shooting?

"We ain't no back-shooters, ma'am," the man on the grass said. "We're huntin' stagecoach robbers and bushwhackin' wimmen killers."

Thackery forced his eyes away from Pinto Vest to look at the woman. *Just shut up!*

The man on the grass pulled his horse around, walked him behind David, and set off at a trot, heading east. The other two followed him. Pinto Vest stayed there a moment, staring at Thackery. Thackery didn't look away. *Man, you ought to be worried about the woman, not me.* Thackery allowed a tiny smile to climb out of his mouth and sit on his face.

Pinto Vest spat a brown gob into the wagon bed and kicked his brown horse viciously in the belly, and the brown ran after the trio.

"Why is it," the woman said as she watched the man in the pinto vest ride away with his head held high. "Why is it men grow up, but they never grow out of boyhood?"

"Why is it," Thackery asked, "a woman couldn't see we were getting out of trouble and would continue to do so if she just kept her mouth shut? You had to tell that man in the vest he wasn't a real lieutenant. If the one on the grass hadn't gone soft over Pea Ridge, we'd both be dead now, instead of talking."

He'd gotten to her with that one. *Found a chink in her armor is what happened.*

She stomped right up to him.

He held his ground.

She smeared grease on his other cheek, spun on her heel, climbed up onto the front wheel, and pulled a rusty wrench from under the driver's seat. "Here. Tighten the axle nut."

She held the wrench out. He thought of Rosie O'Hanrahan of Independence and Clementine Manley and Amanda Bucknell of Kingdom Come. What in Sam Hill was the country coming to breeding such women as these?

"Is it true," he asked, "about Pea Ridge?"

She dropped the proffered wrench. She nodded. Then she spat in the palm of her relatively clean right hand, stuck it out, looked him in the eye, and said, "Truce, Mr. Thackery?"

"Truce." He stuck out his hand, and she dropped hers.

"Spit first, shake second, name third."

He spat. They grasped spit palms. He told his. "Molly," she said. "Tighten the nut, Mr. Thackery," she said.

"If you're Molly, I'm Tom."

"Tighten the nut, Tom."

He picked up the wrench and tightened the right rear nut. He checked the other nuts. They were snugged.

"I thought you'd hold out for a *please*."

He shrugged.

"May I offer a suggestion, Tom?" "Sure."

"It's not a good idea for you to ride down that road the way those guerilla hunters went for a time. Dinner'll be soon. Eat with us?"

It hadn't been an hour since he'd had breakfast. But what did that have to do with eating again?

"Sure."

"Good. Dinner's three hours off. You and I can help the two men who work for me scythe a hayfield." She climbed up onto the wagon. "See that lane cutting off to the right up ahead? That will take us to my farm. It cuts through my orchard. Pick a couple of apples for your horse."

She said, "Heyup," and flicked the reins, and the wagon rumbled away.

Thackery swung up onto the saddle. He considered riding on, considered the odds of running into the four men again. He considered his odds of survival if he did. "David, how bad you want an apple?"

The horse trotted after the wagon. The wagon turned right. David followed it.

Thackery said, "Shit."

The lane led between rows and rows of fruit trees, lined up like soldiers in ranks. Cherry trees were empty of fruit. Peaches weren't ripe yet. Apples and pears were. David stopped and plucked an apple. Molly's wagon bounced and rattled down the lane toward a two-story house, the roof of which showed above the orchard. The top of a barn was also visible. Its hayloft door was hanging open.

Molly turned around on the bench seat. "Hey. Don't let that fleabag eat my whole crop."

Thackery said, "You had to have an apple." The horse ate another.

34

MALONE, MOLLY'S LAST name was.

After turning David loose in the pasture next to her barn, Thackery rode next to Molly in the wagon to her hayfield. Her field was about ten acres, Thackery thought. Two men had laid over a scythe-wide swath down one long side of the rectangular field. They were halfway back in the knee-high hay. Molly set the brake and looped the reins around the handle.

He'd told her he'd cut plenty of hay before, but it had been three years. They climbed down, and Thackery pulled a scythe from the wagon. He stood over the just-mowed hay to practice. His fingers gripped the handles of the tool, and he was transported back to Indiana, to when he was twelve and Paw put a scythe in his hands for the first time.

"It's gonna feel awkward some," Paw had said. It felt awkward, all right.

"Take a couple of swings off to the side. You'll git the hang of it." He took a swing and came close to falling on his butt.

Paw explained how to plant his feet, how to use his arms and shoulders and bend his back to be "boss of the tool." Thackery had been Emerson then, and Emerson grew worried. Paw had never been patient with him before explaining some new job. But Paw had been patient. "You got to make that blade slide level above the ground. You got to cut them little hay stalks off this high above the ground." He held up his thumb and forefinger. "That gets us a goodly amount of hay, and it leaves enough of the stem so the plant don't die. That way we get a couple of mowings this year, and a couple next. Understand?" Emerson hadn't understood, but he nodded. When Paw asked that question, it was always best to say, "Yeah, Paw." Otherwise there'd be a kick to the butt. It didn't take long for the patience to run out. After the butt-kicking started, Emerson pretty quickly became boss of the scythe.

Thackery's muscles, as he took practice swings, recalled the lessons they'd learned when they belonged to Emerson Sharp. *I am the boss of you, Scythe.* He was ready to cut some hay. He planted himself, drew the tool back, and swung it, promptly digging the point of the blade into the soil.

He looked up. Molly shook her head. He preferred the memory of Emerson's paw's boot to Molly's disdain. The thought registered and then flitted away. He drew the blade back and swung it again, attempting to allow this time for the resistance the blade would encounter slicing plant stems. The cut was too high and not level with the ground. After a few more swings, Tom Thackery could cut hay as well as Emerson Sharp.

The other two men reached where Thackery and Molly waited with the wagon.

Willard Egan was stick thin, five ten, and missing his right arm. He had black hair. The other man had black skin. He was huge. Willard was barely as big around as one of the Negro's thighs. Ferdinand, his name was. He didn't have a last name. He'd had one, but it was the family name of the last man to own him. As a freed man, he didn't want that last name or any other. Ferdinand's face, Thackery thought, was good at hiding the thinking going on behind it. Many Negros were like that. Ferdinand, though, couldn't hide the intelligence shining through his mask.

"All right," Molly said. "Everybody knows everybody. Now can everybody get to work?"

Which they did. Molly and Willard swung one-handed cutting tools, slicing foot-wide swathes. By dinnertime, they had more than half the field cut. They stopped to eat. And to pop Thackery's blisters. And he met Lizabetta, Ferdinand's wife. She'd cooked dinner.

Lizabetta was Molly's size. And her friend more than a servant or hireling. After serving the others, Lizabetta sat at the table next to her goliath spouse. Thackery watched them. They seemed to need to touch each other every minute or two. They seemed to need to cast glances at each other every other bite or so. When they did, they smiled longing and need and giving all to each other. Thackery thought of seeing Josh and Nora together. He'd been leaning forward and slumped against the chair back. He'd met Negros he respected. He'd admired a few too. But he was sure he'd never envied Negros before.

"Tom. Tom."

He blinked and faced Molly at her head-of-the-table seat. "You were somewhere far away. Welcome back. I had asked you where you are from. Would you care to tell us?"

Willard and even Lizabetta and Ferdinand had their eyes on him.

"I grew up in Indiana, spent some time in Illinois. I partnered up with a gambler, and we traveled around some. Wound up here in Missouri."

"Traveled around some," Lizabetta said. "You git to any of them big cities?"

"Some," Thackery replied. "Saint Louis, Chicago, Detroit, New Orleans."

"You may have spent some time in cities, but you spent lots more on a farm," Willard said, "based on how you handled that scythe. One time this morning, I thought if Molly hadn't turned you two around, you and Ferdinand would have kept right on heading east and mowing down trees when you run out of hay."

Ferdinand chuckled, and his voice seemed to come from a spot ten feet below the floor. "Dat Mistuh Tom, he a mowin' man, awright!"

"Mr. Ferdinand, I think I'm a morning mowing man." Thackery held up his red palms.

"I'm picking apples this afternoon, Tom," Molly said. "I could use some help. If you'd care to stay."

*****

As they picked apples, Molly tried to get Thackery to talk about himself, but he'd talked about Emerson Sharp all he wanted to. He wasn't Emerson anymore.

She told him about Willard as they filled the empty crates in the wagon. Willard had marched with the Union army to Pea Ridge last year. That's where he lost his arm. But dysentery came closest to killing him in a hospital tent. He and his wife, Tilly, lived in Center City above Tilly's dress shop. He'd worked on the farm before the war. Now, he still did the work of most two-armed men—not Ferdinand, of course. Molly tried again to get him to talk about himself, but she didn't press him.

She told him about Ferdinand. Her husband, Patrick, had bought Ferdinand, freed him, offered him a job and the small house to live in. Ferdinand had married Lizabetta just before the war broke out. Last year, bands of armed men began roaming the countryside and capturing freed Negroes and selling them. Last fall when Willard came back from the war, Ferdinand helped him figure out how to get along left-handed. "And we all decided it would be safer for Ferdinand and Lizabetta to live in town and ride back and forth with Willard in the wagon. Men will do mischief in the daytime, but to do real evil, they seem to prefer the dark of night. That's how we saw it."

When they had the crates full, she said, "I'll drive," and climbed onto the seat. He sat beside her. She clucked the team into motion. "Tom."

He thought she was going to pry again.

"Thank you." His hands rested atop his thighs. She took the reins in one hand and placed the other atop his. "For staying and helping me this afternoon."

Her hand was rougher and more calloused than his, but it felt soft and smooth and warm and dry. He looked at her, and she smiled and melted a big chunk of something in his chest. In her face and eyes, she offered something, something precious. At the same time, he saw her facing off with those four guerilla hunters. She wasn't so much a woman then. She'd been hard with no backing down.

What she stirred up in him with her touch was a lot like what Nora stirred. And he was in love with Nora. Or had been. But now Nora was married to Josh. It didn't seem right to have those same feelings for Molly that he'd had for Nora. Shouldn't there be like a mourning period or something? He had trusted Nora with everything he had to give. Why so soon after that betrayal should he trust another woman?

I killed a woman. Nora probably thinks I betrayed her. And she married another man.

He was Tom Thackery and he was Emerson Sharp, and voices yammered in his head that didn't come from either one of the two.

California. He hadn't thought of California since Molly's wheel fell off. Or Tom Thackery's money under Emerson Sharp's name.

"Molly, you have any whiskey back at the house?"

"There's a jug."

"You willing to share?"

"I'm not drinking. No reason you can't."

*****

After supper, Willard, Ferdinand, and Lizabetta took the wagon loaded with apples to town. In the morning, they'd deliver the load to the riverboat dock before returning to the farm. Molly invited Thackery to sit with her.

Molly's house was a two-story stone-sided box with a single- story wood-sided kitchen built onto the tall box. Thackery had entered the kitchen through a rear door and left that way, too, after dinner. That evening, though, she led him through a parlor to the front porch.

The sun had gone down but hadn't pulled all the light after it yet.

The porch floor was weathered, rough-sawed planks set four inches above the dirt, and it ran the length of the two-story part of the house. Four four-by-four posts supported the porch roof. The base of the post where the kitchen began was charred.

Two weathered rocking chairs sat to the right of the door. Molly sat in one and indicated Thackery should take the other. She stared intently to the north.

From the house, the area scoured of grass funneled down to the lane leading through row upon row of fruit trees to the road to Center City. Across the road, forested terrain rose away to the horizon.

"Look there, Tom Thackery. And imagine you hear a clock. *Tick. Tock. Tick. Tock.* Do you see it? With each *tick*, with each *tock*, another thimbleful of light leaks away. Do you see it? Make your mind be quiet. You'll see."

Make your mind be quiet?

"Shh," she said. "Shh, Tom Thackery." She whispered, "See that gauzy blanket of haze lying over the trees to where the world ends? See how that blanket is woven of purple and orange and blue fibers and how those colors change? *Tick*, change. *Tock*, change."

He stared as she stared. The first thing he saw was how quiet the world had gotten. Then he saw the haze and saw it as a gauzy blanket. He cocked his head a mite, listening for a tick. He heard it. He was sure he heard it.

"You saw it, didn't you?" she asked.

"Yes. I saw it with your eyes."

She stood and looked down at him. It was too dark to see her face. "Tomorrow, Tom Thackery," she said with a voice as soft and gauzy as her blanket lying over the forested hills, "you will see it with your own eyes."

She went inside. To his right, the world had given itself over to night and to the first of the stars. The rest of the stars were almost ready to prick their own holes in the bowl of black. Thackery had the thought that the stars would be looking down at him. To see what he was going to do.

Thackery left the porch, walked through the barn, and led David from the pasture into a stall. "We're leaving in the morning," he said. Then he climbed up into the hayloft, spread his ground cloth, and lay there with his hands under his head, his eyes drinking in darkness.

The next morning, he woke to a voice saying, "No. We ain't leaving."

He grabbed a pistol. The darkness hid him. He didn't cock the weapon. He lay still, listening intently for a sound. Eventually, he felt foolish, found his pants and boots, pulled them on, crawled to the ladder, and climbed down. At the barn door, he stopped. He heard a noise coming from the house.

He found Molly in a rocker, waiting for sunrise. "Coffee, Tom Thackery?"

He may have dreamed the voice that woke him, but that voice turned out to be right.

*****

Tom Thackery, she'd taken to calling him. Ferdinand and Lizabetta called him "Mistuh Tom," and Willard called him Tom. But Molly, she used both his names, and at the end of his second day on her farm, when his name slipped out between her lips, he felt the inside of himself smile. It was her special way to address him.

At dinner, Willard related that, two years ago, Molly's husband, Patrick, and he had joined the Enrolled Missouri Militia. Molly had been upset with Patrick, as had his own wife been with him. But duty called them, and together they answered. They moved to the southwest corner of Missouri to confront a reb army there. Patrick got sick with dysentery and died on the way. During the battle of Pea Ridge, Willard's arm was shattered, and for weeks after, death seemed a more likely prospect for him than survival.

"But, Mistuh Willard," Ferdinand said, "he come back, and he teach dat lef arm a his to shoot better than his right arm did fore dose rebs shot it off of him. Now, wit' one arm, he do the work of two wit' bote they arms."

"What I see," Molly said, "is some men who are good at talking. Maybe you can talk the hay into the barn."

"What you tink, Mistuh Willard?" Ferdinand said. "We have to git up and go out in the field, or can we talk dat hay into the loft from here?"

Ferdinand chuckled, but Thackery saw Willard cock his head to the side, listening intently. He seemed to never let his guard down. He was always on edge, as if it was his duty to be ever vigilant, to protect this little group while they indulged in a few moments of merriment.

In the field, Thackery raked the first-mowed hay into rows. Molly and Willard turned the half-cured stalks to the sun. Ferdinand finished the cutting. Lizabetta cleaned up the kitchen, and then she drove the wagon as Thackery pitchforked the fodder onto it.

That evening, after the others returned to town, Thackery and Molly again sat on the porch and rocked side by side and regarded the vista to the north. It was easier this second time to push his mind to be quiet or for it to decide to be that way.

"This place, Tom Thackery, has a history. Would you care to hear it?"

He was disappointed. He'd expected her to speak more about the things her eyes saw that his couldn't. But he said, "Of course, Mrs. Molly."

He was pretty sure she was pleased that he had inserted a bit more formality in his form of address.

The original white settler had been a man named Oswilder. He had a wife, a young son, and a younger daughter. Oswilder began clearing fields for planting in 1812. He built a one-room wooden house and a small barn, and he had cleared some forty acres by 1820. Then a half dozen young Cherokees set out from the eastern part of what became the Indian Territory. They'd filled their bellies with white men's whiskey and smeared their faces with red men's war paint. They were warriors, they convinced each other, the way their ancestors had been warriors. These young warriors killed and scalped the Oswilder family and burned down their house.

In 1835, a widowed German woman moved to America with her two sons. They settled in a place called Orchard Farm, not far from the confluence of the Mississippi and Missouri Rivers. In 1845, the youngest son, Herman Wille, age eighteen, appreciating that he would inherit neither the family's farmland nor their general store, loaded a wagon with sapling fruit trees and headed west. When Herman found this place, all that was left of the Oswilder house was a stone chimney. The fields were being reclaimed by the forest.

"Herman bought this place and built this house," Molly said. "That post"—she pointed to the one with the charring at its base—"was the only reusable piece of lumber from the original buildings. He wanted some piece of Oswilder in the new house. And Herman planted the orchard. It's the largest and finest in this part of the state."

In 1856, young Patrick Malone was on his way to Kansas City, where he hoped to join a wagon train going west. He stopped in the saloon at Center City short of funds and looking for temporary work. Herman was in the saloon, having a beer after selling a wagonload of peaches. He offered Patrick Malone a job. The two hit it off, and Patrick accepted permanent employment vice temporary.

"The next year, I started working in the saloon there in Center City. Patrick found me there and convinced me to marry him." It had grown dark as Molly had rolled out the story. Thackery heard her sigh. "He didn't have to work up a sweat convincing me. We married, and Herman built that small house in back for us."

By that time, Herman had grown his farm to one hundred acres. He decided it was time for him to marry. Herman wrote his mother and asked her if she would send to Germany for a wife for him. He also sent a bank draft for his bride's passage from Germany across the Atlantic and up the Mississippi.

The mother wrote back saying it would take one or two years for the woman to arrive in Orchard Farm. When Herman's intended arrived, his mother would have the older brother bring the woman to him.

Two years later, Herman received a letter from his mother. The woman he sent for had arrived in Orchard Farm, but Herman's older brother decided he needed a Frau more than his sibling. The older brother married the woman.

Herman exploded. He would go to Orchard Farm. He would shoot his brother. He would take this woman who had been promised to him.

Patrick managed to calm him down, but with the anger gone out of him, so, too, had his spirit departed.

"For vat I do all dis?" Herman asked Patrick.

"I can't tell you why you did it," Patrick told him. "I can only tell you it was a good thing, a very good thing you built here with your heart and your hands."

Two days later, Herman called Patrick and Molly into his kitchen. "Ve are partners. Dis paper makes it so. You sign."

Patrick argued.

"You vant I sell to Center City Land Management? Dey kick you out."

Patrick signed the document. The Malones were to deposit half the farm's earnings into a bank account for Herman. Herman himself headed west. He had to get farther away from Orchard Farm. He made it to Kansas City, where he got into an argument with a Mormon. Herman shouted it was a sin against God for a man to have more than one wife. He pulled a knife. The Mormon pulled a pistol.

"Mr. Wille had been drunk some," a sheriff had written.

Molly stopped her recitation, but the rockers continued to squeak. To the north, star jewels adorned the sky above the blackness on earth.

"That's the history of this place," she said. "It is my history, Tom Thackery."

"But you didn't tell me your history. You told Herman Wille's and Patrick's."

"I did tell you mine. Before Patrick took me from that saloon and made me Molly Malone, I had no history. I had not begun to be."

Thackery thought about Weekes Daley and, before the man had become Weekes, how he had changed his name by the day of the week. His objective had been to leave as little trace of himself behind as possible, as if he could pass through life and not leave a history of his passing. And Weekes had never spoken of his beginnings. Just like Molly. *Just like Tom Thackery.*

The shadow figure of Molly Malone rose from her rocker. "Sleep well, Tom Thackery." Then she went inside. He went to the barn and slept in air perfumed by new hay.

36

THE NEXT NIGHT on her porch, Molly Malone and Tom Thackery took to their rockers with half the sun still above the horizon. Thackery waited for Molly to speak first. He thought if he opened his mouth, he'd spoil something. He wouldn't be able to make his mind be quiet. His eyes would not be able to see what hers saw. Maybe she wouldn't invite him to sit with her again.

The last sliver of orange-yellow fire disappeared. *As I blinked my eyes*, he thought.

"My husband, Patrick Malone, told me once that I should watch the sun set, not stare directly at it, but to watch it out of the side of my eye. After it had gone down, he asked me if I had noticed how the sun moved. Did it move fast? Did it move slow? Patrick Malone asked questions like that when we sat out here in the evenings. He never expected me to answer, but after putting his question to me, he always gave me a few minutes for it to settle in my mind. That night, he said, 'Did you notice that you could see the motion, see the sun move? In a way, it is like you can see time move and with it, you see your life slipping away. Did you see that, Molly Malone?'"

Molly turned away from the west and looked at Thackery. Her eyes sparkled. She faced to the north. "Then Patrick Malone said, 'Did you notice that the sun wasn't in a hurry to go down? Did you see that, Molly Malone? That is the sun saying our future will move like that.

At a pace we can keep up with. We will have joys. We will have sorrow. Times for laughter, times for tears. But neither will stay too long. Do you see how perfectly He arranged that?'"

She turned to him again. Now shadows hid her eyes. "Patrick Malone said that it was important for us to sit out here in the evening and see the hills, to watch the sun set. 'A farm,' he said, 'will suck the juice out of a man and woman if you let it. But twenty or thirty minutes on our porch at the end of a day, Molly Malone, do you see what a difference it makes?'"

He heard her breathe and held his breath lest the sound of it disturb her and the stillness that settled with dusk.

"Patrick Malone," she whispered, "why did you go off to war and die before you even got there? Such a waste that was. Do you see that, Patrick Malone?"

It felt to Thackery like Molly had taken a dipperful of cistern water and dumped it into his open chest.

She placed her hand on his arm. His held breath gushed out.

"This farm, Tom Thackery, was beginning to suck the juice out of me. Thank you for sitting with me."

She rose and went inside. He rose and walked to the barn.

He admired and envied Patrick Malone. He admired and envied Patrick Malone's wife. The things she could see, that he could not, until she taught his eyes.

Dusk had not sucked all the light from inside the barn. David waited with his head over the stall door. Thackery put his hand on the horse's head.

"I'm not sure what happened," he said. "Mrs. Molly needed some help with something, I think. I think I helped her. I feel kind of good about that."

He tousled David's forelock and climbed up to the loft.

He lay there with the new-hay smell in his nose. "She might not need us here anymore," he said. In his head, he saw the sun. It was not too bright to look at directly. It was on the far side of the world. It did not move fast. Nor slow. But he could see it move.

The sun. On the far side of the world. It had begun to move fast. Tom Thackery tried to slow it down, but the sun moved faster. He tried harder, and it moved faster still.

"Tom Thackery."

He was on the far side of the world, and the voice came from very far away.

"Tom Thackery."

A woman. Maw never called. Always Paw called. His lids were closed but his eyes knew light had fallen onto his face. He was confused. He was on the far side. Where it was light.

"Tom Thackery."

Molly Malone held a lantern in her hand. Her head and shoulders were above the edge of the loft. "Good morning, Tom Thackery. Coffee's on."

When he got to the kitchen, he found the table set for only two.

"They are staying in town today," Molly said.

After they ate, they took mugs of coffee onto the porch. "Today, Tom Thackery, we need to watch the sun come up."

He told her about his dream, about trying to get the sun to stop moving too fast.

She'd dreamed about the sun too. "I thought if I waited until the sun came up, I'd find that you'd gone."

"I thought you wanted me to leave."

"I do not."

"I'm glad. You make good coffee, Molly Malone."

She reached for his hand. "You make my heart smile, Tom Thackery."

The porch wasn't wide enough to place the rockers side by side looking east. Molly took hers and placed it on the packed dirt in front of the house and indicated she wanted his close by. The August air was heavy and thick. The only color the sun was able to push through the thick blanket of haze was gray. They watched as a hint of blue appeared, and then a slice of orange fire peeked above the cloud that

Thackery thought had gotten too heavy to float in the sky and had settled onto the earth.

Molly stood. "Come, Tom Thackery."

"Please. Another minute. Or two. My heart, Molly Malone, it wants to smile, but it is afraid to do so." She sat again. He scooted his rocker around to face her. "I am Tom Thackery. Before I was him, I was Emerson Sharp. I want you to know about Emerson. I have to tell you his history, and then I have to see what is in your eyes. Then I'll know if I can let my heart smile."

He told her about Indiana, about Maw and Paw and his brother John and the graves, about the Barlows and Simmonses, Weekes Daley and Josh Ewing. Barlows dead by his hand. Saint Joseph gamblers dead by his hand. He told her about riding with guerillas on an ambush. He told her about killing the woman and the girl. Then he took a deep breath and let it out and waited for her to judge.

She sat forward on her rocker. "If Patrick Malone were here, he'd say, 'You are a good man, Tom Thackery.' I know by how you carry these deaths on your heart."

"And you, Molly Malone, what do you say?"

She kissed the tip of her forefinger, rocked forward, and pressed a promise to his lips. Then she stood up again.

"Do you see, Tom Thackery, how high the sun is in the sky? Did I not tell you we had things to do? Can we be about it, then?"

The first thing they did was to bury a box with Patrick Malone's black suit neatly folded with his white shirt atop it, and on that, Molly had placed the black ribbon she used to secure her ponytail. There was a plain white limestone marker next to ones for the Oswilder family and for Herman Wille. Herman had been buried in Kansas City, but Patrick Malone wanted a marker for him next to Oswilder. Ferdinand would carve a stone with Patrick's name and birth and death dates on it.

Then after the sun burned off the dew, Thackery and Molly loaded the last hay from the field onto the wagon and then hoisted it into the barn with the big four-pronged fork and pulley rope tied to one of the draft horses.

He shaved. She bathed and brushed her hair. He took a bath. Then she led him by the hand up to her bedroom. She showed him where to hang his suit and white shirt in the chifforobe. Taking his hands in hers, she looked into his eyes, and he into hers, and he loosened the reins on his heart so that it could smile.

*****

It was different at Molly Malone's dinner table. Thackery had considered them all to be open and friendly before, but he had been a guest. Now, though, he had been admitted to the family. It showed most in Ferdinand. The first few days Thackery ate with them, Ferdinand barely spoke. But tonight he rambled on and talked more than all the others put together. Mostly he spoke about the war.

Last year, it sure looked like the Union was going under. Then Mr. Lincoln started off 1863 with his Emancipation Proclamation. What would that mean if the "'federates" beat the "fed'rals"? Ferdinand thought that if the Confederates won, that proclamation would make the Southerners mad and they'd take it out on the Negroes. But now things looked different. The Union won big battles in Pennsylvania and in that Vicksburg. Mr. Lincoln, he needed more soldiers. Not enough volunteered, so he set up a thing called a draft. Still, he wasn't getting enough men to fight.

"Dey's taking Negroes in the army. I think I sign up," Ferdinand said.

Sudden horror, like a horse had stepped on her foot, splashed over Lizabetta's face. She didn't scream, but she did jump up and bolt out the back door. Molly hurried after her.

Willard glared across the table at Ferdinand, and he glared back.

"You think I shoulda tole her before?" Ferdinand asked. "Why? I know how she act."

Willard looked at Thackery. Thackery shrugged.

"Listen, Ferdinand," Willard said. "There's another way for you to fight. North of Molly's farm, there's a parcel of that forest land for sale. What would it mean if a Negro owned that property, cleared it, built his own farm? That'd be worth more than one man going off to war and getting shot."

"I wouldn't be going to let the rebs shoot me. I be goin' to shoot dem."

"That was exactly what I thought I was going to do at Pea Ridge. But once the shooting starts, shooters got nothing to say about what happens. The bullets take over and they have everything to say. When I got shot, 150 of us were charging up this rise through a stand of trees. The rebs cut loose and the bullets ripped limbs from trees, cut down saplings and men like we were little stalks of hay, and the bullets were like Ferdinand with his scythe, and he mowed us down." Willard leaned across the table. "And look at you. Skinny as I am, a bullet found me. You, hellfire, man, thick as those bullets were, you'd have been hit five, maybe ten times."

Ferdinand glared at Willard. Thackery thought Willard had scored a few points in the argument. Ferdinand was chewing on what his friend had said.

Ferdinand turned. "Wha' choo tink, Mistuh Tom?"

Thackery had been thinking about Lieutenant Miller. Miller fought because he did not want despots back east to tell the folks out west how to conduct their lives, but all the men under the lieutenant, and even Quantrill himself, as best he could tell, fought to avenge wrongs done to Missourians by Kansans and Union soldiers. In Ferdinand, he could see clearly the cause the man wanted to fight for. Thackery had sat at two dinner tables now where whites and Negroes ate together, but those were probably the only two households in the state of Missouri where that could happen. Ferdinand wanted that to be the rule, not the rare exception.

Thackery said, "You should think about Lizabetta. You should listen to Willard. He's been to the war." Thackery didn't mention Patrick Malone, but he didn't think he had to. "You should think about doing what Willard suggested, buying that property. A colored man owning land, that would be doing something more important than shooting even a passel of rebs. That's what I think."

"How I do that? I ain't got no money. Nobody be lendin' me some. Who let a Negro own property roun' here?"

"I have some set aside," Willard said. "I think it's enough to get us started. I think I can get a loan and buy the property from the land company. And we'll be partners. We can cut the trees down and sell the logs to pay off the loan."

"We be partners?"

"Partners."

"Before you go to the bank," Thackery said, "you should have this all planned out. Which sawmill you'll sell logs to, how much they'll pay you for a load of logs, how long it'll take to clear the land. Put that all down on a piece of paper and take it to the bank, odds are, you'll get your loan."

"Meantime, Ferdinand," Willard said, "you best go out and do some talking of your own to Lizabetta."

37

W ITH HAY IN and oats not ready to harvest, Thackery traveled to Saint Louis. By riverboat. Molly insisted he not travel by himself on roads patrolled by Union soldiers, guerilla hunters, and Confederate army recruiters, and all of them hunting each other, and all of them eager to find someone to shoot or hang.

In Boatman's Bank, with the help of the vice president he and Weekes always dealt with, he transferred Emerson Sharp's money into an account belonging to Tom Thackery. When he walked out of the bank, he was surprised he wasn't elated at recapturing his fortune. He felt more like he'd lost something. It was the final and complete demise of Emerson Sharp, but nowhere was there a stone with Emerson's name on it proclaiming that he had walked the earth for a period of time.

On the trip to Saint Louis, Thackery played cards. The last bout of poker lasted eighteen hours. At the end, he was up $700. On the return to Center City, Thackery sat on deck and read or watched the scenery slide by and thought about who and what he used to be and what he was now. Molly was happy with writing her history as if she'd been plopped onto earth as a fully grown person. Thackery, however, could not erase Emerson and Maw and Paw. He couldn't erase Weekes Daley. He couldn't erase Josh, or Nora, or Miller, or Quantrill, or Iago-renamed- Horse, or Roan. By the time the side-wheeler maneuvered to dock at Center City, the mugwumps gripped him, and he was desperate for Weekes to tell him, "Assume the stance." He was desperate for someone to slap him.

But it was interesting watching the *Big Muddy* work the sidewheels, one wheel plowing water, thrusting ahead, while the other wheel backed to swing the bow in to the pier, then reversing the directions of both wheels to swing the stern to shore. During the trip, some passengers had toured the pilothouse as well as below to the big room housing the steam boiler. He hadn't gone, busy as he was ineffectually handling the mugwumps. There was something about Molly Malone's history and about his history that bothered him. He couldn't figure out what it was.

Lines were heaved over to shore fore and aft, and the vessel blew its whistle, which echoed up and down the river, stirring large birds into startled flight. Ashore, a line of wagons, cued up back from the pier, awaited the embarkation and debarking of clots of passengers aboard and ashore.

Molly sat on the driver's seat of the lead wagon. Ferdinand sat on the rear of the wagon bed, his legs dangling. Thackery waved his hat, but several men were waving hats. Ferdinand saw him and pointed him out to Molly. Even from the distance, he could see her face light up with pleasure at seeing him.

The vessel swung a gangway into position with a boom, and Thackery, in the middle of two dozen, mostly men, crowded to get ashore as if, he thought, they'd been sailors on a whaling vessel and out at sea for a year.

She was standing by the front wheel when he reached her. He took her hands. "Molly Malone, it is heaven itself to see you again."

She looked so fine. Pants, white blouse, with the small ponytail secured by a red ribbon under the brim of her straw hat and her cheeks so deliciously bronzed by the sun.

"And you, Tom Thackery," she said, beaming a beatific radiance, "are a sight for my hungry eyes. We start harvesting the oats tomorrow."

"What?"

Ferdinand gave off a chuckle that growled up from down in his boots.

"What are you laughing at?"

"Oh, nuttin'. Nuttin' atall, Mistuh Tom."

"Tom Thackery," Molly said, "you want to stand here all day jawing, or will you drive the wagon down to the dock and help Ferdinand unload the crates of peaches?"

Molly didn't wait for an answer but walked off and up the gangway and onto the boat.

Thackery watched her engage a man on the second deck. As she spoke, he wrote on a paper on a clipboard.

"Hey," the driver of the second wagon in line hollered, "how about moving your rig?"

Thackery climbed onto the seat and moved the rig.

*****

That night on the porch, Molly asked, "What's wrong, Tom Thackery?"

"Nothing's wrong with me. I thought maybe while I was gone, you might have decided you liked it better the way you had it before."

"We have been together for a month. Did you expect it would be fresh and pure between us forever?"

He faced her. "I did."

She touched his cheek with her hand.

Later, she said, "I like having you in my life, Tom Thackery. I like having you on my porch and in my bed. You make me feel safe, like I don't have to sleep with one eye open."

She rolled onto her side and kissed him and settled back with an arm draped over his chest. He laid an arm over her back. "Mmmm," she said.

He wanted to tell her about the mugwumps, that he thought, deep down, he was afraid of losing her.

But she slept.

He couldn't.

The next day, Willard showed up for dinner after being absent for four days. He had secured the loan, he'd purchased the property, and they could begin logging it.

"You done it, Mistuh Willard! You done it. Les go. We git stawted."

"Ferdinand," Willard said, "Mrs. Molly needs help with the oats. We can help her in the morning and work the forest in the afternoon. There's time to work it. We have all winter."

"Dey ain't no time," Ferdinand said. "Lizabetta having a baby. Dat chile be borned in our own house on our own land."

Lizabetta clouded up. She smacked Ferdinand on his shoulder. "Dat not how we was gonna tell dis."

"It how I say it."

"You, Ferdinand. Propity owner. An' me, I'se jus' a piece a dat propity!"

"Why you givin' me dat, woman?"

Molly smacked the table. Her plate and silver ware jumped. "Quiet. Everybody. Willard, you and Ferdinand go work your land. Lizabetta, do you know any of your people in town who would work for me?"

"I knows—"

"Hush, Ferdinand. You got your head in the clouds." A smile flickered briefly on Molly's lips. "I am happy for you, really. But I have property too. Lizabetta has her feet on the ground. You worry about your place. Lizabetta will help me find another hand."

That night, from the porch, Molly and Thackery didn't look at the scenery. They listened to Ferdinand's ax bite into tree trunks. They listened to Ferdinand's trees crash to the ground. Half the property and half the value of the lumber belonged to Willard, but Ferdinand was the one making noise.

Willard hired two Negros to help Ferdinand. For his part, Willard sharpened axes and drove the log wagon to the sawmill. He had also begun talking with the bank and the land office about purchasing another fifty acres adjoining their property.

Late in August, word reached Center City that Quantrill had raided Lawrence, Kansas, and killed two hundred. "Murdered two hundred unarmed men and boys," some said. Others said, "Sneaking, horse-stealing, back-shooting Jayhawks. Quantrill caught 'em with their pants down and give 'em what they had coming is what he done."

The night the story hit town, there was a fistfight in the Center City saloon. The next night, as another argument sprang to life, four men pulled pistols and shoved the Quantrill sympathizers out the door. The four sympathizers included the blacksmith, the proprietor of the general store, and two drummers. They disappeared. Probably shot, weighted with rocks, and dumped in the river, some said. The next day, the widow dressed in black and opened the general store at the normal time. She would hear no word of sympathy. She had no time for idle chitchat. A Negro who understood iron and forges and hammering moved into the blacksmith shop. No one said a word against the new smith. The town needed him.

On the first of September, Thackery was ready with his surprise.

They couldn't hear Ferdinand's ax from the porch that evening. They could hear his trees crash to the ground, though. The smell from the brush pile he and Willard had burned that afternoon hung on the still air. There was enough haze above the horizon that a man could look directly at the big orange ball of sun. The haze diminished not only the brightness of the sun but its warmth as well. Molly wore a shawl over her shoulders.

He waited for her to say something. She only rocked. His surprise pushed to get out.

"Molly, when I was in town this morning, I went to the land office. The Kirkpatrick farm to the south of yours is 150 acres." Excitement gilded his voice. "I had no idea it was so big. Tomorrow, I will go in and buy it. I told you about Dutzow's Corner. I told you about the Bucknell farm out west of here. Do you see, combining our farms, we'll be the Bucknells and the Dutzow of Center City?" He got down on a knee. "Molly Malone, will you marry me?"

She looked to the west. The edge of the world had sliced off the bottom half of the sun. As she turned back to face him, she wiped a tear.

A hand squeezed Thackery's heart. Molly could be such a tough woman. It was incredibly tender to see that tear. He'd remember it always.

"I am ... happy for you, Tom Thackery. I thought there was something missing in you. I didn't know what it was. But I see now. You didn't have a dream. Now you do."

"A dream? I guess it is a dream. It is you and me together building something grand right here."

"It's your dream, Tom Thackery. Do you not see what it does to mine?"

She stood, kissed the tip of her finger, and pressed it to his lips. Then she went inside her house.

It hadn't happened to him often playing cards, but a few times, he'd calculated the odds at 90 percent that he'd win a hand. And lost. When that happened, and Weekes had guaranteed it would happen occasionally, you made your heart and head go cold; you nodded and smiled congratulations to the winner; you quickly assessed the mistake in your calculation; and then you set about winning your money back. Or you walked away from the table. That's what Weekes had told him.

There wasn't any way to win anything back here.

The last sliver of sun seemed to hang on to the edge of the world and then it let go. To the north, a tree crashed and sent its vibration through the earth to Molly Malone's porch.

His heart and head were cold.

Thackery pushed himself up. His feet carried him to the barn. He wrapped his coffeepot and skillet in rags and placed them in his saddlebags. He saddled David, mounted, and rode him out of the barn.

Molly was on the porch. She walked out into the yard and called his name.

Thackery turned David to ride over to her. She handed up a stuffed-full flour sack in one hand and the ring he'd bought for her and left on her rocker.

He took the flour sack. "Lizabetta doesn't have a ring. Maybe Ferdinand would like to give her one." He tipped his hat. "You were God's own blessing to me, Molly Malone."

"David," he said.

The horse trotted away from the house and entered the lane through the orchard.

"I know what you're thinking," Thackery said. "You were thinking Molly Malone has one fine barn and that it would be one fine place to spend the winter and that if we were lucky, we might be here for next year's apple crop. That was your dream. Wasn't it?"

They reached the end of the lane, and Thackery turned the horse left with his knee. "This is what we're going to do, David. Spend the night in Center City. In the morning, we'll buy supplies. Then we'll head south and find Lieutenant Miller's widow. Was going to do that in the winter, after we had all the crops in."

David cantered away from Molly Malone's lane. Ahead of them, a patch of below-the-horizon sunlight smeared the sky like glowing snail slime.

"Next week," Thackery said, "we'd have started harvesting the corn. Not our business now, though. We'll go to Joplin, then on to Texas, and figure out how to get to California from there."

Thackery pulled up where the land sloped away to the river, and off to his right, lighted windows in the houses and businesses defined the layout of Center City. He turned in the saddle to look down the dark road.

He thought about Molly Malone building a life for herself on the remnants of what must have been a hard, bad past. Nora, too, had ugly things to get over and grow out of. Both of them had done so. "All I do, David," he said, "is lay down trails that run off the end of the world. I'm not sure I want to be Tom Thackery anymore. Maybe I should change my name again and start over. Like Molly did."

He'd thought when Molly buried Patrick Malone's things, she was burying her attachment to him, freeing herself to be Mrs. Tom Thackery. She had liked being with him. That had been obvious. He wanted to get the proposing done right this time. He'd bought a permanent engagement ring, not a temporary one. She had liked being with him, but she did not want to marry him. He should have seen that. If she married him, she would become Mrs. Molly Thackery. She would lose what she had become, had made of herself. He wasn't sure how to put his head around what had happened and the logic of it.

She had needed something from him. He gave it without really understanding what he was doing. She took what she needed. And paid for the taking—not in coin but in teaching his eyes and senses things about the world even Weekes hadn't been able to show him.

She didn't need him anymore and sent him away. She had the two Negros Lizabetta found for her. One of them, freedman Caleb Samson, along with his wife, now lived in the small house on her farm.

As he looked down the dark road that had taken him from her farm to the ridge overlooking the river, what she'd done hit him. Molly Malone had used Tom Thackery just like he had used saloon girls.

From a back corner of his mind, a notion formed that he should be angry at Molly Malone. He wasn't. He couldn't be angry at her. She had given him more than he'd ever given to a saloon girl.

He turned around and looked down on the river, a wide swath of molten lead preventing him from going farther in that direction, and there was no way to turn around and go back.

"Shit," he said through clenched teeth.

He rode down the hill and turned right on River Street and pulled up at Tilly's Dress Shop. The lights were on in the second-story living quarters. He mounted the stairs in back and knocked.

Tilly answered the door.

"Is Willard home, ma'am?"

"No. He and Ferdinand sleep out on their land some nights. I don't expect him tonight."

"All right. Well, I'll ride out and say goodbye to them in the morning."

"Say goodbye? We thought you and Molly—"

Thackery shook his head. "I'm sorry I disturbed you, ma'am. I shouldn't have come."

It had seemed like a good idea to say goodbye to Willard and to Ferdinand. Now it seemed like a very bad idea. What he needed to do was to buy his supplies in the morning and ride away and leave it to Molly to say what happened.

At the foot of the stairs, Thackery stopped. By the light spilling out her back door, he knew Tilly Egan was watching him. It was no time for looking back, though.

The saloon was the last building on River Street before the road leading down to the river. Across the road sat the livery stable. He intended to put David up and sleep there as well. First, he'd have two whiskies.

He drank off half the first and swallowed, and the whiskey reached into his lungs and grabbed out a handful of air and took it to the pit of his stomach and puddled warm there. Then he could breathe again. He stood at the bar with a half dozen other men. They all faced or leaned on the bar. Thackery turned to take in the tables. One hosted a six-man card game. Two men sat at another table. One was midtwenties, with a black mustache, and a head taller than his companion. The shorter one's hat rested on their table. He was bald on top. These two studied intently the two men at the next table. The latter two, Thackery decided, weren't men but boys. One of them might be sixteen; the other was younger. They had a bottle in the middle of their table. The younger reached for the whiskey.

The older grabbed his hand. "You best slow down."

The younger pulled his hand with the bottle free, poured his glass full, and chugged it.

"Come on," the older said. "I'm going up to the room."

"Go if you want." The younger refilled his glass.

"Come on. Bring the bottle."

Thackery drank off the rest of his glass and ordered a refill.

From the card game: "Pair of sixes bets." "Ten dollars." "Your ten and one more jist like it."

Mumbled conversation buzzed along the bar. Thackery sipped the second whiskey.

The two men got up from their table, walked over to the boys' table, pulled out chairs, and sat.

"Where you fellows from?" Baldie asked.

Conversation along the bar ceased. Two men left their drinks on the bar and walked out the front door. Those at the poker table turned to watch the table with four.

"Ain't from nowhere," the younger replied.

"Everybody's from someplace," Black Mustache said.

"Red Legs burned us out of Osceola two years ago. We moved north, and this year, the federals burned us out again. Killed Paw. Maw and our sister they stuck in jail, and the jail collapsed and killed 'em both. We ain't got no place to be from no more," the younger one said.

"You're *secesh*," Baldie said.

The other three at the bar headed for the door. Two from the poker table grabbed up their money and crowded out after the others.

"We ain't nothing, mister," the older boy said. "We're on our way to our uncle's place up by Columbia."

"I'll tell you what we ain't," the younger said.

Jesus, kid!

"We ain't Red Legs, and we ain't federal."

Black Mustache smiled. "Then you're *secesh*." He reached inside his coat, and Baldie reached for a belt gun.

Thackery drew his pistol and cocked it. "Everybody stay real still."

"You best back out of this, mister," Black Mustache said.

"Bartender," Thackery said. "Move down to this end of the bar so I can see you."

The bartender did as instructed. He had a glass and a towel in his hands. His eyes were big, and he licked his lips.

"You two put your hands on the table," Thackery ordered.

Baldie had his back to Thackery. Thackery saw him look at Black Mustache. He was going to try something. The two kids sat on their chairs with their mouths hanging open. The bartender was a statue with a glass and a towel in his hands.

"Baldie," Thackery said. "Whatever you're thinking of doing, don't."

Thackery took two strides and jammed his pistol against Baldie's ear while keeping his eyes locked on Black Mustache. "Hands on the table. Do it. Now."

Black Mustache eased his hands up, and Baldie did too.

"Git," Thackery snapped, and the poker players didn't ask if he was talking to them. One of them left a pile of bills on the table.

"Didn't ask for no help." The younger one glared up at Thackery.

"Get him out of here," Thackery ordered the older one.

"I ain't going," the young one said. "These is jist like Jayhawkers and federals. Cain't git away from 'em. I'm going back and joining Quantrill. Wish I'd been with him in Lawrence."

Thackery shoved Baldie into Black Mustache. His chair went over, and Baldie landed on top of him. Thackery stepped around the table and smashed a left fist into the jaw of the younger kid, and he spun out of his chair. He sprawled on his side on the floor.

Thackery disarmed Baldie and Mustache and ordered them to lie on their bellies with their arms above their heads.

"Kid," Thackery said to the older, "keep these two covered."

The kid stood.

"You don't have a gun. You know how to use one?"

"Not a handgun. No, sir."

"Shit." They had to move. "Pull Baldie's boots off."

"You ain't taking my—"

Thackery kicked Baldie in the ribs. Then he ordered Black Mustache to stand and punched him in the belly. Black Mustache bent over and Thackery smashed a knee into his face, and he went over backward.

As Thackery pulled Black Mustache's boots off, he asked, "What the hell are you kids doing here?"

The older kid stood there holding Baldie's boots.

Thackery holstered his pistol and pulled his Bowie. "Well." He slit through the waistband and belt of Black Mustache's pants and pulled them off him.

"We killed Mr. Lattimer and run away," the older one said.

Thackery ripped the shirt and long johns from unconscious Black Mustache. "Who's Lattimer?"

Thackery wadded up the rags of clothing and piled them with the boots.

"When the federals killed our paw, they were going to shoot my brother and me too."

Thackery kicked Baldie in the ribs again. Baldie moaned and rolled into a ball.

"Lattimer had a farm next to ours. He talked the federals into letting him take us. He treated us like niggers. Davey told him so. Lattimer laughed and said, 'Niggers cost money. You was free.' And this morning, he was going to whip me for spilling oats. Davey stuck a pitchfork in his back. We took his money and two horses and run all day. Once we crossed the river, Davey said we was safe. He wanted a whiskey. 'Ain't ever' day you kill a man,' he said."

"Shit." Thackery looked at the bartender. "You have a shotgun back there?"

He nodded.

"Get it, kid."

Thackery told the bartender to lie on the floor. Then he ripped the strings off the man's apron and tied his hands behind his back.

The younger kid moaned and rolled onto his side and puked. Black Mustache moaned and raised his hands to his bloody nose. Baldie glared up at Thackery, and Thackery kicked him again. Baldie screamed.

Thackery pulled the younger one up and slung him over his shoulder, and he puked some more. Thackery felt it wet his pant leg.

"Kid, pick up those boots and clothes and follow me."

Thackery headed for the side door. Outside, he told the older kid to hide the clothes in the bushes behind the building. Thackery carried the younger one to the hitching rail in front of the saloon. Five horses were tied up there. Two were plow horses. Two probably belonged to Baldie and the other one. The older kid came running around to the front of the saloon.

"Get up on this one," Thackery told him. After the kid mounted, he slung the young one across his brother's lap. Then he handed the reins to the other riding horse to him. There was no place to put the shotgun. Thackery handed the two pistols he'd taken. "Stick these in your belt. Now, get up the hill, and go like hell. People are going to come after us."

The older kid turned his horse up the hill. "Giddup," he said. Two rifles banged from the river side of the livery stable, and the older kid fell, and his brother did too. Another rifle banged, and a bullet whanged off a post holding up the roof over the boardwalk in front of the saloon. Thackery swung up onto David and headed him north, away from the livery stable. At the first cross street, he turned up the hill and, at the second street, turned left. At the end of the street, David slowed and entered forest.

"Shit, David, maybe I should have shot Baldie and Black Mustache right off and skedaddled. Maybe those kids would have made it."

David found a game trail. It paralleled the river and headed north. Sticking to the trail would make it easier for guerilla hunters to track him, but just then, putting distance between them and Center City was important.

"Weekes Daley said once, 'God gives each of us a certain amount of luck.' You know what I think happened, that day back in '60, when I ran away from Indiana, somehow I got my hands on not only my own luck, but I spent those two dumb kids' luck as well. Shit. Didn't even learn their names."

Then Thackery stopped talking and started listening to the night.

38

THACKERY CROSSED A major east-west road and entered the woods on the other side. Lights from Columbia lit the night like dawn happening in the middle of the world instead of at the edge. He stepped down and watched and listened at his back trail. He considered taking the road through Columbia and then, comfortably east of Center City, heading southwest to Joplin and from there on to Texas, as he planned. But he decided he had to be sure he was not pursued before exposing himself to travelers on main roads.

Setting out again, he headed David northeast. He rode hunkered over with his head low over David's neck to avoid branches and limbs scraping his face. It wouldn't do to have something happen to his eyes.

Those *poor dumb kids* kept coming to mind. Much as he'd been three years prior. He'd been lucky. They hadn't. "Shit," he mumbled.

Nora. That look on her face when he ran into her on Doc Hofstedler's porch, he thought she loved him as he did her. But then she thought he'd killed a woman and a girl, and she wouldn't even let him explain. Not that there was any way to explain it. *They made me go with them. I didn't kill the woman and girl. It was Lieutenant Miller did that.* Even saying it to himself sounded weak and lame, and it convicted him much more than exonerated.

Molly Malone. They'd spoken with each other like he'd never talked with a woman before. She'd taken him into her bed the way no woman had before. He'd thought she would want him there till *death do us part*. And not the way Deborah Simmons had said it back in Indiana.

David came out of woods to a cornfield. Already harvested. The stalks cut and bound into tepees. Across the field, a dark farmhouse, a dark barn stood like black paper cutouts. The moon was big and round and directly above. Dogs started barking. Thackery thought the people back in Center City would be able to hear the racket. He hopped down and pulled a half dozen ears from a shock and stuffed them in the sack Molly had handed him as she dismissed him, telling him she was Molly Malone and she would not be Molly Thackery.

She wouldn't talk about what she'd been before Patrick Malone married her. Patrick had taken her from a saloon, though.

If anyone would understand what it felt like to be treated like a saloon girl, Molly would.

Thackery wondered why her treatment of him didn't make him angry. It didn't. It could have caused the mugwumps to grab him. It didn't do that, either. He didn't know if Molly would remember him, or if she'd write the last couple of chapters of her history without him in it. But he would remember her. She was one saloon girl he would remember.

Vigilance.

David made better time walking along the edge of the field of stubbles and tepees. Dogs at the next farm joined the barking, baying cacophony. They passed two more farmhouses. Also with dogs. These had lamplight spilling out a window. Then the forest swallowed them again, and the howling and yapping dropped behind and finally, blessedly, ceased.

He stepped down and walked until his legs became more tired than the rest of him.

The September morning was clear, clean, and chill. Thackery stopped beneath a hickory tree on a rise and dropped the ears of corn on the ground for David. The horse set to crunching the kernels from the cobs. Thackery put the telescope in his pocket and climbed the tree until he could see above the forest. He took his time glassing to both sides of the way he'd come. He was about convinced no one tracked him.

Then a horse exited trees and started crossing a meadow. Pinto Vest. Three other riders trailed him. He couldn't see faces. Two black hats, a tan hat, on two black horses and a sorrel. Pinto Vest leaned to the side. Tracking, Thackery thought.

Tracking him.

An idea occurred. Thackery hustled down out of the tree. He scoured up stones to circle a fire pit. He placed the coffeepot on the stones and laid the foundation of a fire. With a little more time, he would have got the fire going. But he figured he'd set the stage well enough. He climbed up onto David and gigged him into a gallop running away from the four riders. A hundred yards away from the hickory tree, he pulled up, hopped down, and led the horse twenty yards off the game trail. Then he headed back toward Pinto Vest, paralleling the track he'd left.

Bushwhacking may have been distasteful before, but in his present situation, it was just what he needed. Pinto Vest was the leader. He was sure. And Pinto Vest must have a base close to Center City. Everybody in Center City knew Tom Thackery had an association with Molly Malone, Willard Egan, and Ferdinand. If Pinto Vest returned to Center City without having caught him, Vest would likely take out his hate on Thackery's friends. Bushwhacking was nothing compared to that.

Thackery stopped opposite the hickory tree, pulled David down onto his knees, and rolled him onto his side. He waited. Not long.

Black Hat on the sorrel followed Thackery's trail to the foot of the hickory tree. Black Hat dismounted and picked up his coffeepot. "Over here," Black Hat called.

A rider crashed through the brush to the far side of the hickory. Tan Hat.

Black Hat showed Tan Hat the coffeepot. "Spooked him, I reckon."

"About got him, I reckon." Tan Hat grinned.

Thackery shot Tan Hat. He fell from the saddle, and his horse bolted down the trail to the southwest. Black Hat drew a belt gun and whirled around, and Thackery shot him. He fell over backward. Black Hat's sorrel bobbed its head, but it stayed put.

Thackery stayed still and waited for the ringing in his ears to subside. *What would Pinto Vest have done?*

Pinto Vest, he decided, was back down the trail to the south. He'd sent his three companions ahead. He was south. The other rider, on the other black? The man on the sorrel had followed Thackery's trail flanked off to the west. Odds were the remaining rider, apart from Pinto Vest, was east. Thackery waited for the ringing in his ears to quit. He listened. He heard nothing and pulled David to his feet and walked to where the sorrel stood ground-hitched. After retrieving the pistols from the two downed guerilla hunters, he mounted the sorrel, led David by the reins, and set off at a good pace, heading west. After thirty minutes, he turned south. A half hour in that direction, he figured, would be enough to get behind Pinto Vest. Then he could come up on his rear and get the man off his tail forever.

Fifteen minutes later, Thackery reined the sorrel to a stop. A picture of Pinto Vest had formed in his head. In the picture, Pinto Vest hunkered down in a bushwhack next to the trail Thackery had followed before. Waiting for Thackery to ride up that trail again.

Thackery recalled looking into the man's dark brown eyes across the bed of Molly Malone's wagon. It had been a long time, he remembered thinking, since those eyes had looked on anything that the man didn't hate. In those eyes, Thackery had seen hate and no intelligence. That had been a mistake. The man was not dumb. He was a tracker. He would smell an ambush. That's why he'd sent Black and Tan Hats ahead.

Thackery considered the odds. Pinto Vest could be lying in ambush along Thackery's trail. He could be trailing him from the spot of Thackery's ambush.

West, he decided, and headed the sorrel that way.

Thackery checked the guerilla hunter's saddlebags and found a corn fritter and fried bacon wrapped in paper. Coffee, too, but there was no time for that. Something to eat, though, was good. Otherwise, he thought, they'd be able to trail the sound of his stomach grumbling.

He kept to the woods. When he came to roads, he checked for riders or wagons before crossing. He skirted towns and avoided game trails for the most part. Occasionally, he came to areas of scrub brush tangled with vines, and game trails were the only way around and through those. Early afternoon, he stopped below the crest of a rise and studied his back trail. Just as he was about to collapse the spyglass, he saw a man leading a horse walk across a small clearing.

The man studied the ground. Reading his trail. He wasn't wearing a vest. Thackery thought Pinto Vest would be the tracker. The man stood up and raised his eyes and looked right at Thackery. It was Pinto Vest, but he'd removed his distinctive garb. Unless the man had extraordinary vision, he wouldn't be able to see Thackery without the aid of binoculars or a glass such as his, but he had the sense that Pinto Vest knew he was there, knew he was being watched.

Thackery forced himself to study Pinto Vest's right flank. He wanted to find the other man. If he couldn't shake Pinto Vest, maybe he could get them to a place where, if he couldn't kill both of them, he might be able to stop Pinto Vest. There. The other rider was some yards to the north of Thackery's trail.

Shit!

Another rider, a like distance to the north of his trail. Thackery glassed Pinto Vest's other flank. Two more of them.

Shit!

Pinto Vest had started with three hunters. He'd killed two.

Now there were five of them!

Pinto Vest was the key. With the others out on the flanks, maybe Thackery could head right for him, work another ambush, and after he shot Pinto Vest, escape to the east.

Pinto Vest, now I'm hunting you.

A pistol popped. Pinto Vest had disappeared under the forest canopy, but Thackery was sure he was the one who'd fired. He glassed to the north. The flank riders were converging on the trail.

Thackery swore. Pinto Vest knew what he was thinking.

He mounted David and led the sorrel, pressing on to the west.

At noon, Thackery came to a spot affording a view of the way he'd come. Pinto Vest was there with his hunters out on the flanks, but close to him. Thackery pushed on and came to a small town sitting astride a major north-south road. He thought it was probably the road connecting Moberly to Columbia. Heading west out of the small town was a smaller road heading due west. Thackery switched back to the sorrel, skirted around the town, picked up the road, and kicked the sorrel into a gallop. He ran the animal until he felt him tire, and then he slowed to a trot, and without stopping, he switched to David and galloped him until he tired.

He passed wagons and riders and paid them no mind. He kept up his pace. At midafternoon, he left the road at a bridge over a stream and watered the horses and allowed them to graze in a meadow for fifteen minutes. Mounting the sorrel, he pushed on west until he came to an intersection with businesses occupying the four corners. He turned south. He knew Pinto Vest would still be behind him. Odds were perhaps fifty-five to forty-five he could pull off what he planned. Well. More like fifty-one to forty-nine.

He was headed for the ferry across the Missouri at a town called Sandy Shore. He wanted to get there before the sun set and the ferry stopped. He thought he could make it. He kept the sorrel at a trot for a time and then ran him again until the horse was played out. Thackery stopped, stripped the saddle and bridle from the sorrel, and slapped it across the rump, and the animal tore off across a field of hay stubble.

He mounted David and arrived at the Sandy Shore ferry landing with the low sun smearing a hot streak of orange-yellow fire on the lead-colored surface of the east-west-running Missouri.

The ferryman looked up at Thackery. "A horse is fifty cents. I ain't making another run for fifty cents."

"How much do you want to take me across?" Thackery asked.

"Hunnert dollars." The skinny man grinned through his grizzled whiskers and spat brown juice into the river.

"I see it this way. You take me across and I'll give you five dollars, or I'll throw you in the river and pull myself across for free."

"Huh. Five's fair."

After they beached on the south shore, Thackery said, "Tie the raft up."

"Why would I do that? My place is over there in Sandy Shore."

Thackery pulled his Bowie knife and held it over the guide rope next to the pole to which it was secured.

"Hey, hey. Wait. My canoe is on the other side."

"I noticed that. Now tie it off or you and the ferry are going downstream."

"Damn you, mister."

"Tie it off. And stop cussing me or I won't pay you."

Thackery cut the rope and gave him twenty dollars.

"Twenty goddamned dollars. What you're doin', it's worth a hunnert."

"How about I keep the money and throw you in the river?"

"Shit," the ferryman said.

At the first town they came to, Thackery bought David two scoops of mashed corn and oats at the livery stable. He walked across the street to the café and bought fried chicken and biscuits for himself. Back at the stable, he purchased another two scoops of mash in a sack and pushed on. He ate as David plodded them first south, and then when they picked up the road connecting Jefferson City and Sedalia, he turned west.

Just before the sun came up, David clattered over a wooden bridge. The ridge to the east of the lane to Bucknell's place rose dark and high to his left. He stopped and stepped down. His butt was glad. His legs weren't. The rest of him was cold and stiff. His head buzzed with fatigue like a hive that had been bumped, not hard enough to set the little buggers off into a homicidal, suicidal quest for revenge, just enough to a wake a few of them to buzz-grumble a bit.

No one on the road east or west. He stepped into the saplings on the bank above the stream. After a few steps, he was steadier on his feet. He pressed farther south along the bank than he'd gone before. Dawn leaked enough light for him to see the slope of the ridge was less steep here. He started up and gave David slack in the reins to make his way up at his pace.

Above the ridgetop, tree leaves formed a canopy. Scrub brush festooned the ground up to the level of David's withers. Pushing through the brush made noise, but if he took it slow, it wasn't bad, even in the stillness and chill of dawn that drove night beasts to their nests early and encouraged the denizens of day to stay in theirs a bit longer.

Thackery came to the place where he'd hidden Quantrill's money. With a few steps, he could peer down on the road. A few steps in another direction, he could see the gate with the bell. Another few steps, and Bucknell's front porch was in view.

He stripped the saddle and rubbed David down with the blanket and then laid the blanket atop the brush. He removed the bridle, looped a rope around David's neck, tied him to a sapling, and opened the bag of mash for him.

David needed a rest, as did he. Thackery rolled up in his ground cover. When he woke, he'd push on south, either atop the ridge or at the base of it along the stream. Hopefully, Pinto Vest lost his trail. If not, the bastard could chase him to Texas if he wanted.

Thackery exhaled a big breath, and with it, marrow-deep weariness from his arms and legs. His last thought was that Bucknell would never know he came back.

39

A BELL TINKLED.

Thackery opened his eyes and squinted at a sliver of sunlight slicing through the leaves above him. The sun was directly overhead. He pushed himself up, stretched, and moved his head, working kinks out of his neck.

He patted David on the neck and spoke softly to him. Then he pushed through the brush to where he could see Bucknell's gate. Nothing there. A few steps to his left and he saw the front of the house. A man in a tan suit sat astride a white horse looking up at Celia Bucknell standing on her porch. The man took his hat off and bobbed his head to the woman. Then he put the hat back on and climbed down. A Negro man took the reins of the white and led it around the porch toward the rear of the house.

Derby Hat climbed the steps and held out a bouquet of flowers to Celia. He had another bouquet in his other hand.

From the rear of house, a black-haired boy—no. It was the girl, Amanda. Amanda raced across the lot between the house and the barn.

Derby Hat held the door open for Celia Bucknell and then followed her inside.

From the far side of the barn, a horse, Roan, with Amanda riding bareback, tore out of the barn and galloped along the paddock fence and disappeared, screened by foliage.

Derby Hat must have come to court Amanda. Huh.

It brought to mind Paw sending Emerson Sharp to court Deborah Simmons. Deborah didn't run away. Instead, she'd, in effect, promised to make Emerson's life miserable *until death do us part.*

William Bucknell appeared from behind the rear corner of the house. He cupped his hands around his mouth and hollered, "Amanda, come back! Right now!"

Roan's hooves continued pounding the dirt as the only answer to William.

That was Bucknell business.

Thackery walked back to David and saddled him. Then he looked at the contents of the flour sack Molly had handed to him. Nothing in it but clothes and gun-cleaning gear. He kept one black suit and one work shirt and pants. He rolled those in his ground cloth and stashed another suit and other shirts and pants under the log where he'd hidden the money. He had a skillet, coffeepot, and tin cup. Coffee from the sorrel's rider. He loaded the gear into his saddlebags and stashed the one from sorrel under the log. He stowed powder tin, balls, and gun-cleaning gear in the other pocket of the bags. He kept the flour sack Molly had given him. Two sets of saddlebags were a pain to manage, but a sack came in handy from time to time.

As long as he could move freely enough through the brush, he intended to stay atop the ridge as he headed south. He intended to stay afoot and lead David until he cleared Bucknell's property.

Riders, a number of them, thundered over the wooden bridge. Thackery spoke to David and then worked his way to where he could see the road. Six riders. One of them was Pinto Vest. He was wearing it again. He stopped at the head of Bucknell's lane. The hunters circled around him. He pointed back to the stream. One rider peeled off and headed back toward the bridge. Pinto Vest sent another on toward Kingdom Come; then he took his hat off and mopped sweat off his forehead with a shirtsleeve. Recognition flashed in Thackery's brain. Pinto Vest's hatless face ... he was Tan Coat, the man who'd shot Iago-renamed-Horse. He remembered the face from when he'd shot the man's hat off.

Thackery hurried back to David and pulled his rifle from the scabbard. When he got back to a vantage point with a view of the road, the riders and Pinto Vest Tan Coat were gone. A bell rang. He made his way to where he could see the front of Bucknell's house.

Bucknell stood on his porch, his legs apart, a double-barrel shotgun cradled across his white shirt. Pinto Vest with his riders spread apart enough so they covered the length of the porch and faced Bucknell. Pinto Vest appeared to begin to dismount. But he stopped and stayed in the saddle.

Thackery heard a crashing through the brush along the top of the streambed behind him. The man was in a hurry and not trying to be quiet. He'd find the place where he and David had climbed the slope that morning.

Bucknell hollered, "Ben! Absalom!"

Ben stood in the open barn door with a rifle pointed at the riders. Absalom stepped out from behind the far side of the porch with a rifle as well.

Then Thackery heard someone pushing through the brush atop the ridge, heading right for him. That guerilla hunter? Already? Thackery spoke to David to keep him quiet. He laid the rifle down against the hiding place log, and he pulled David down onto his knees and onto his side. He'd made noise. Whoever was approaching continued to do so, apparently making too much noise himself to hear David.

Thackery dropped to the ground and started crawling. Close to the ground, the brush was devoid of leaves. He could see a few yards.

"Well, lookee here." A man.

"Let go." *Amanda?*

"Ow. Kick, bite, scratch all you want, little missy." The man chuckled. "Oh, yeah. I like 'em feisty."

Thackery took his hat off and eased up.

A black-bearded, round-shouldered, big-bellied grinning man held Amanda Bucknell by the arm. She struggled and kicked and hissed. Thackery dropped back to his knees and crawled closer. As the two struggled, they made a fair amount of noise. Thackery moved fast to where he could see their legs as they danced in a circle. When the man's legs appeared in front of him, Thackery jumped up and rammed his Bowie into the man's back. He grunted. Thackery pulled the knife free, grabbed a handful of greasy hair, pulled the man's head back, and cut his throat.

Thackery looked up from the dead man. Amanda stood with her hands to her side. The front of her shirt had been ripped away. A trail of blood had splattered across her breasts. He raised his eyes to find hers looking into him.

From below the ridge, a rifle banged. A shotgun boomed. Rifles and pistols were fired and another shotgun blast. And then that silence infused with weight and depth that followed a sudden spasm of violence set upon the ridge and the house below for a heartbeat.

"Father!" Amanda screamed and tore off down the hill.

"Stop, Amanda. Stop." Thackery pictured her busting out of the trees down below and whoever was still standing all juiced up with the smell of gunpowder and being shot at and shooting men down, and even if all the targets were down, still filled with a need to kill, and anything that moved—

Thackery ran after her. Amanda ran like a deer through the brush and down the slope. He raised his right arm in front of his face to shield it from branches and pushed harder. He almost had her when she busted clear of the brush at the foot of the ridge and onto the cleared lot in front of the barn and the house.

Four men lay sprawled on the dirt below the porch. Up on the porch, Bucknell leveled his shotgun at Thackery. William Bucknell, next to his father, raised a rifle. Ben Bucknell stood in the doorway to the barn with a rifle coming up to his shoulder.

Shit! He'd come out of the brush a step behind the girl with a Bowie raised as if to stab her. He dove to the right. Bucknell's shotgun barked, and Ben's rifle banged and a bullet twipped past his ear. Thackery lay on his belly and stayed still.

"No!" Amanda screamed. "He saved me!" Amanda had turned and was running back toward him. "Don't shoot him!"

Bucknell shouted for his daughter to stop.

Bobby Bucknell was in the open hayloft door reloading a

breechloader. Ben Bucknell, in front of the barn, on the ground level, reloaded his rifle. Mr. Bucknell started down the porch steps.

Amanda threw herself on Thackery's back.

"Aman—" A rifle banged. Mr. Bucknell dropped his shotgun. It clattered down the steps. He grabbed his chest and sat back on the top step.

A puff of gunsmoke blossomed in the trees at the far edge of the cleared space. Thackery rolled to the left, heaving the girl off his back. He drew the pistol from the holster on his hip and fired at the smoke. Thackery fired three times. Bobby's rifle banged from the hayloft. Thackery fired twice more.

"Absalom!" Bobby shouted. "The man's down! Check him!"

Absalom ran out from edge of the house to the bushwhacker's hide.

On the porch, William knelt to one side of his father, holding an arm. Celia supported him on the other side. Bucknell had his hands over a red stain on his white shirt.

Ben had Amanda by an arm. She struggled just as she had with the guerilla hunter up on the ridge. Ben had his rifle in his right hand and was trying to point the weapon at Thackery.

"Amanda!" Celia shrieked and stood up, letting go of her husband. "Cover yourself!"

Mr. Bucknell's chin sagged onto his chest. William lowered him back onto the porch.

Amanda went still, staring at her father. Ben kept hold of her arm and raised the rifle at Thackery. Amanda lunged and grabbed the barrel of the rifle, and it fired into the dirt.

"Bobby," Ben said, "shoot him."

Thackery, still on the ground, looked up at Bobby in the hayloft.

"Tom Thackery!" Bobby said.

"Shoot him," Ben said.

"No, Bobby. One of them"—Amanda pointed at the bodies below the porch—"grabbed me up on the ridge. Thackery killed him. He saved me."

"Shoot him, Bobby," Ben snarled.

Amanda kicked Ben on the side of his knee. He grimaced, grabbed his knee, and staggered back a step.

Thackery jumped up, shucked his coat, and draped it over Amanda's shoulders.

Amanda looked up at Bobby. "He saved me."

"You little bitch!" Ben growled and hobbled toward Amanda.

Thackery stepped around her. Ben took a clumsy swing.

Thackery parried it.

"It's like Amanda said, Ben." Ben came at him again, and Thackery caught him on the chin with an uppercut. Ben's head snapped back, he spun sideways and dropped to his hands and knees.

Amanda held the coat closed in front of her and ran to the porch.

Bobby hustled out the barn door and helped Ben up.

Thackery picked up Ben's rifle.

Ben jerked Bobby's rifle away from him. Thackery dropped the rifle and drew the pistol from his shoulder holster and cocked it. "Do you wanna be dead?" Thackery asked. "Do you?"

Ben didn't answer.

"Well, Ben, I'd rather not kill you, so there ought to be a way out of this. Take your rifle back, Bobby."

Bobby did and let the hammer down.

"We should check on your father."

Bobby moved to help Ben walk, but Ben jerked his arm away. Thackery stayed a step behind as Ben hobbled to the porch and up the steps.

Thackery stayed below. Mr. Bucknell's lower legs hung over the top of the porch. Thackery couldn't see his face. Amanda knelt beside him. Clarice was on her knees by his head. Celia and William stood looking down at husband and father.

"Absalom," Mr. Bucknell wheezed. "Get him."

Ben called him, and Absalom hurried across the yard and up the steps.

"Absalom," Bucknell said, "look after my boys."

"Ben," Bucknell said. "William. You need to listen to Absalom."

"Father." Amanda sniffed and stared down at him.

Thackery saw a tear trickle down her cheek. He saw Bucknell's hand reach up to wipe away his daughter's tear.

"Ben." Bucknell's voice was a whisper. "What do you need to do first?"

"Get you in the house," Ben said, "and send Absalom for the doctor."

"Tell him, Absalom."

"We needs to git dese mens buried."

"Listen to him, Ben." Bucknell panted a couple of short breaths. "William, ride to town. Tell Clementine Manley what happened. Only her."

Bucknell's hand dropped away from Amanda.

Amanda wiped away fresh tears.

"Get in the house, Amanda," Celia snapped. "Get yourself properly dressed."

Amanda stood up. She looked down at Thackery. She put a little smile on her face. Just for him, he thought. He felt it in his stomach. The smile came off like a rudely ripped-off mask. She looked at her mother a moment; then she turned to Bobby. Something passed between them. Thackery wasn't sure what it was.

Amanda walked into the house. Bobby clumped up the steps and started to follow his sister into the house.

"Bobby," Celia said. "stay here. Help your brothers with this other Quantrill guerilla."

"Ain't no Quantrill guerillas here, missus," Absalom said. Celia turned away from Bobby, and he entered the house. "Dose dere on the ground, they's militia. Union. And deh ain't no bedder dan dat Quantrill. Mistuh Thackry, he ain't wit' 'em."

"Union? Why would Union men attack us?" Celia demanded.

"'Cause dey's snakes more dan dey's Union. They just strike whatever comes in front a them."

Just then, the man with the white horse and the derby hat rode out of the barn and headed for the gate.

"Whoa up there, Mistuh Simpson Manley!" Absalom shouted. "Whoa up!"

The man reined up and looked over his shoulder at the porch. "I … I'm going home."

Absalom pointed at him. "You stay right dere."

"What do you think you're doing?" Ben demanded. "Talking to a white man like that."

"I'se talking to a man who kin do a lotta harm to the Bucknell fambly, he git to Kingdom Come first. You, Mistuh William. Your daddy, he say you be uncommon smart. Dat be so, you see you need to do what he said. You git dere firstest. Take one of dese horses." The guerilla hunters' mounts stood ground-hitched near their fallen riders. "You make dat Mistuh Simpson keep his mout shut, and you be telling the story to Missus Clementine."

William started descending the steps.

"Wait," Celia said. "Thackery. He's with Quantrill. The militia were chasing him. He led them here."

Thackery was surprised it had taken them so long to think of that.

"Missus," Absalom said. "He ain't done no such thing. Din't you hear dat one talking wit' your husbin?" He pointed to Pinto Vest. "He say he know you all sell horses to the guerillas. 'It was time,' he say, 'the Bucknells got showed the error of they ways.'

"Now, Mistuh Bucknell, he lyin' there on his porch like he no different dan dose in the dirt. Clarice, you help the missus and Mistuh Ben git him inside. You show dem how to take care a him."

William mounted Pinto Vest's horse. "Come on, Simpson." The two of them headed for the gate.

The two women had Bucknell by the legs. Ben backed his father's torso through the front door.

"It be a shame," Absalom said, "dat a man like him can be brought down by a bushwhacker."

Absalom turned to Thackery. "You up for some grave diggin'?"

40

"WHY YOU DON'T wait till the mawnin', Mistuh Thackry? Ain't nobody be chasing you no more."

"I'll feel better getting a few miles between me and this place by sunup. I think I brought you all enough trouble."

"Dis part of the state, dey's a lot of troubles. Soon or late, some of it was gonna fine us."

"Sure you don't want to come along to California, Mister Absalom?"

"A part of me wants dat, but the biggest part knows I gots to stay here wit' Clarice and the chilrens."

"Ben and William and Mrs. Bucknell, they seem to me to bring out the worst in each other."

"Dat's true. But the missus be taking Miss Amanda back east. Tomorra', right after dey buries Mistuh Bucknell. Mistuh Ben and Mistuh William, dey daddy was uncommon good to me, and dey be needing help."

"A pleasure to make your acquaintance, Mr. Absalom."

"Good luck on dat trip of yours, Mistuh Thackery. I hope dat California be the land of milk and honey." Thackery tipped his hat and said, "David."

The big black set off from Absalom's house next to the paddock fence. Pinto Vest's chestnut with one white stocking followed on the lead rope.

The huge harvest moon hung above the horizon, shining cold silver on the world. Just in the time he'd spoken with Absalom, the cold settled on his shoulders with the same weight and substance as a high August sun sat hot on a dark shirt. He pulled a glove on his left hand and kept his right in his coat pocket.

They rounded the far end of the paddock and followed the lane between the paddock and more fenced pasture to the south. Thackery could see that the south pasture was divided into two parts. One held cows and horses. One had no animals. He thought about Ben Bucknell. Ben did not have farming in his blood. He needed Absalom, all right. Absalom would know when to shift the animals from one pasture to the other to enable the grass to recover.

Beyond the pasture, they turned right and rode along the edge of a field of stubble and shocks of corn, with the ridge rising dark to their left. The cornfield was separated from one that had grown grain by a strip of trees. Past the grain field, he passed through another boundary strip of saplings and onto a hayfield.

Quiet. The bugs and birds of summer were snuggled in their nests. The horses' hooves made a lot of noise. The air was still, as if it were too cold and heavy to move.

He wrinkled his nose. Dust. There was dust in the air.

He hopped down and studied the ground. The moonlight was enough to make out the fresh prints amid the wheel tracks and half-weathered-out horseshoe marks. Two riders.

It was ten thirty. They couldn't have passed more than thirty minutes ago, he thought.

More guerilla hunters? Bushwhackers? Bad enough meeting either of them in daylight.

About fifty or sixty yards ahead of him, the field gave over to forest.

David bobbed his head. His ears stood up. Thackery pulled a pistol from a saddle holster. He flexed his fingers, working function back into stiff joints.

"Mr. Thackery" came from the darkness ahead of him. "Bobby? Bobby Bucknell?"

"Yes, sir."

"Jesus, kid. I was this close to shooting."

Two riders rode out of the woods and headed for him.

"Who's with you?"

"I am."

"Amanda!"

They rode up to him and stopped.

"What in God's name are you doing out here?"

"We want to go with you, Mr. Thackery," Bobby said.

"Like hell. Get back to your house where you belong."

"We left," Amanda said, "and we're not going back."

"Suit yourself, but you're not coming with me."

*****

The next morning, with the sun up fair, Thackery found what he was looking for: a place that stunk of skunk.

He stopped David and climbed down. "I'm fixing breakfast here."

"Suit yourself," Amanda said. "I'm riding on a bit. Bobby, you staying in the stink or coming with me?"

"With you," he said.

Thackery watched them ride on. "Shit," he said and followed them.

Clear of the stink, Amanda stopped and gathered stones to ring a fire pit as Bobby gathered wood and shaved up tinder and lit a fire. Thackery stripped the saddles off the horses and tied their neck ropes to trees so they could graze. Amanda made coffee and fried bacon.

They sat around the fire and ate.

Thackery sipped coffee. "Passable." He'd hoped it would get a rise out of her. "I hoped you'd get tired and go back. You stuck to me all night. Why are you so all fired set on leaving your home?"

"It's not our home anymore," Bobby said. "Ben and William are not Father."

"Mother is going back east. She said if I refused to marry Simpson Manley, I was to go with her. I said I would not go. Ben said I sure would go with her. I said I was leaving and they'd have to shoot me to stop me."

"We all argued," Bobby said, "and we said awful things to each other. Finally, Ben said, 'Go, then. You are no longer part of this family.'"

"Look—it's not too late. I can take you back. We can talk to Ben, get Absalom to weigh in."

"Ben hates you most of all," Bobby said. "Says you were the reason Father was killed."

"Tom Thackery, we are either going with you, or we'll just trail you like we did last night," Amanda said.

"We'll pass through Springfield. You can go with me that far."

"We're going to California with you, Tom Thackery." "Amanda—"

"By the way, Tom Thackery, I changed my name too." He looked at her.

She smiled. "I'm Amanda Kate." "Amanda Kate?"

"After Quantrill's wife," Bobby said.

"You admire Quantrill?" Thackery asked.

"No. I admire his wife." She used a rag to pull the coffeepot off the fire. "More passable?"

"Shit," he said. He held out his cup.

After they finished, they cleaned up the cook site and rode on for an hour and stopped near water and graze.

"We'll stop for four hours," Thackery said.

"I'll take the first watch," Bobby said. "How about if I go back along the way we came a few yards and watch from there? That all right, Mr. Thackery?"

"That'll do. You have a timepiece?"

He did.

"Give me an hour and a half. Then wake me."

Thackery spread his ground cloth out and placed saddlebags for a pillow. He rolled the cover over him. Amanda Kate watched him. He put his hat over his eyes, took a deep breath, and let it out.

He heard Amanda Kate get up and walk toward him. A ground cloth flapped. He slipped his hat back. She'd spread her cover next to his.

"What are you doing?"

"Why, Tom Thackery, I am lying beside you."

"You're a girl."

"I'm two years older than Kate was when she was married." "You expect me to marry you?"

"I do, Tom Thackery."

"You looked down your nose at me."

"But then I got to know you."

"You don't know anything about me."

"I do. I know enough for now."

She leaned over and kissed him.

"You know what else I expect, Tom Thackery?"

He shook his head.

"I expect you to shave and take a bath. You smell like a skunk."

"Shit."

"And this crude language, Tom Thackery, that will have to stop."

"Rats."

Amanda Kate lifted the flap of his ground cover and slipped in beside him.

"Amanda Kate, are you sure about this?"

"I've been sure since I saw you in Kingdom Come for the horse races. That's why Mother tried to get me married off to Simpson."

"Uh, Bobby—"

"I told him he was to keep the watch for three hours."

"I wonder if William Quantrill has as much trouble with his Kate as I am bound to have with mine."

"Even though you smell like a skunk, I find you … passable, Tom Thackery."

"No chance I'm going to get the last word in, is there?"

"None."

Sometimes it seemed like the good Lord hit a man with a series of big, heavy things, one after another, not giving a man time to deal with one issue before another was on him.

He had to slow this thing down.

He flipped the ground cover back.

"What's the matter?"

"Let me think a minute."

Amanda Kate propped herself on an elbow.

Thackery walked two paces away from her and turned around.

"Stand up, Amanda Kate."

"Why?"

"Stand up."

She did. He walked to her and knelt on one knee.

"Will you marry me, Amanda Kate?"

"I have given myself to you. We are already married."

"No. Maybe that's how Kate Quantrill did it, but we will do this properly. Will you marry me, Amanda Kate? We'll be in Springfield in three days. Will you marry me in Springfield, Amanda Kate?"

AUTHOR'S NOTE

I DEVELOPED AN interest in the Civil War in Missouri period and setting while I was researching my wife's family history. It turned out that her great-great-grandfather, John Wilke, emigrated to America in 1840 with his mother, a widow, and an older brother, Herman. During the Civil War, John served as a private in the militia, while Herman was an officer. One night, shortly after the end of the war, a disgruntled Southern sympathizer broke into Herman's house intending to shoot the Yankee officer, but Herman carried a pistol at all times and wounded his would-be assailant, who fled into the night.

My interest piqued, I reread *The Devil Knows How to Ride,* a Quantrill bio by Edward Leslie. I acquired *My Dear Molly, The Civil War Letters of Captain James Love,* and a number of other books about guerillas, regulators, guerilla hunters, Red Legs, Border Wars, and Slicker Wars. And, of course, organized violence was a regular feature of life in Missouri since before John Wilke ever settled in Orchard Farm, Missouri. The Mormon Wars, for instance.

At any rate, I found it an interesting period and decided to write a short story set in the western half of Missouri at the time of Quantrill's raid on Lawrence, Kansas. An editor read the story and suggested I build a novel around the character, which I was reluctant to do. I had other things I wanted to write, but, for some reason, a spirit moved me to give it a go. And *Guerilla Bride* happened.

Thanks to the St. Charles County Historical Society, my Coffee and Critique Group, and the super editors at iUniverse, Sarah E. in particular, and even thanks to the one who talked me into all this extra work.

www.ingramcontent.com/pod-product-compliance
Lightning Source LLC
Chambersburg PA
CBHW030707190726
48286CB00001B/217